SON of SHAOLIN

BOOK 1: THE BEGINNING

SON OF SHAOLIN: BOOK ONE. First printing: September 2017
Published by Image Comics, Inc. Office of publication: 2701 NW Vaughn St., Suite 780, Portland, OR 97210. Copyright © 2017 Size 13 Productions Inc. All rights reserved. "Son of Shaolin," its logos, and the likenesses of all characters herein are trademarks of Size 13 Productions Inc., unless otherwise noted. "Image" and the Image Comics logos are registered trademarks of Image Comics, Inc. No part of this publication may be reproduced or transmitted, in any form or by any means (except for short excerpts for journalistic or review purposes), without the express written permission of Size 13 Productions, Top Cow Productions Inc., or Image Comics, Inc. All names, characters, events, and locales in this publication are entirely fictional. Any resemblance to actual persons (living or dead), events, or places, without satiric intent, is coincidental. Printed in the USA. For information regarding the CPSIA on this printed material call: 203-595-3636 and provide reference **#RICH-761223**.

For international rights, contact: foreignlicensing@imagecomics.com. ISBN: 978-1-5343-0323-2.

Original subway map by Jug Cerovic, Architect www.inat.fr

For any additional information about Son of Shaolin, email info@sonofshaolin.com.
Want more info? Check out: www.topcow.com for news & exclusive Top Cow merchandise!
To find the comic shop nearest you, call 1-888-COMICBOOK.

STRANGE TURN

For Strange Turn Entertainment
Ryan Kalil - CEO
Aroop Sanakkayala - COO

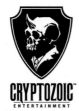

CRYPTOZOIC ENTERTAINMENT

For Cryptozoic Entertainment
John Nee - Co-Founder & Co-CEO
Matt Hoffman - Director of Special Projects

SIZE 13

For Size 13 Comics
Jay Longino - Founder / Partner
ROAR - Founder / Partner

TOP COW PRODUCTIONS, INC.

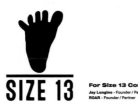

For Top Cow Productions, Inc.
Marc Silvestri - CEO
Matt Hawkins - President & COO
Elena Salcedo - Vice President of Operations
Henry Barajas - Director of Operations
Vincent Valentine - Production Manager
Dylan Gray - Marketing Director

image

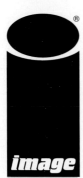

IMAGE COMICS, INC.
Robert Kirkman—Chief Operating Officer
Erik Larsen—Chief Financial Officer
Todd McFarlane—President
Marc Silvestri—Chief Executive Officer
Jim Valentino—Vice President

Eric Stephenson—Publisher
Corey Murphy—Director of Sales
Jeff Boison—Director of Publishing Planning & Book Trade Sales
Chris Ross—Director of Digital Sales
Jeff Stang—Director of Specialty Sales
Kat Salazar—Director of PR & Marketing
Branwyn Bigglestone—Controller
Kali Dugan—Senior Accounting Manager
Sue Korpela—Accounting & HR Manager
Drew Gill—Art Director
Heather Doornink—Production Director
Leigh Thomas—Print Manager
Tricia Ramos—Traffic Manager
Briah Skelly—Publicist
Aly Hoffman—Events & Conventions Coordinator
Sasha Head—Sales & Marketing Production Designer
David Brothers—Branding Manager
Melissa Gifford—Content Manager
Drew Fitzgerald—Publicity Assistant
Vincent Kukua—Production Artist
Erika Schnatz—Production Artist
Ryan Brewer—Production Artist
Shanna Matuszak—Production Artist
Carey Hall—Production Artist
Esther Kim—Direct Market Sales Representative
Emilio Bautista—Digital Sales Representative
Leanna Caunter—Accounting Analyst
Chloe Ramos-Peterson—Library Market Sales Representative
Marla Eizik—Administrative Assistant
IMAGECOMICS.COM

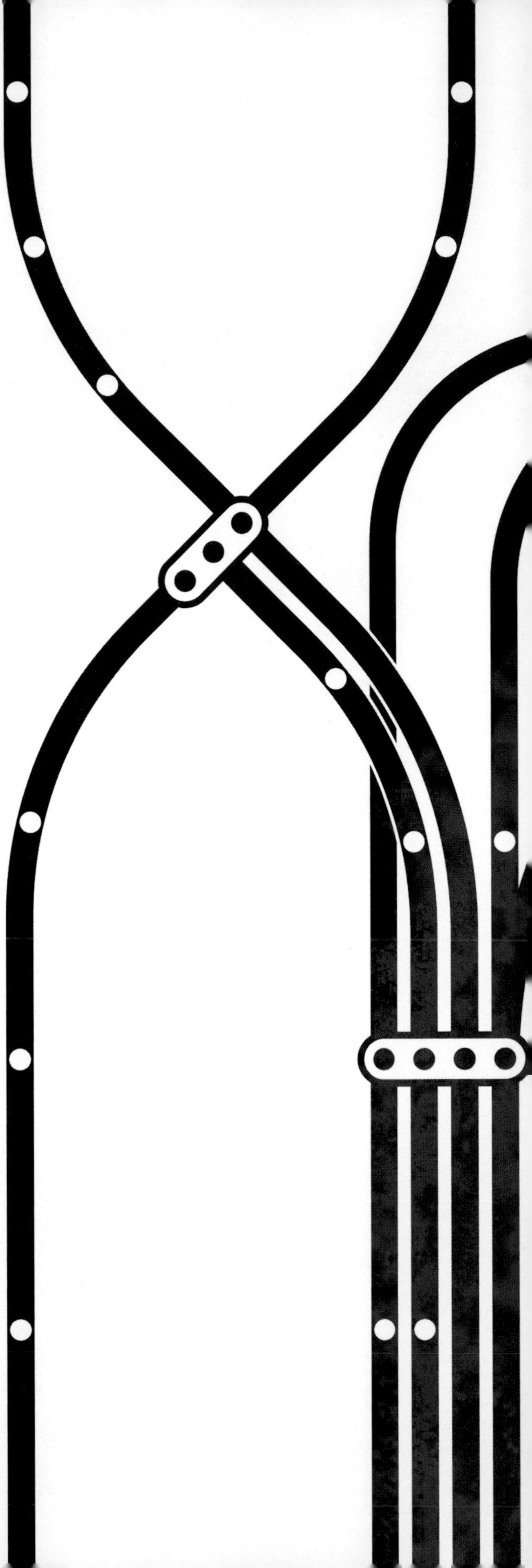

JAY
LONGINO
CREATOR AND WRITER

CAANAN
WHITE
ARTIST

DIEGO
RODRIGUEZ
COLORIST

Harlem
148 St

SIMON
BOWLAND
LETTERER

LOUISE
SIMONSON
AND
SHAHRIAR
FOULADI
EDITORS

CAANAN WHITE
COVER ARTIST

FISHBRAIN
DESIGN

When I was a kid I loved comic books. I know a lot of kids love comic books, but I *LOVED* comic books.

I was a weird kid — your typical grade school outlier, a dreamer who loved to read and spent most of my free time reveling in fantasy — at the movies, at the controller of an arcade game, and most of all, reading books.

Comic books were an escape. But more than that, they offered up a universe where grand injustices were correctable, where cruelties could be righted, where even deaths could be reversed. For a nerdy little girl who was the only black kid at her school, an outsider who was bullied frequently and felt injustices keenly, the idea of punching out the villain and saving the little guy was the most delicious of fantasies.

I wanted to be a superhero so badly. Maybe my schoolyard injustices were limited to teasing and social isolation, but I knew the larger world was a terrible place. I read the newspaper, and watched the news, and I knew bigger cruelties were perpetrated everywhere, every day. And I knew that as a kid, there was nothing I could do. I felt injustice keenly, but even more keenly, I felt my inability to change what an unkind place the world could be. I was just an ordinary kid, my meager powers cruelly deserting me each time my last life expired at the arcade.

Superhero lore provided not just an outlet for me, but a lifeway. Superheroes

Photo: Robert Adam Mayer

wore their mantle reluctantly. They didn't want to put everyone and everything they cared about at risk to save the lives of strangers. They didn't want to live alone for fear of putting loved ones in danger. Superheroes saved the world because they had to. Because it was a duty. An obligation. *A destiny.*

The beloved superheroes of my youth didn't save the world because they wanted to. They saved it because they had no other choice. It was who they were, woven into the fabric of their Adamantium bones or the misshapen platelets of their irradiated blood. They were obligated by their abilities to serve. With great power comes great responsibility. And that responsibility was as much a burden as it was a gift. Because what these reluctant superheroes really wanted was just to be *an ordinary kid.*

"I WANTED TO BE A SUPERHERO SO BADLY."

Like me.

I loved the ordinariness at the center of the superhero's saga — that despite their magical powers or indestructibility, they always just wanted to live a simple life — to love, to sleep, to caress a loved one without crushing their bones to dust or drawing the unwanted attention of an intergalactic warlord. I related to superheroes in so many ways, save one. Almost none of them looked like me.

Not much has changed since I was a kid. There are still so few superheroes of color, you can count them on a hand or two.

The beauty of the superhero saga is that they can be anyone, from anywhere. All they need is a good heart and a sense of duty. From Wolverine to Peter Parker to Green Lantern to Cyborg, the essence of that saga is that there is a hero in all of us, that we are all capable of greatness. Luke Skywalker was just an orphaned farm boy, Neo a faceless office worker, mired in the mundane. Katniss was just a girl from District 12 until, reluctantly, she became much, much more.

When I was a kid I would read those books, and watch those movies, and dream I was a hero — that I could save the world, even though I never saw anyone who looked like me in those stories. But in this story, and in others like it finally emerging, there rests an expanded universe that doesn't just represent our world more accurately, but the essence of the superhero saga more perfectly — that there is a hero in ALL of us, and that any of us could be a Jedi Knight, or a galactic law enforcer, or the last descendant of an ancient Shaolin master.

There is greatness buried deep in each of us. And with that knowledge, comes great responsibility.

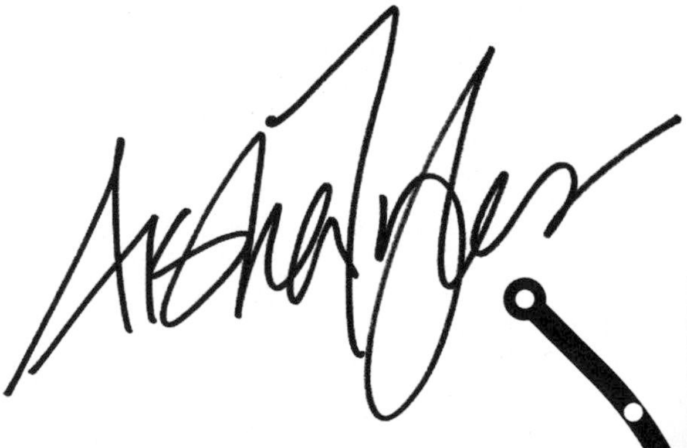

Aisha Tyler is an actor, director, comedian, writer and producer.

You might know her from *Archer, Criminal Minds, Whose Line Is It Anyway, The Talk, Friends, Talk Soup*, the *Santa Clause* movies, or maybe from *Halo, Gears of War*, or *Watch Dogs*. She's also the creator of the cocktail company Courage+Stone.

Tyler graduated from Dartmouth College.

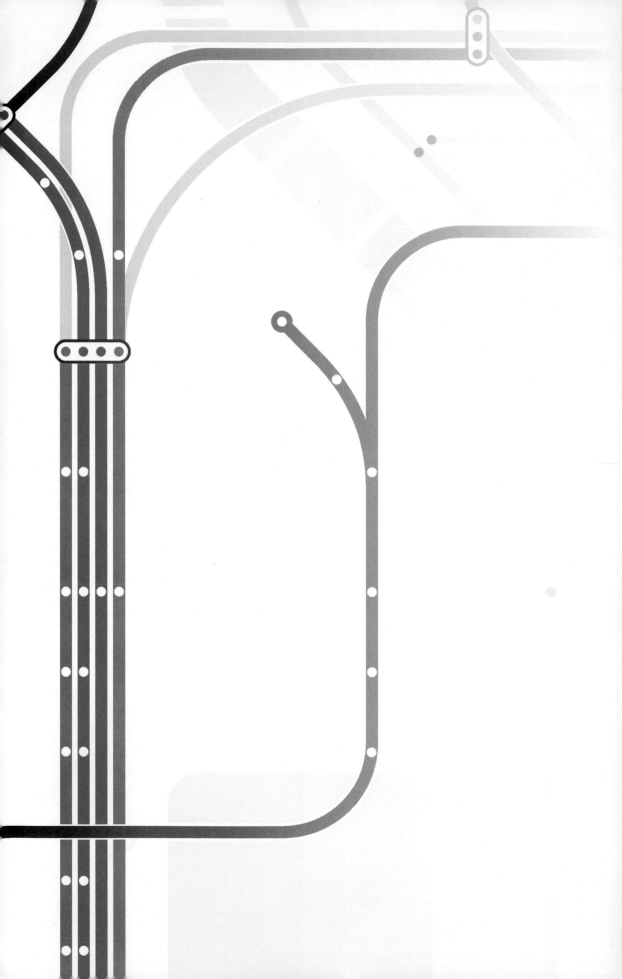

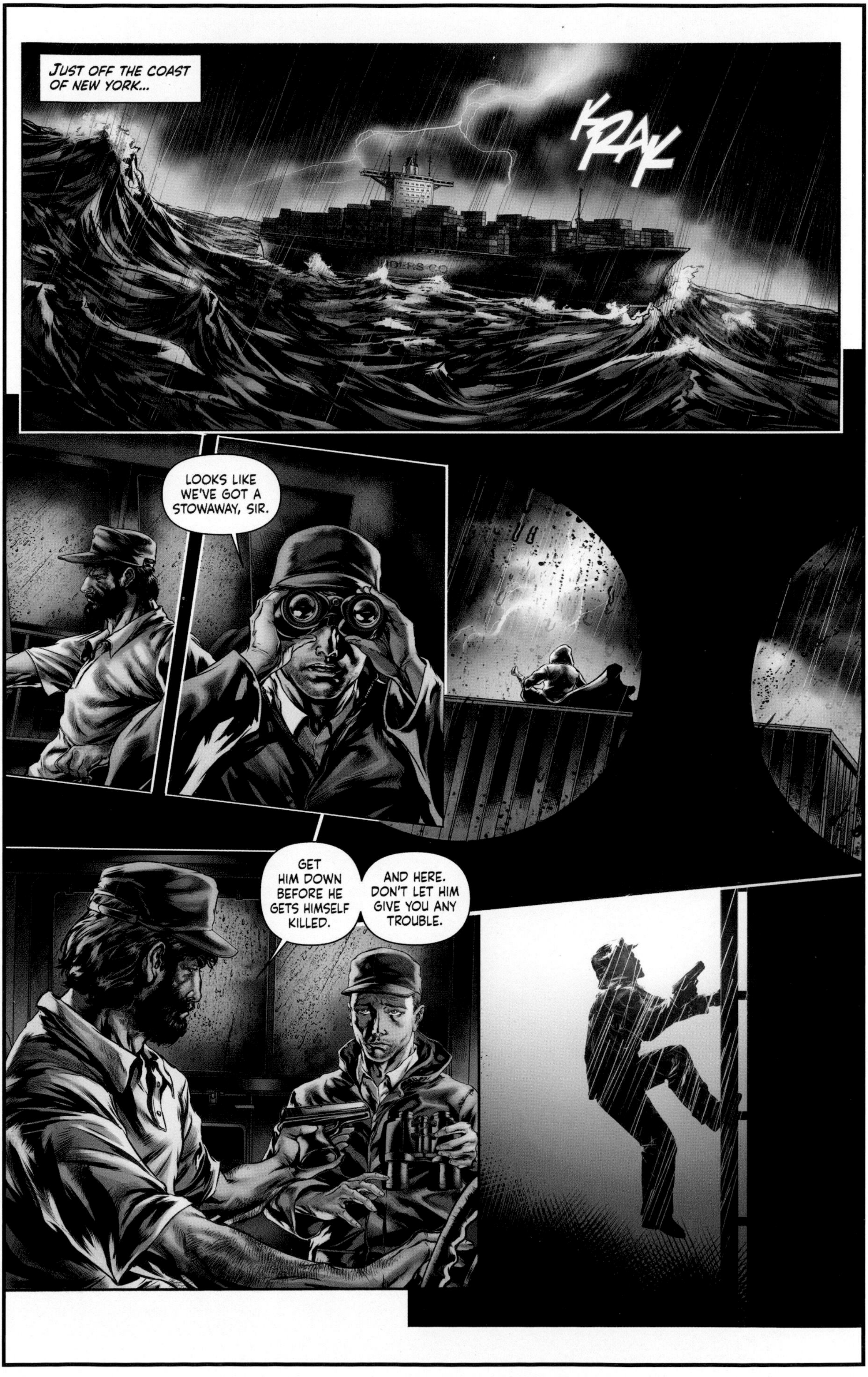

JUST OFF THE COAST OF NEW YORK...
KRAK
LOOKS LIKE WE'VE GOT A STOWAWAY, SIR.
GET HIM DOWN BEFORE HE GETS HIMSELF KILLED.
AND HERE. DON'T LET HIM GIVE YOU ANY TROUBLE.

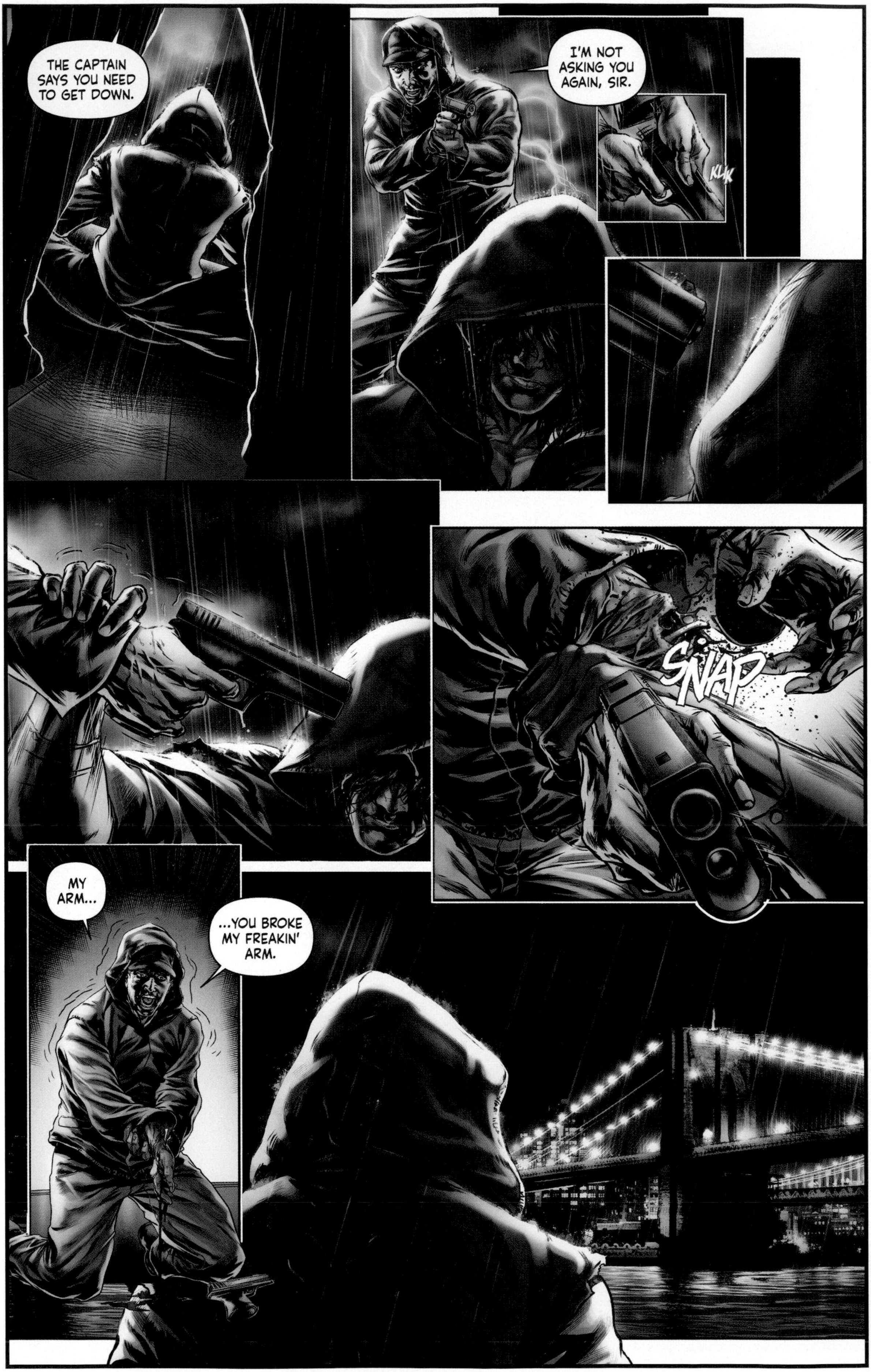
THE CAPTAIN SAYS YOU NEED TO GET DOWN.
I'M NOT ASKING YOU AGAIN, SIR.
KLIK
SNAP
MY ARM...
...YOU BROKE MY FREAKIN' ARM.

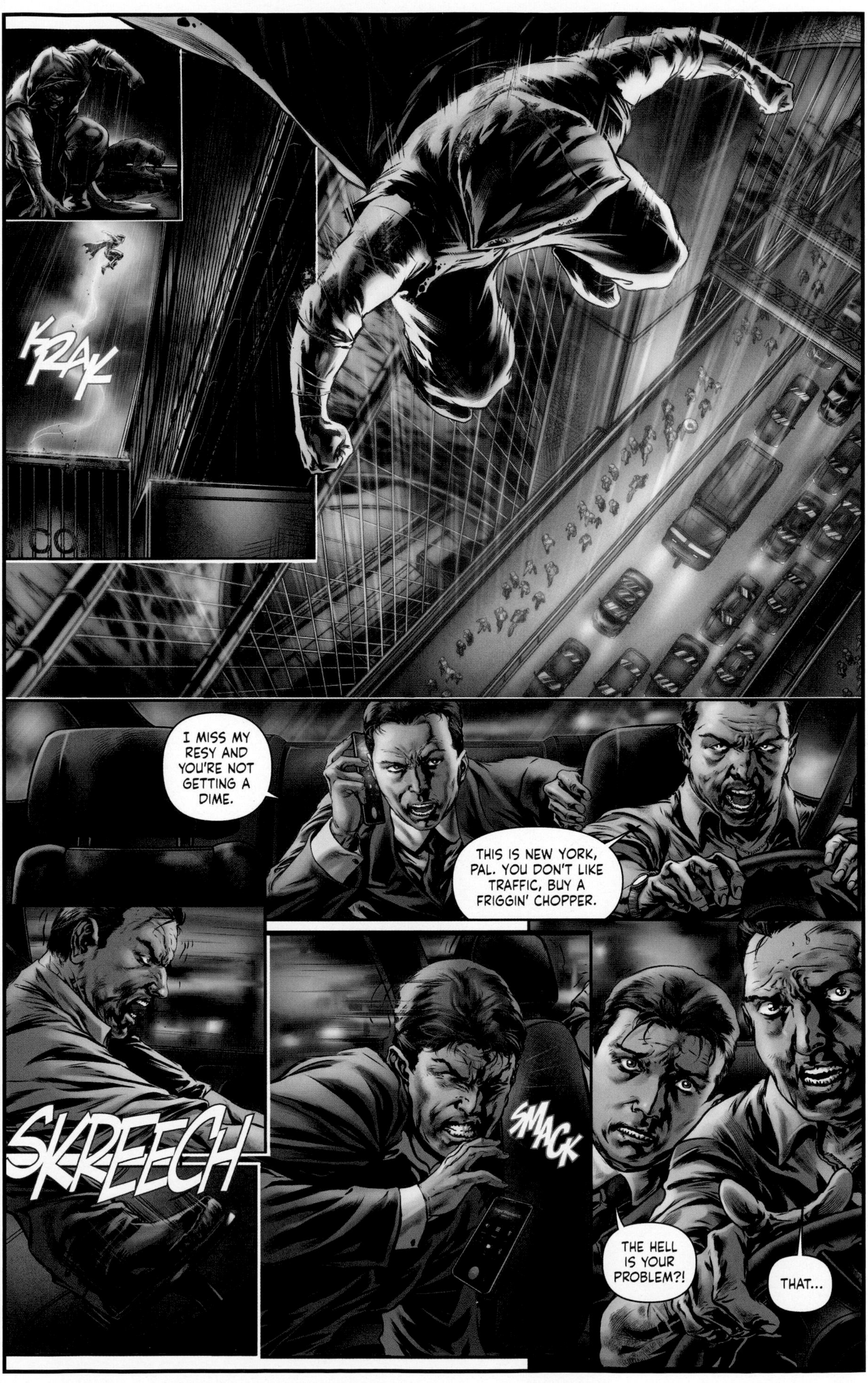
KRAK
I MISS MY RESY AND YOU'RE NOT GETTING A DIME.
THIS IS NEW YORK, PAL. YOU DON'T LIKE TRAFFIC, BUY A FRIGGIN' CHOPPER.
SKREECH
SMACK
THE HELL IS YOUR PROBLEM?!
THAT...

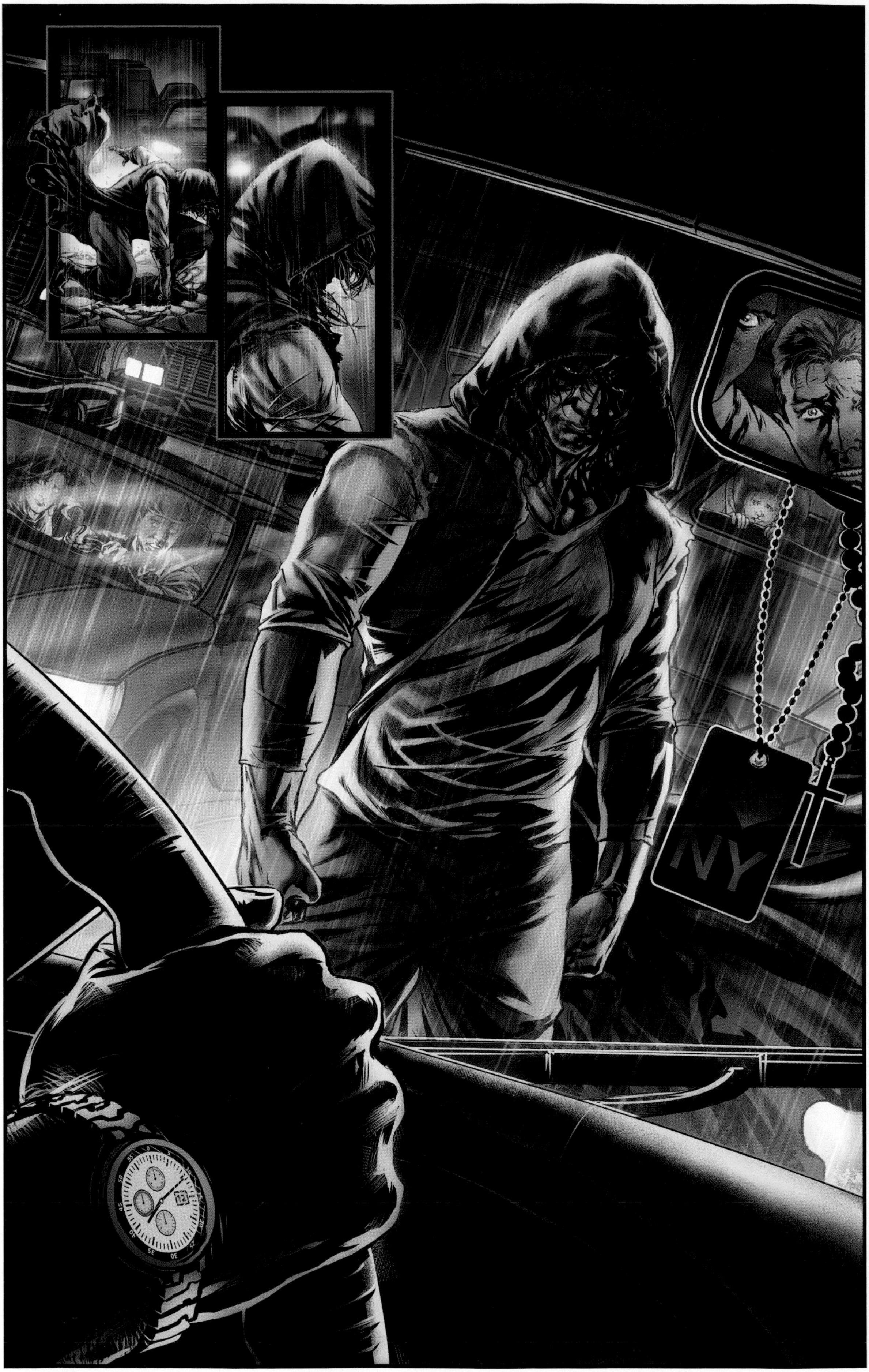
NY

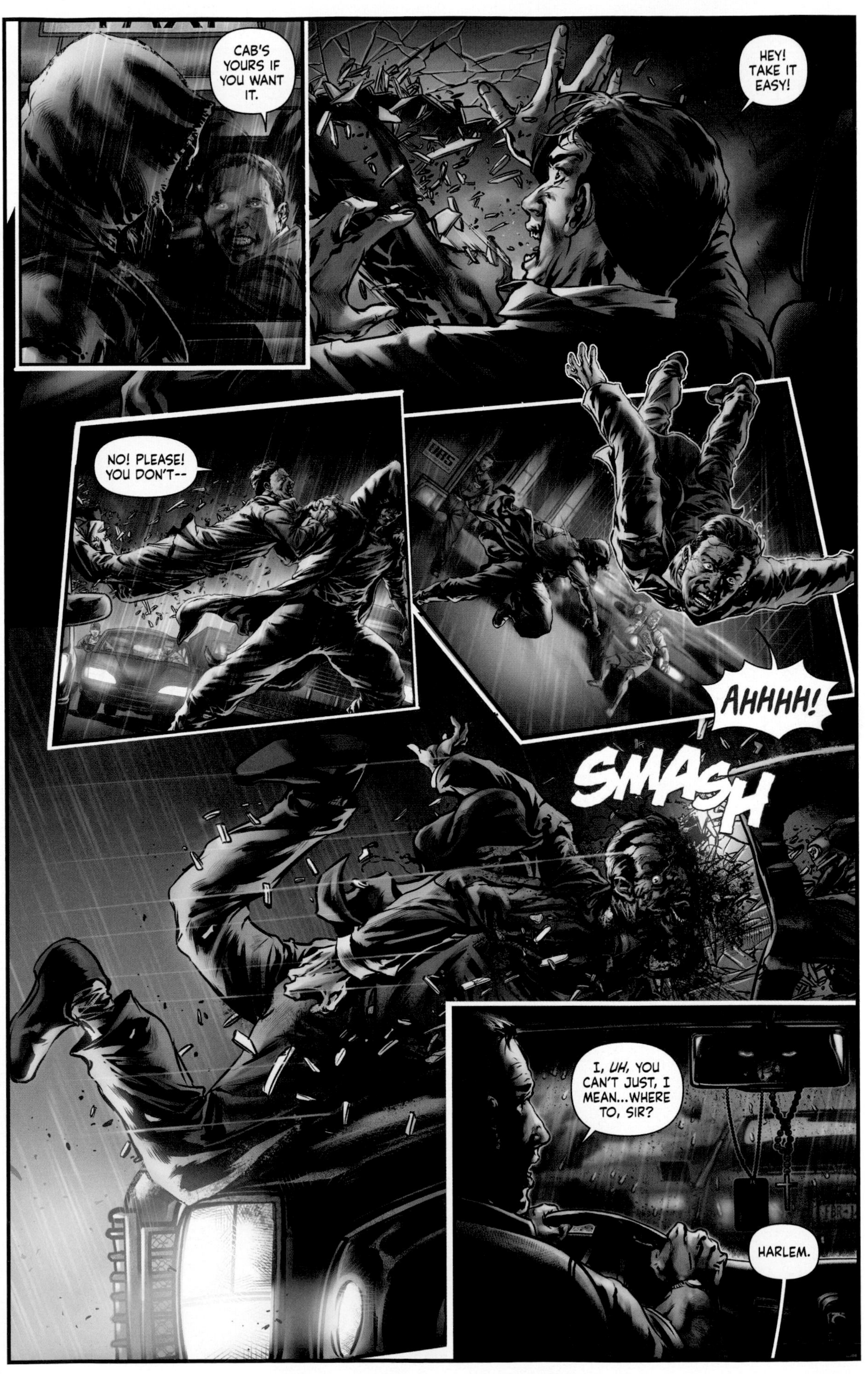
CAB'S YOURS IF YOU WANT IT.
HEY! TAKE IT EASY!
NO! PLEASE! YOU DON'T--
AHHHH!
SMASH
I, UH, YOU CAN'T JUST, I MEAN...WHERE TO, SIR?
HARLEM.

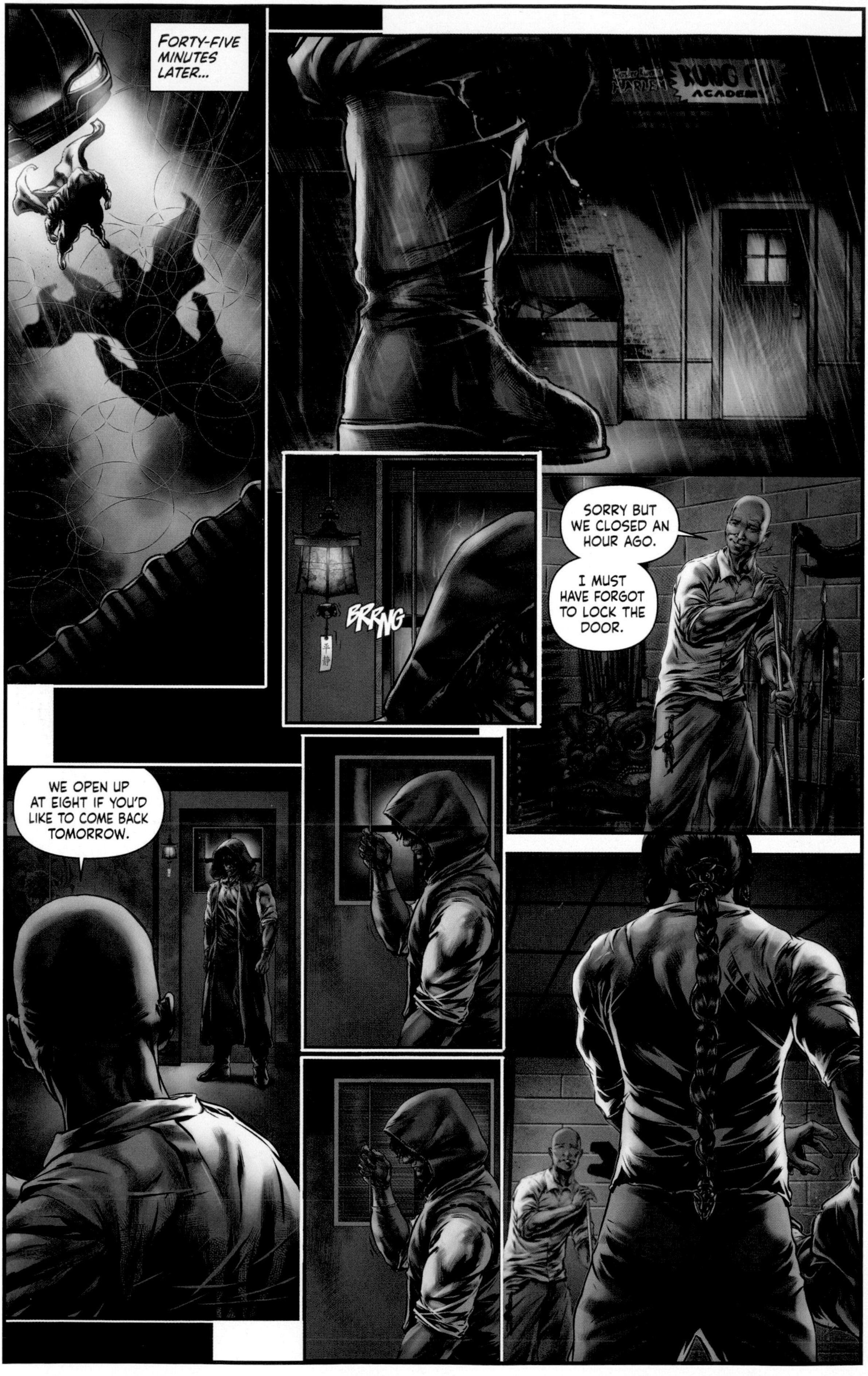
FORTY-FIVE MINUTES LATER...
BRRNG
SORRY BUT WE CLOSED AN HOUR AGO.
I MUST HAVE FORGOT TO LOCK THE DOOR.
WE OPEN UP AT EIGHT IF YOU'D LIKE TO COME BACK TOMORROW.

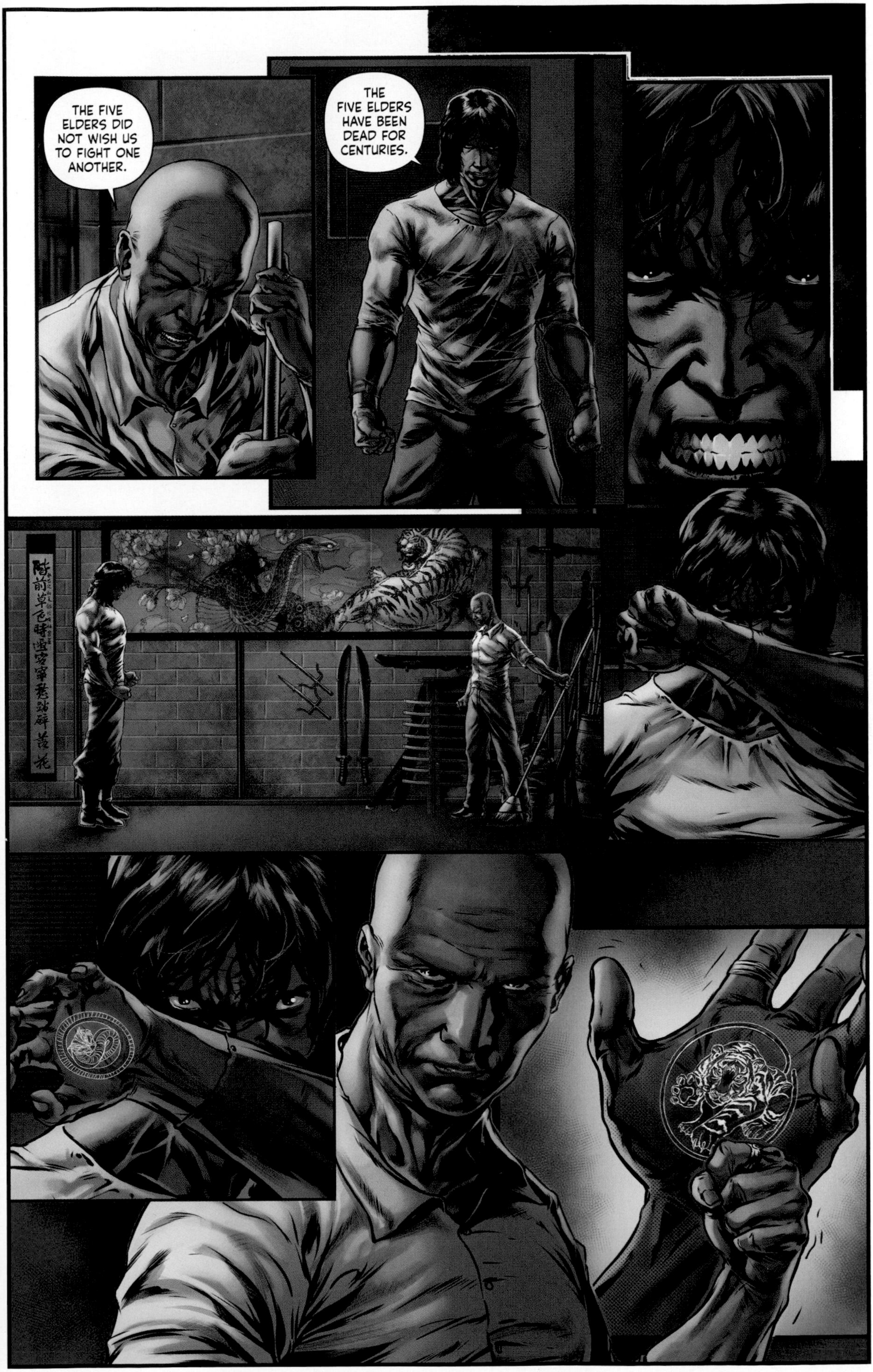
THE FIVE ELDERS DID NOT WISH US TO FIGHT ONE ANOTHER.
THE FIVE ELDERS HAVE BEEN DEAD FOR CENTURIES.

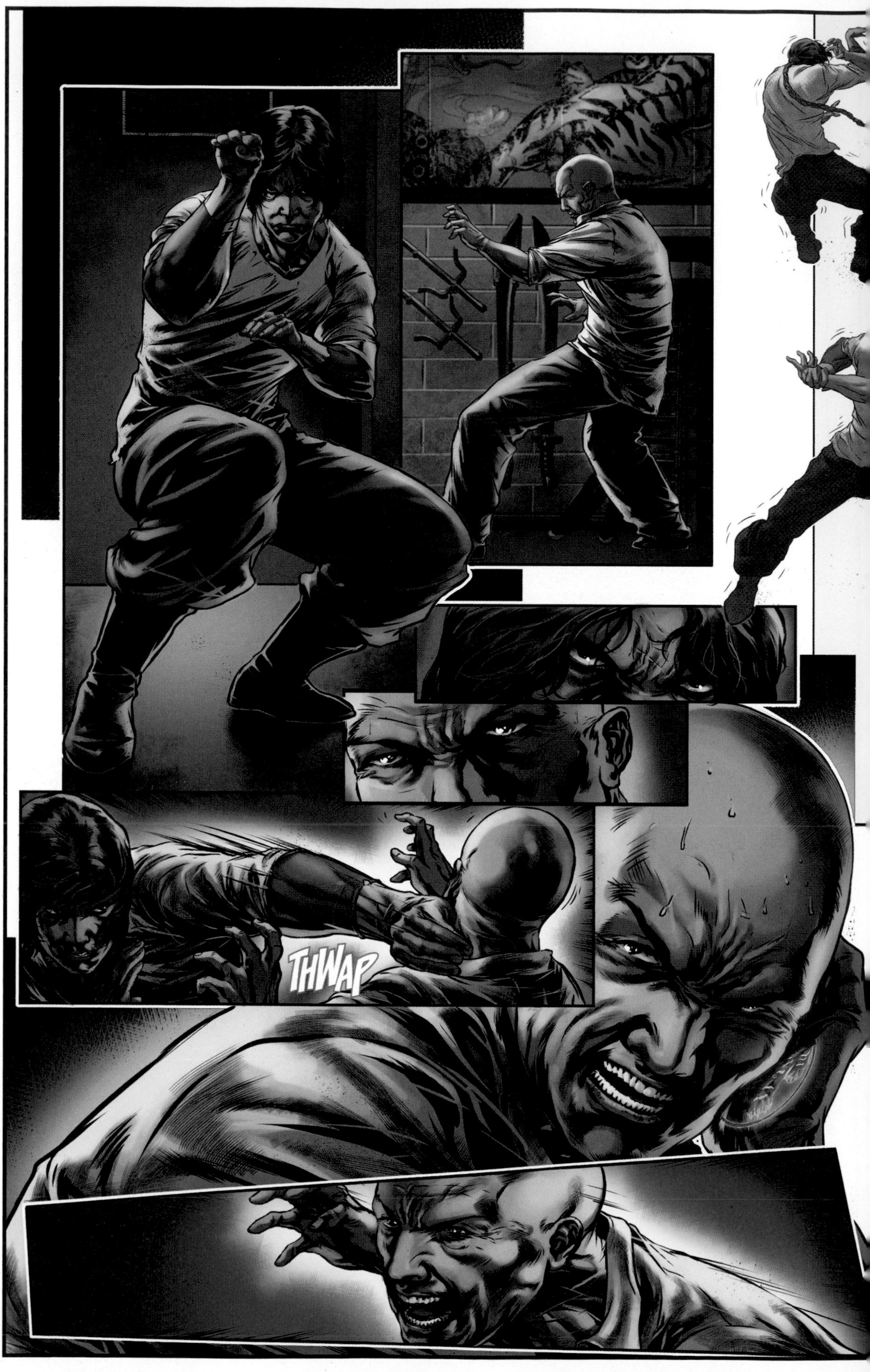
THWAP

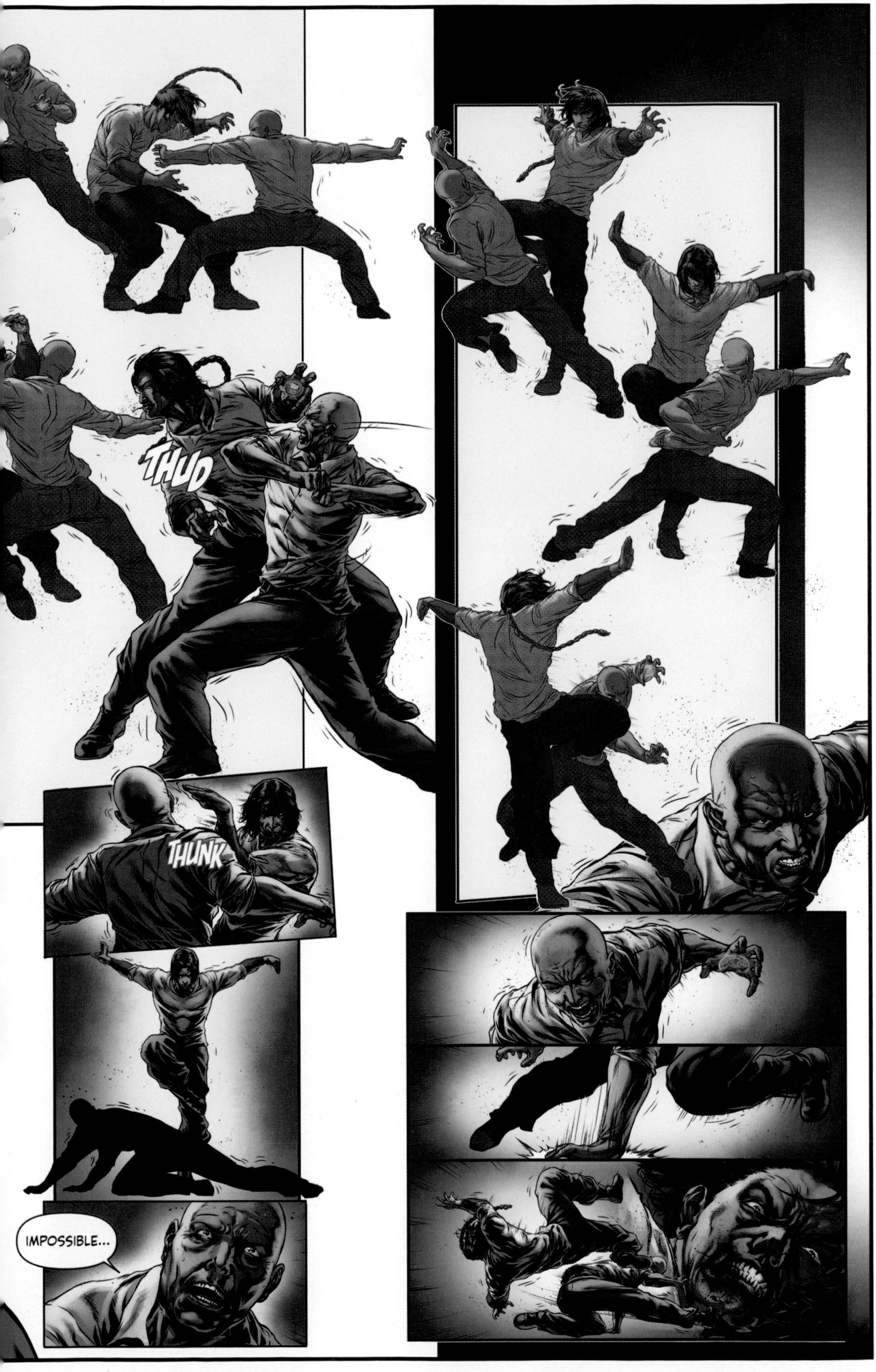

THUD
THUNK
IMPOSSIBLE...

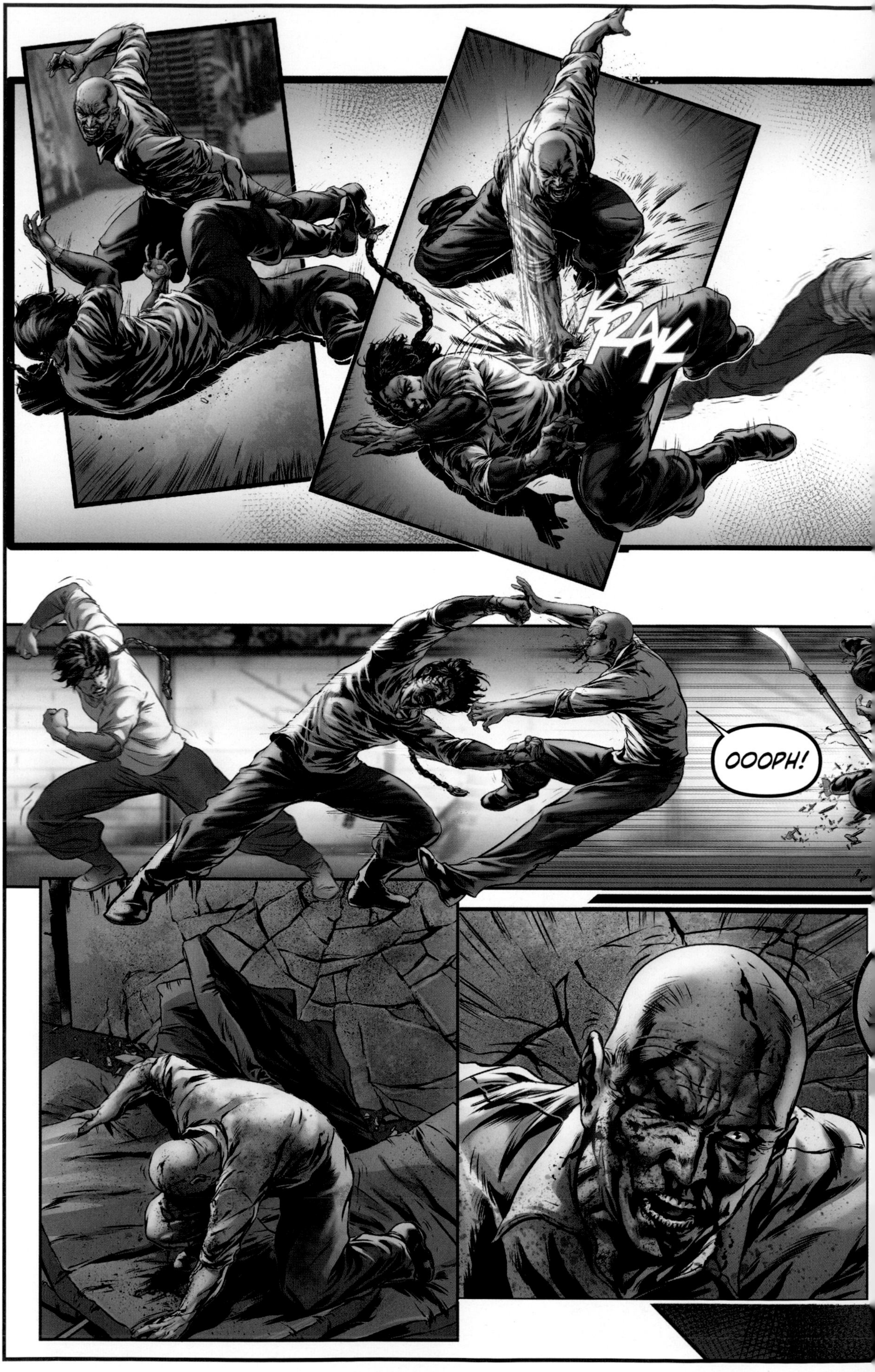
KRAK
OOOPH!

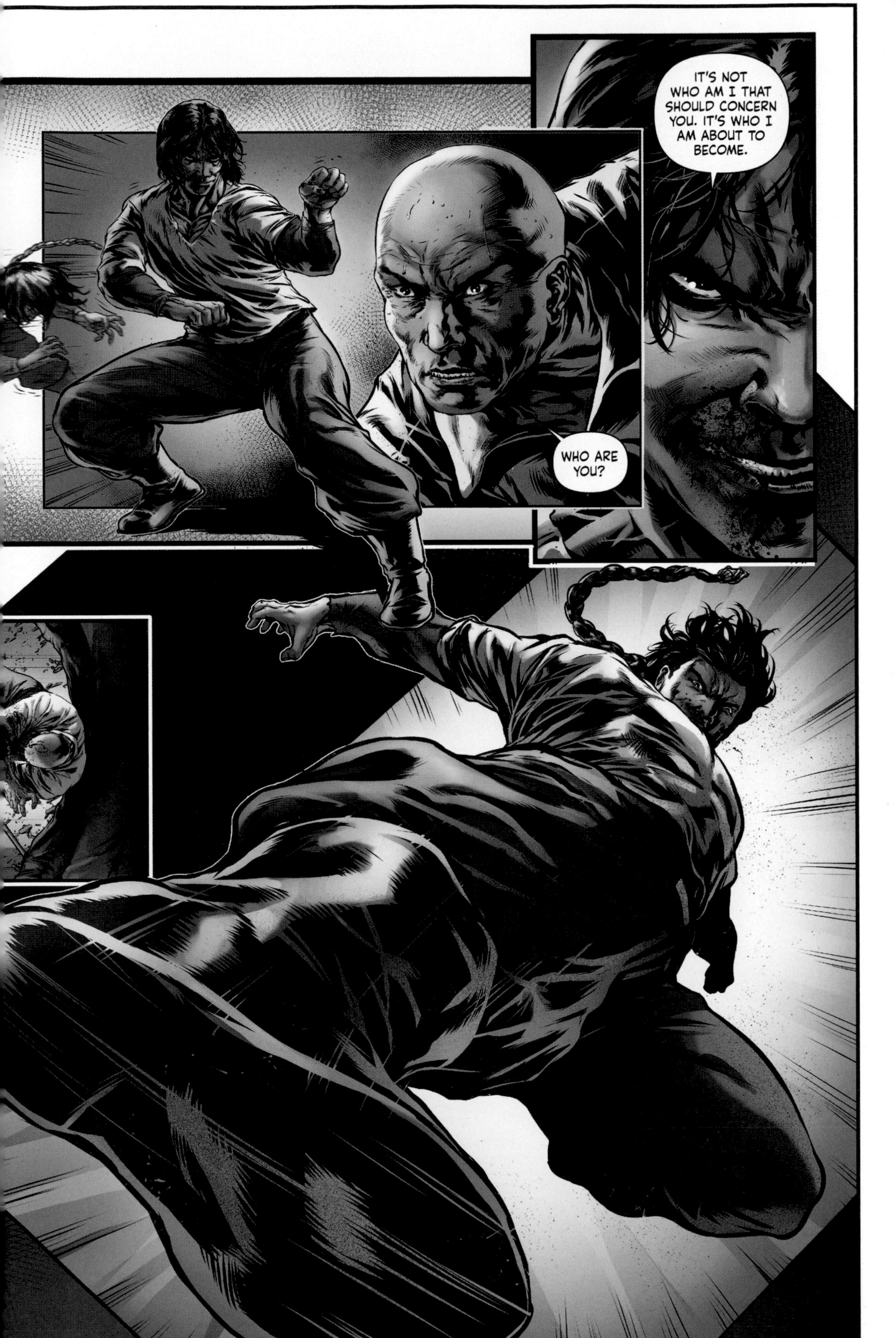
WHO ARE YOU?
IT'S NOT WHO AM I THAT SHOULD CONCERN YOU. IT'S WHO I AM ABOUT TO BECOME.

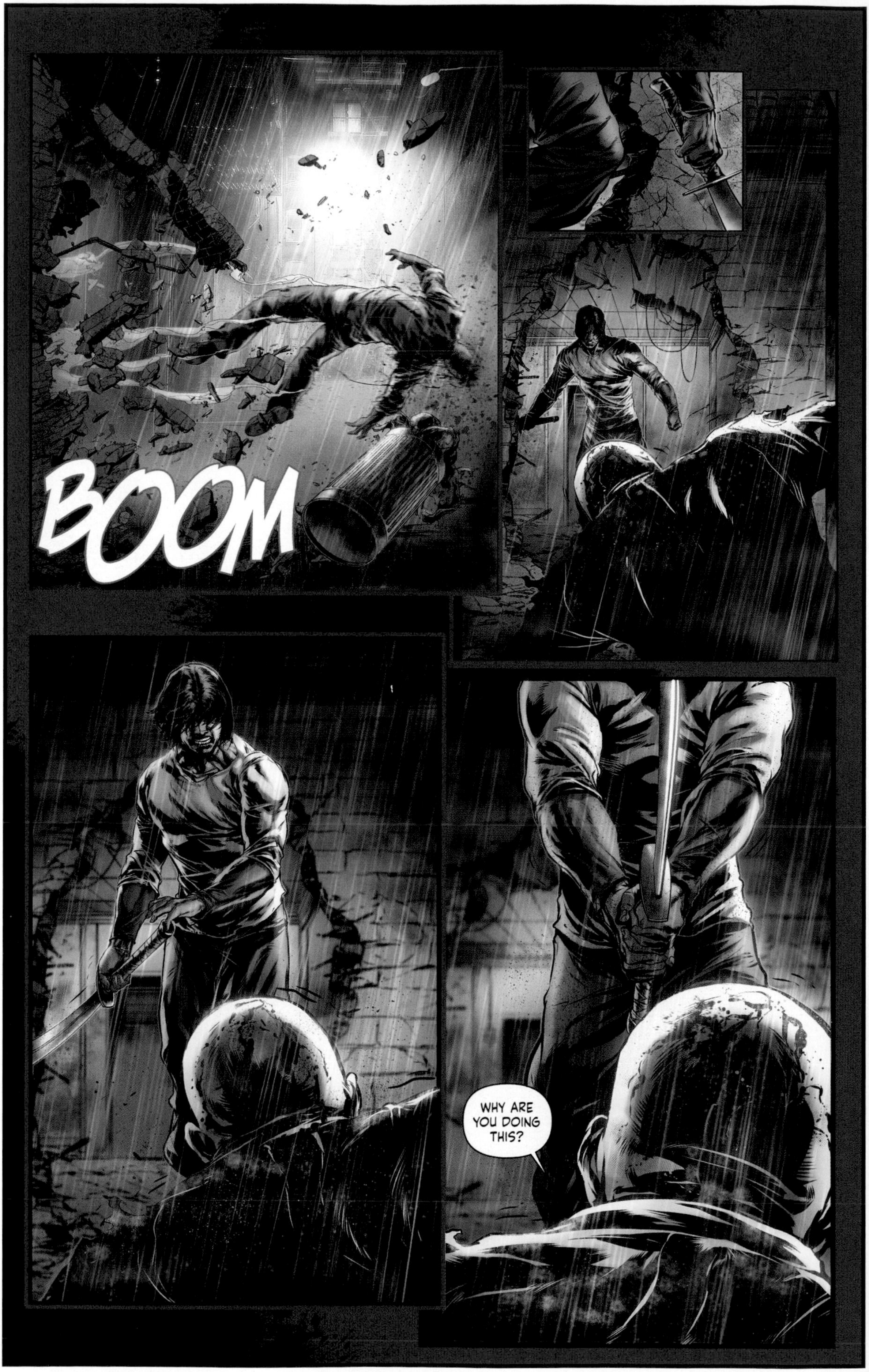
BOOM
WHY ARE YOU DOING THIS?

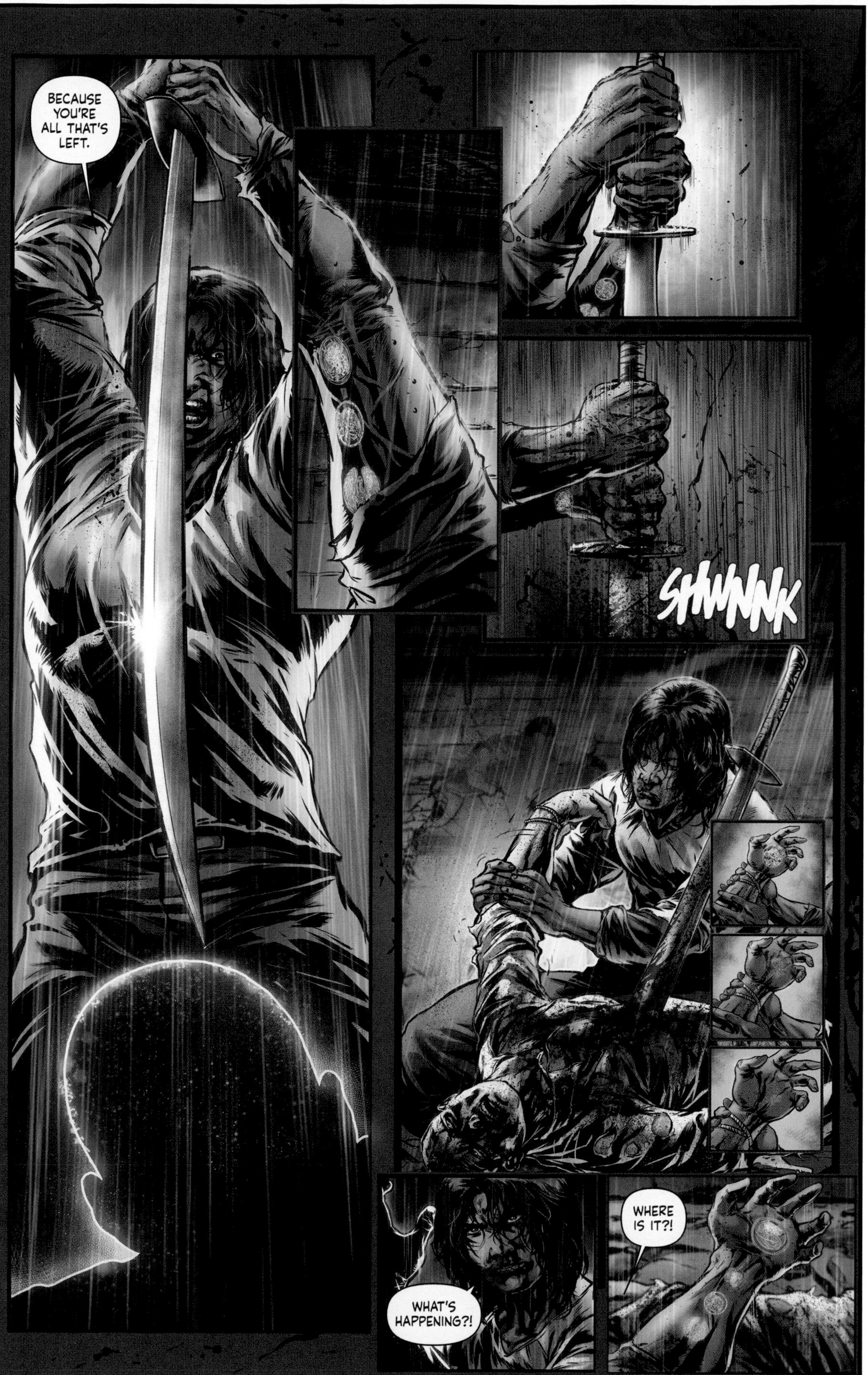
BECAUSE YOU'RE ALL THAT'S LEFT.
SHWNNK
WHAT'S HAPPENING?!
WHERE IS IT?!

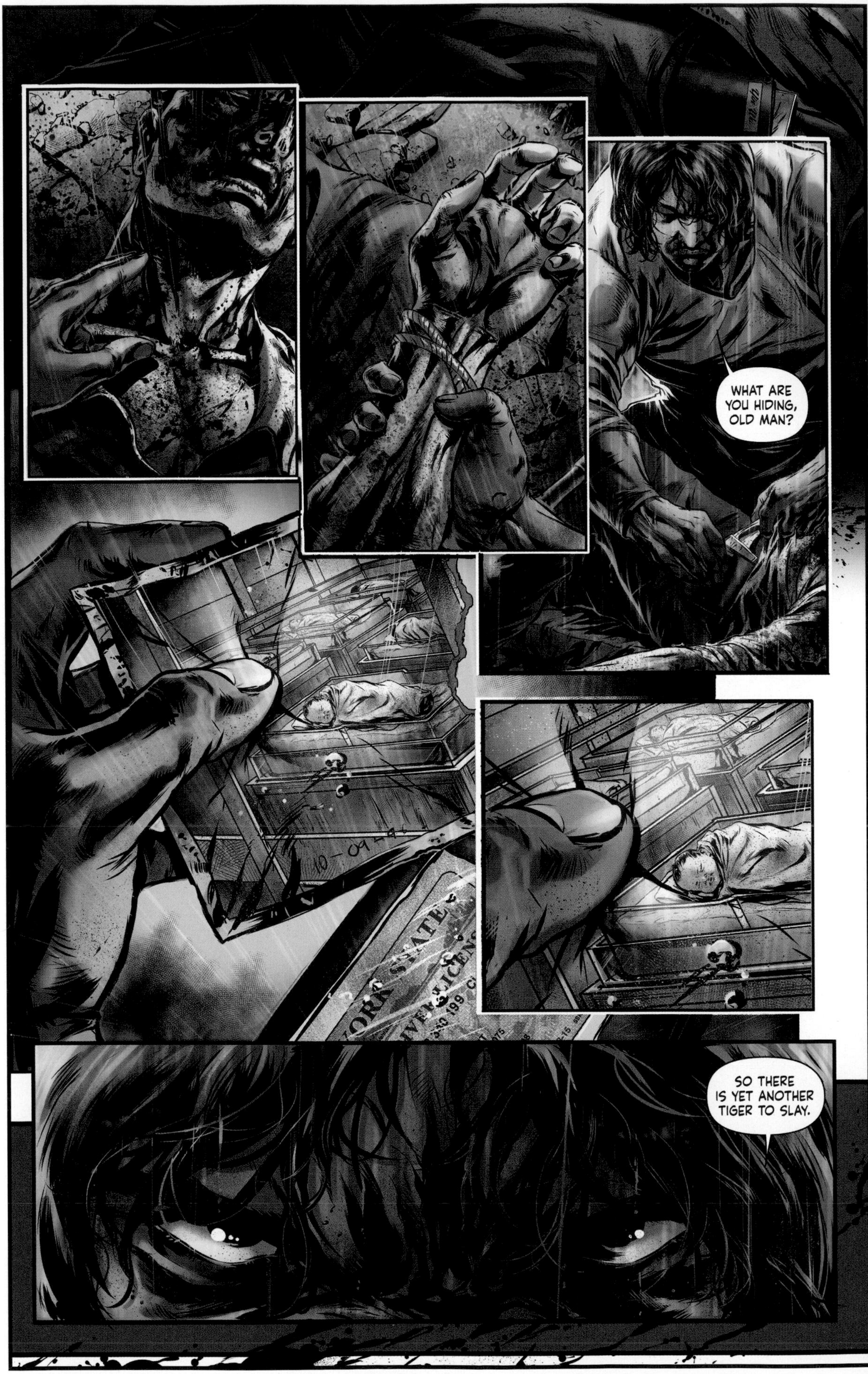
WHAT ARE YOU HIDING, OLD MAN?
SO THERE IS YET ANOTHER TIGER TO SLAY.

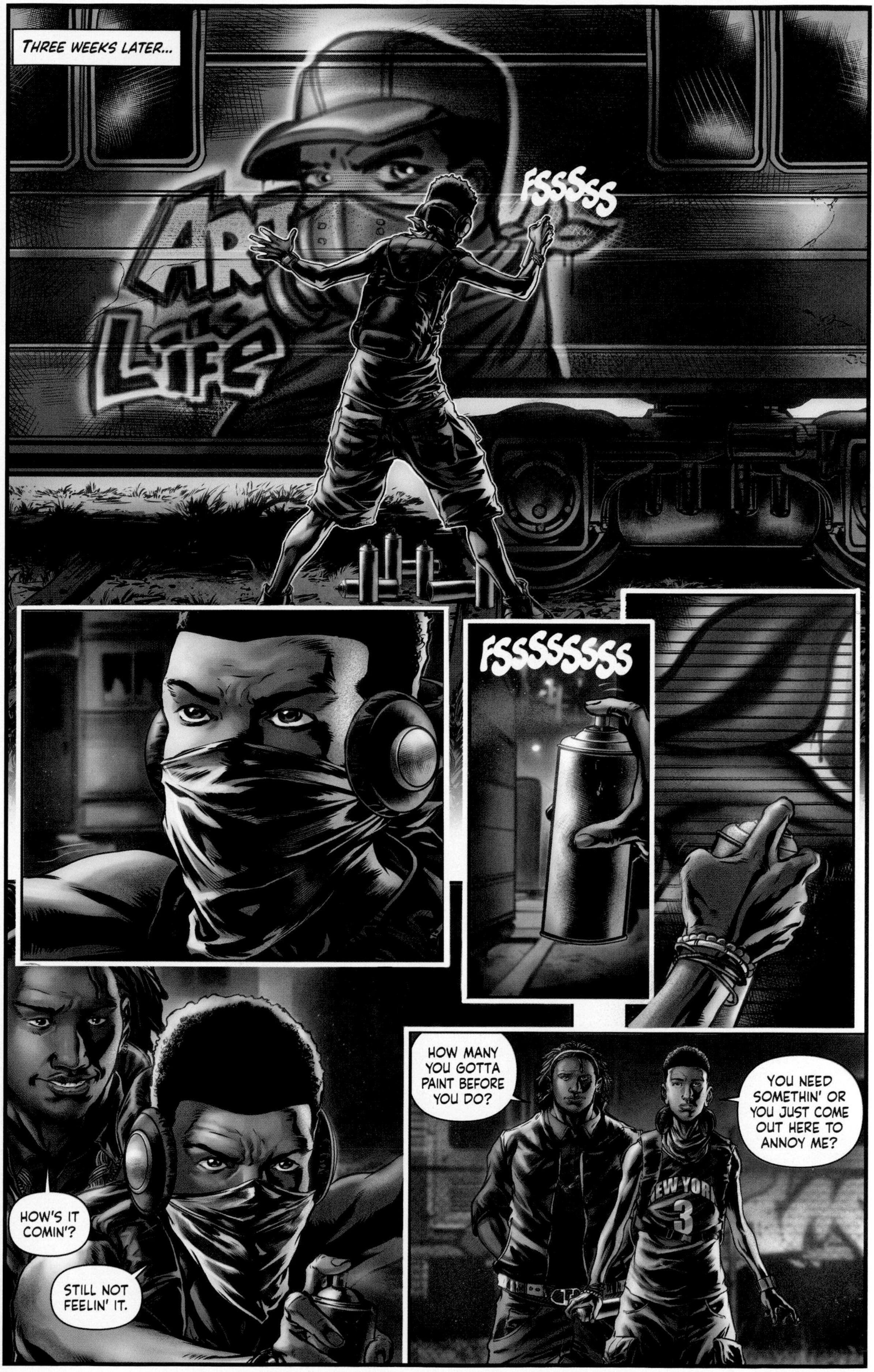
THREE WEEKS LATER...
FSSSSS
ART IS LIFE
FSSSSSSSS
HOW'S IT COMIN'?
STILL NOT FEELIN' IT.
HOW MANY YOU GOTTA PAINT BEFORE YOU DO?
YOU NEED SOMETHIN' OR YOU JUST COME OUT HERE TO ANNOY ME?
NEW YORK 3

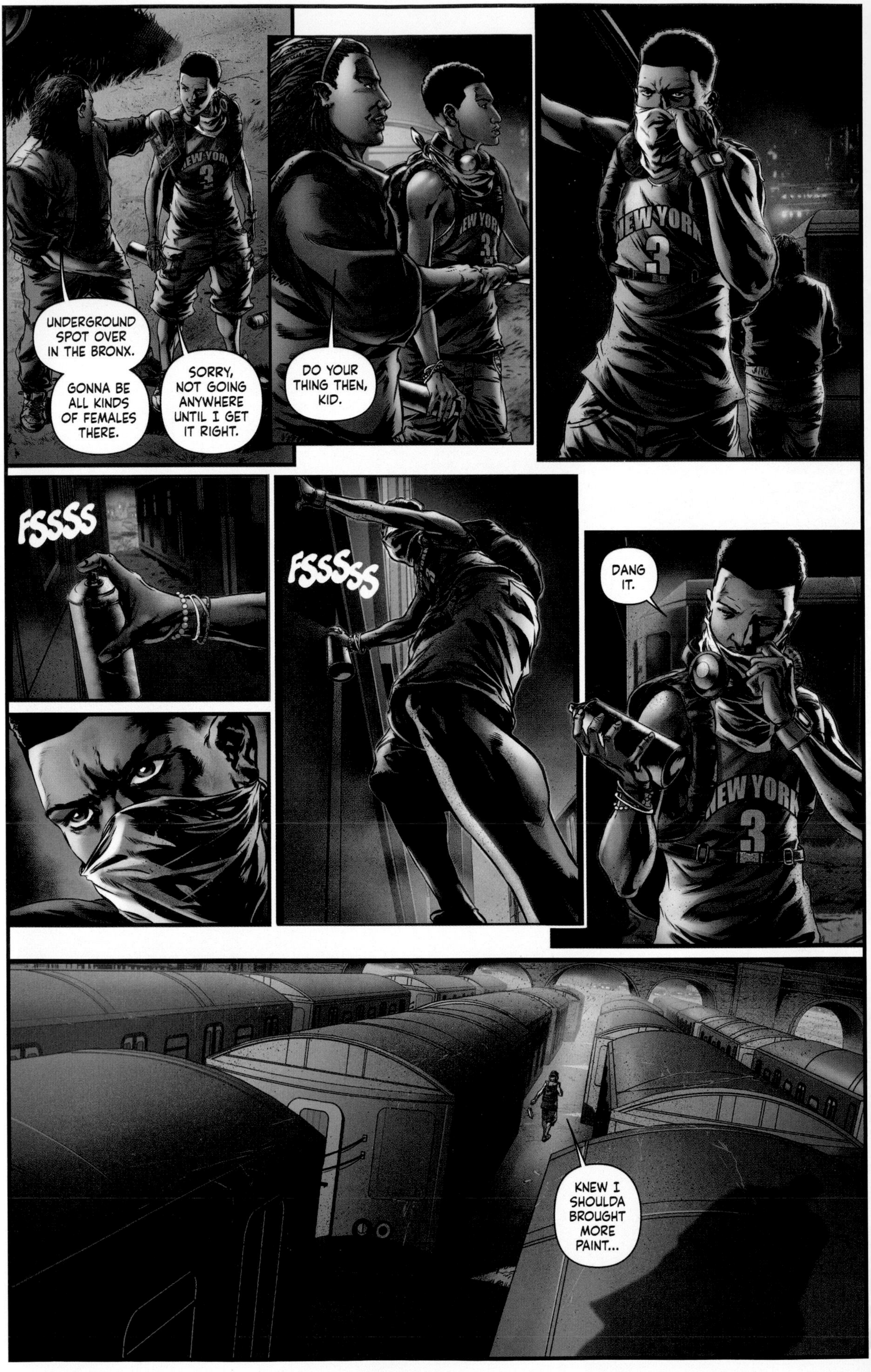
UNDERGROUND SPOT OVER IN THE BRONX.
GONNA BE ALL KINDS OF FEMALES THERE.
SORRY, NOT GOING ANYWHERE UNTIL I GET IT RIGHT.
DO YOUR THING THEN, KID.
FSSSS
FSSSSS
DANG IT.
KNEW I SHOULDA BROUGHT MORE PAINT...

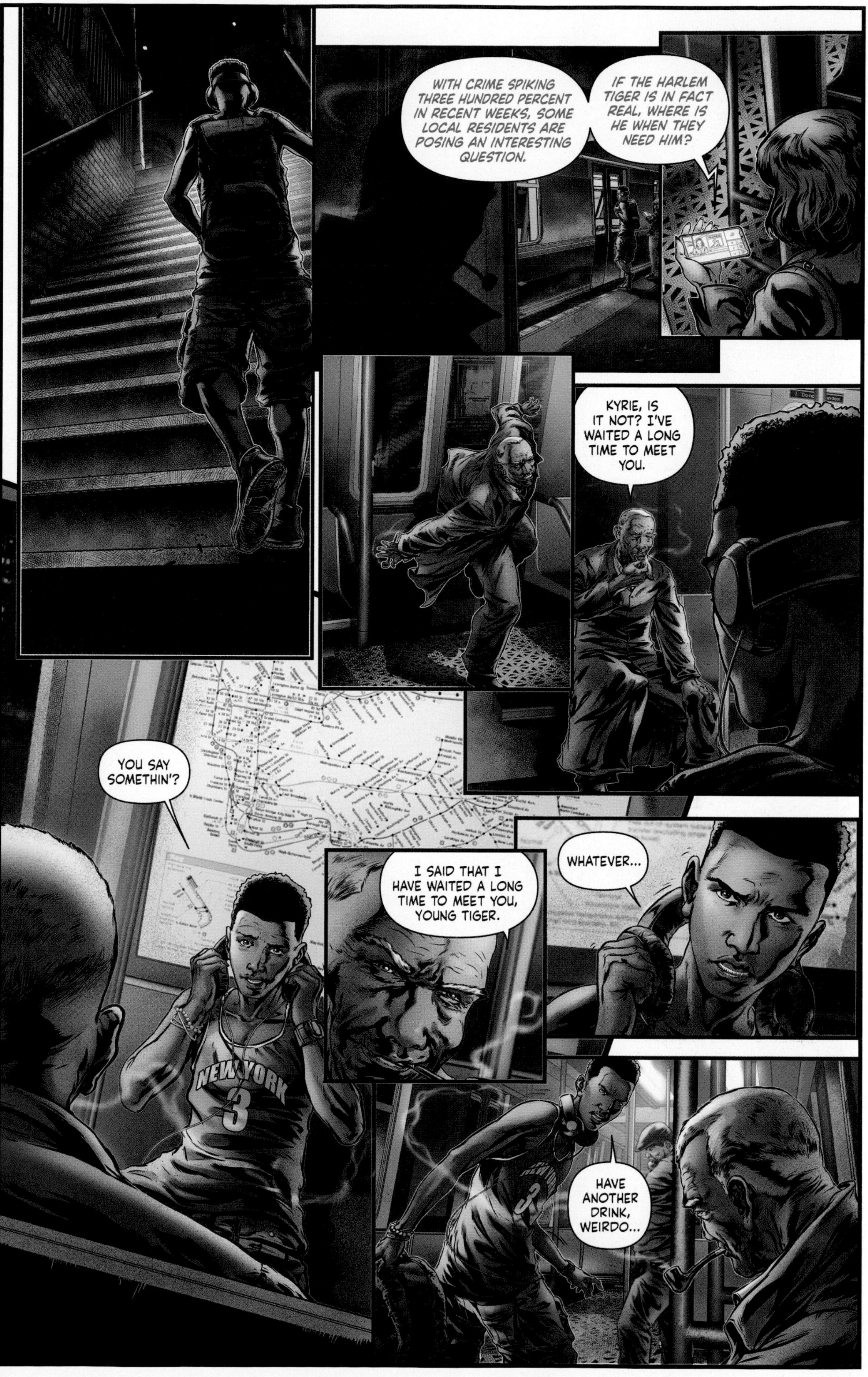

WITH CRIME SPIKING THREE HUNDRED PERCENT IN RECENT WEEKS, SOME LOCAL RESIDENTS ARE POSING AN INTERESTING QUESTION.
IF THE HARLEM TIGER IS IN FACT REAL, WHERE IS HE WHEN THEY NEED HIM?
KYRIE, IS IT NOT? I'VE WAITED A LONG TIME TO MEET YOU.
YOU SAY SOMETHIN'?
I SAID THAT I HAVE WAITED A LONG TIME TO MEET YOU, YOUNG TIGER.
WHATEVER...
HAVE ANOTHER DRINK, WEIRDO...
NEW YORK 3

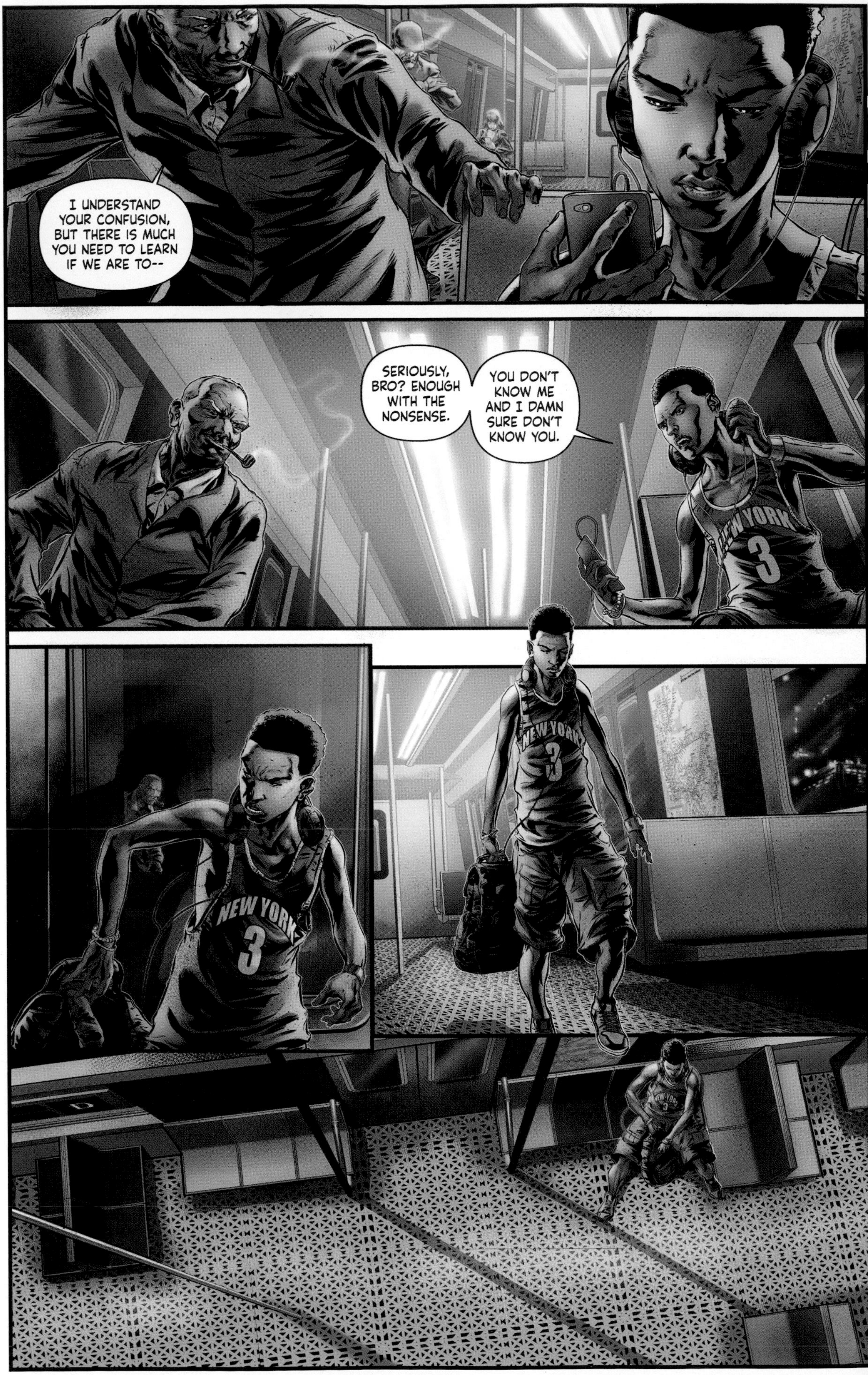
I UNDERSTAND YOUR CONFUSION, BUT THERE IS MUCH YOU NEED TO LEARN IF WE ARE TO--
SERIOUSLY, BRO? ENOUGH WITH THE NONSENSE.
YOU DON'T KNOW ME AND I DAMN SURE DON'T KNOW YOU.
NEW YORK 3
NEW YORK 3
NEW YORK 3

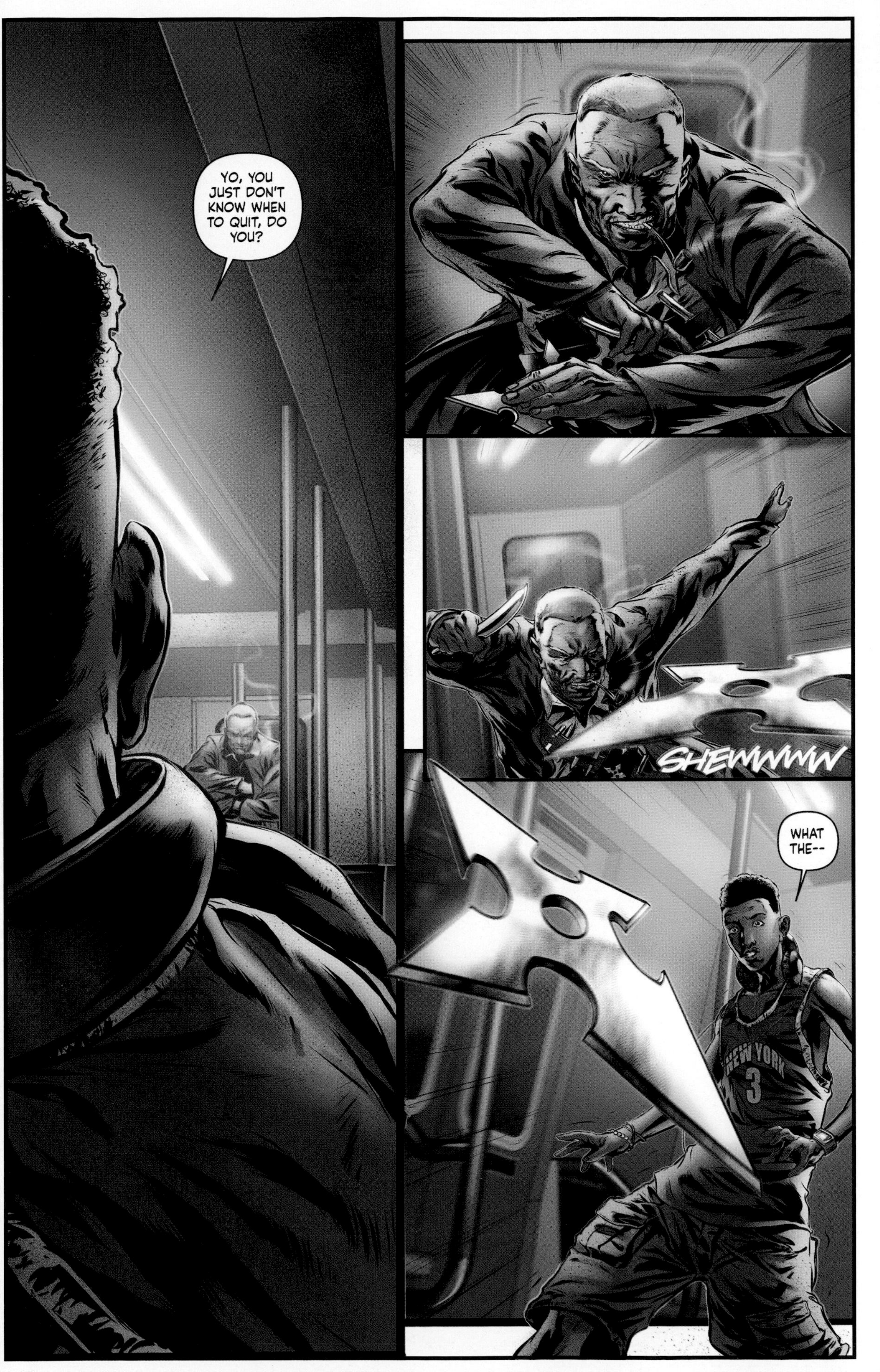
YO, YOU JUST DON'T KNOW WHEN TO QUIT, DO YOU?
SHEWWWW
WHAT THE--
NEW YORK
3

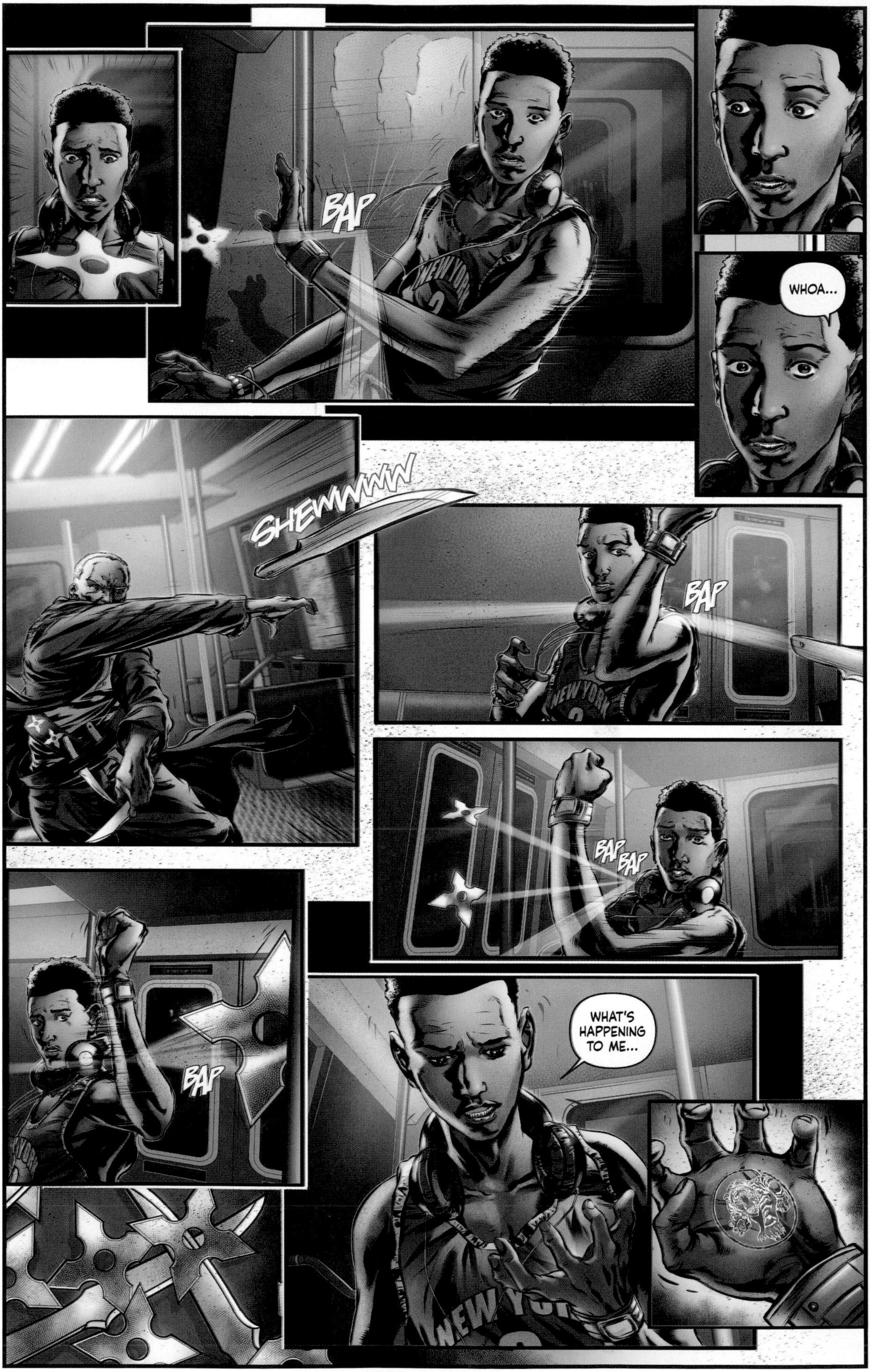
BAP
WHOA...
SHEWWWW
BAP
BAP BAP
BAP
WHAT'S HAPPENING TO ME...

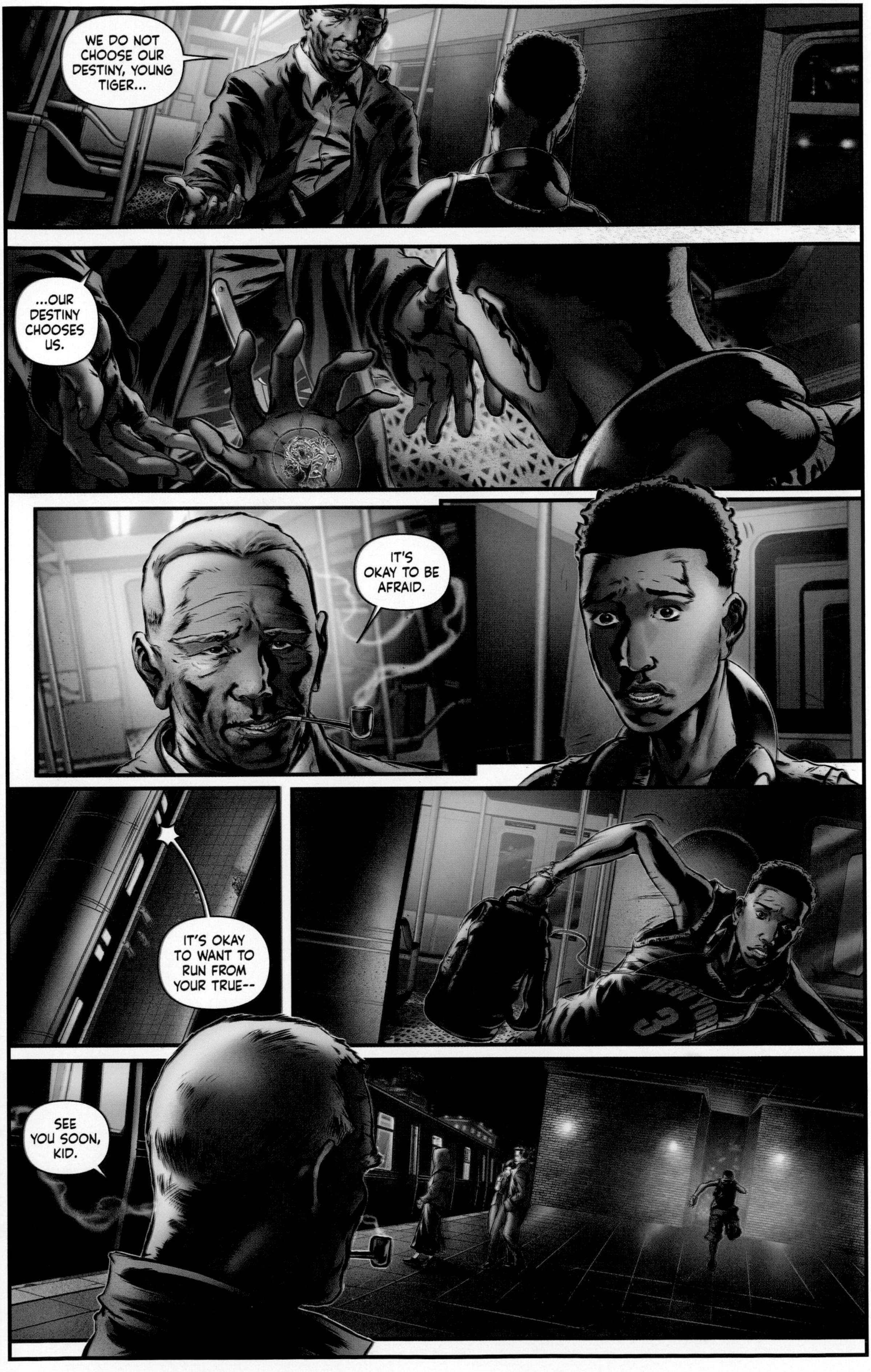
WE DO NOT CHOOSE OUR DESTINY, YOUNG TIGER...
...OUR DESTINY CHOOSES US.
IT'S OKAY TO BE AFRAID.
IT'S OKAY TO WANT TO RUN FROM YOUR TRUE--
SEE YOU SOON, KID.

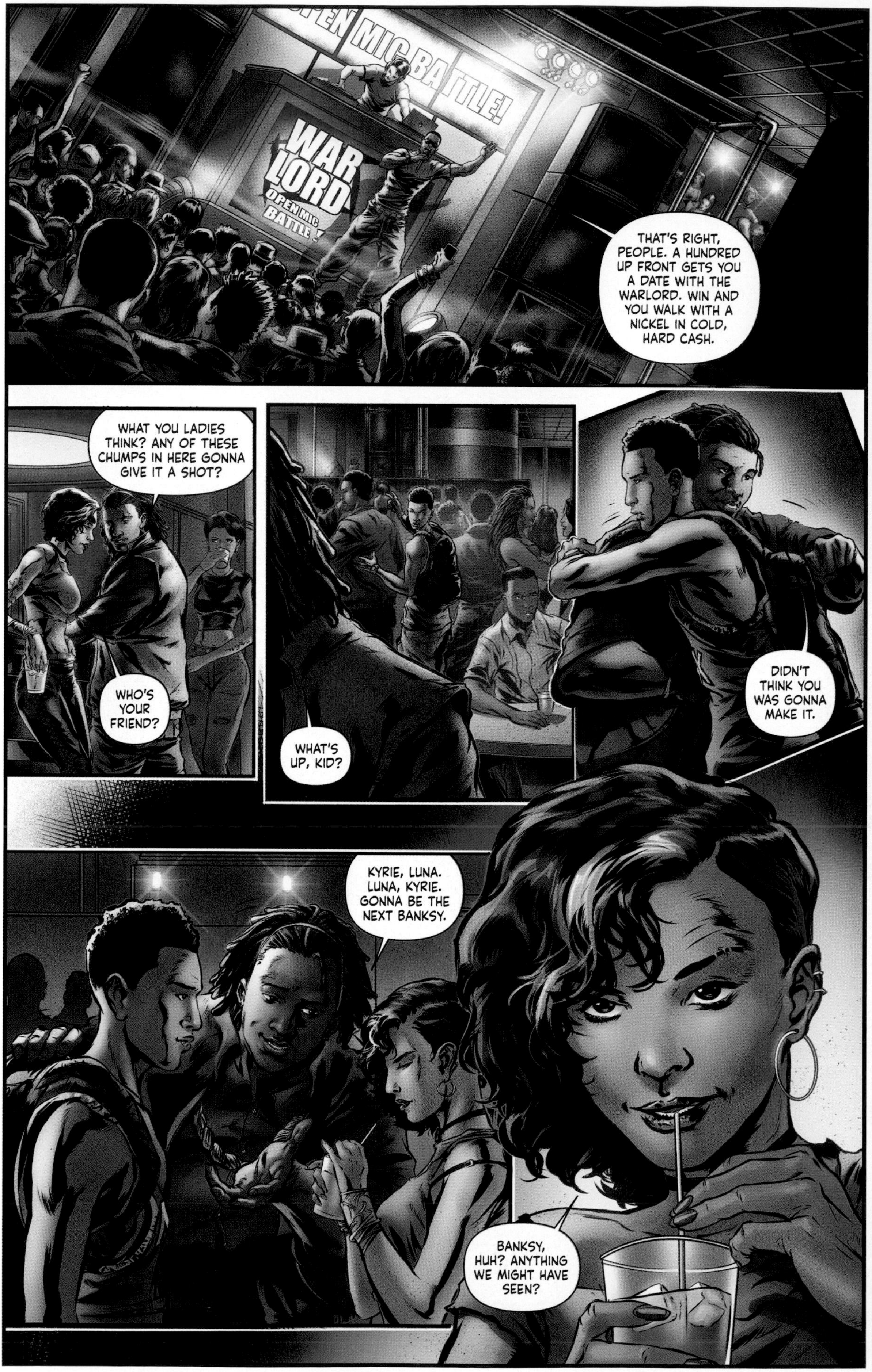
OPEN MIC BATTLE!
WAR LORD
OPEN MIC BATTLE!
THAT'S RIGHT, PEOPLE. A HUNDRED UP FRONT GETS YOU A DATE WITH THE WARLORD. WIN AND YOU WALK WITH A NICKEL IN COLD, HARD CASH.
WHAT YOU LADIES THINK? ANY OF THESE CHUMPS IN HERE GONNA GIVE IT A SHOT?
WHO'S YOUR FRIEND?
WHAT'S UP, KID?
DIDN'T THINK YOU WAS GONNA MAKE IT.
KYRIE, LUNA. LUNA, KYRIE. GONNA BE THE NEXT BANKSY.
BANKSY, HUH? ANYTHING WE MIGHT HAVE SEEN?

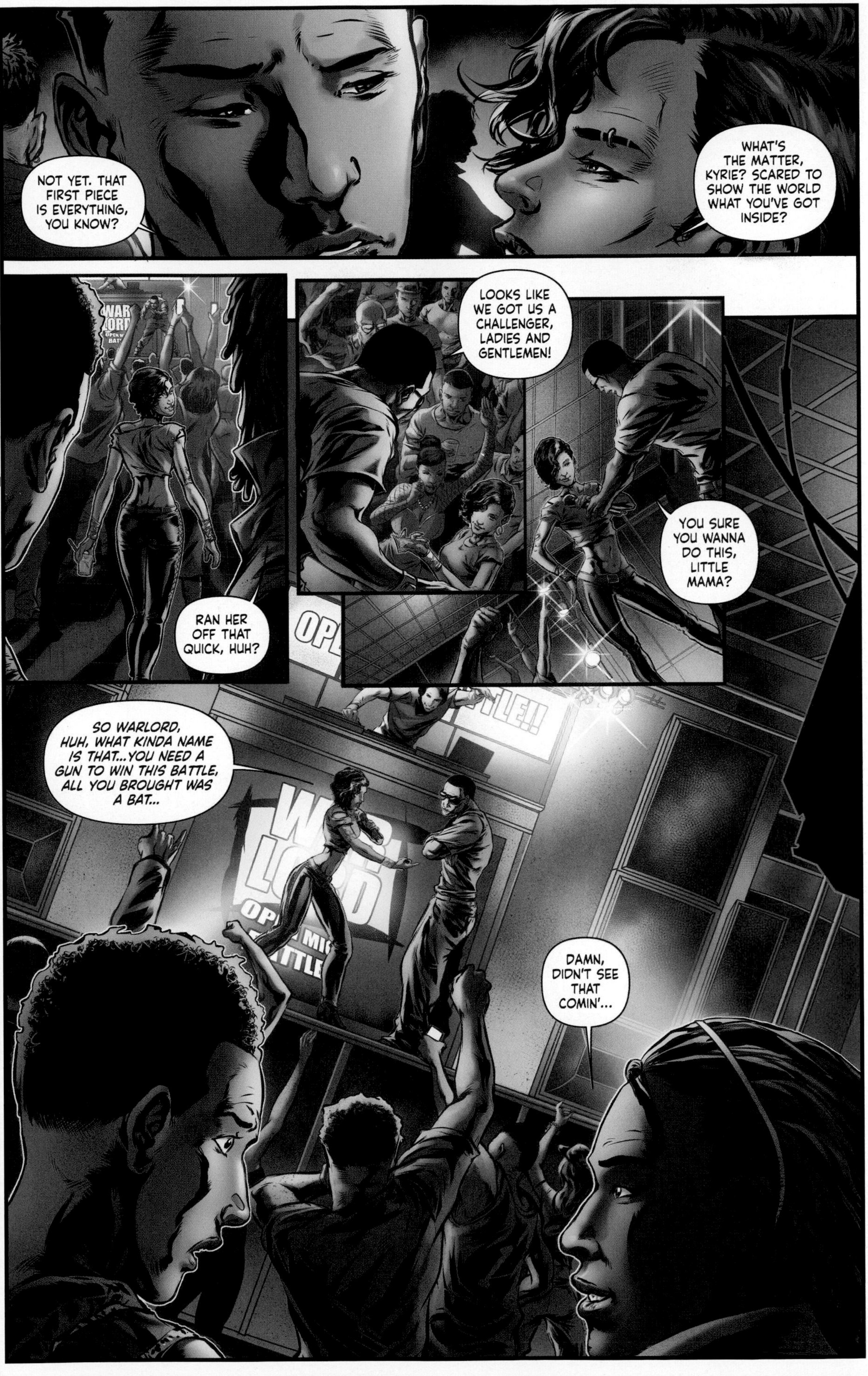
NOT YET. THAT FIRST PIECE IS EVERYTHING, YOU KNOW?
WHAT'S THE MATTER, KYRIE? SCARED TO SHOW THE WORLD WHAT YOU'VE GOT INSIDE?
WAR LORD
RAN HER OFF THAT QUICK, HUH?
LOOKS LIKE WE GOT US A CHALLENGER, LADIES AND GENTLEMEN!
YOU SURE YOU WANNA DO THIS, LITTLE MAMA?
SO WARLORD, HUH, WHAT KINDA NAME IS THAT...YOU NEED A GUN TO WIN THIS BATTLE, ALL YOU BROUGHT WAS A BAT...
DAMN, DIDN'T SEE THAT COMIN'...

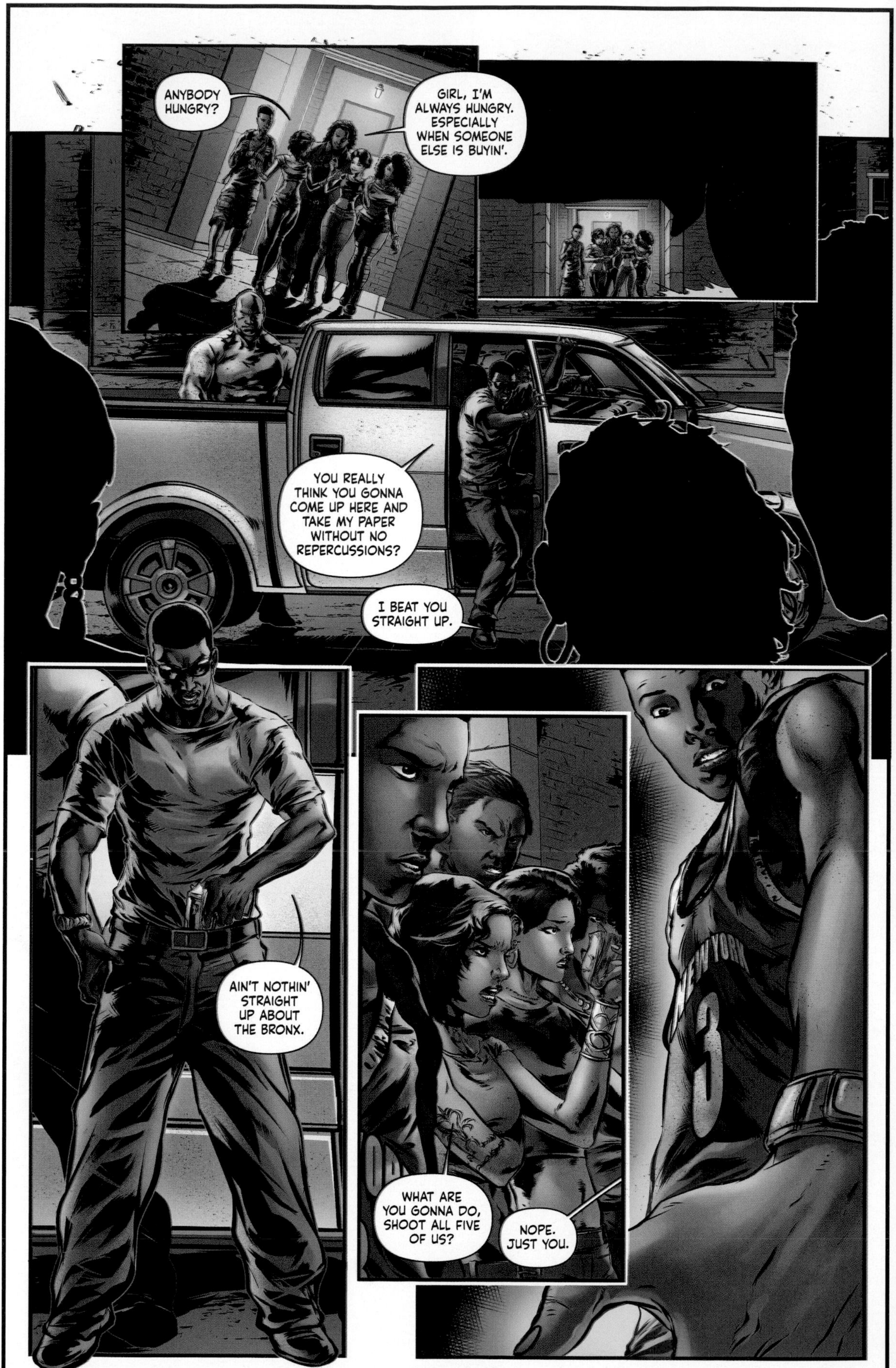
ANYBODY HUNGRY?
GIRL, I'M ALWAYS HUNGRY. ESPECIALLY WHEN SOMEONE ELSE IS BUYIN'.
YOU REALLY THINK YOU GONNA COME UP HERE AND TAKE MY PAPER WITHOUT NO REPERCUSSIONS?
I BEAT YOU STRAIGHT UP.
AIN'T NOTHIN' STRAIGHT UP ABOUT THE BRONX.
WHAT ARE YOU GONNA DO, SHOOT ALL FIVE OF US?
NOPE. JUST YOU.

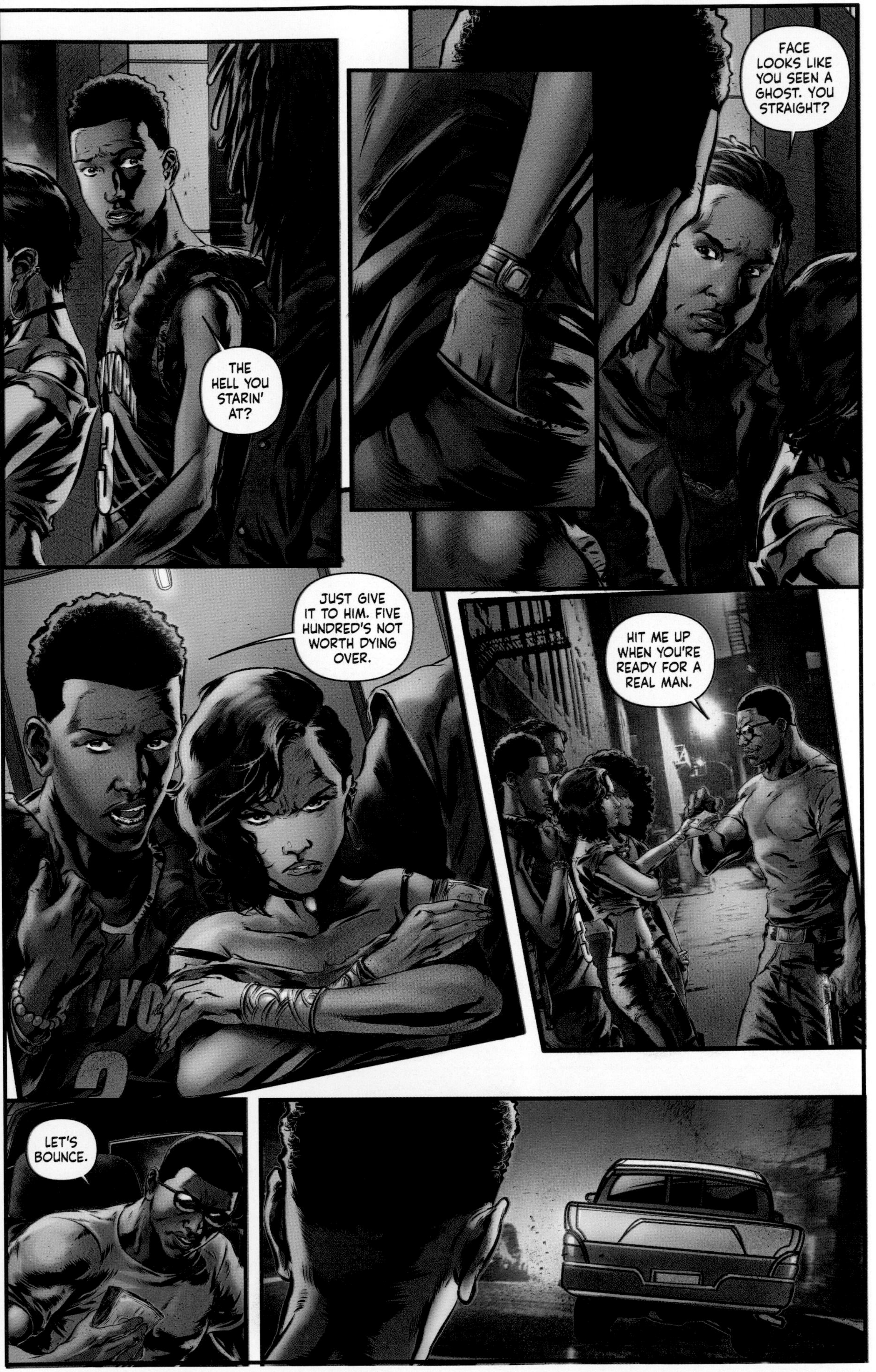
THE HELL YOU STARIN' AT?
FACE LOOKS LIKE YOU SEEN A GHOST. YOU STRAIGHT?
JUST GIVE IT TO HIM. FIVE HUNDRED'S NOT WORTH DYING OVER.
HIT ME UP WHEN YOU'RE READY FOR A REAL MAN.
LET'S BOUNCE.

MAKE SURE THEY'RE ON THERE TIGHT. PEOPLE AROUND HERE BEEN ACTING CRAZY OF LATE.

HARLEM HOAGIES

LET'S GO, SON. REGULARS ARE GETTIN' RESTLESS.

LUNCH RUSH IS COMING SO TRY NOT TO GET LOST.

THIS ADDRESS EVEN IN RANGE?

SAID HE'D PAY EXTRA.

HARLEM HOAGIES, CAN YOU HOLD?

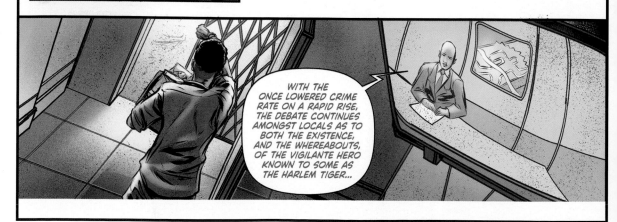

WITH THE ONCE LOWERED CRIME RATE ON A RAPID RISE, THE DEBATE CONTINUES AMONGST LOCALS AS TO BOTH THE EXISTENCE, AND THE WHEREABOUTS, OF THE VIGILANTE HERO KNOWN TO SOME AS THE HARLEM TIGER...

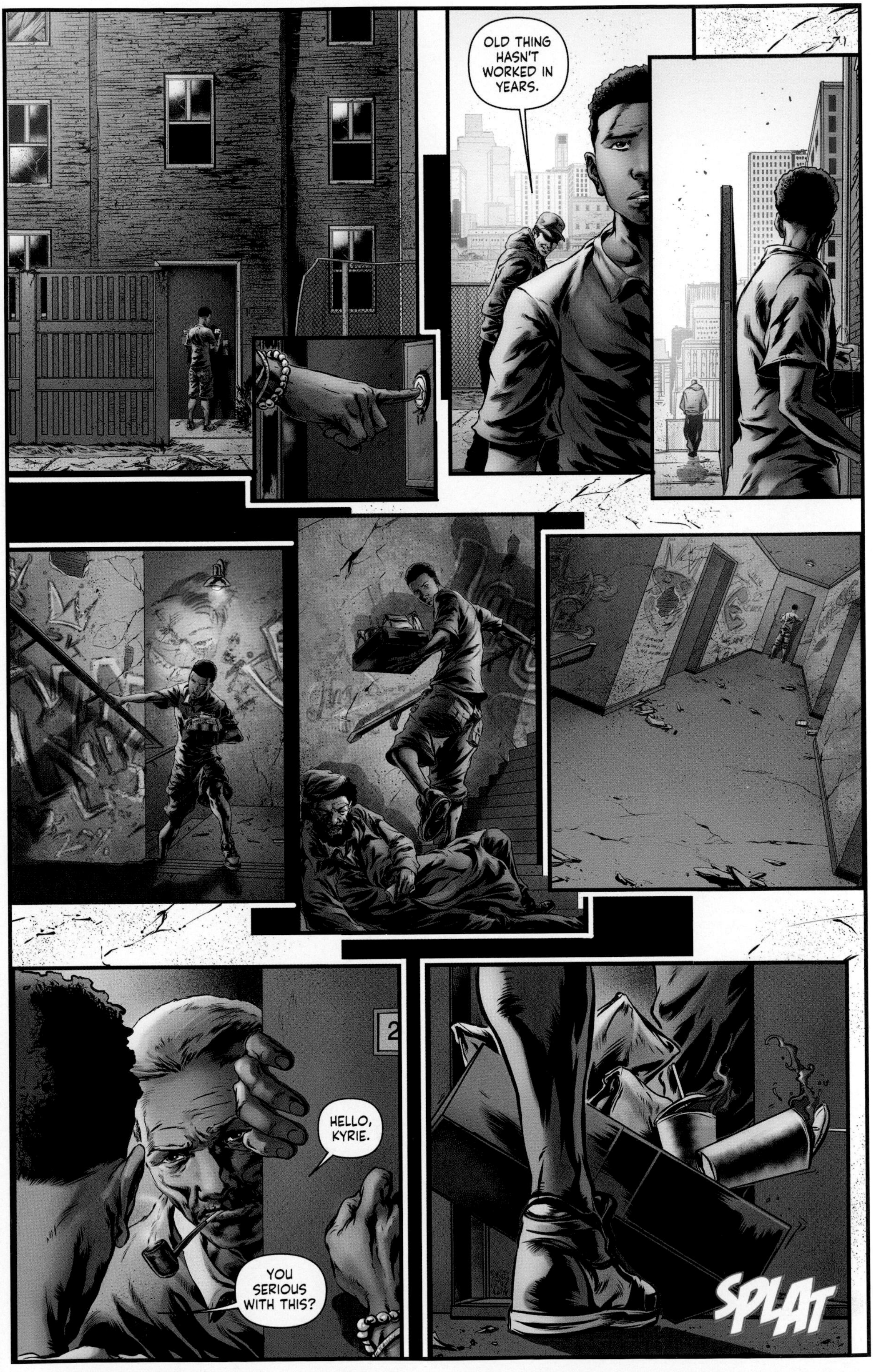
OLD THING HASN'T WORKED IN YEARS.
2
HELLO, KYRIE.
YOU SERIOUS WITH THIS?
SPLAT

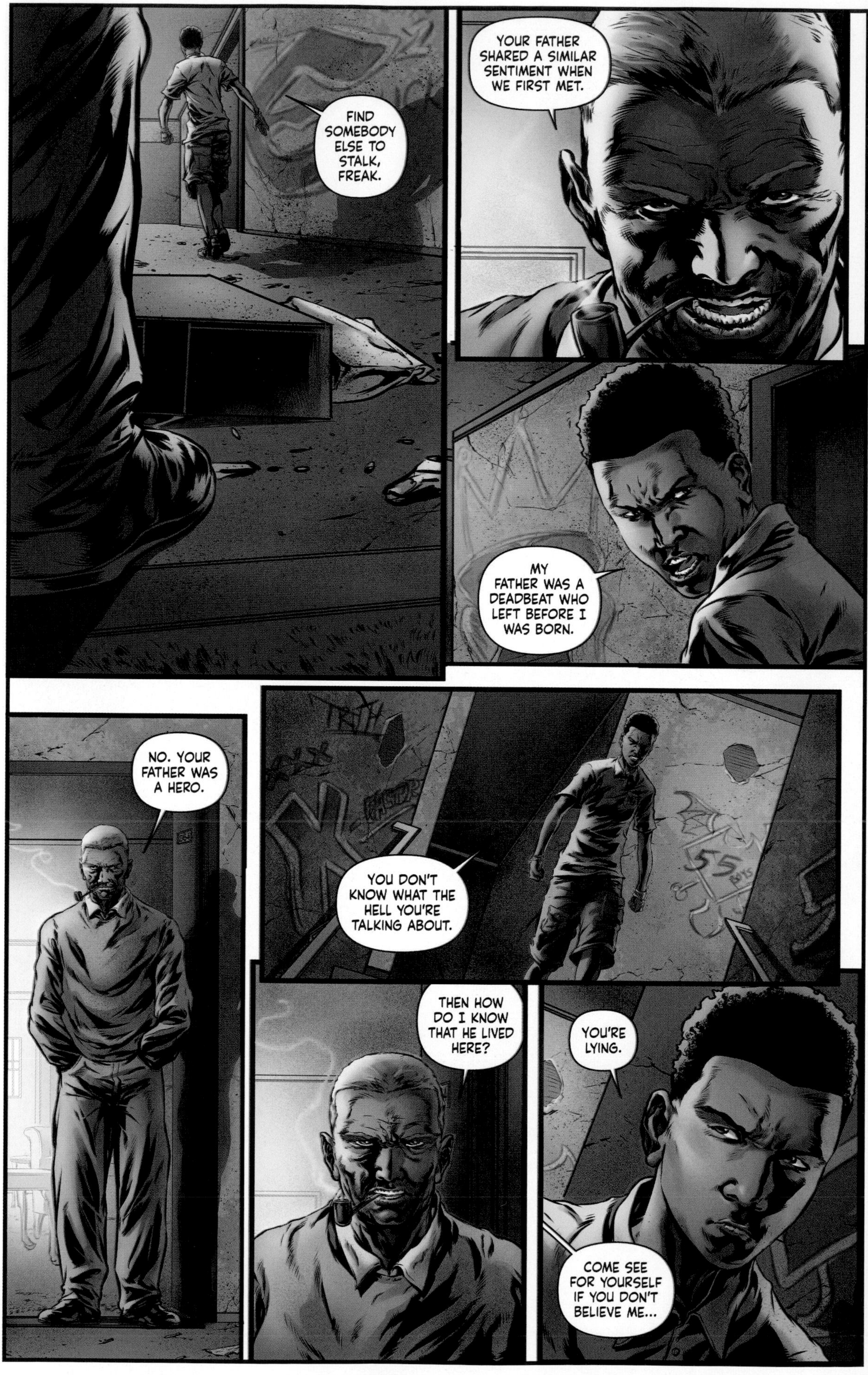
FIND SOMEBODY ELSE TO STALK, FREAK.
YOUR FATHER SHARED A SIMILAR SENTIMENT WHEN WE FIRST MET.
MY FATHER WAS A DEADBEAT WHO LEFT BEFORE I WAS BORN.
NO. YOUR FATHER WAS A HERO.
YOU DON'T KNOW WHAT THE HELL YOU'RE TALKING ABOUT.
THEN HOW DO I KNOW THAT HE LIVED HERE?
YOU'RE LYING.
COME SEE FOR YOURSELF IF YOU DON'T BELIEVE ME...

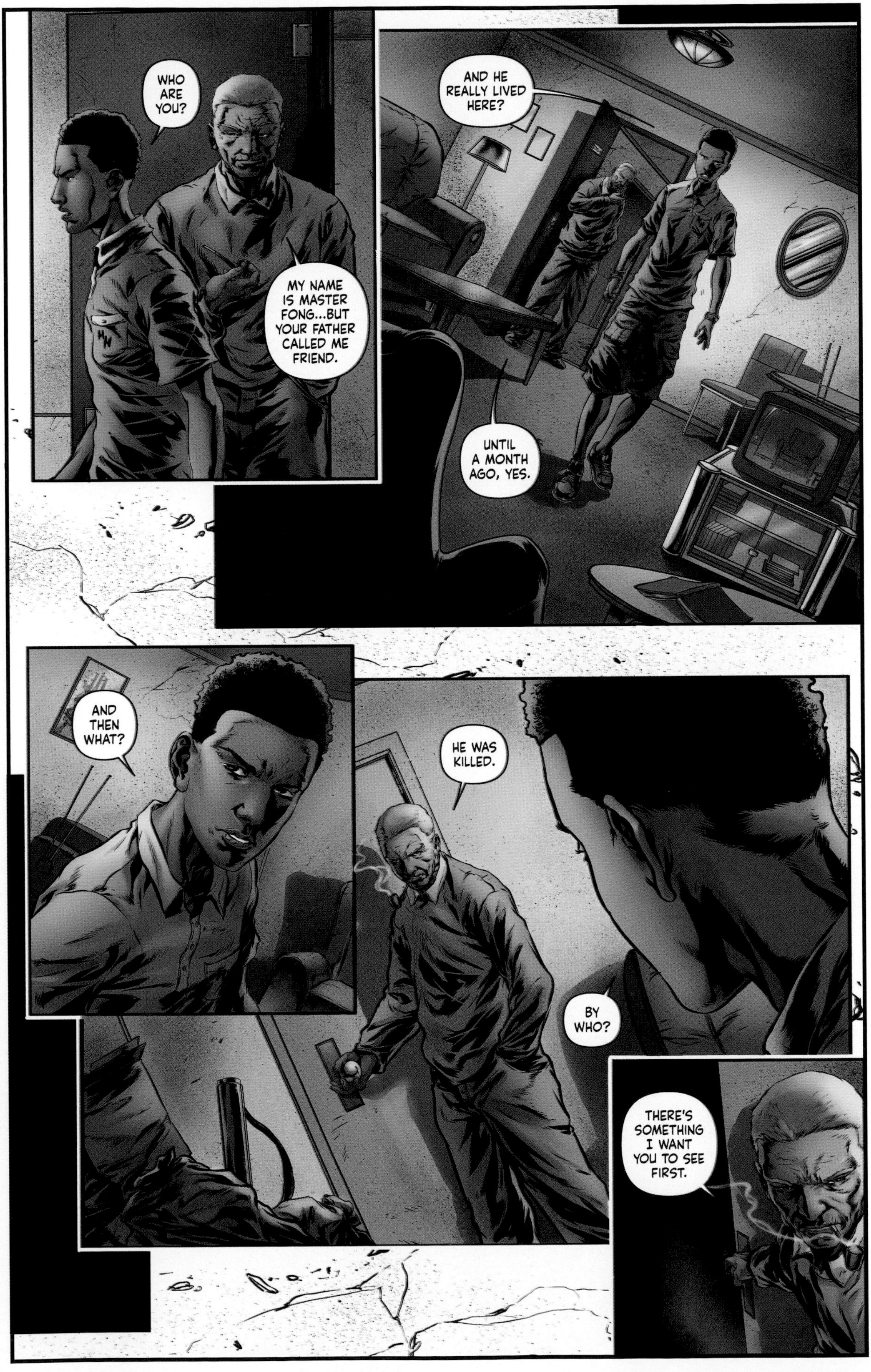
WHO ARE YOU?
MY NAME IS MASTER FONG...BUT YOUR FATHER CALLED ME FRIEND.
AND HE REALLY LIVED HERE?
UNTIL A MONTH AGO, YES.
AND THEN WHAT?
HE WAS KILLED.
BY WHO?
THERE'S SOMETHING I WANT YOU TO SEE FIRST.

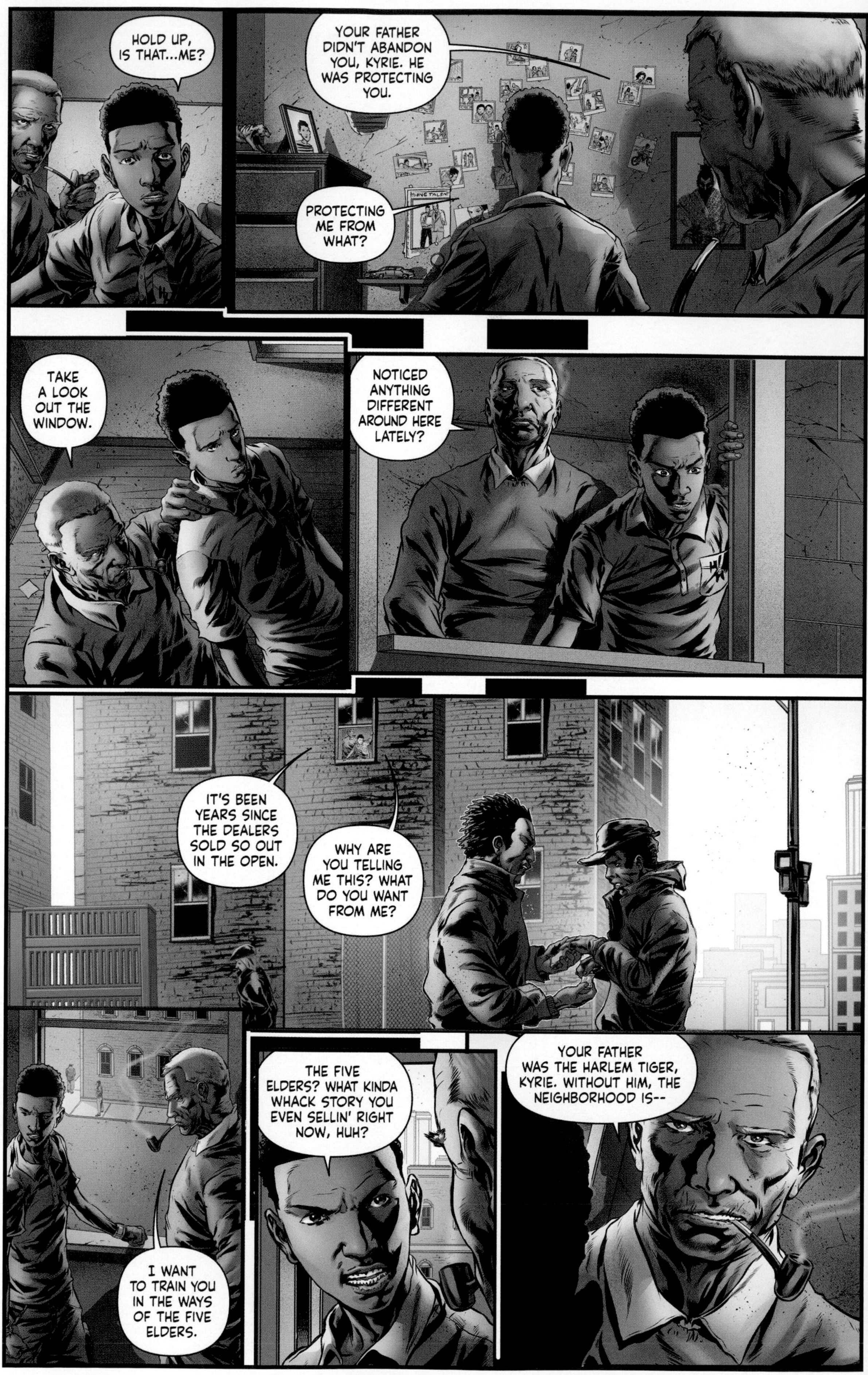
HOLD UP, IS THAT...ME?
YOUR FATHER DIDN'T ABANDON YOU, KYRIE. HE WAS PROTECTING YOU.
PROTECTING ME FROM WHAT?
TAKE A LOOK OUT THE WINDOW.
NOTICED ANYTHING DIFFERENT AROUND HERE LATELY?
IT'S BEEN YEARS SINCE THE DEALERS SOLD SO OUT IN THE OPEN.
WHY ARE YOU TELLING ME THIS? WHAT DO YOU WANT FROM ME?
I WANT TO TRAIN YOU IN THE WAYS OF THE FIVE ELDERS.
THE FIVE ELDERS? WHAT KINDA WHACK STORY YOU EVEN SELLIN' RIGHT NOW, HUH?
YOUR FATHER WAS THE HARLEM TIGER, KYRIE. WITHOUT HIM, THE NEIGHBORHOOD IS--

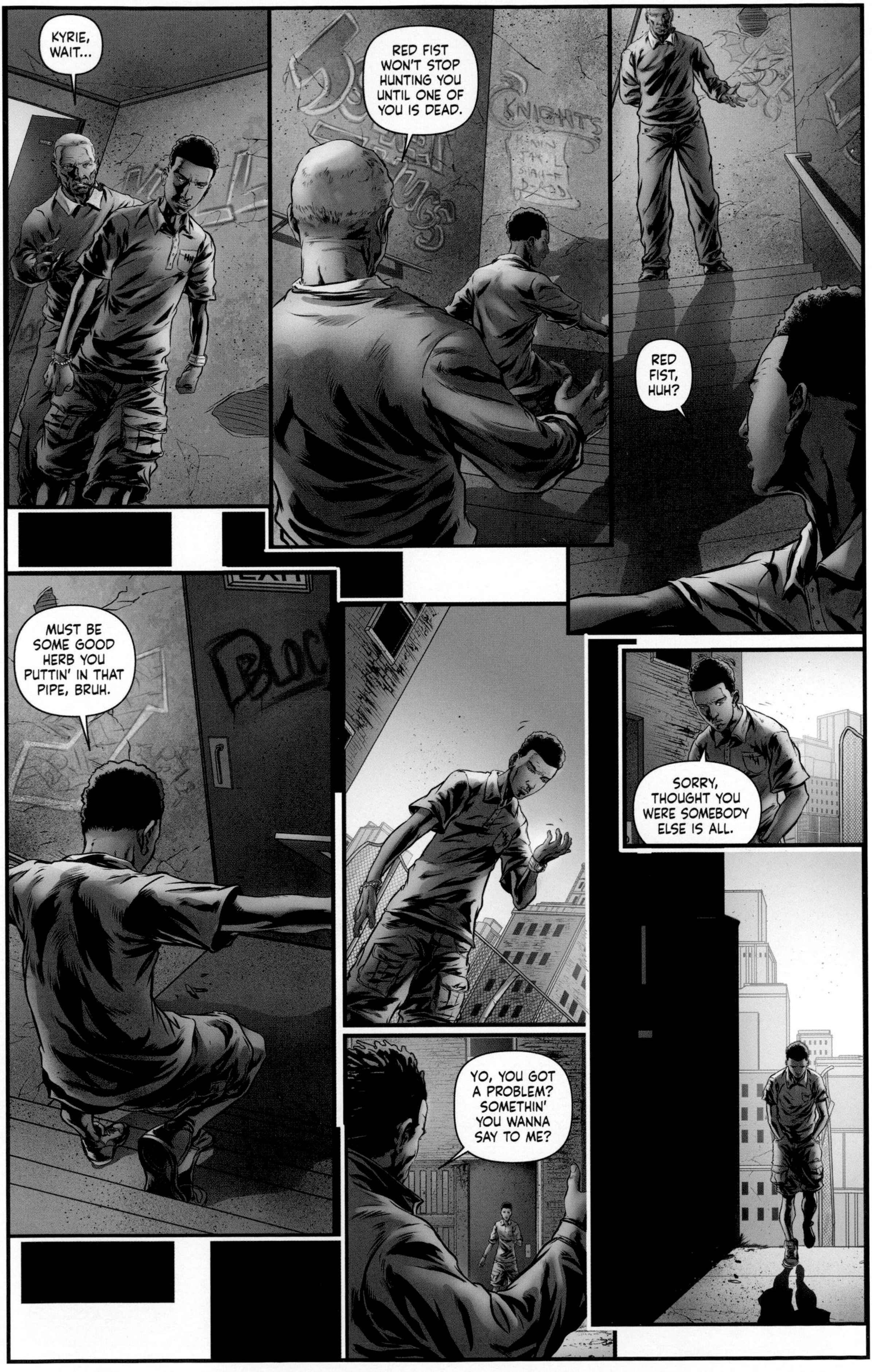
KYRIE, WAIT...
RED FIST WON'T STOP HUNTING YOU UNTIL ONE OF YOU IS DEAD.
RED FIST, HUH?
MUST BE SOME GOOD HERB YOU PUTTIN' IN THAT PIPE, BRUH.
YO, YOU GOT A PROBLEM? SOMETHIN' YOU WANNA SAY TO ME?
SORRY, THOUGHT YOU WERE SOMEBODY ELSE IS ALL.

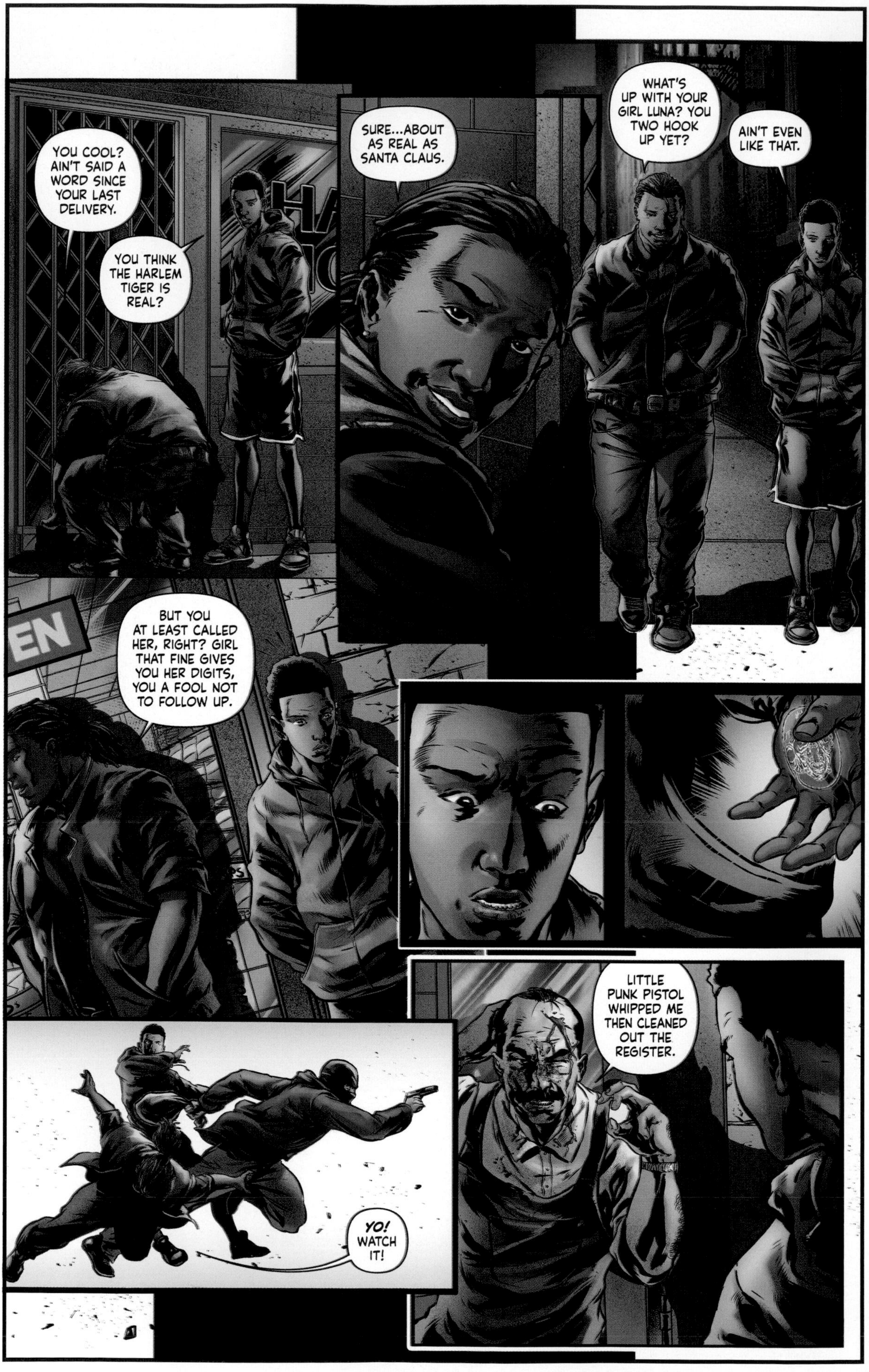
YOU COOL? AIN'T SAID A WORD SINCE YOUR LAST DELIVERY.
YOU THINK THE HARLEM TIGER IS REAL?
SURE...ABOUT AS REAL AS SANTA CLAUS.
WHAT'S UP WITH YOUR GIRL LUNA? YOU TWO HOOK UP YET?
AIN'T EVEN LIKE THAT.
BUT YOU AT LEAST CALLED HER, RIGHT? GIRL THAT FINE GIVES YOU HER DIGITS, YOU A FOOL NOT TO FOLLOW UP.
LITTLE PUNK PISTOL WHIPPED ME THEN CLEANED OUT THE REGISTER.
YO! WATCH IT!

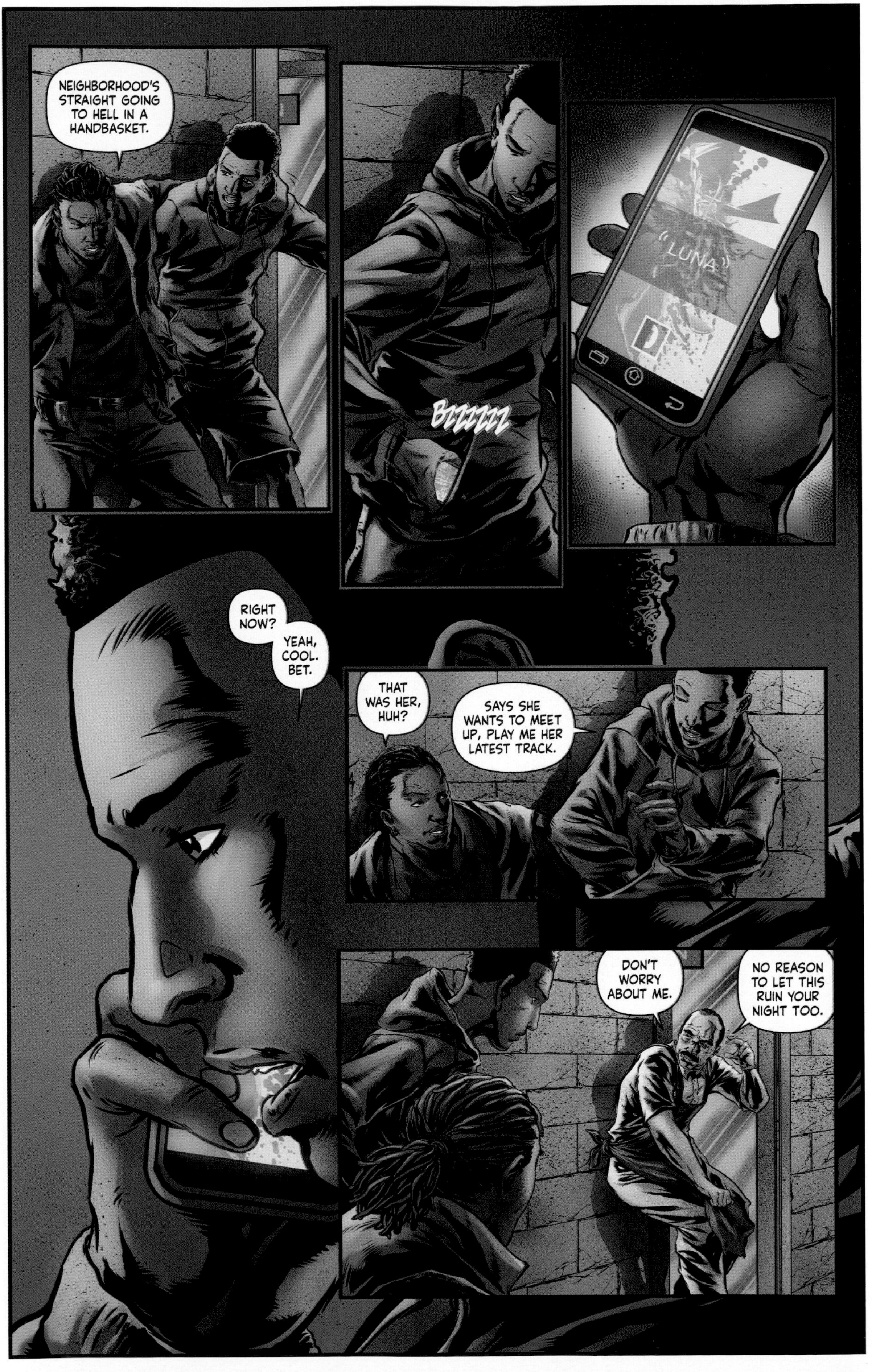
NEIGHBORHOOD'S STRAIGHT GOING TO HELL IN A HANDBASKET.
Bzzzzzz
"LUNA"
RIGHT NOW?
YEAH, COOL. BET.
THAT WAS HER, HUH?
SAYS SHE WANTS TO MEET UP, PLAY ME HER LATEST TRACK.
DON'T WORRY ABOUT ME.
NO REASON TO LET THIS RUIN YOUR NIGHT TOO.

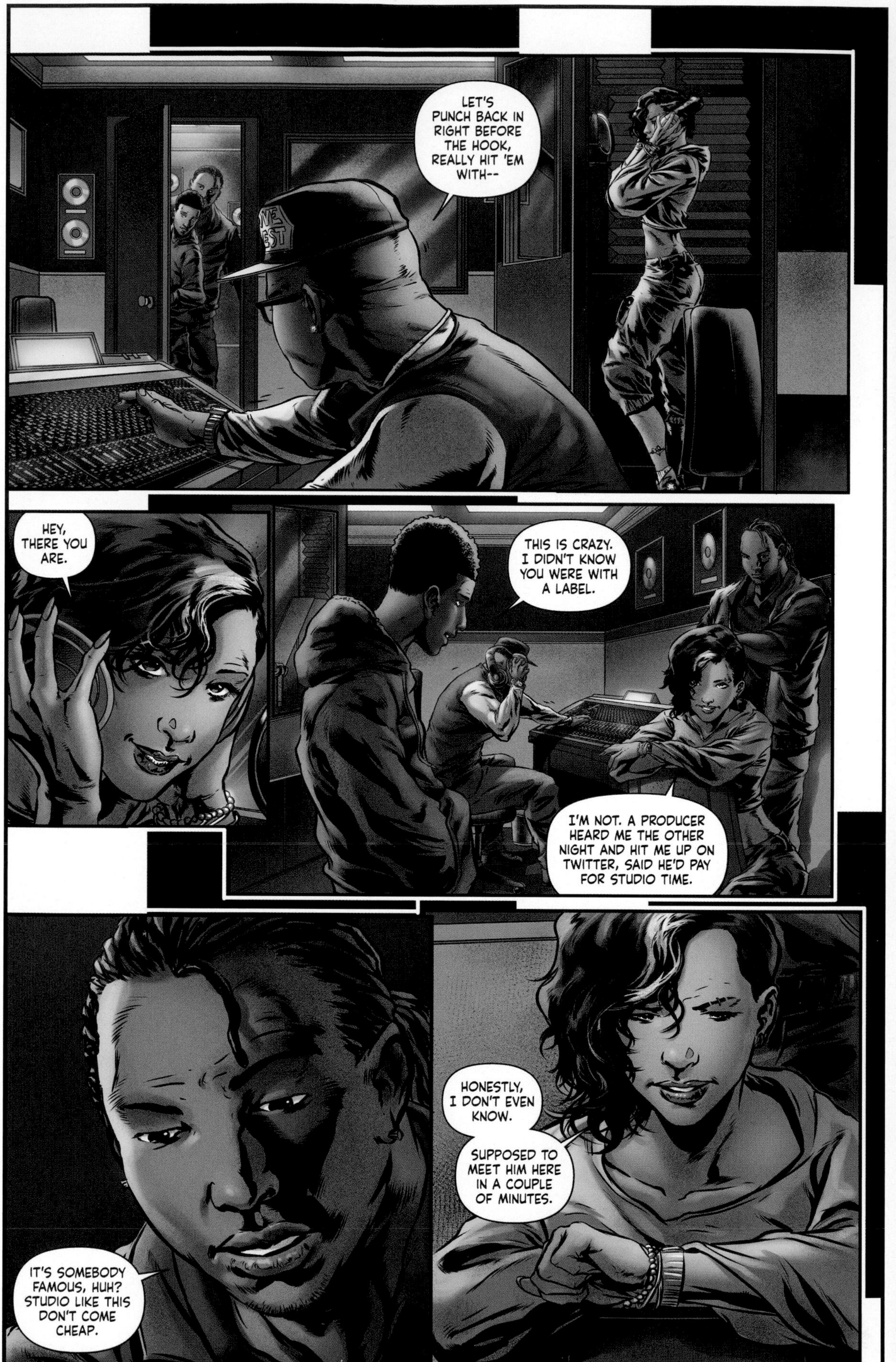
LET'S PUNCH BACK IN RIGHT BEFORE THE HOOK, REALLY HIT 'EM WITH--
HEY, THERE YOU ARE.
THIS IS CRAZY. I DIDN'T KNOW YOU WERE WITH A LABEL.
I'M NOT. A PRODUCER HEARD ME THE OTHER NIGHT AND HIT ME UP ON TWITTER, SAID HE'D PAY FOR STUDIO TIME.
IT'S SOMEBODY FAMOUS, HUH? STUDIO LIKE THIS DON'T COME CHEAP.
HONESTLY, I DON'T EVEN KNOW.
SUPPOSED TO MEET HIM HERE IN A COUPLE OF MINUTES.

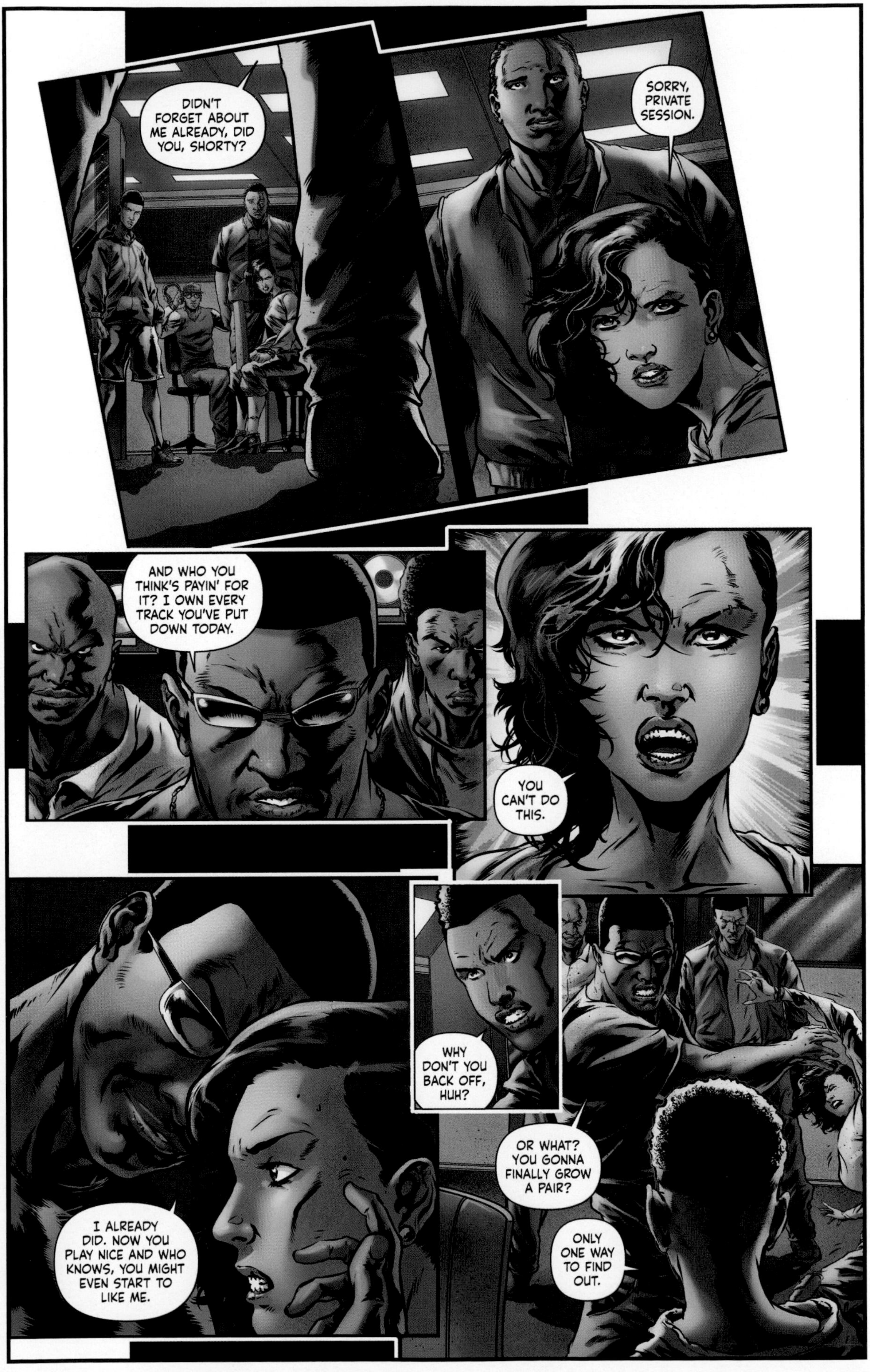
DIDN'T FORGET ABOUT ME ALREADY, DID YOU, SHORTY?
SORRY, PRIVATE SESSION.
AND WHO YOU THINK'S PAYIN' FOR IT? I OWN EVERY TRACK YOU'VE PUT DOWN TODAY.
YOU CAN'T DO THIS.
I ALREADY DID. NOW YOU PLAY NICE AND WHO KNOWS, YOU MIGHT EVEN START TO LIKE ME.
WHY DON'T YOU BACK OFF, HUH?
OR WHAT? YOU GONNA FINALLY GROW A PAIR?
ONLY ONE WAY TO FIND OUT.

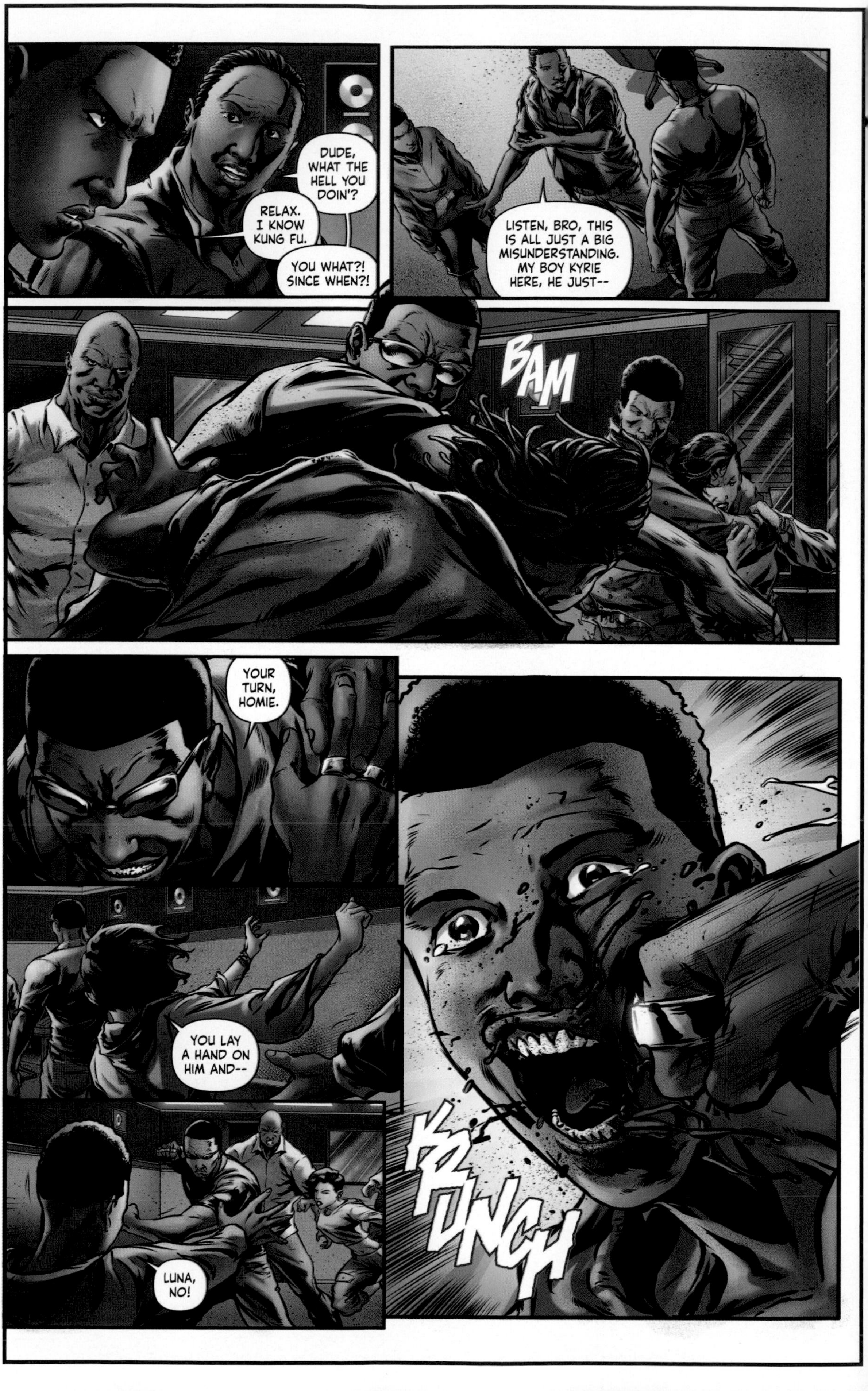
DUDE, WHAT THE HELL YOU DOIN'?
RELAX. I KNOW KUNG FU.
YOU WHAT?! SINCE WHEN?!
LISTEN, BRO, THIS IS ALL JUST A BIG MISUNDERSTANDING. MY BOY KYRIE HERE, HE JUST--
BAM
YOUR TURN, HOMIE.
YOU LAY A HAND ON HIM AND--
LUNA, NO!
KRUNCH

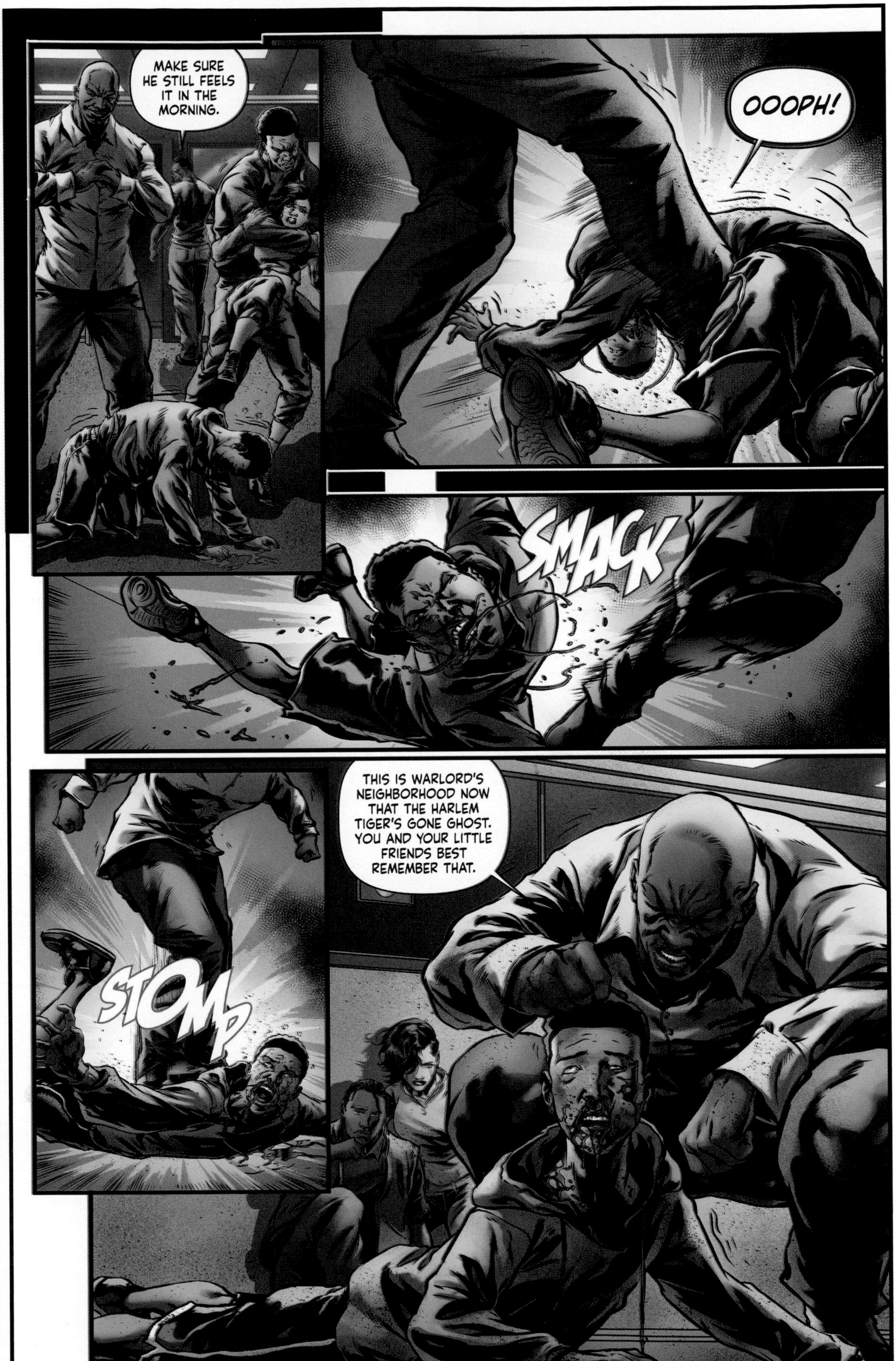
MAKE SURE HE STILL FEELS IT IN THE MORNING.
OOOPH!
SMACK
STOMP
THIS IS WARLORD'S NEIGHBORHOOD NOW THAT THE HARLEM TIGER'S GONE GHOST. YOU AND YOUR LITTLE FRIENDS BEST REMEMBER THAT.

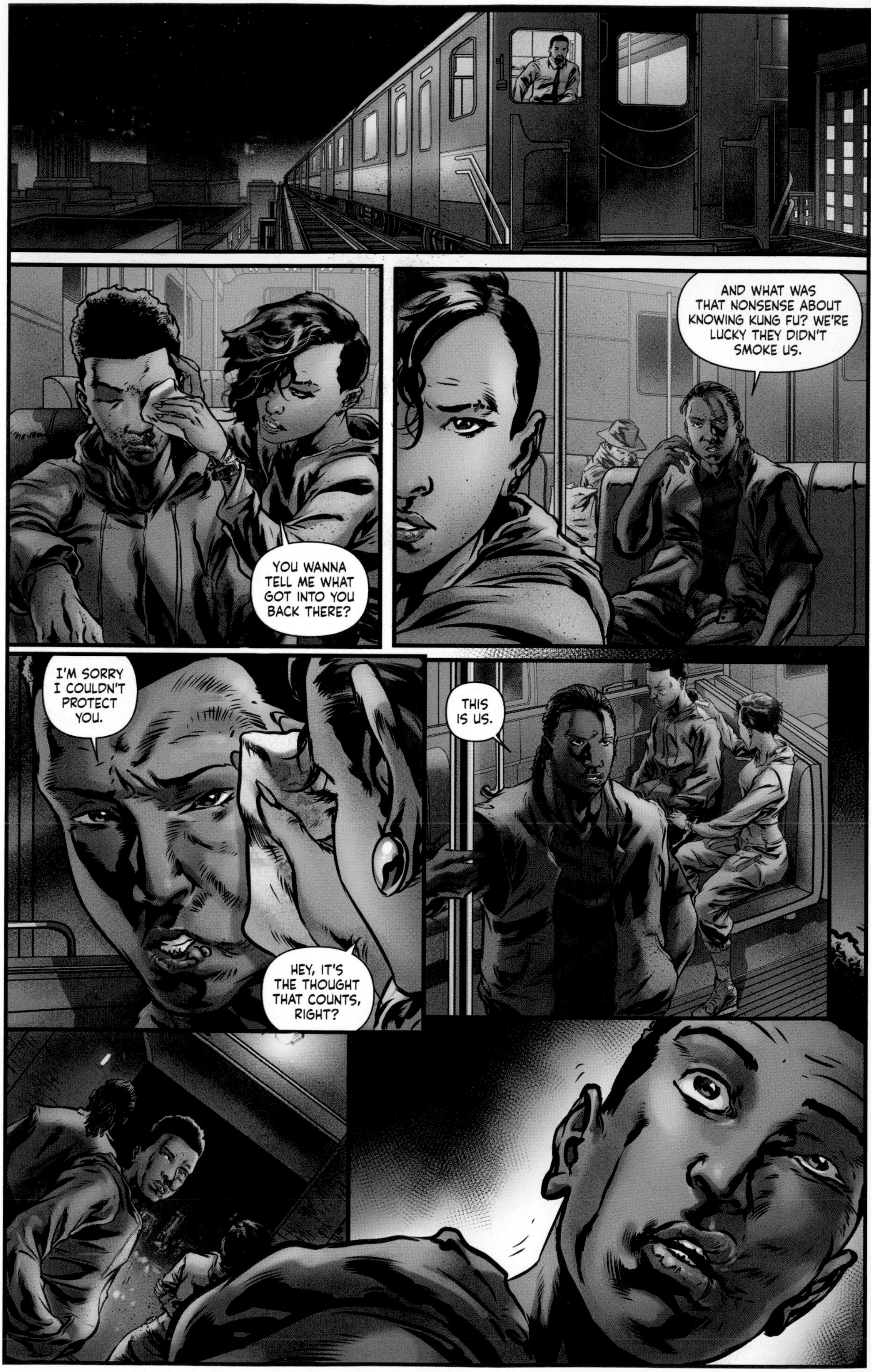
YOU WANNA TELL ME WHAT GOT INTO YOU BACK THERE?
AND WHAT WAS THAT NONSENSE ABOUT KNOWING KUNG FU? WE'RE LUCKY THEY DIDN'T SMOKE US.
I'M SORRY I COULDN'T PROTECT YOU.
HEY, IT'S THE THOUGHT THAT COUNTS, RIGHT?
THIS IS US.

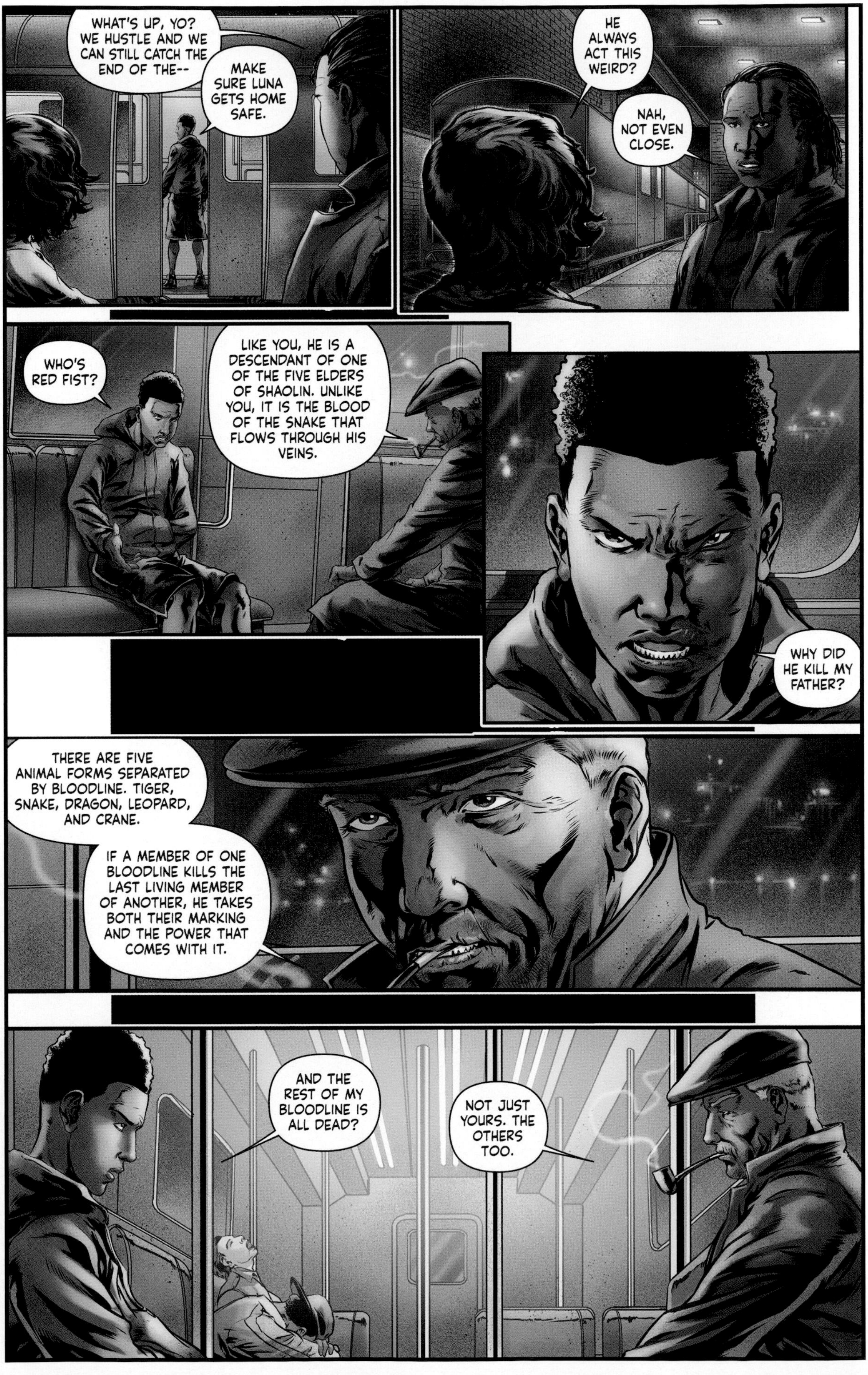

WHAT'S UP, YO? WE HUSTLE AND WE CAN STILL CATCH THE END OF THE--
MAKE SURE LUNA GETS HOME SAFE.
HE ALWAYS ACT THIS WEIRD?
NAH, NOT EVEN CLOSE.
WHO'S RED FIST?
LIKE YOU, HE IS A DESCENDANT OF ONE OF THE FIVE ELDERS OF SHAOLIN. UNLIKE YOU, IT IS THE BLOOD OF THE SNAKE THAT FLOWS THROUGH HIS VEINS.
WHY DID HE KILL MY FATHER?
THERE ARE FIVE ANIMAL FORMS SEPARATED BY BLOODLINE. TIGER, SNAKE, DRAGON, LEOPARD, AND CRANE.
IF A MEMBER OF ONE BLOODLINE KILLS THE LAST LIVING MEMBER OF ANOTHER, HE TAKES BOTH THEIR MARKING AND THE POWER THAT COMES WITH IT.
AND THE REST OF MY BLOODLINE IS ALL DEAD?
NOT JUST YOURS. THE OTHERS TOO.

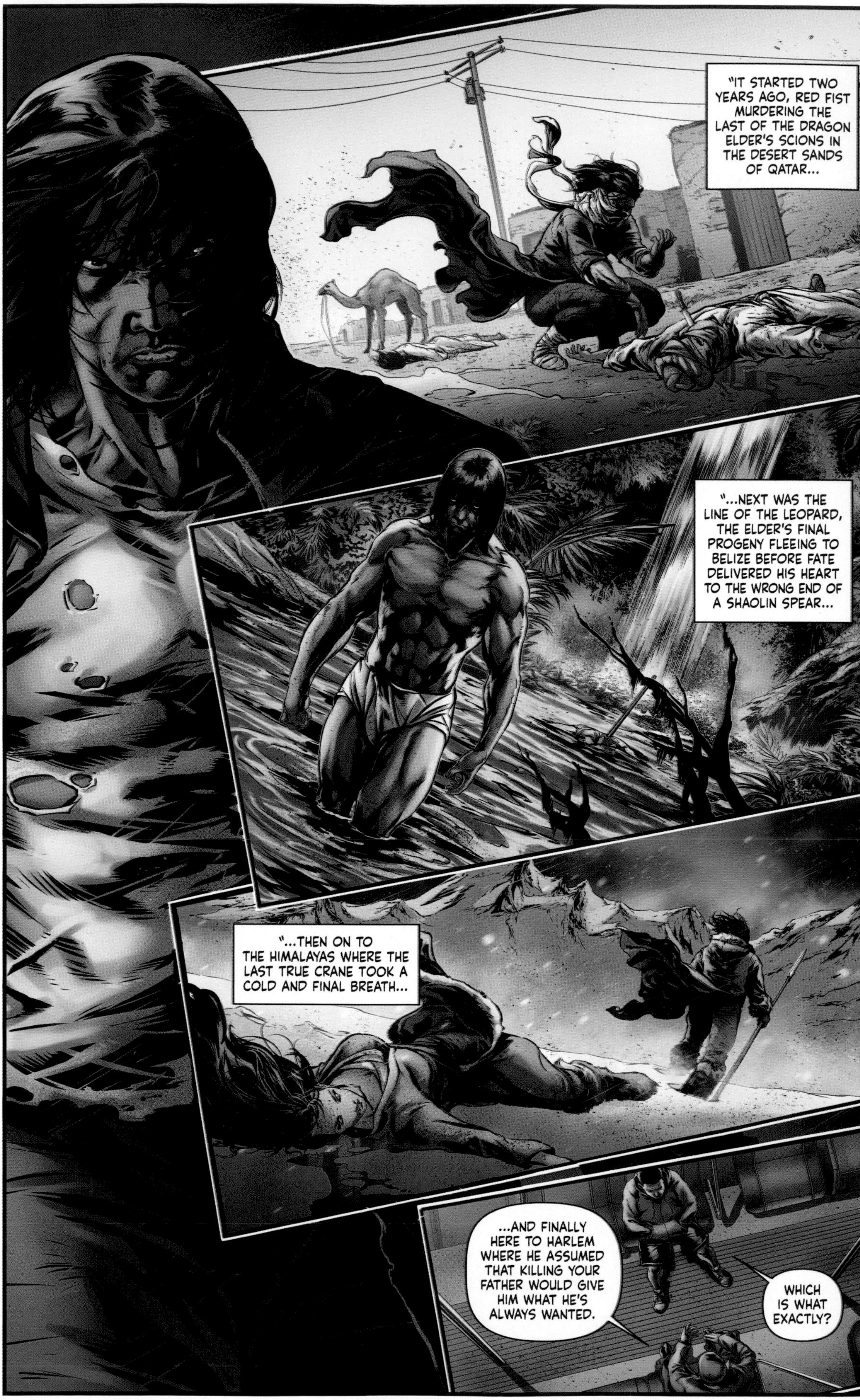
"IT STARTED TWO YEARS AGO, RED FIST MURDERING THE LAST OF THE DRAGON ELDER'S SCIONS IN THE DESERT SANDS OF QATAR...
"...NEXT WAS THE LINE OF THE LEOPARD, THE ELDER'S FINAL PROGENY FLEEING TO BELIZE BEFORE FATE DELIVERED HIS HEART TO THE WRONG END OF A SHAOLIN SPEAR...
"...THEN ON TO THE HIMALAYAS WHERE THE LAST TRUE CRANE TOOK A COLD AND FINAL BREATH...
...AND FINALLY HERE TO HARLEM WHERE HE ASSUMED THAT KILLING YOUR FATHER WOULD GIVE HIM WHAT HE'S ALWAYS WANTED.
WHICH IS WHAT EXACTLY?

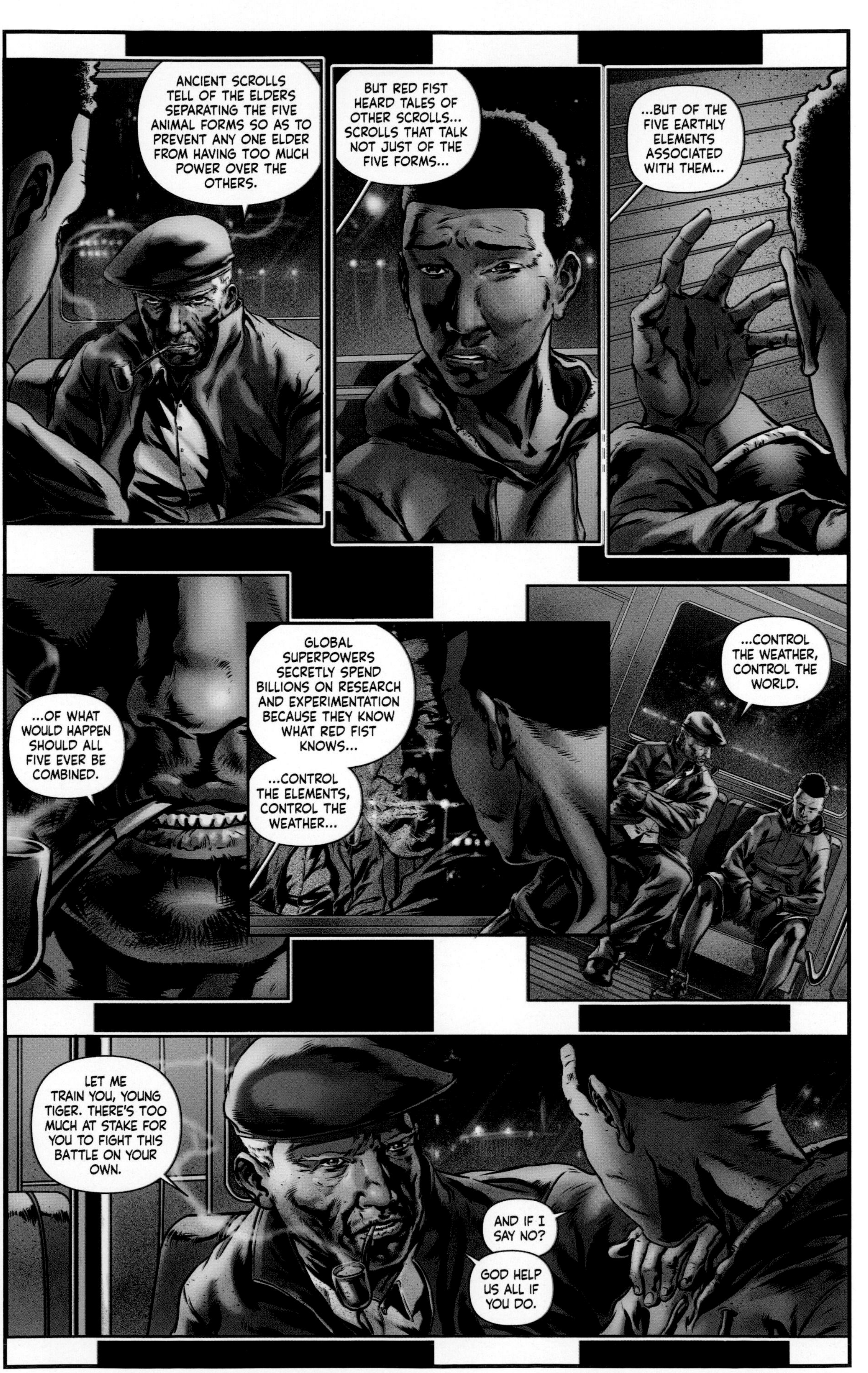
ANCIENT SCROLLS TELL OF THE ELDERS SEPARATING THE FIVE ANIMAL FORMS SO AS TO PREVENT ANY ONE ELDER FROM HAVING TOO MUCH POWER OVER THE OTHERS.
BUT RED FIST HEARD TALES OF OTHER SCROLLS... SCROLLS THAT TALK NOT JUST OF THE FIVE FORMS...
...BUT OF THE FIVE EARTHLY ELEMENTS ASSOCIATED WITH THEM...
...OF WHAT WOULD HAPPEN SHOULD ALL FIVE EVER BE COMBINED.
GLOBAL SUPERPOWERS SECRETLY SPEND BILLIONS ON RESEARCH AND EXPERIMENTATION BECAUSE THEY KNOW WHAT RED FIST KNOWS...
...CONTROL THE ELEMENTS, CONTROL THE WEATHER...
...CONTROL THE WEATHER, CONTROL THE WORLD.
LET ME TRAIN YOU, YOUNG TIGER. THERE'S TOO MUCH AT STAKE FOR YOU TO FIGHT THIS BATTLE ON YOUR OWN.
AND IF I SAY NO?
GOD HELP US ALL IF YOU DO.

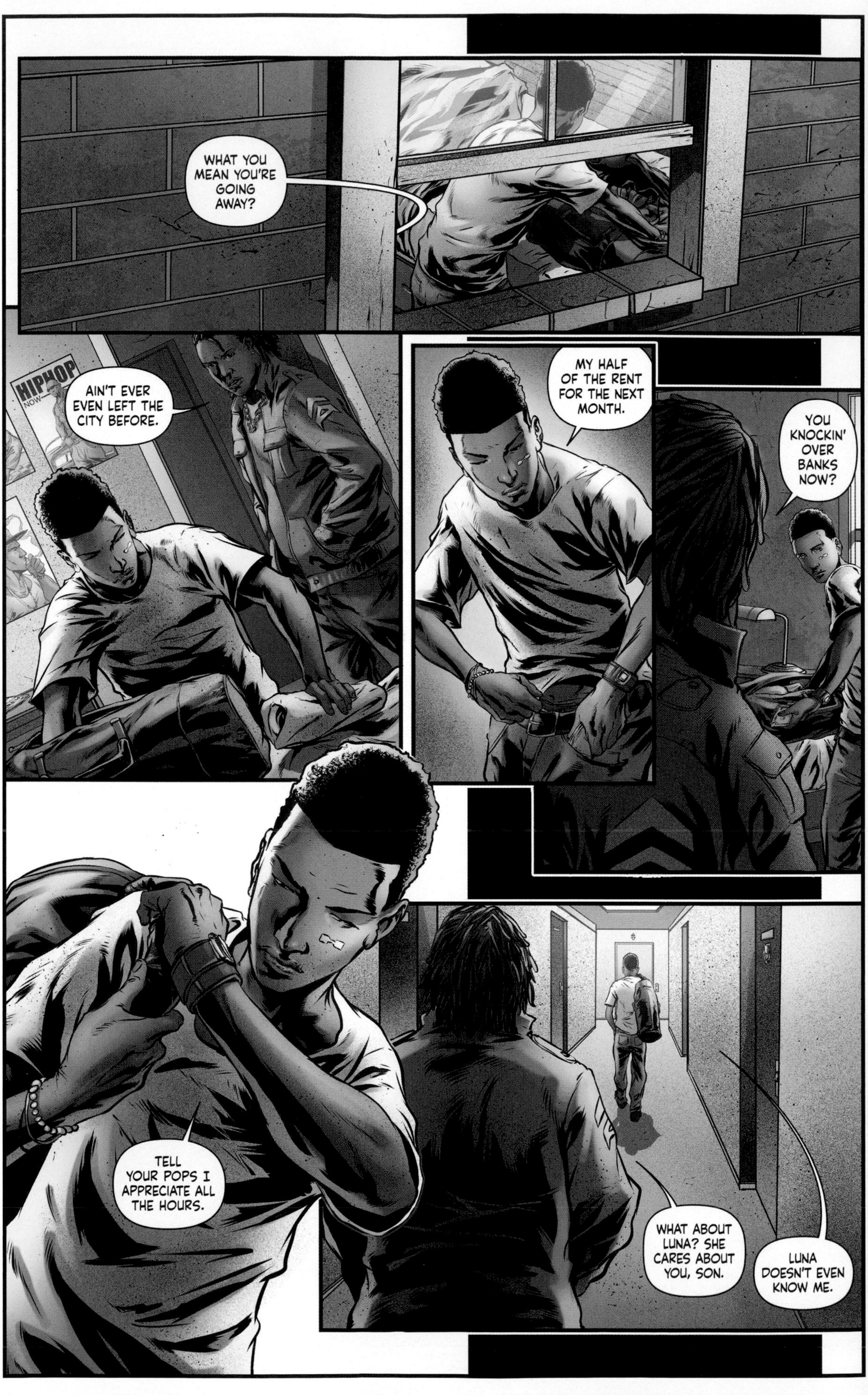

WHAT YOU MEAN YOU'RE GOING AWAY?
AIN'T EVER EVEN LEFT THE CITY BEFORE.
HIPHOP NOW
MY HALF OF THE RENT FOR THE NEXT MONTH.
YOU KNOCKIN' OVER BANKS NOW?
TELL YOUR POPS I APPRECIATE ALL THE HOURS.
WHAT ABOUT LUNA? SHE CARES ABOUT YOU, SON.
LUNA DOESN'T EVEN KNOW ME.

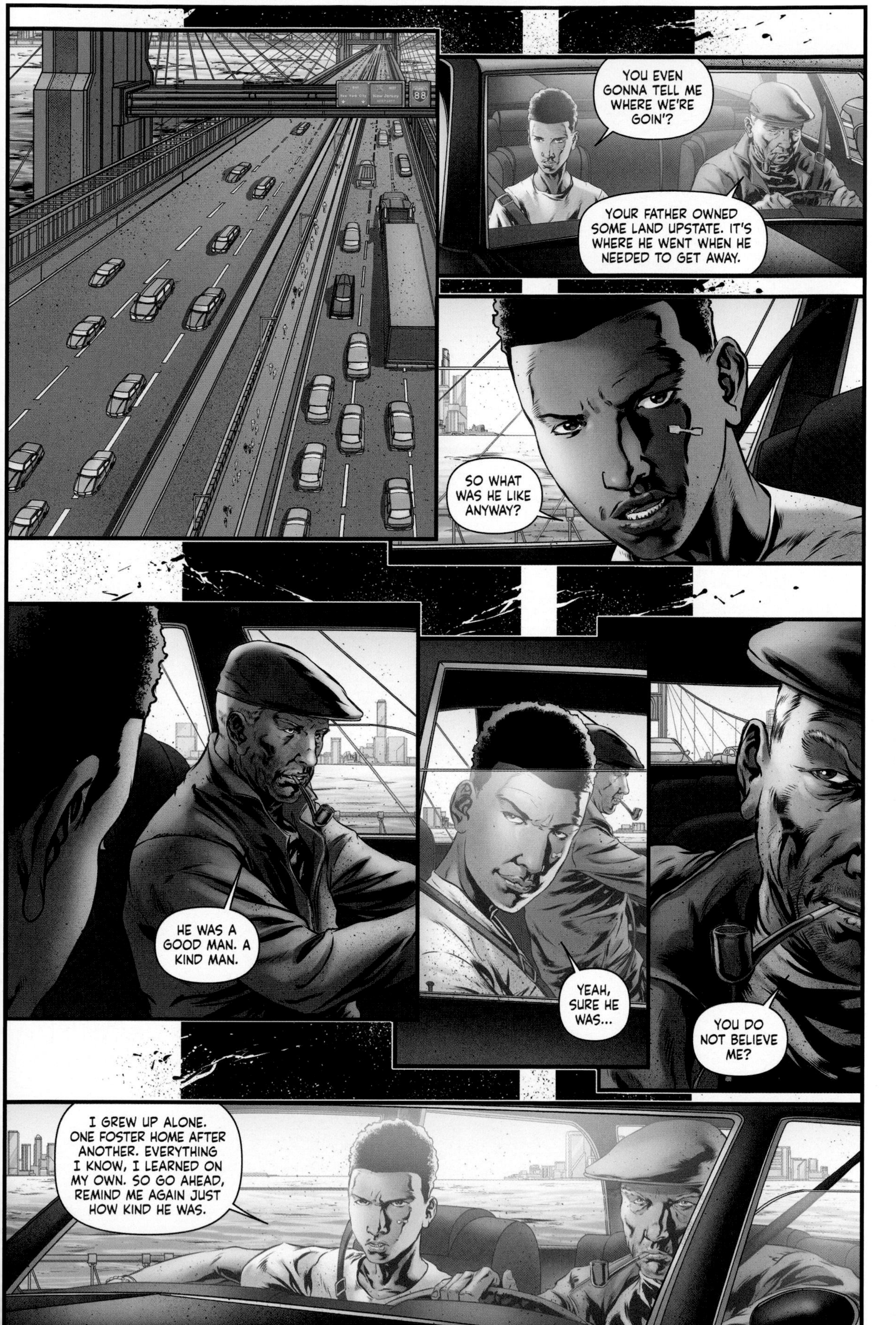
New York City
New Jersey
88
YOU EVEN GONNA TELL ME WHERE WE'RE GOIN'?
YOUR FATHER OWNED SOME LAND UPSTATE. IT'S WHERE HE WENT WHEN HE NEEDED TO GET AWAY.
SO WHAT WAS HE LIKE ANYWAY?
HE WAS A GOOD MAN. A KIND MAN.
YEAH, SURE HE WAS...
YOU DO NOT BELIEVE ME?
I GREW UP ALONE. ONE FOSTER HOME AFTER ANOTHER. EVERYTHING I KNOW, I LEARNED ON MY OWN. SO GO AHEAD, REMIND ME AGAIN JUST HOW KIND HE WAS.

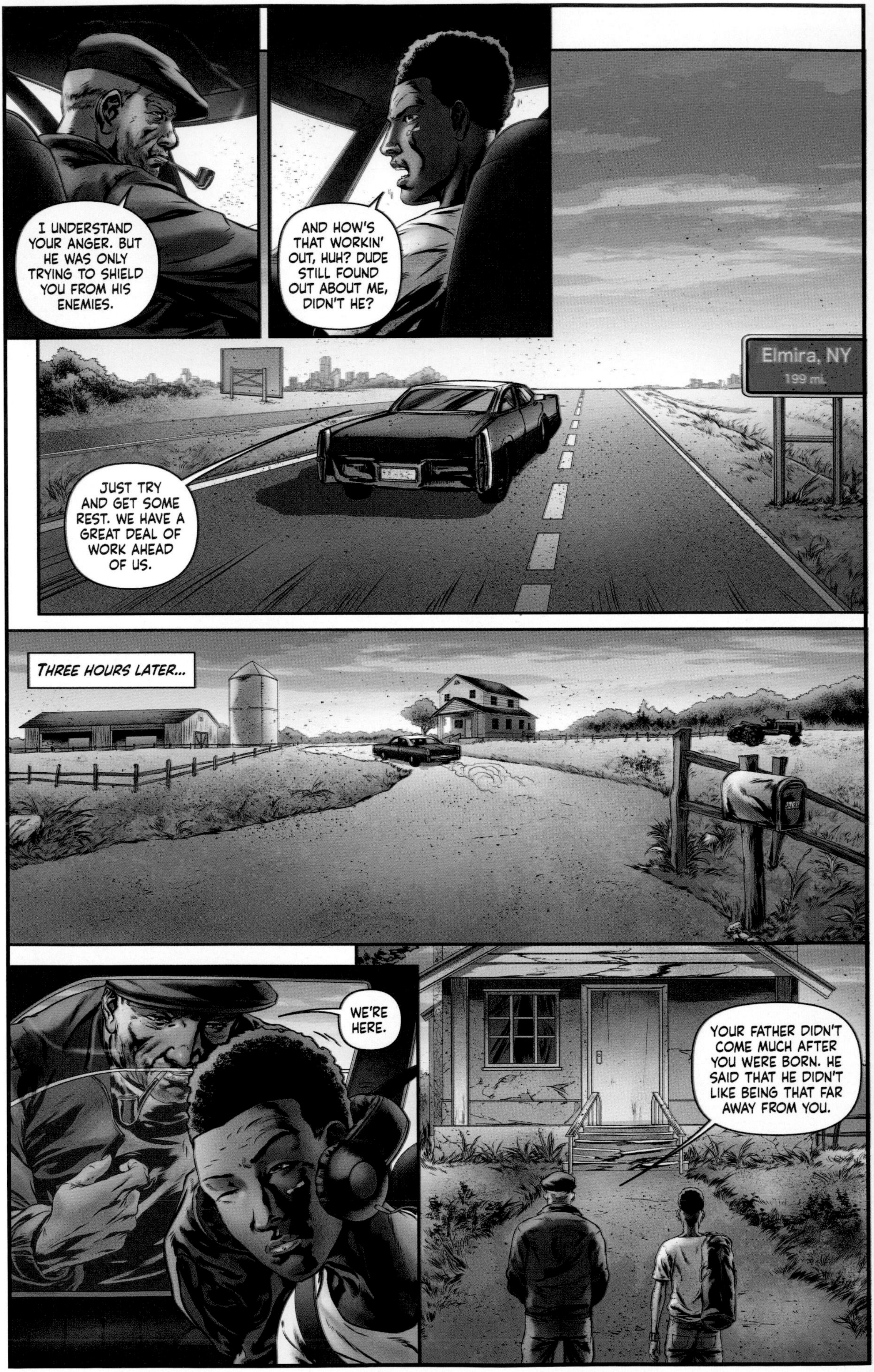
I UNDERSTAND YOUR ANGER. BUT HE WAS ONLY TRYING TO SHIELD YOU FROM HIS ENEMIES.
AND HOW'S THAT WORKIN' OUT, HUH? DUDE STILL FOUND OUT ABOUT ME, DIDN'T HE?
Elmira, NY
199 mi.
JUST TRY AND GET SOME REST. WE HAVE A GREAT DEAL OF WORK AHEAD OF US.
THREE HOURS LATER...
WE'RE HERE.
YOUR FATHER DIDN'T COME MUCH AFTER YOU WERE BORN. HE SAID THAT HE DIDN'T LIKE BEING THAT FAR AWAY FROM YOU.

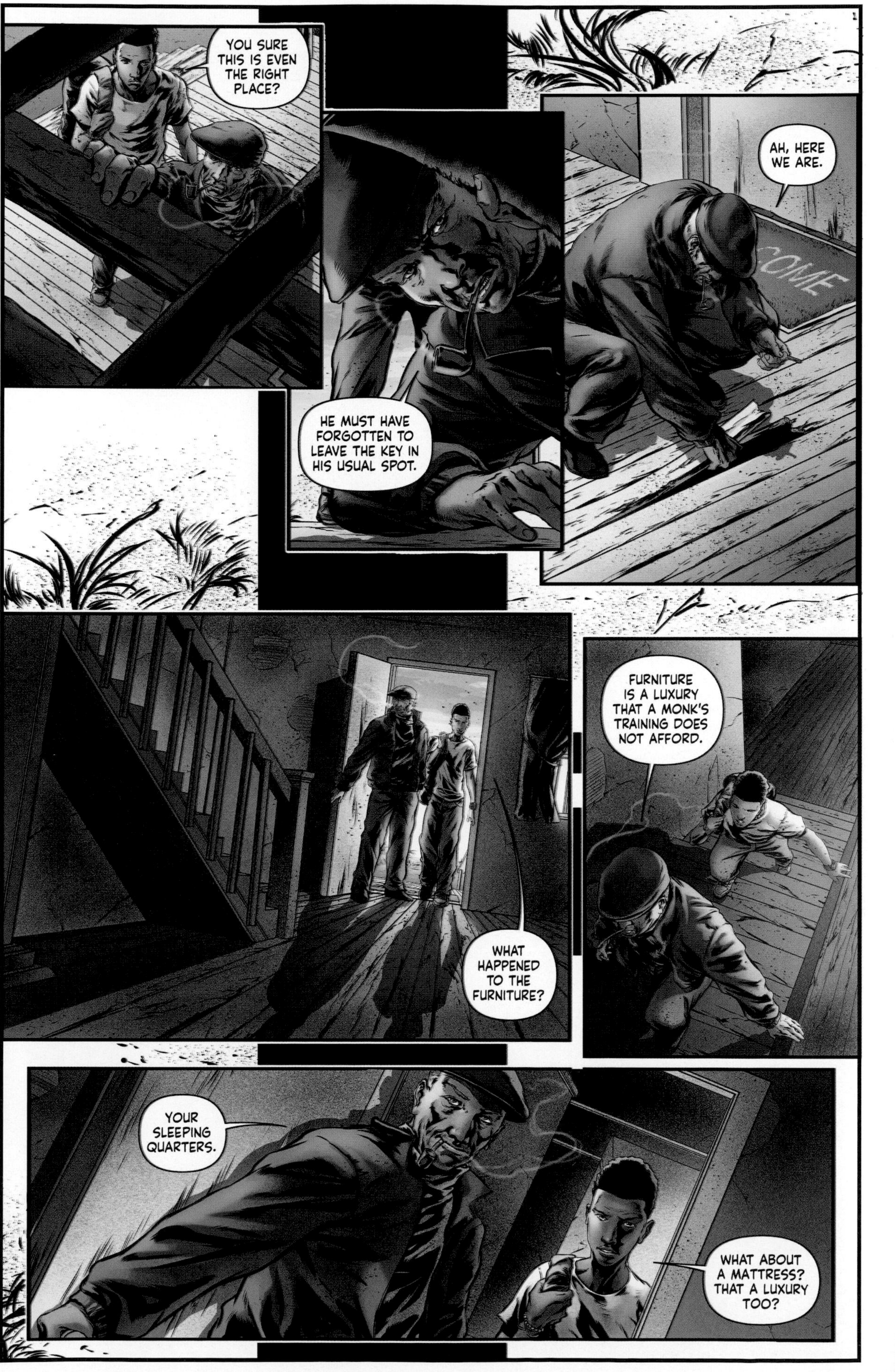

YOU SURE THIS IS EVEN THE RIGHT PLACE?
HE MUST HAVE FORGOTTEN TO LEAVE THE KEY IN HIS USUAL SPOT.
AH, HERE WE ARE.
COME
WHAT HAPPENED TO THE FURNITURE?
FURNITURE IS A LUXURY THAT A MONK'S TRAINING DOES NOT AFFORD.
YOUR SLEEPING QUARTERS.
WHAT ABOUT A MATTRESS? THAT A LUXURY TOO?

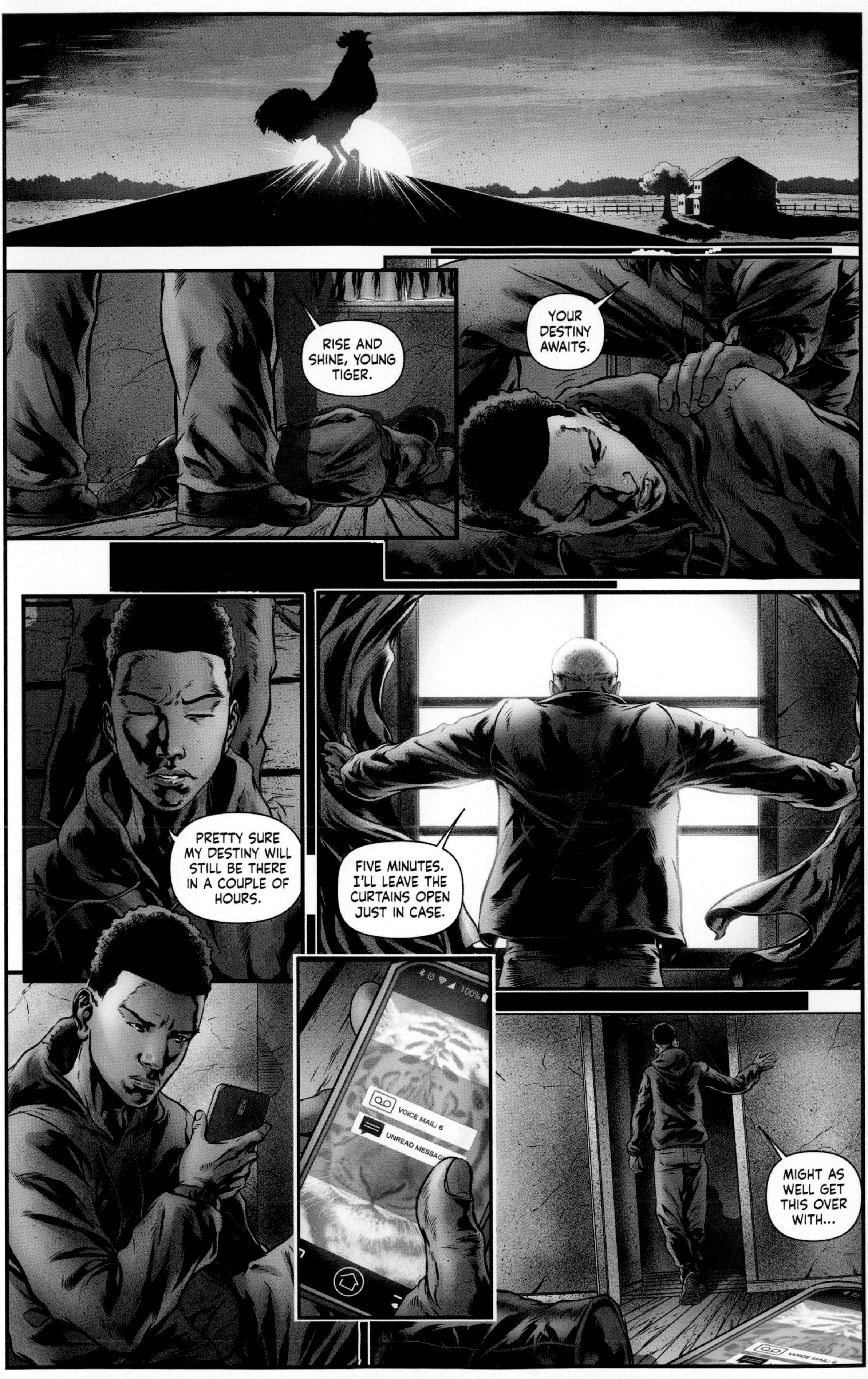
RISE AND SHINE, YOUNG TIGER.
YOUR DESTINY AWAITS.
PRETTY SURE MY DESTINY WILL STILL BE THERE IN A COUPLE OF HOURS.
FIVE MINUTES. I'LL LEAVE THE CURTAINS OPEN JUST IN CASE.
100%
VOICE MAIL: 6
MIGHT AS WELL GET THIS OVER WITH...

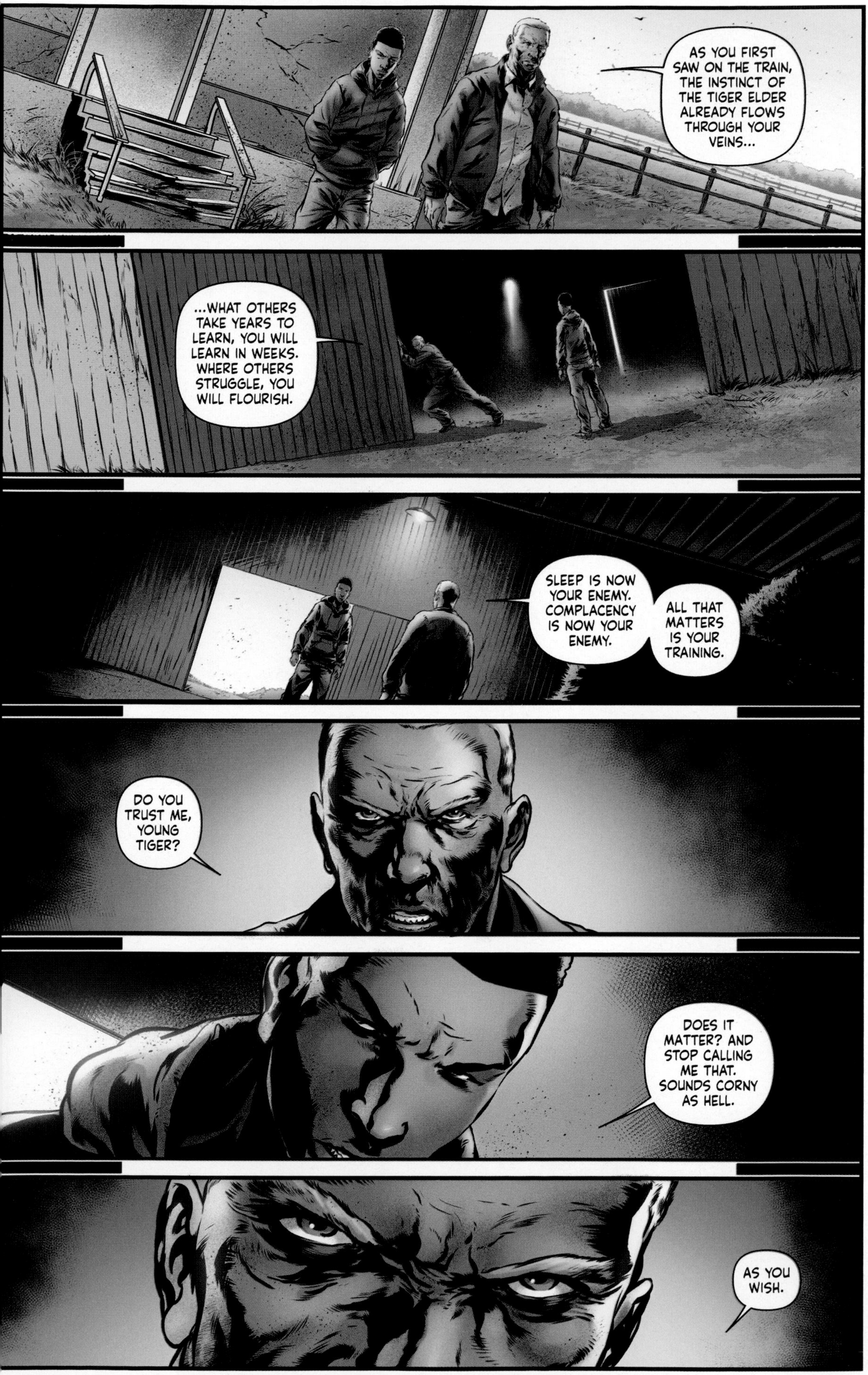
AS YOU FIRST SAW ON THE TRAIN, THE INSTINCT OF THE TIGER ELDER ALREADY FLOWS THROUGH YOUR VEINS...
...WHAT OTHERS TAKE YEARS TO LEARN, YOU WILL LEARN IN WEEKS. WHERE OTHERS STRUGGLE, YOU WILL FLOURISH.
SLEEP IS NOW YOUR ENEMY. COMPLACENCY IS NOW YOUR ENEMY.
ALL THAT MATTERS IS YOUR TRAINING.
DO YOU TRUST ME, YOUNG TIGER?
DOES IT MATTER? AND STOP CALLING ME THAT. SOUNDS CORNY AS HELL.
AS YOU WISH.

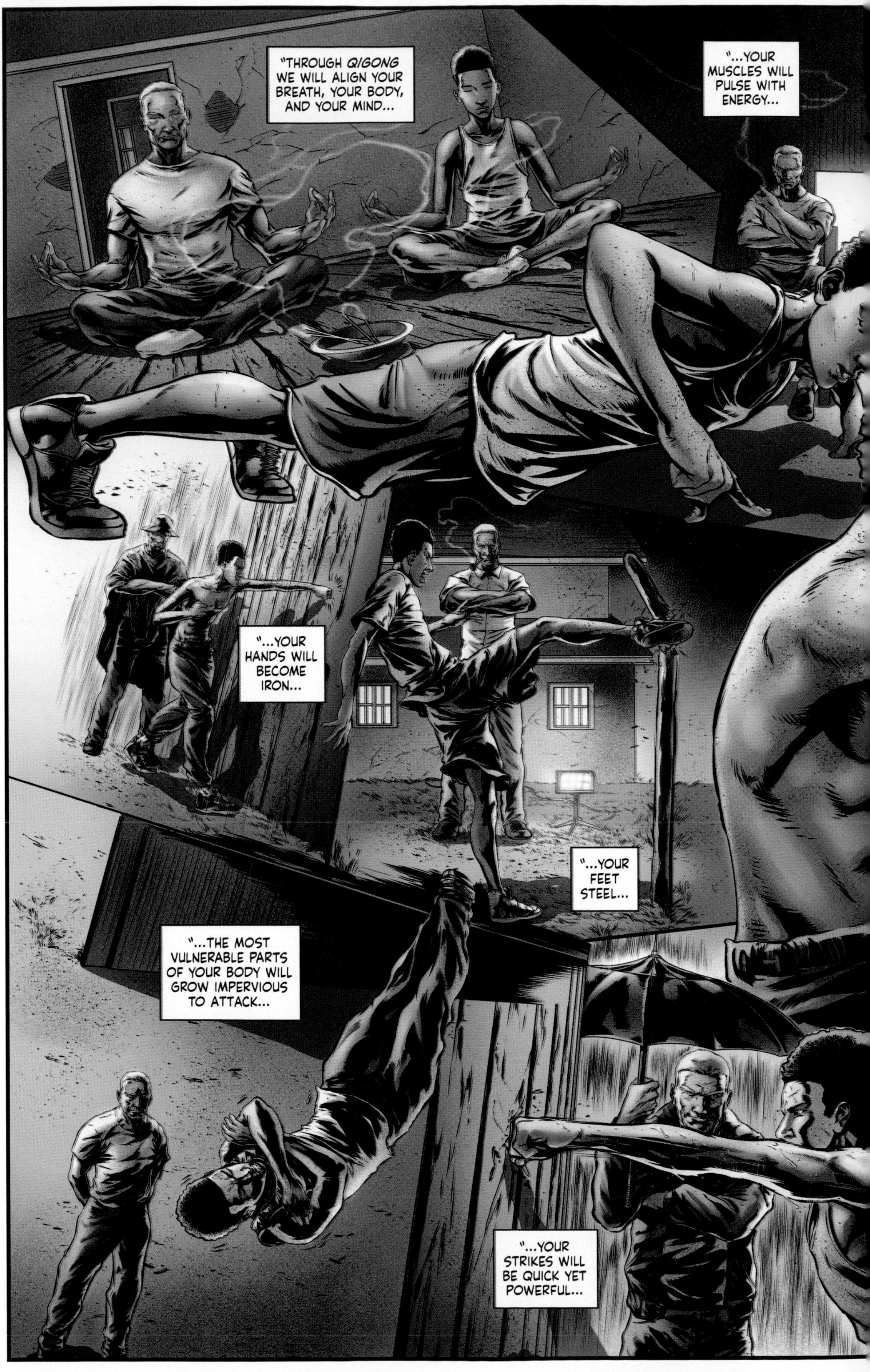
"THROUGH *QIGONG* WE WILL ALIGN YOUR BREATH, YOUR BODY, AND YOUR MIND...
"...YOUR MUSCLES WILL PULSE WITH ENERGY...
"...YOUR HANDS WILL BECOME IRON...
"...YOUR FEET STEEL...
"...THE MOST VULNERABLE PARTS OF YOUR BODY WILL GROW IMPERVIOUS TO ATTACK...
"...YOUR STRIKES WILL BE QUICK YET POWERFUL...

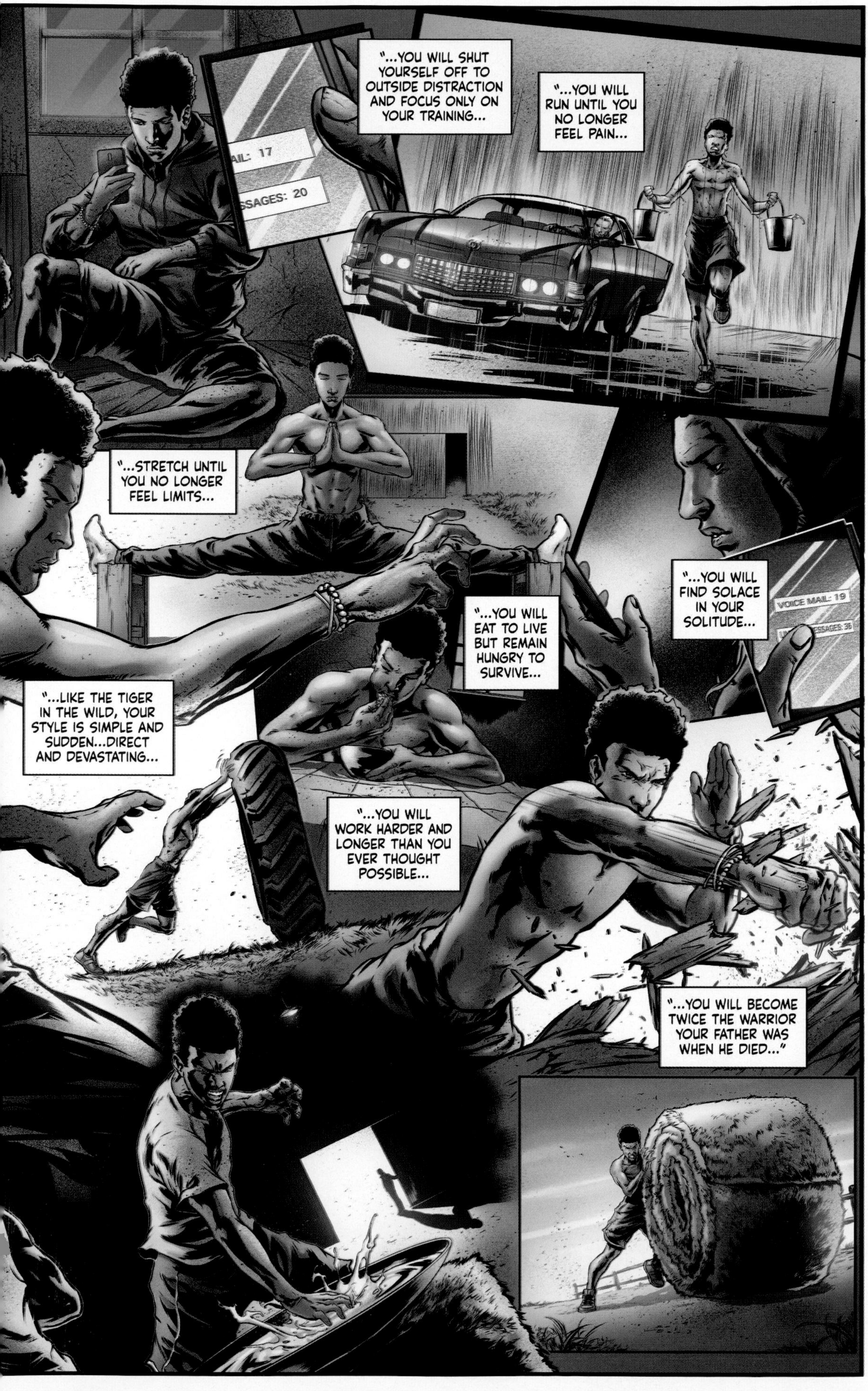
"...YOU WILL SHUT YOURSELF OFF TO OUTSIDE DISTRACTION AND FOCUS ONLY ON YOUR TRAINING...
"...YOU WILL RUN UNTIL YOU NO LONGER FEEL PAIN...
"...STRETCH UNTIL YOU NO LONGER FEEL LIMITS...
"...YOU WILL FIND SOLACE IN YOUR SOLITUDE...
VOICE MAIL: 19
"...YOU WILL EAT TO LIVE BUT REMAIN HUNGRY TO SURVIVE...
"...LIKE THE TIGER IN THE WILD, YOUR STYLE IS SIMPLE AND SUDDEN...DIRECT AND DEVASTATING...
"...YOU WILL WORK HARDER AND LONGER THAN YOU EVER THOUGHT POSSIBLE...
"...YOU WILL BECOME TWICE THE WARRIOR YOUR FATHER WAS WHEN HE DIED..."

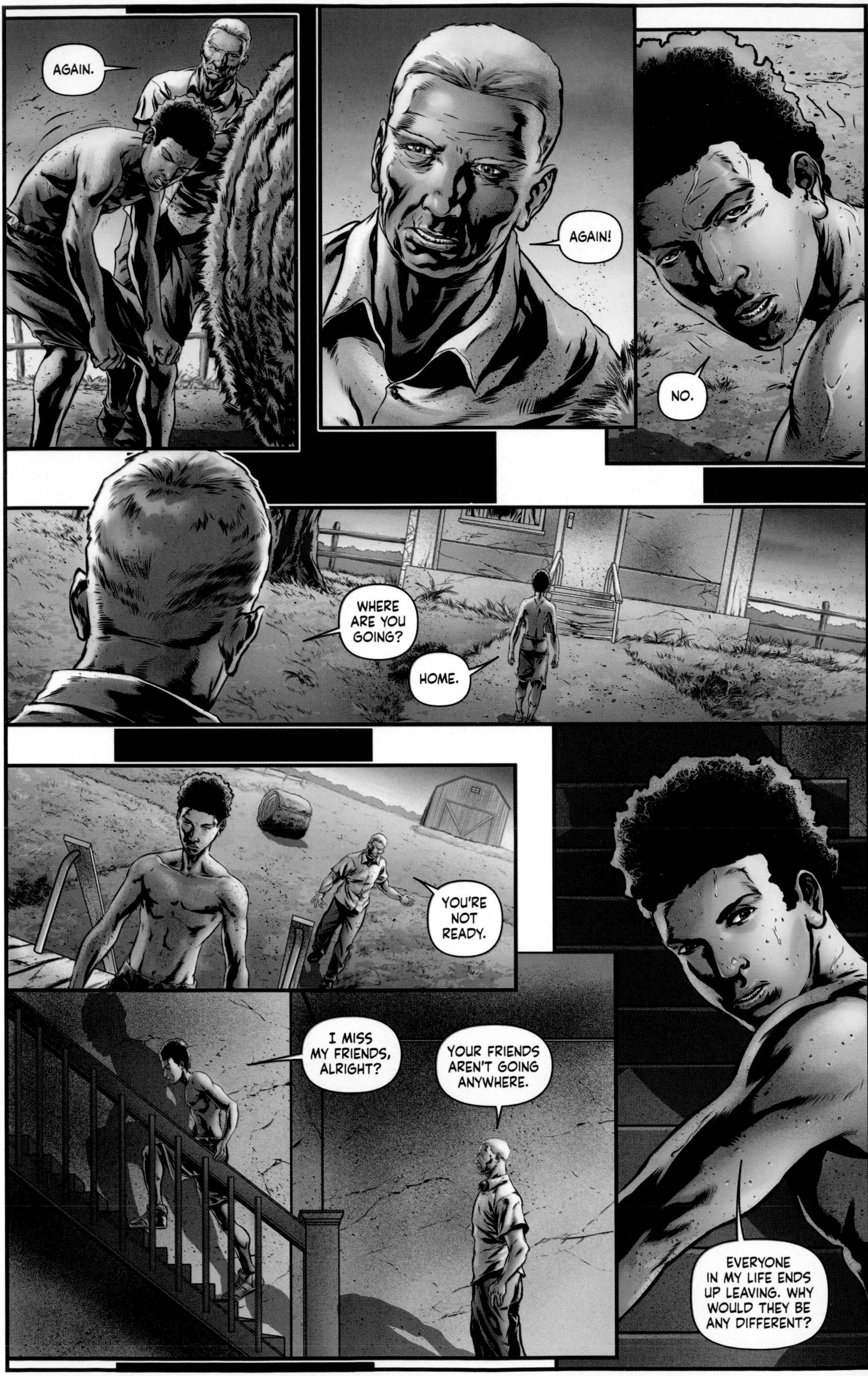
AGAIN.
AGAIN!
NO.
WHERE ARE YOU GOING?
HOME.
YOU'RE NOT READY.
I MISS MY FRIENDS, ALRIGHT?
YOUR FRIENDS AREN'T GOING ANYWHERE.
EVERYONE IN MY LIFE ENDS UP LEAVING. WHY WOULD THEY BE ANY DIFFERENT?

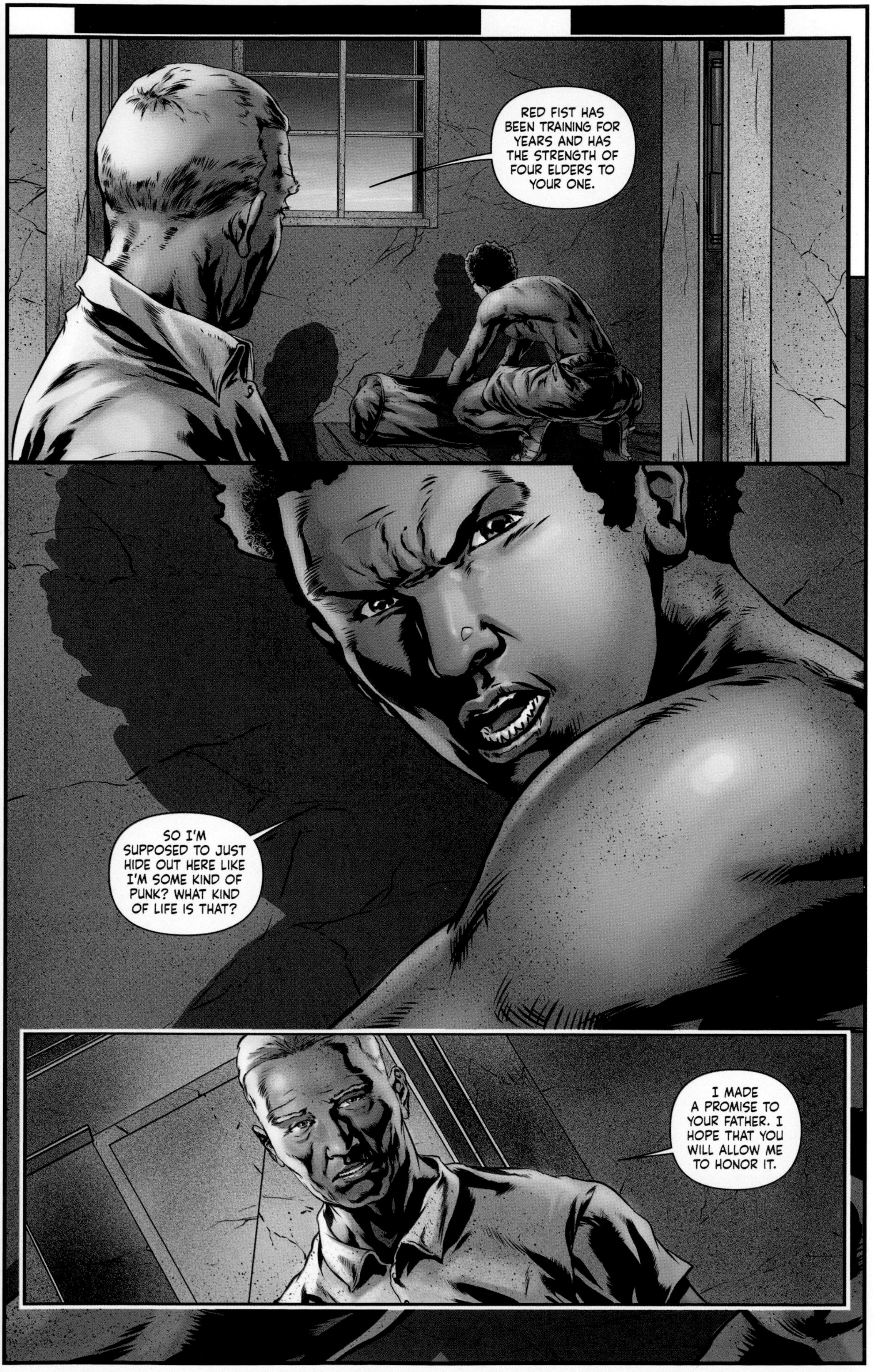
RED FIST HAS BEEN TRAINING FOR YEARS AND HAS THE STRENGTH OF FOUR ELDERS TO YOUR ONE.
SO I'M SUPPOSED TO JUST HIDE OUT HERE LIKE I'M SOME KIND OF PUNK? WHAT KIND OF LIFE IS THAT?
I MADE A PROMISE TO YOUR FATHER. I HOPE THAT YOU WILL ALLOW ME TO HONOR IT.

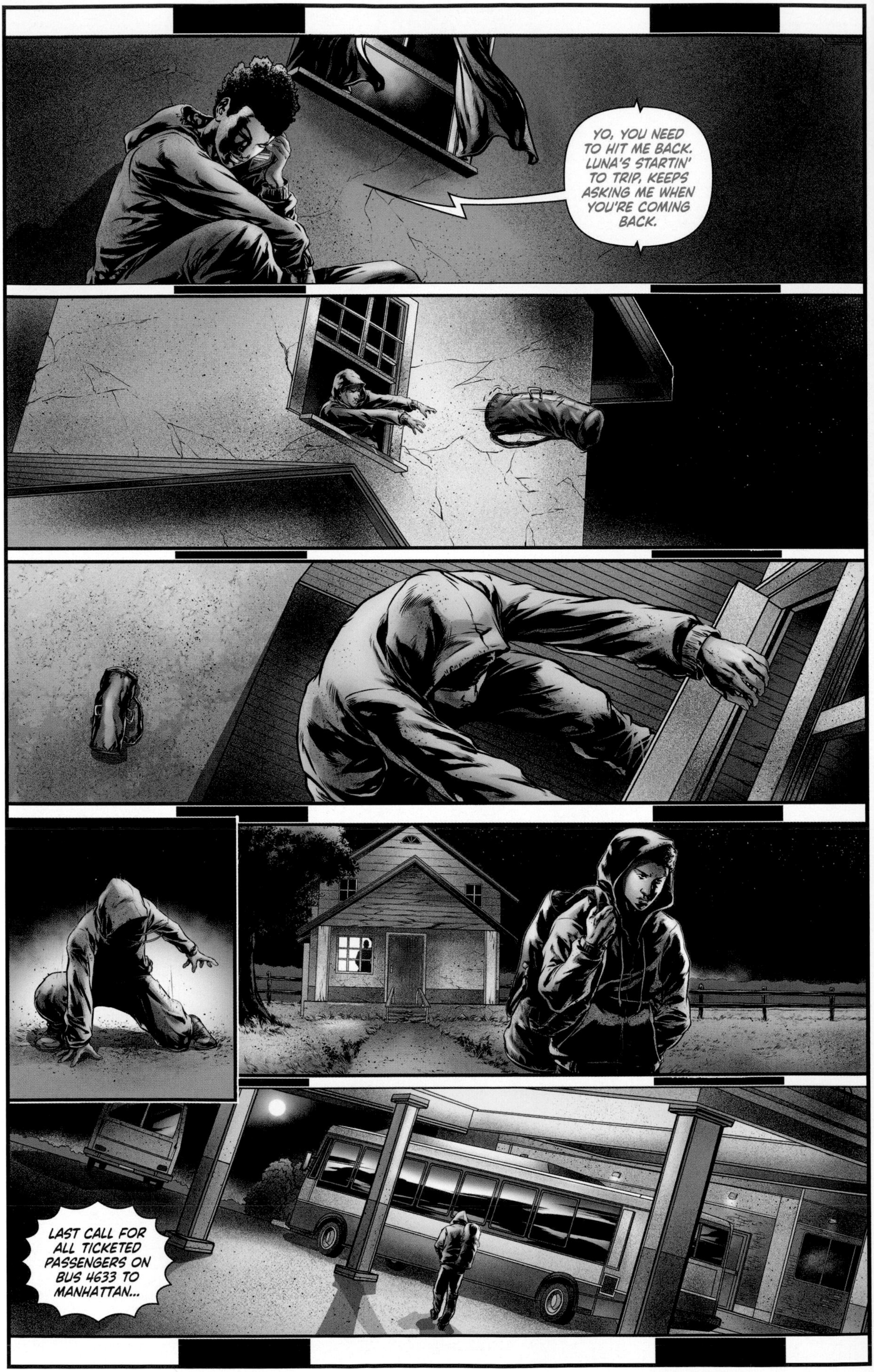
YO, YOU NEED TO HIT ME BACK. LUNA'S STARTIN' TO TRIP, KEEPS ASKING ME WHEN YOU'RE COMING BACK.
LAST CALL FOR ALL TICKETED PASSENGERS ON BUS 4633 TO MANHATTAN...

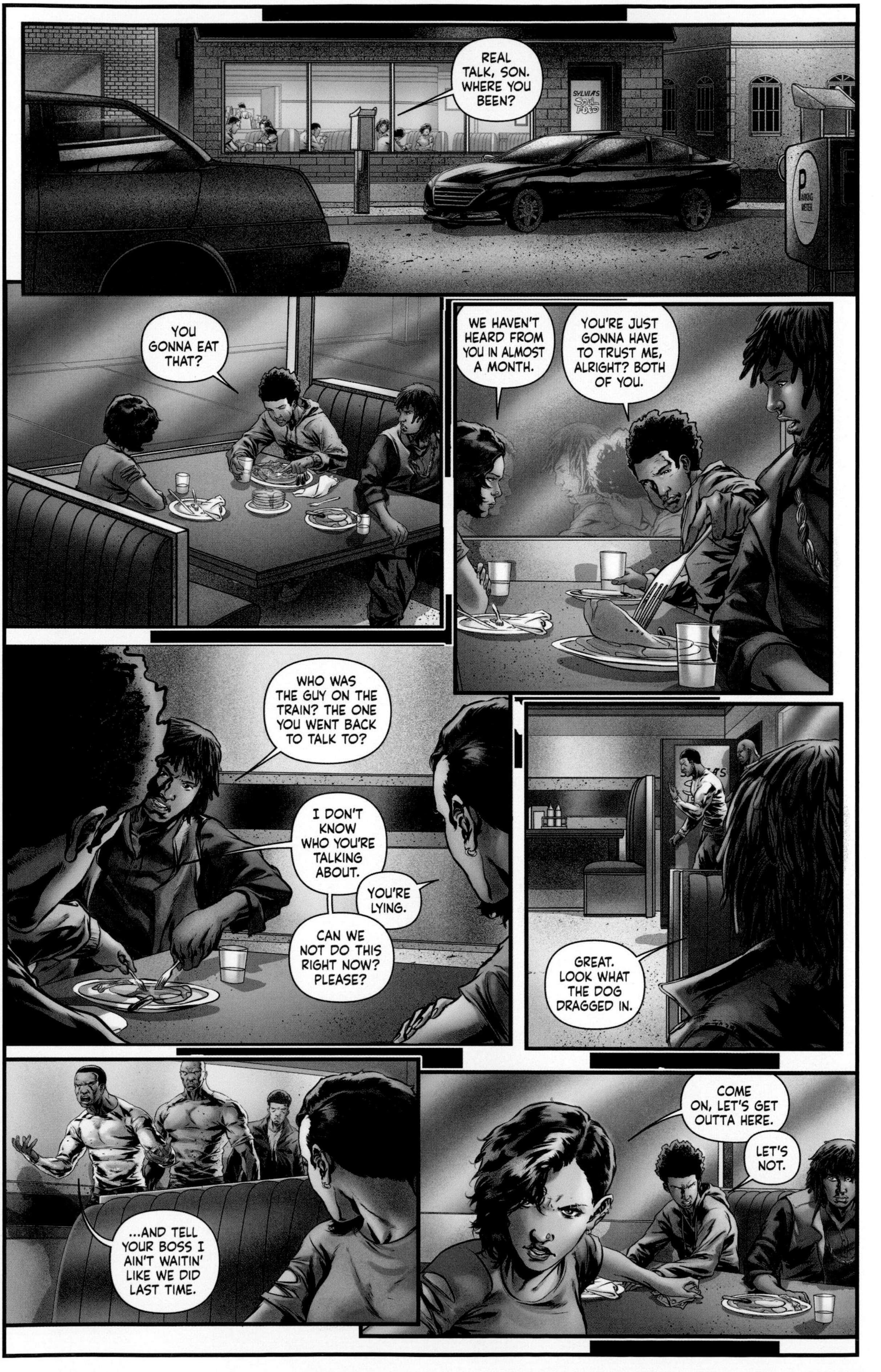
REAL TALK, SON. WHERE YOU BEEN?
SYLVIA'S SOUL FOOD
PARKING METER
YOU GONNA EAT THAT?
WE HAVEN'T HEARD FROM YOU IN ALMOST A MONTH.
YOU'RE JUST GONNA HAVE TO TRUST ME, ALRIGHT? BOTH OF YOU.
WHO WAS THE GUY ON THE TRAIN? THE ONE YOU WENT BACK TO TALK TO?
I DON'T KNOW WHO YOU'RE TALKING ABOUT.
YOU'RE LYING.
CAN WE NOT DO THIS RIGHT NOW? PLEASE?
GREAT. LOOK WHAT THE DOG DRAGGED IN.
...AND TELL YOUR BOSS I AIN'T WAITIN' LIKE WE DID LAST TIME.
COME ON, LET'S GET OUTTA HERE.
LET'S NOT.

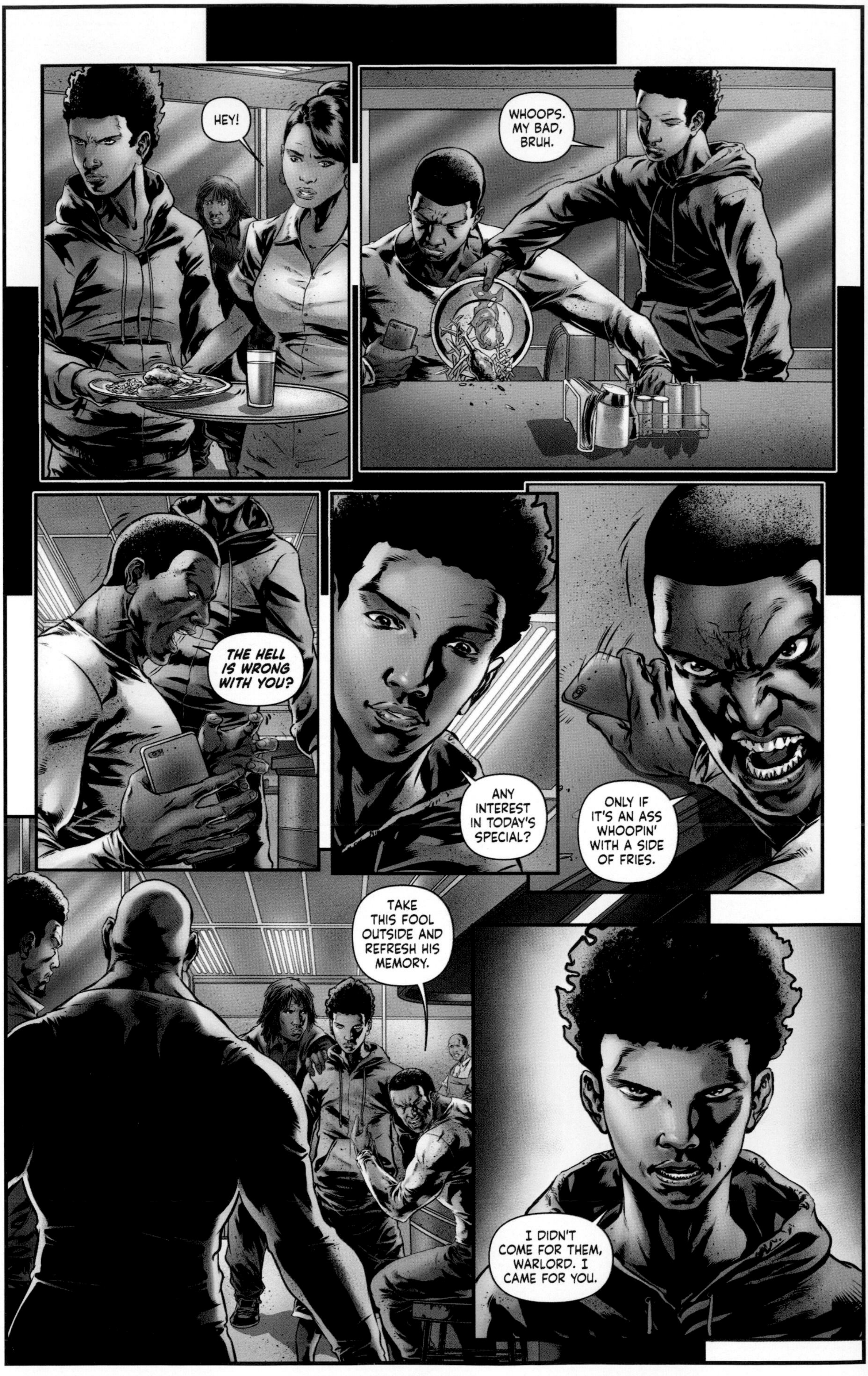
HEY!
WHOOPS. MY BAD, BRUH.
THE HELL IS WRONG WITH YOU?
ANY INTEREST IN TODAY'S SPECIAL?
ONLY IF IT'S AN ASS WHOOPIN' WITH A SIDE OF FRIES.
TAKE THIS FOOL OUTSIDE AND REFRESH HIS MEMORY.
I DIDN'T COME FOR THEM, WARLORD. I CAME FOR YOU.

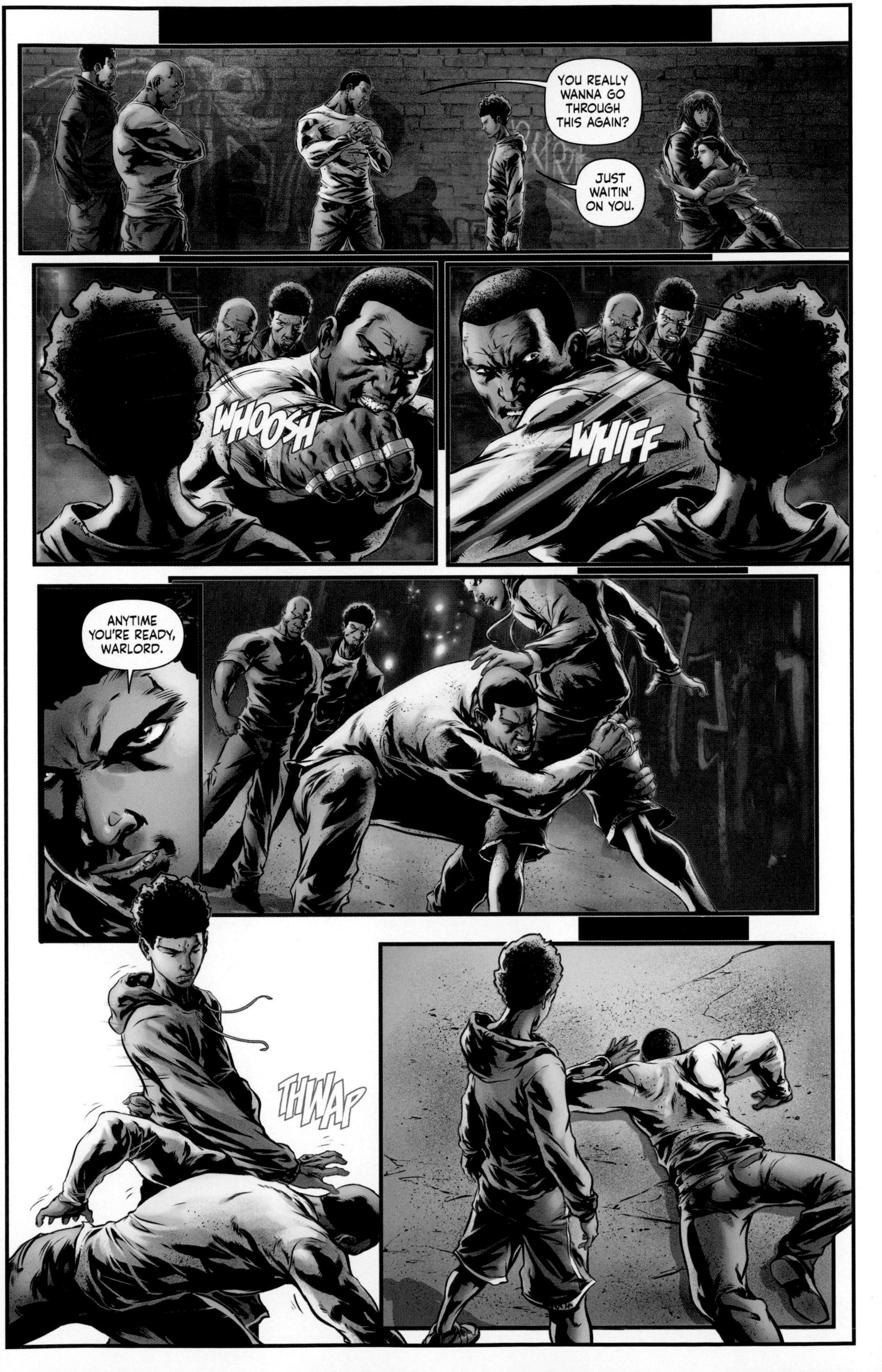
YOU REALLY WANNA GO THROUGH THIS AGAIN?
JUST WAITIN' ON YOU.
WHOOSH
WHIFF
ANYTIME YOU'RE READY, WARLORD.
THWAP

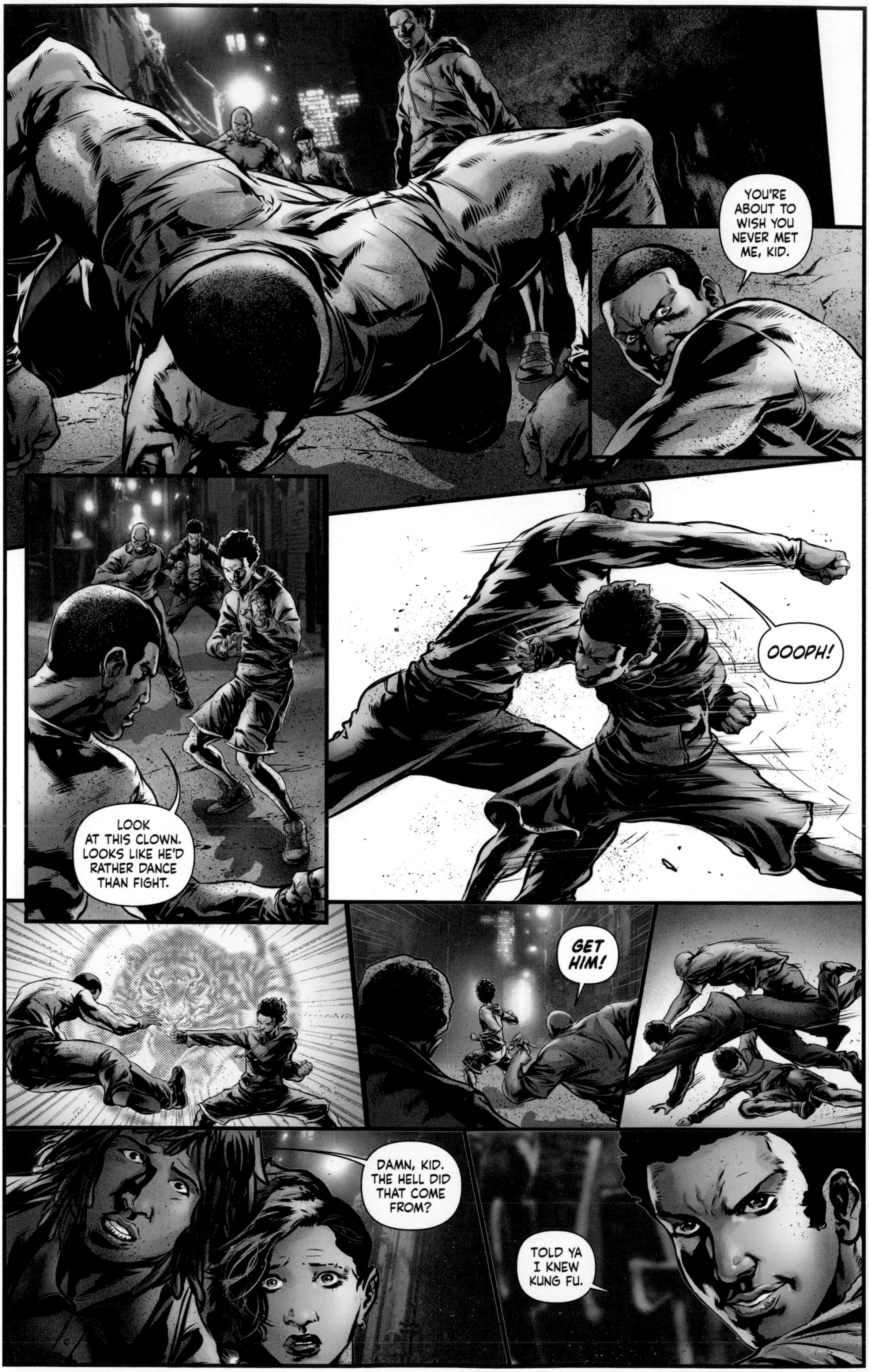
YOU'RE ABOUT TO WISH YOU NEVER MET ME, KID.
LOOK AT THIS CLOWN. LOOKS LIKE HE'D RATHER DANCE THAN FIGHT.
OOOPH!
GET HIM!
DAMN, KID. THE HELL DID THAT COME FROM?
TOLD YA I KNEW KUNG FU.

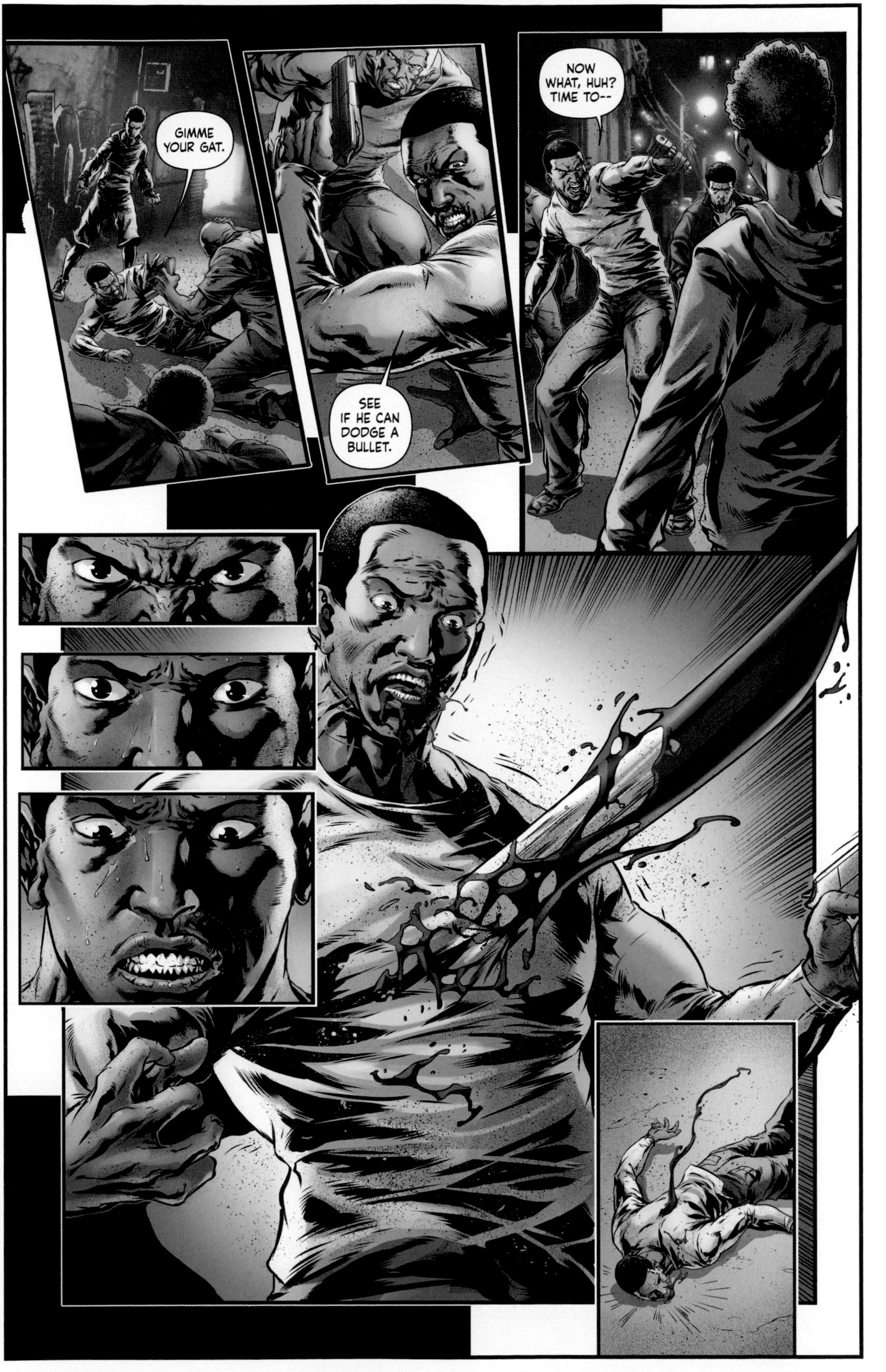
GIMME YOUR GAT.
SEE IF HE CAN DODGE A BULLET.
NOW WHAT, HUH? TIME TO--

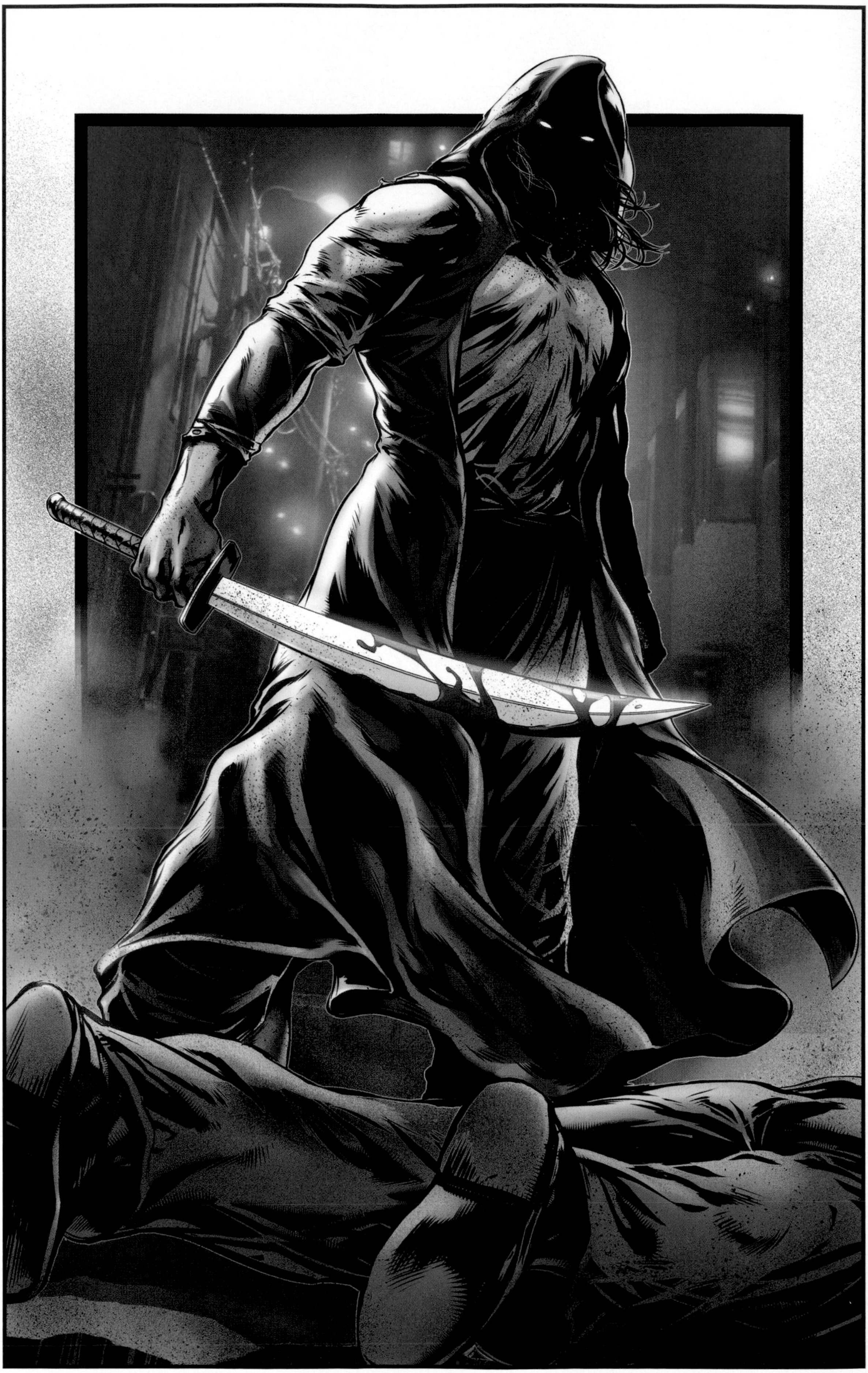

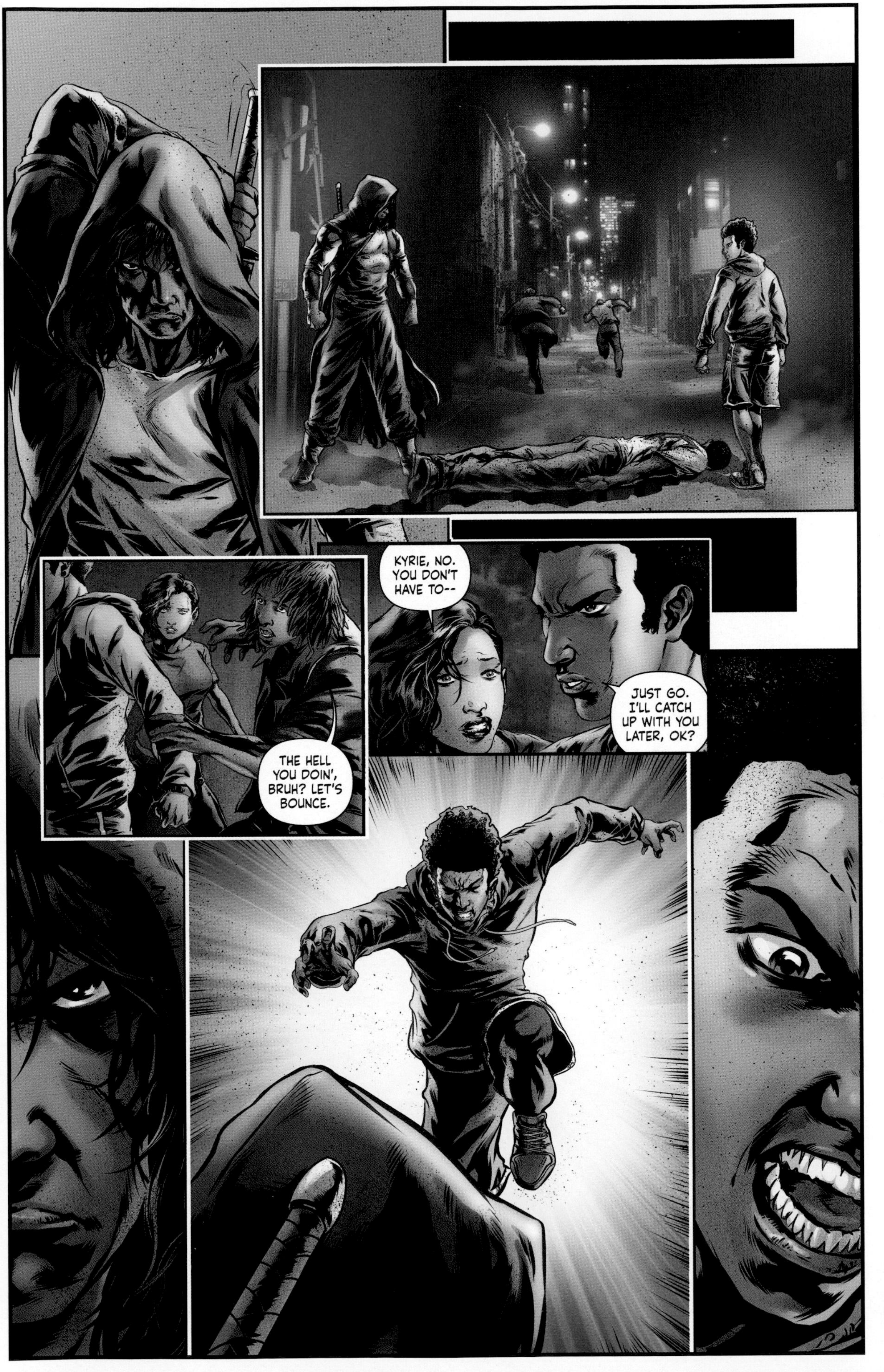
[redacted]
[redacted]
THE HELL YOU DOIN', BRUH? LET'S BOUNCE.
KYRIE, NO. YOU DON'T HAVE TO--
JUST GO. I'LL CATCH UP WITH YOU LATER, OK?

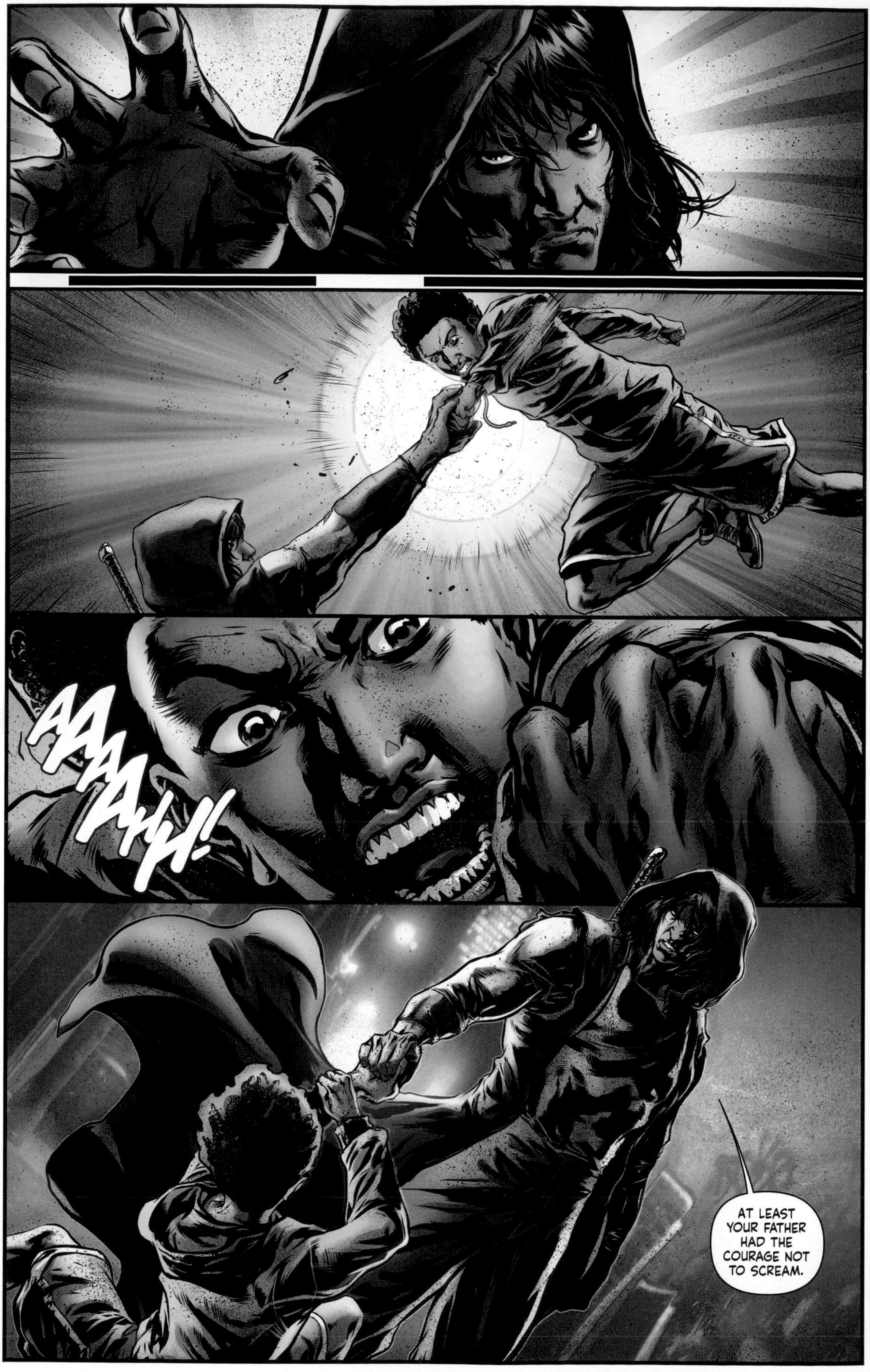
AAAAAHH!!
AT LEAST YOUR FATHER HAD THE COURAGE NOT TO SCREAM.

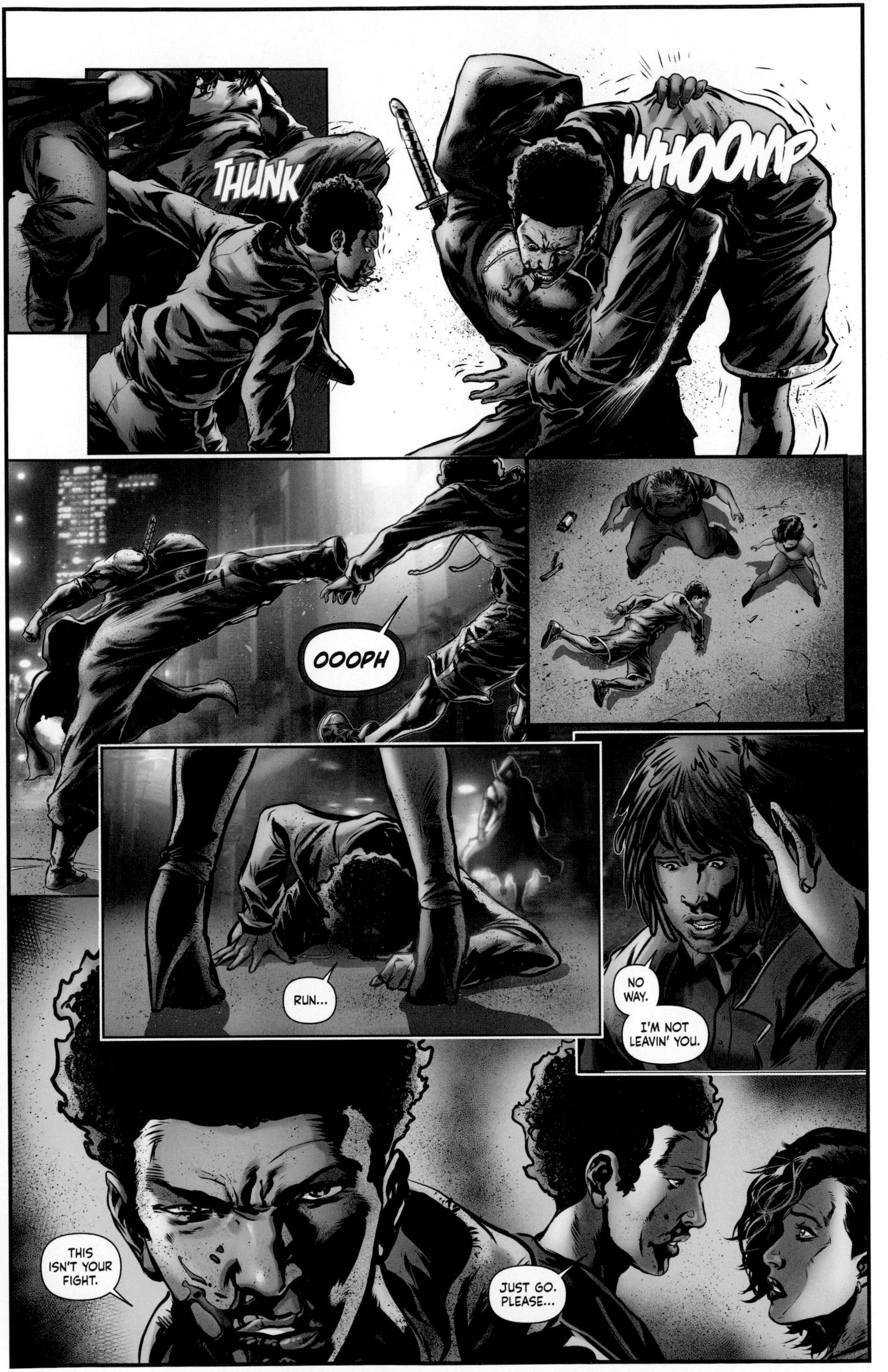
THUNK
WHOOMP
OOOPH
RUN...
NO WAY.
I'M NOT LEAVIN' YOU.
THIS ISN'T YOUR FIGHT.
JUST GO. PLEASE...

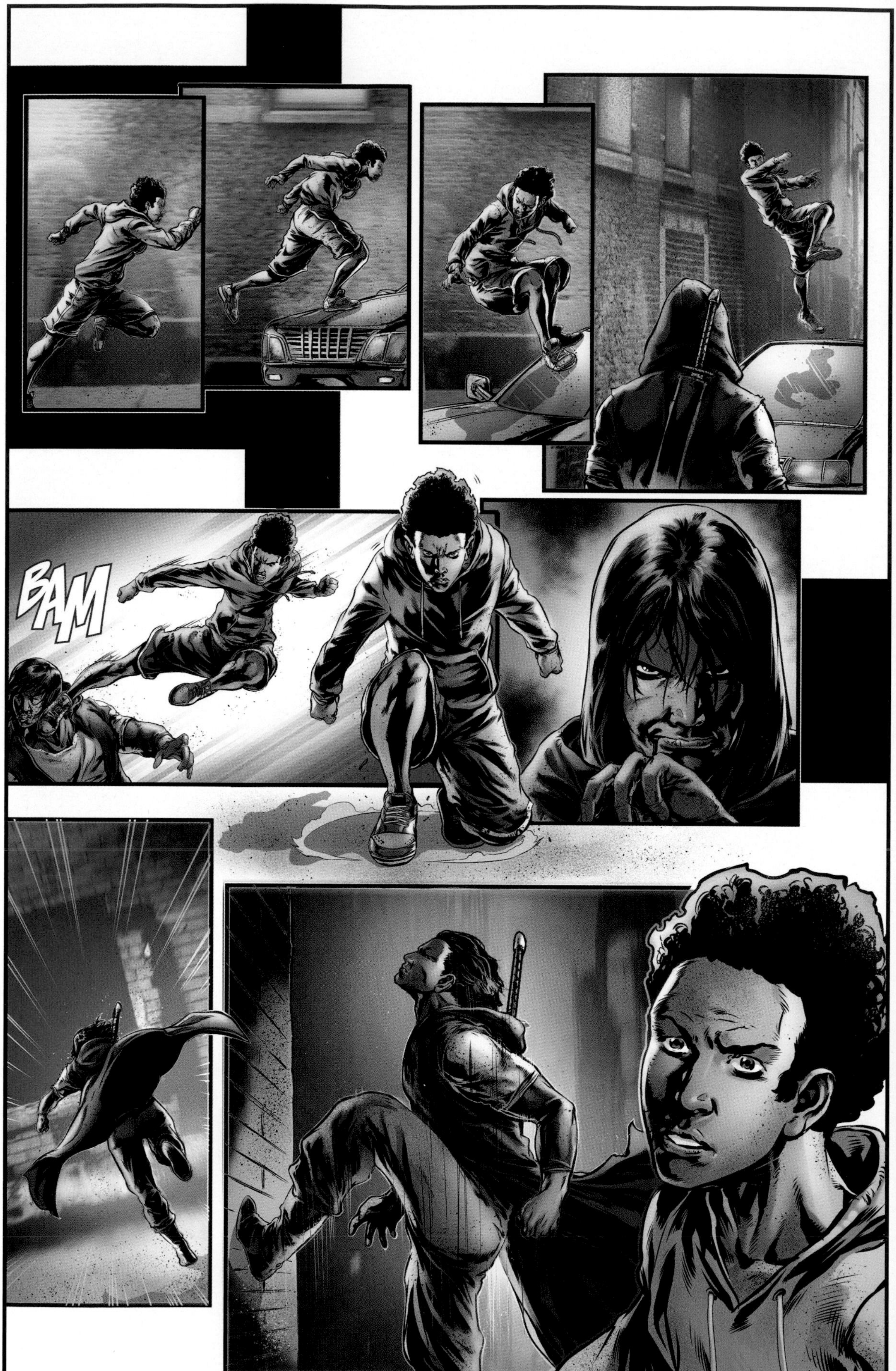
BAM

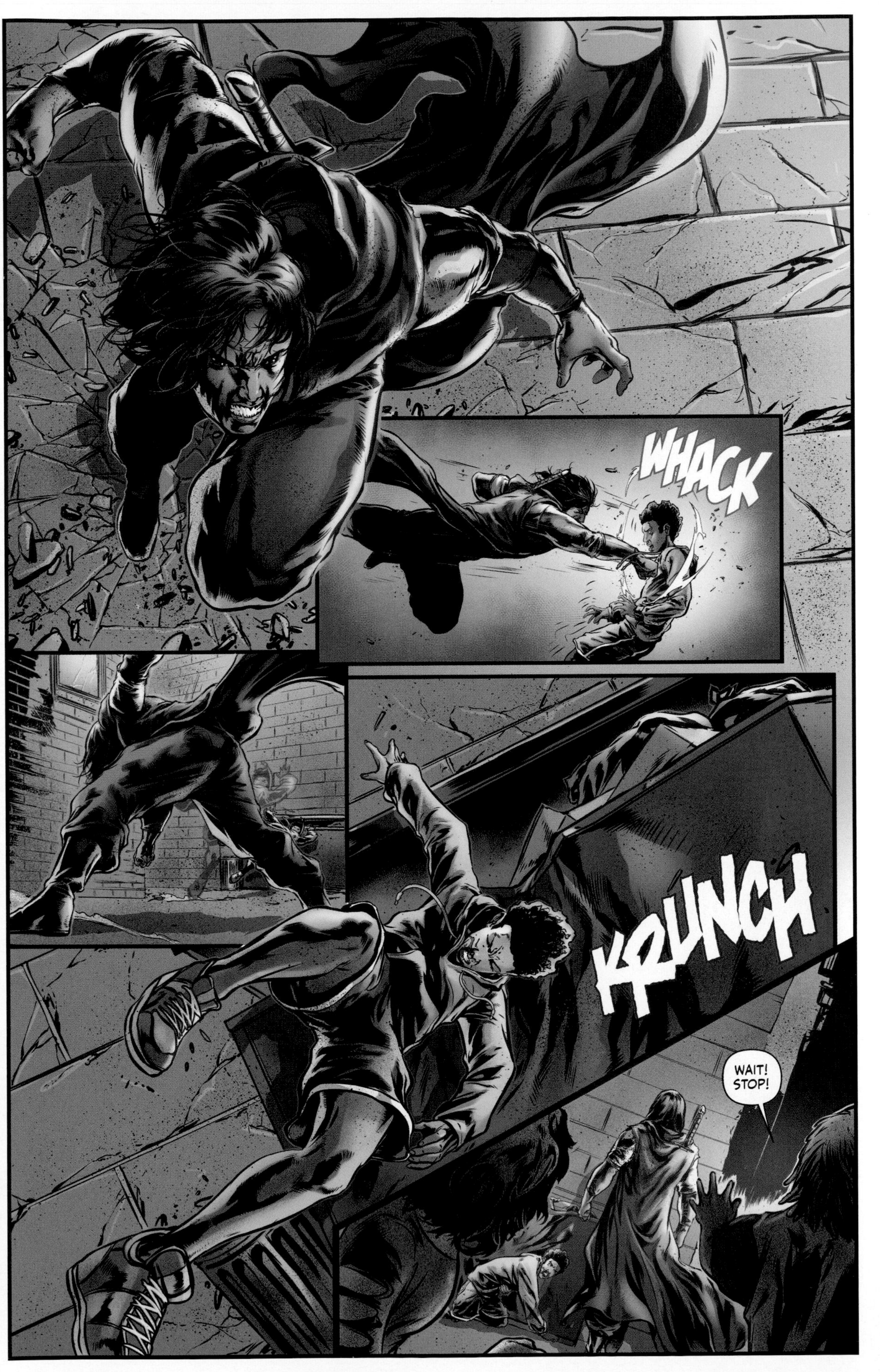
WHACK
KRUNCH
WAIT! STOP!

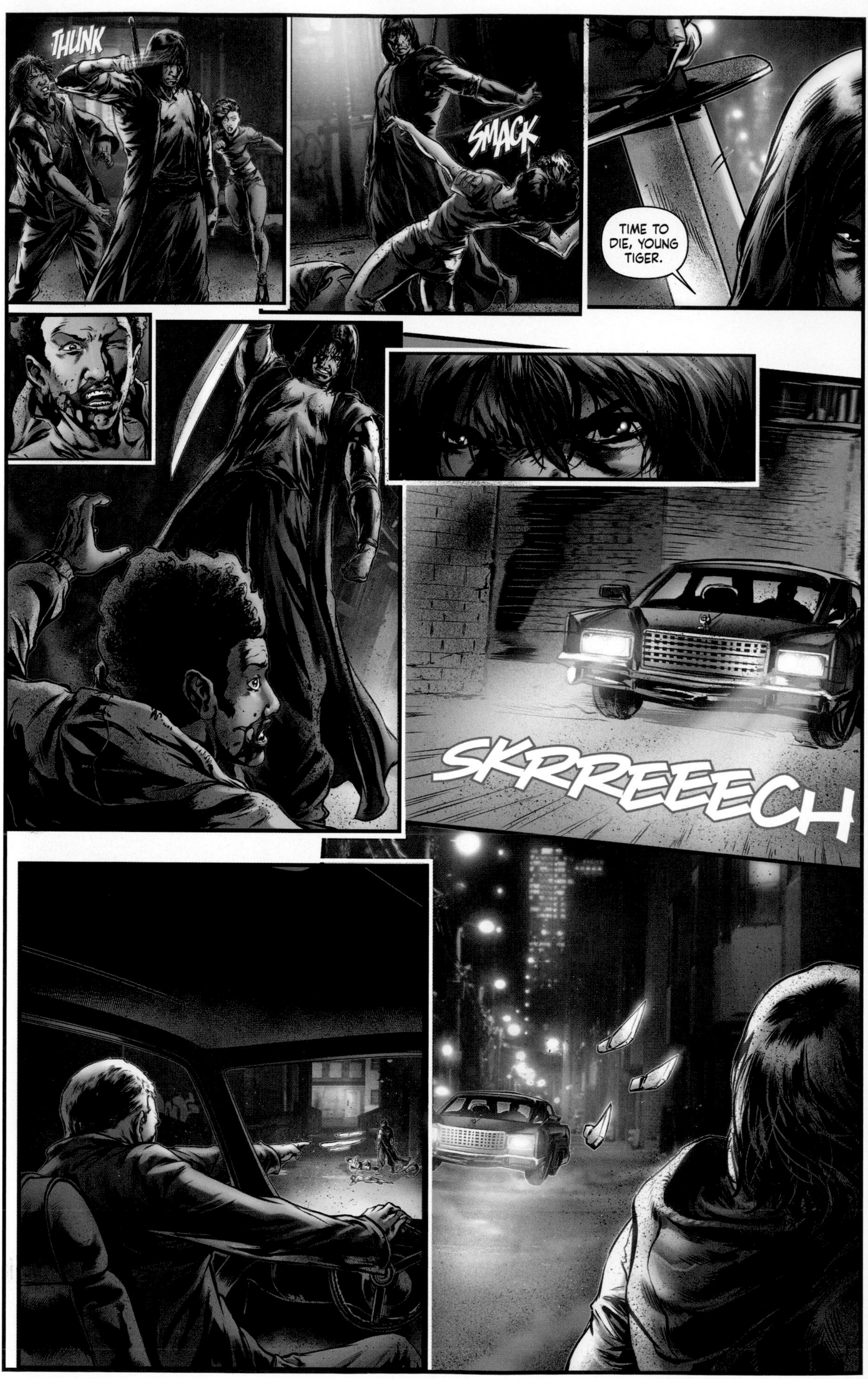
THUNK
SMACK
TIME TO DIE, YOUNG TIGER.
SKRREEECH

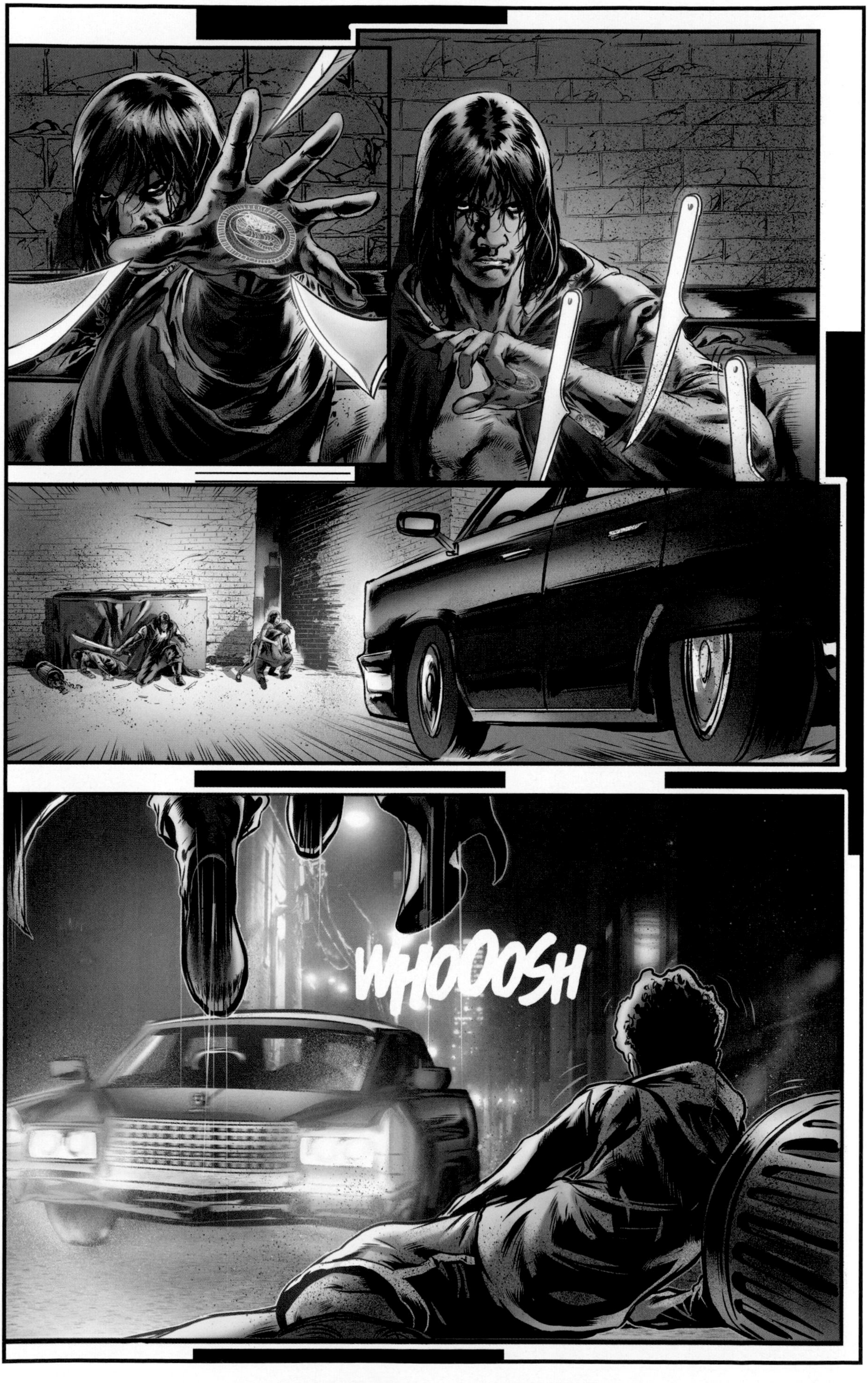
WHOOOSH

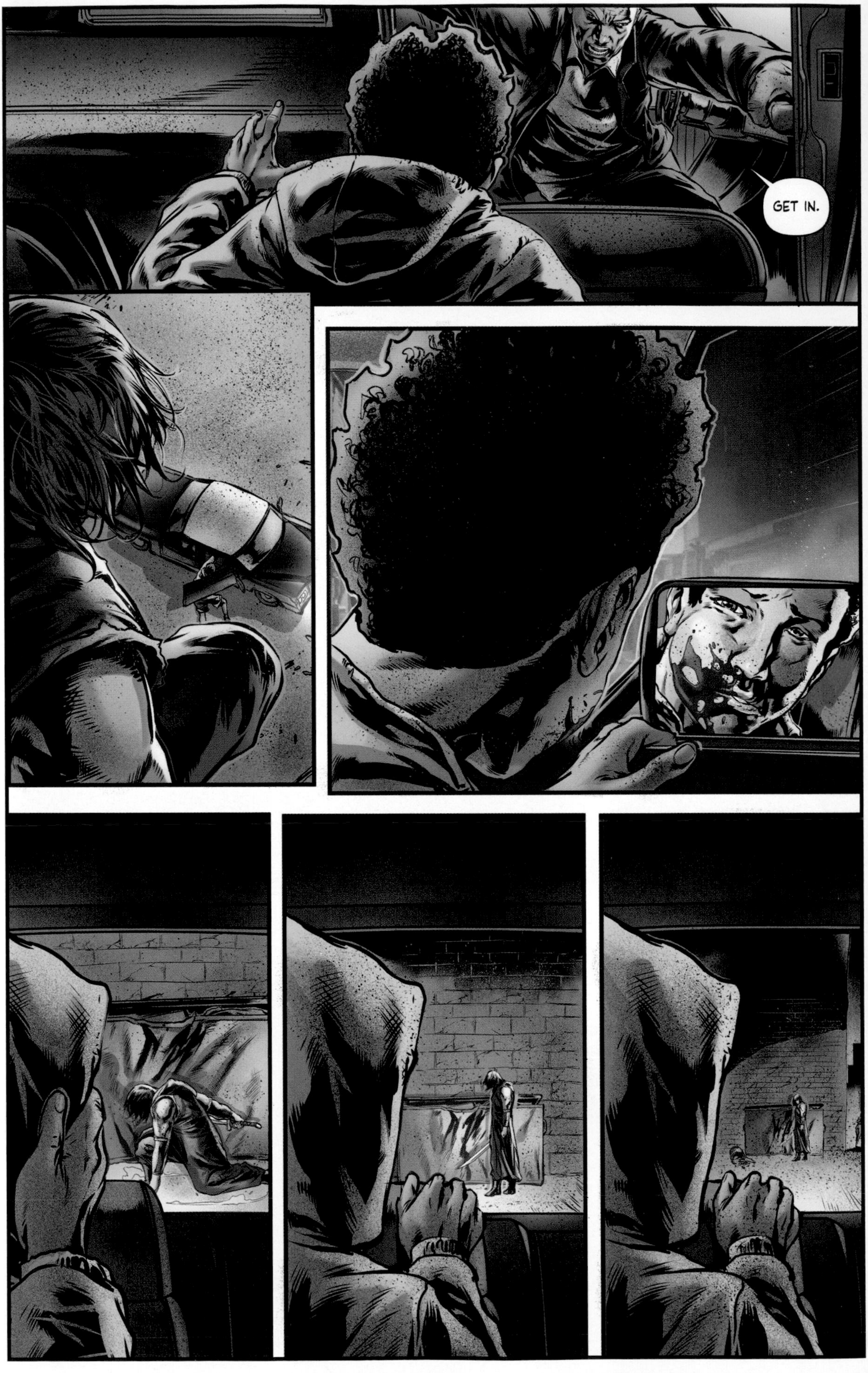
GET IN.

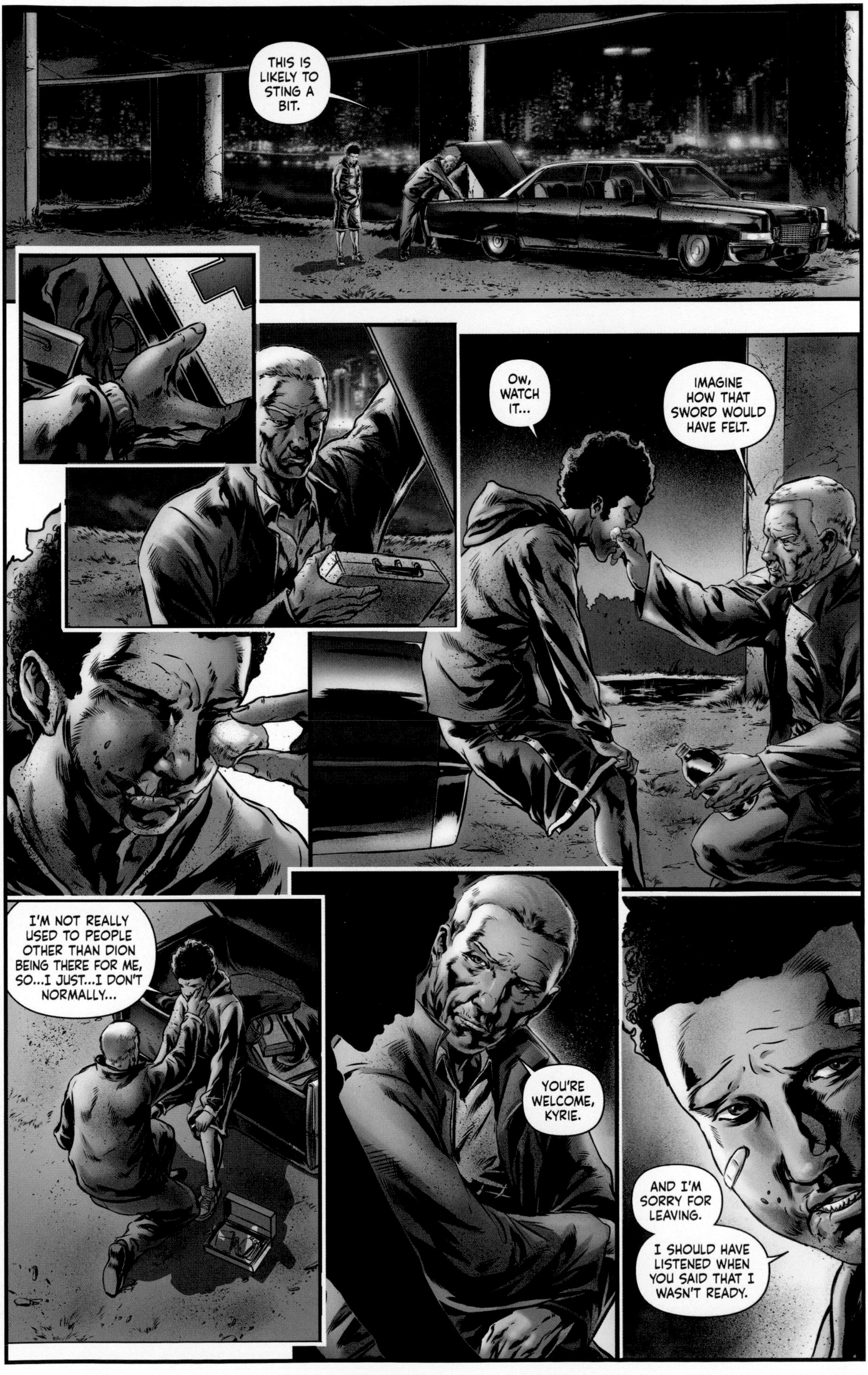
THIS IS LIKELY TO STING A BIT.
OW, WATCH IT...
IMAGINE HOW THAT SWORD WOULD HAVE FELT.
I'M NOT REALLY USED TO PEOPLE OTHER THAN DION BEING THERE FOR ME, SO...I JUST...I DON'T NORMALLY...
YOU'RE WELCOME, KYRIE.
AND I'M SORRY FOR LEAVING.
I SHOULD HAVE LISTENED WHEN YOU SAID THAT I WASN'T READY.

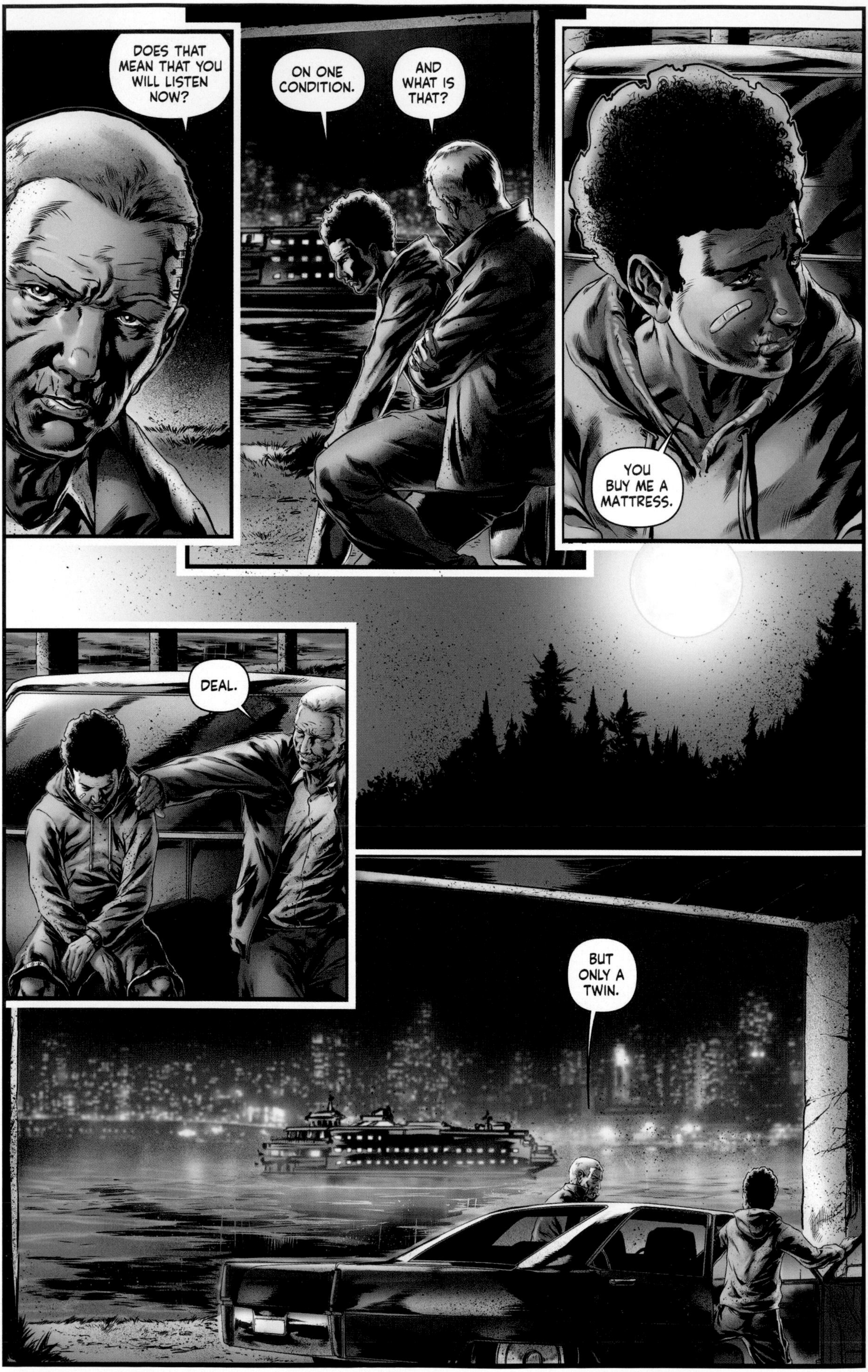
DOES THAT MEAN THAT YOU WILL LISTEN NOW?
ON ONE CONDITION.
AND WHAT IS THAT?
YOU BUY ME A MATTRESS.
DEAL.
BUT ONLY A TWIN.

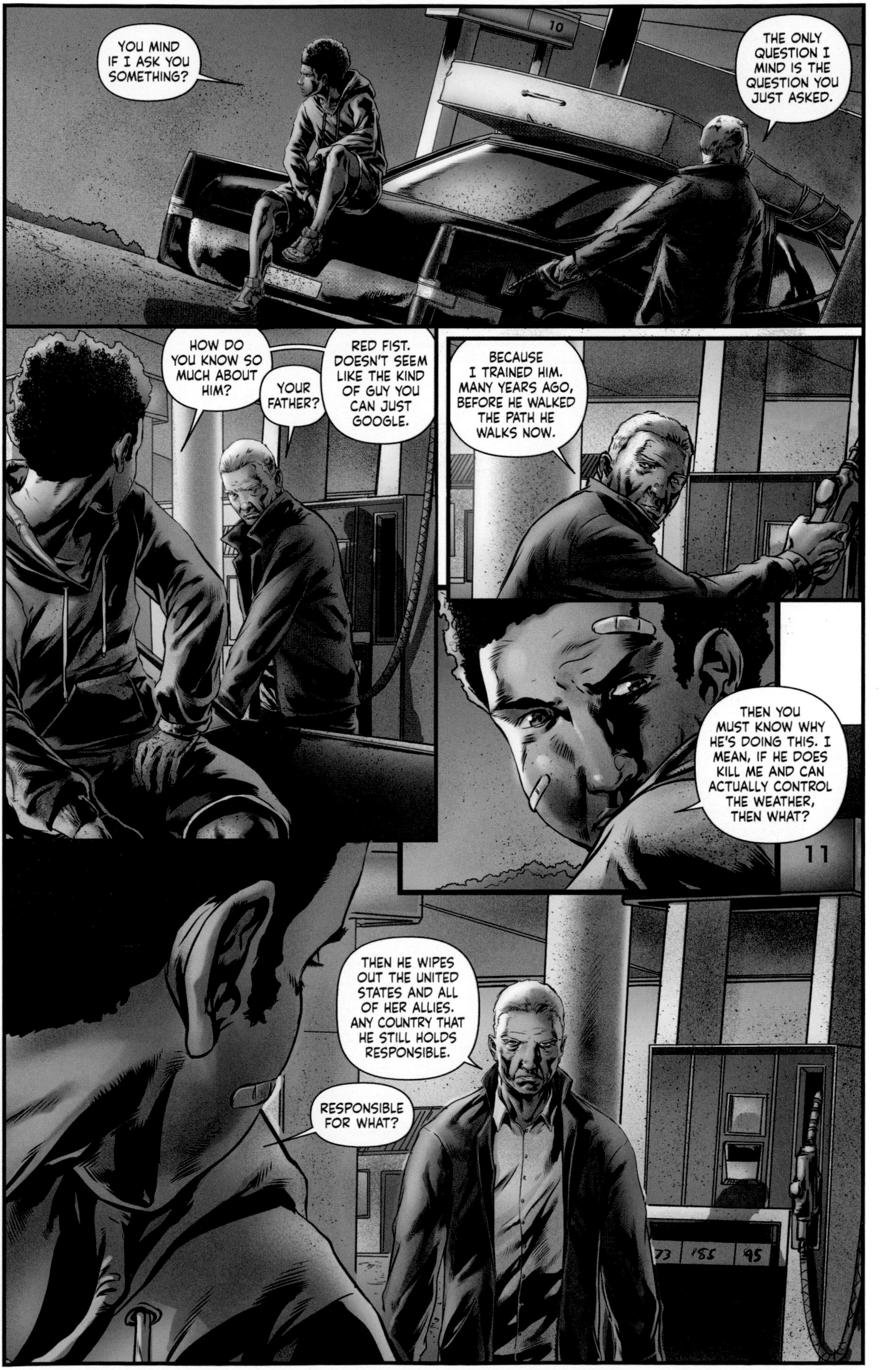

YOU MIND IF I ASK YOU SOMETHING?
THE ONLY QUESTION I MIND IS THE QUESTION YOU JUST ASKED.
10
HOW DO YOU KNOW SO MUCH ABOUT HIM?
YOUR FATHER?
RED FIST. DOESN'T SEEM LIKE THE KIND OF GUY YOU CAN JUST GOOGLE.
BECAUSE I TRAINED HIM. MANY YEARS AGO, BEFORE HE WALKED THE PATH HE WALKS NOW.
THEN YOU MUST KNOW WHY HE'S DOING THIS. I MEAN, IF HE DOES KILL ME AND CAN ACTUALLY CONTROL THE WEATHER, THEN WHAT?
11
THEN HE WIPES OUT THE UNITED STATES AND ALL OF HER ALLIES. ANY COUNTRY THAT HE STILL HOLDS RESPONSIBLE.
RESPONSIBLE FOR WHAT?

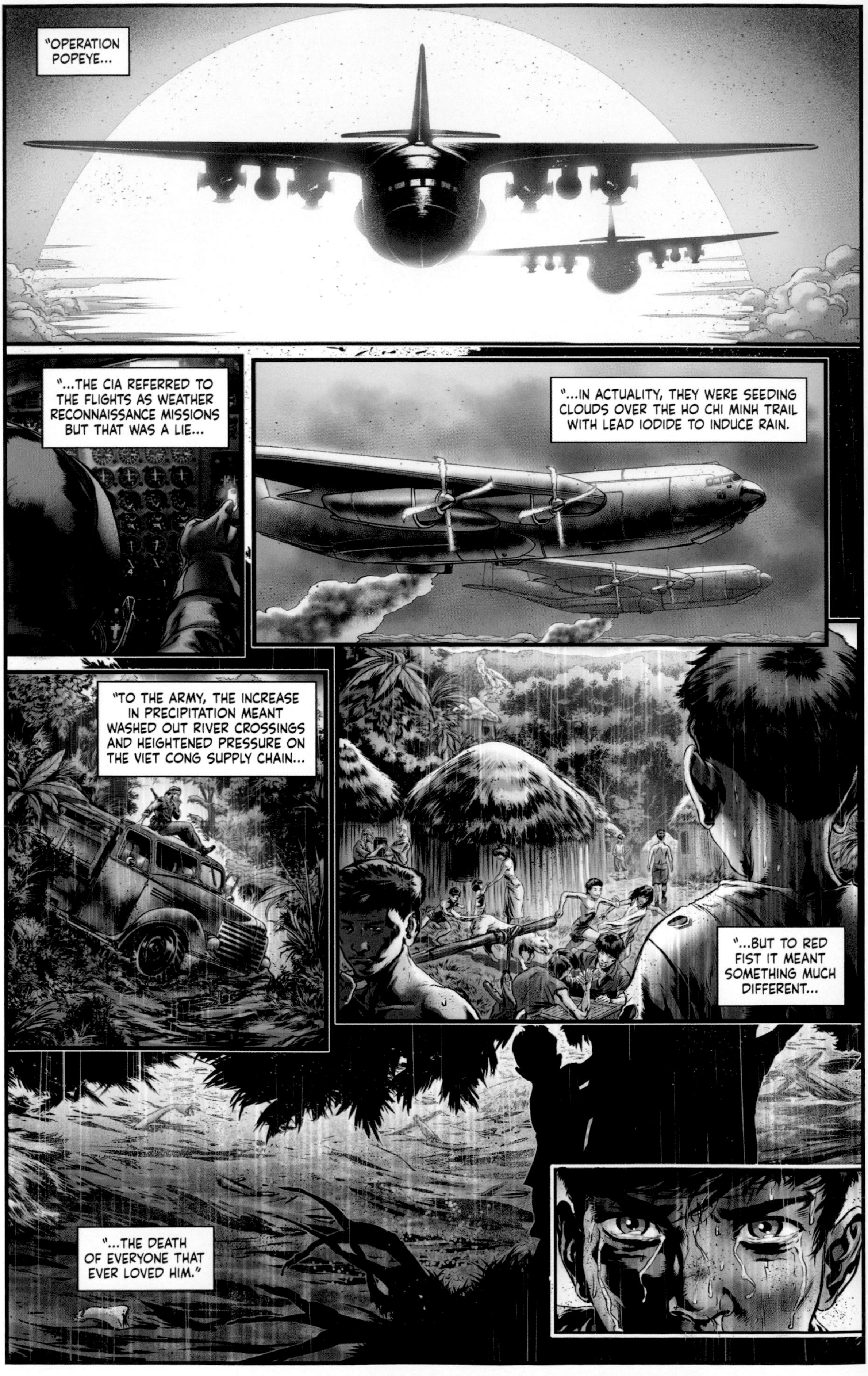
"OPERATION POPEYE...
"...THE CIA REFERRED TO THE FLIGHTS AS WEATHER RECONNAISSANCE MISSIONS BUT THAT WAS A LIE...
"...IN ACTUALITY, THEY WERE SEEDING CLOUDS OVER THE HO CHI MINH TRAIL WITH LEAD IODIDE TO INDUCE RAIN.
"TO THE ARMY, THE INCREASE IN PRECIPITATION MEANT WASHED OUT RIVER CROSSINGS AND HEIGHTENED PRESSURE ON THE VIET CONG SUPPLY CHAIN...
"...BUT TO RED FIST IT MEANT SOMETHING MUCH DIFFERENT...
"...THE DEATH OF EVERYONE THAT EVER LOVED HIM."

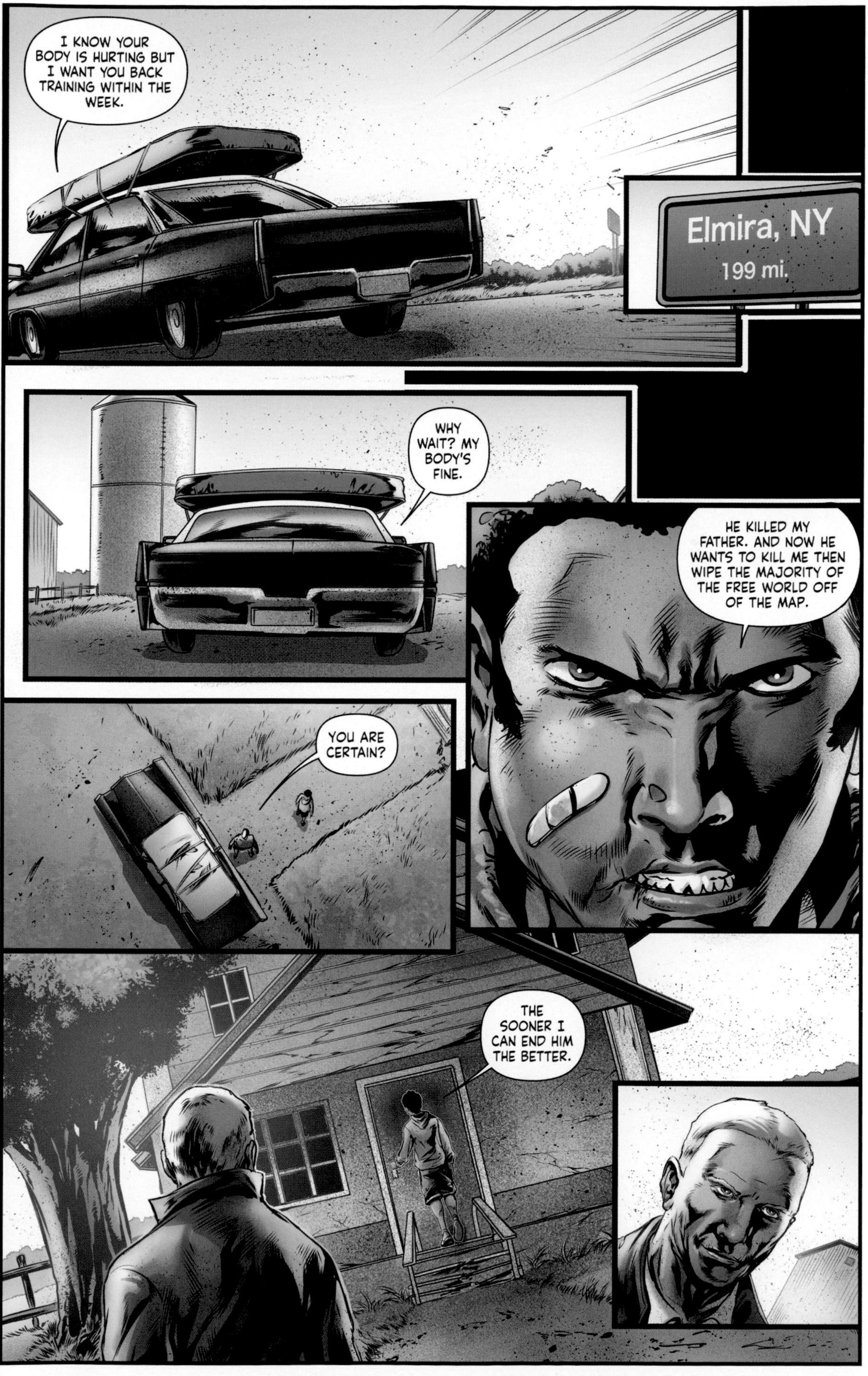
I KNOW YOUR BODY IS HURTING BUT I WANT YOU BACK TRAINING WITHIN THE WEEK.
Elmira, NY
199 mi.
WHY WAIT? MY BODY'S FINE.
HE KILLED MY FATHER. AND NOW HE WANTS TO KILL ME THEN WIPE THE MAJORITY OF THE FREE WORLD OFF OF THE MAP.
YOU ARE CERTAIN?
THE SOONER I CAN END HIM THE BETTER.

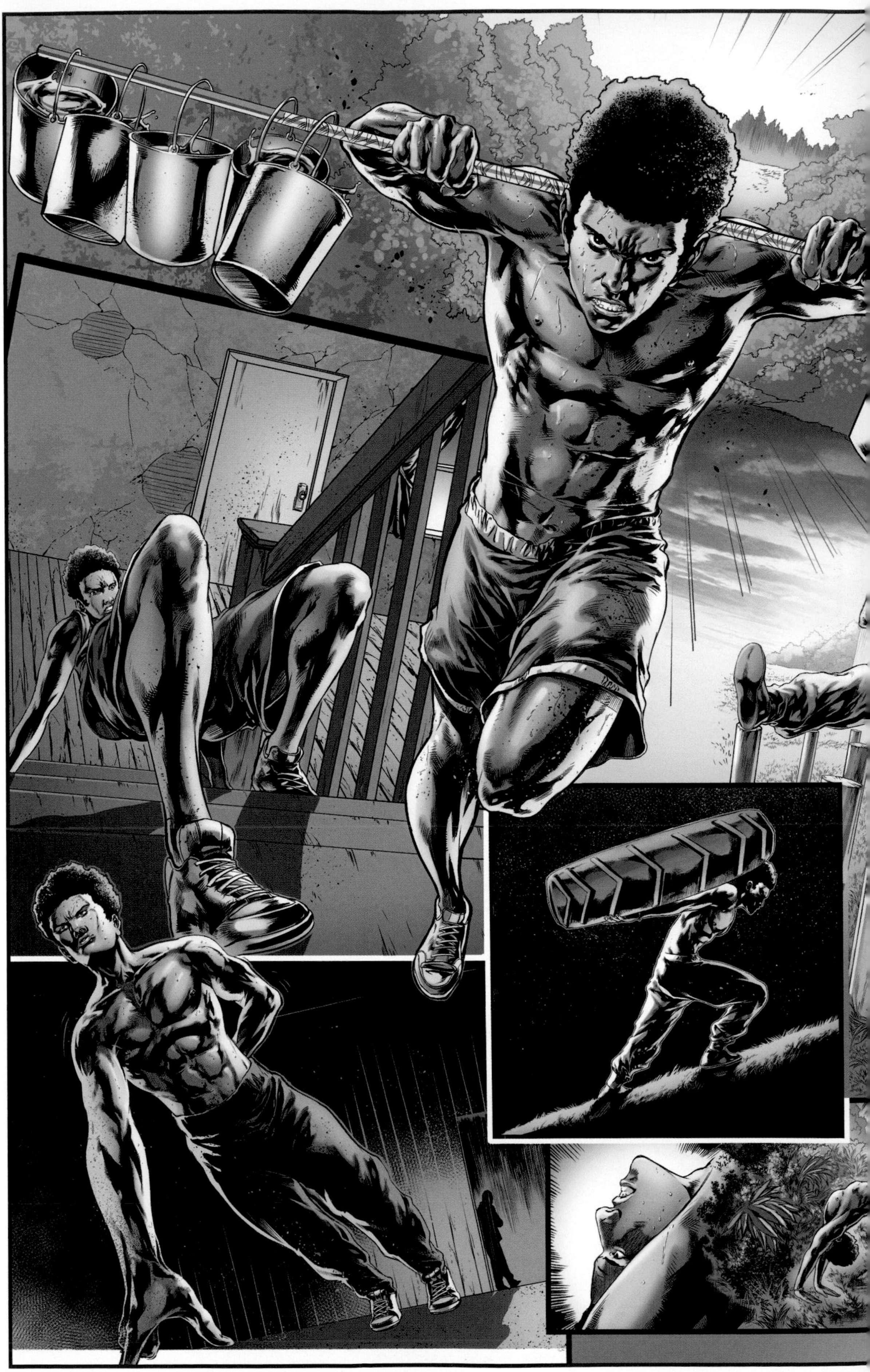

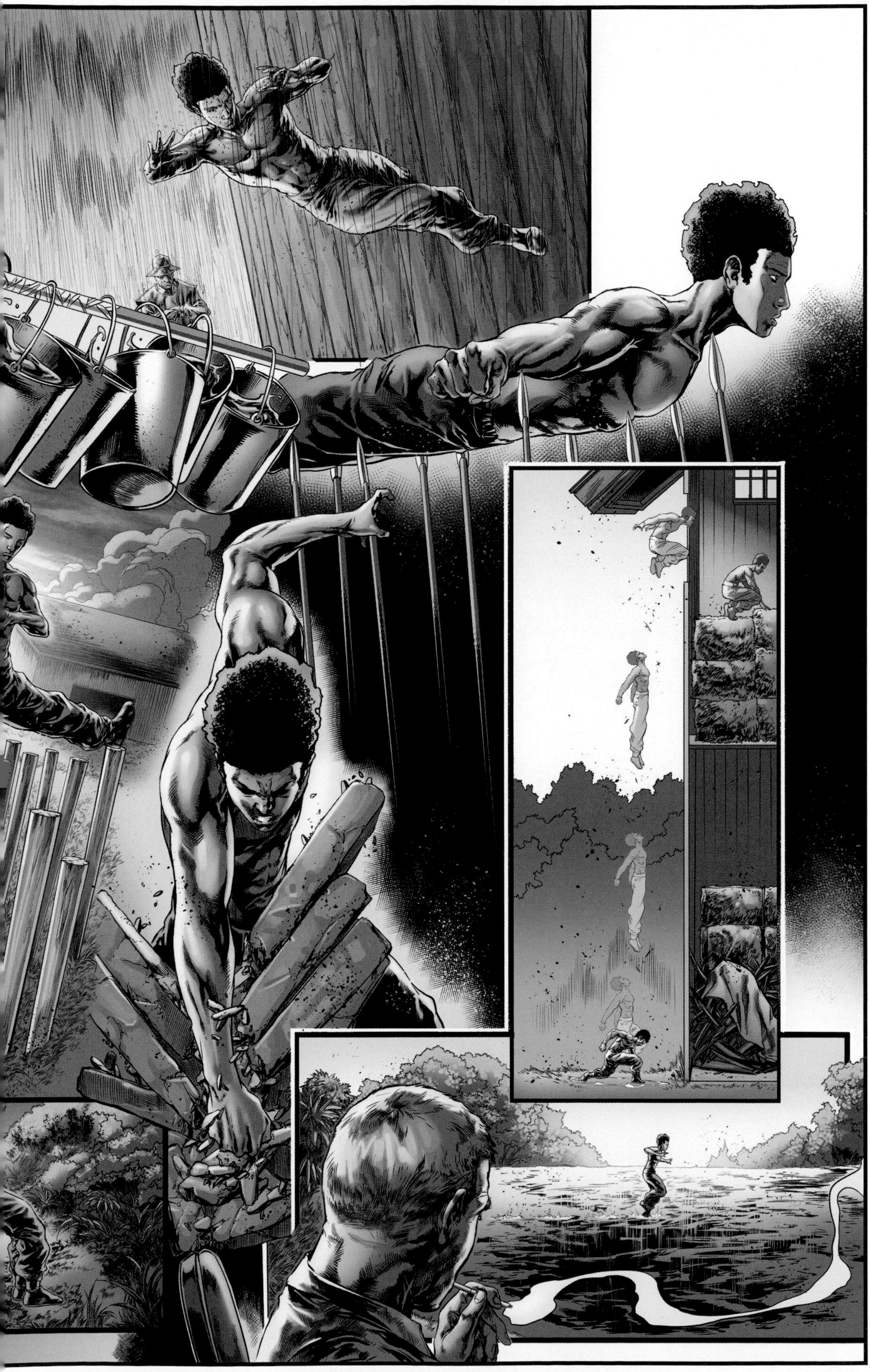

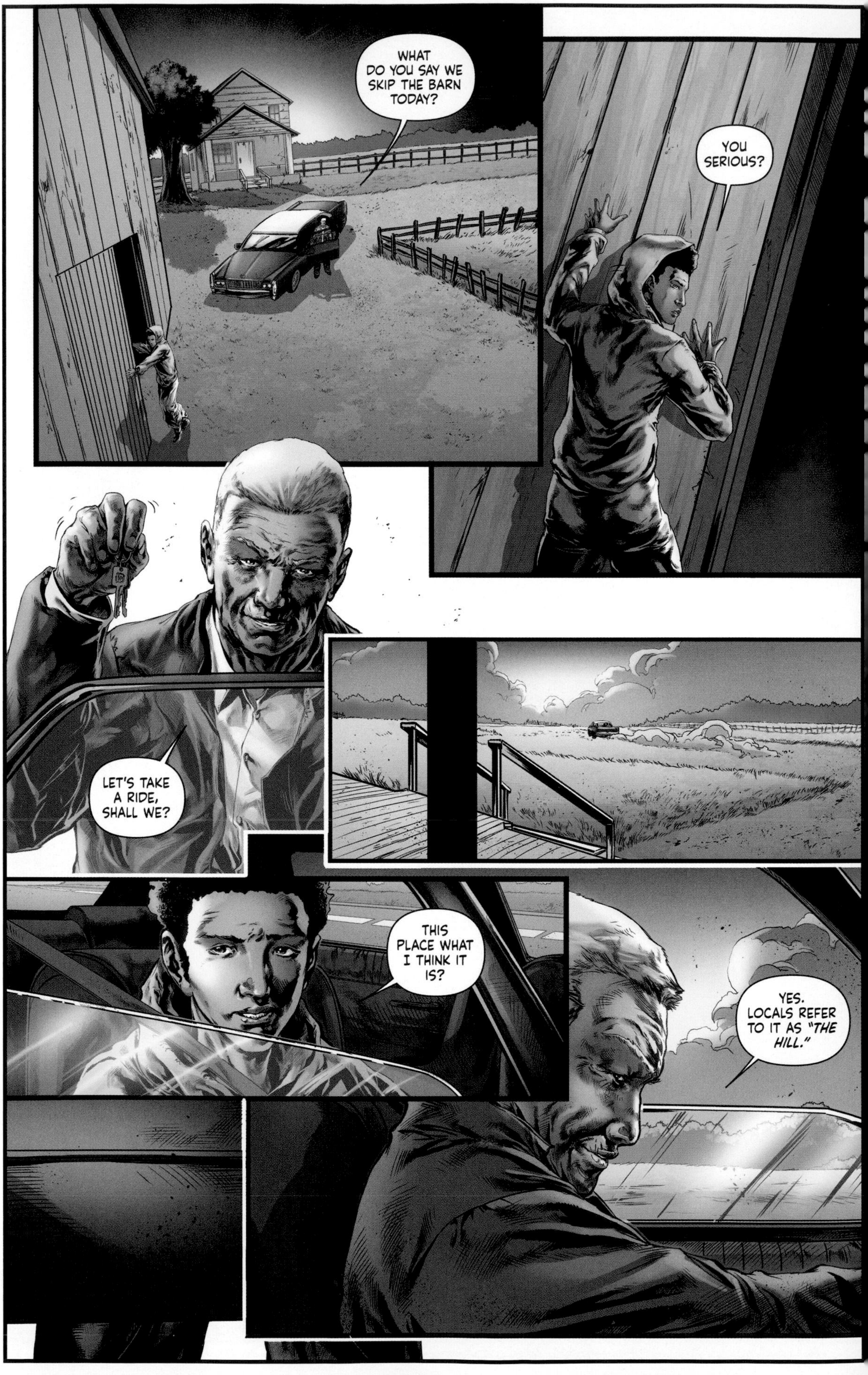
WHAT DO YOU SAY WE SKIP THE BARN TODAY?
YOU SERIOUS?
LET'S TAKE A RIDE, SHALL WE?
THIS PLACE WHAT I THINK IT IS?
YES. LOCALS REFER TO IT AS *"THE HILL."*

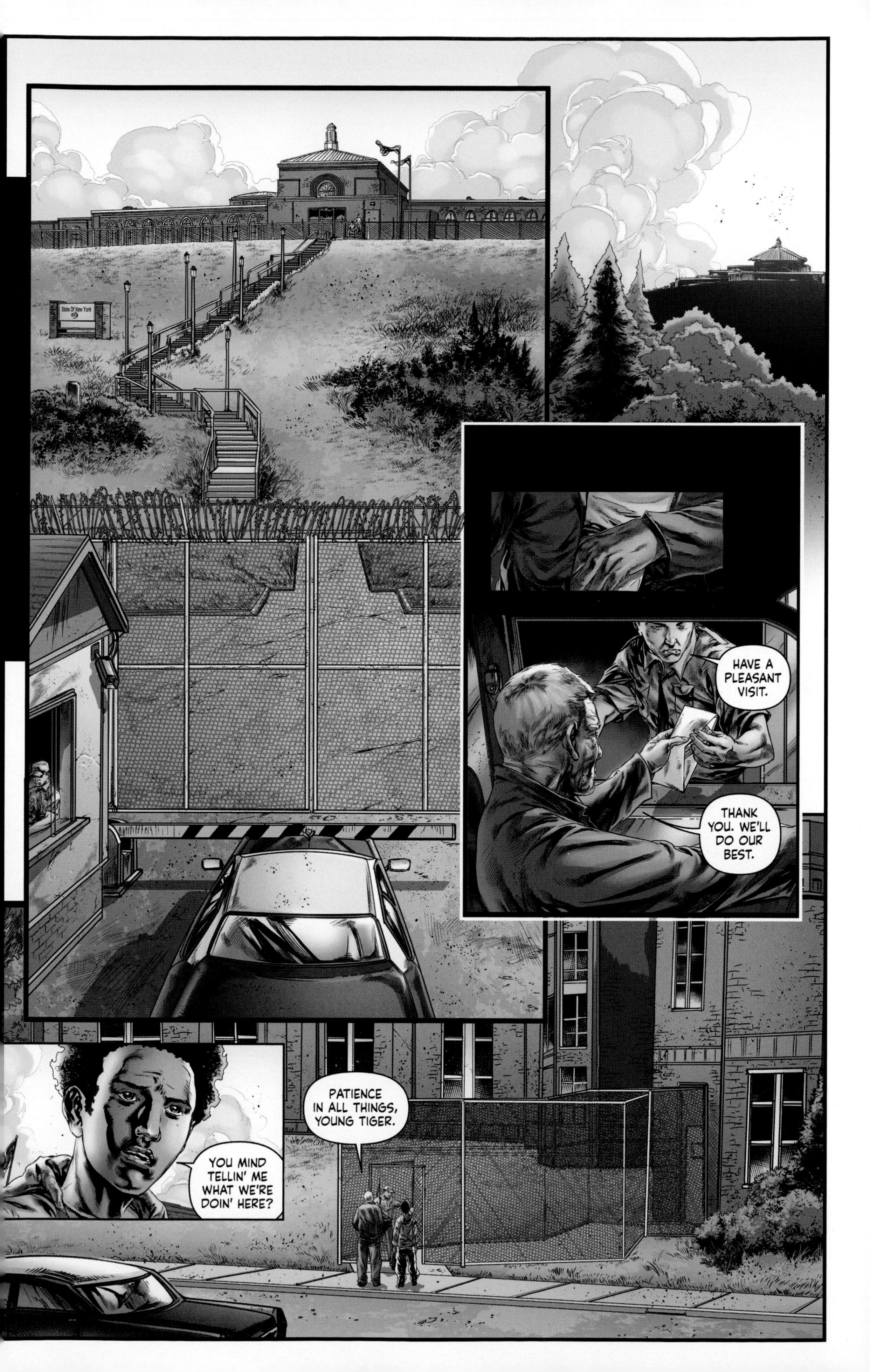
State Of New York
HAVE A PLEASANT VISIT.
THANK YOU. WE'LL DO OUR BEST.
YOU MIND TELLIN' ME WHAT WE'RE DOIN' HERE?
PATIENCE IN ALL THINGS, YOUNG TIGER.

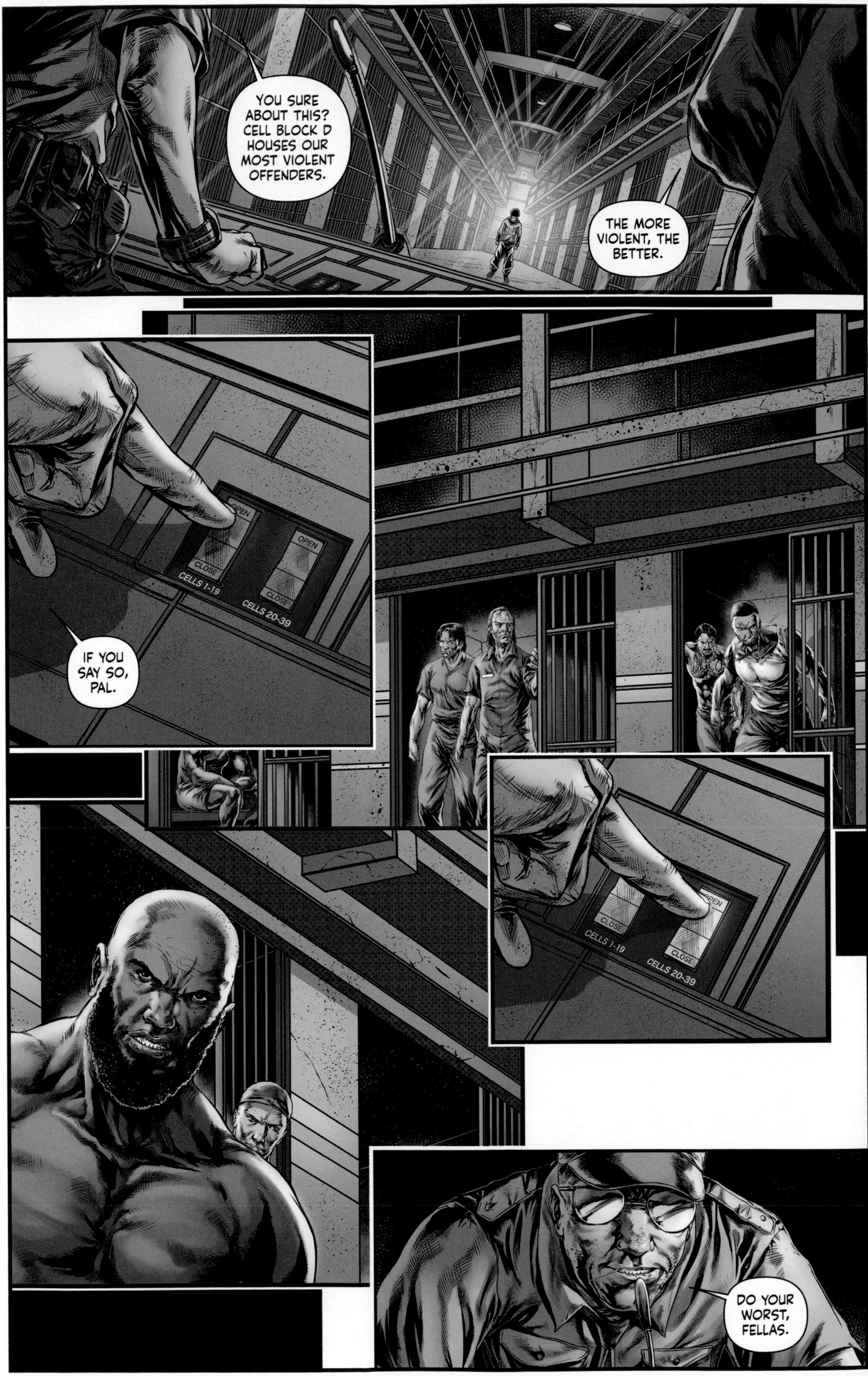
YOU SURE ABOUT THIS? CELL BLOCK D HOUSES OUR MOST VIOLENT OFFENDERS.
THE MORE VIOLENT, THE BETTER.
OPEN
CLOSE
CELLS 1-19
OPEN
CLOSE
CELLS 20-39
IF YOU SAY SO, PAL.
OPEN
CLOSE
CLOSE
CELLS 1-19
CELLS 20-39
DO YOUR WORST, FELLAS.

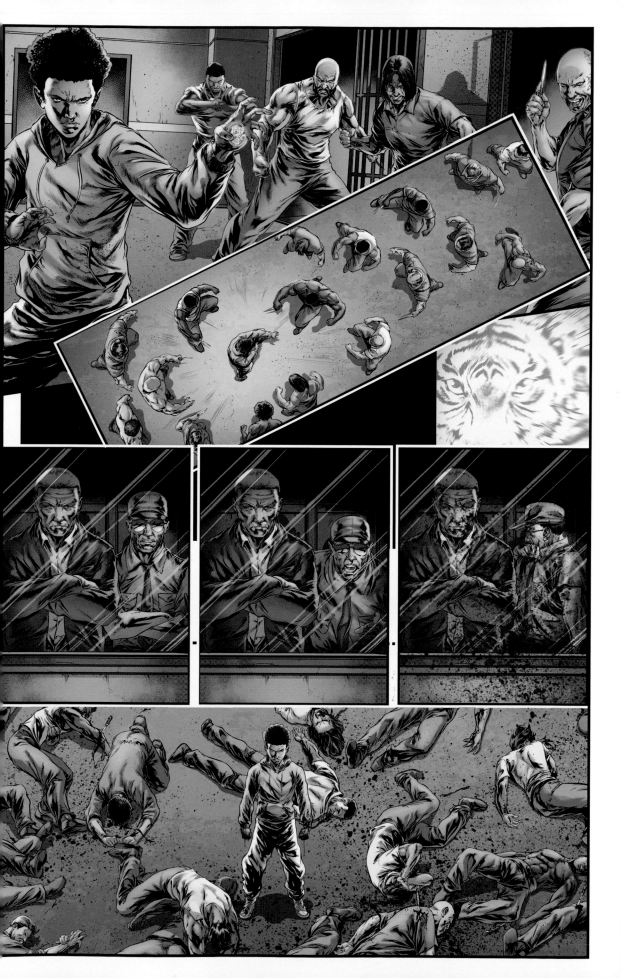

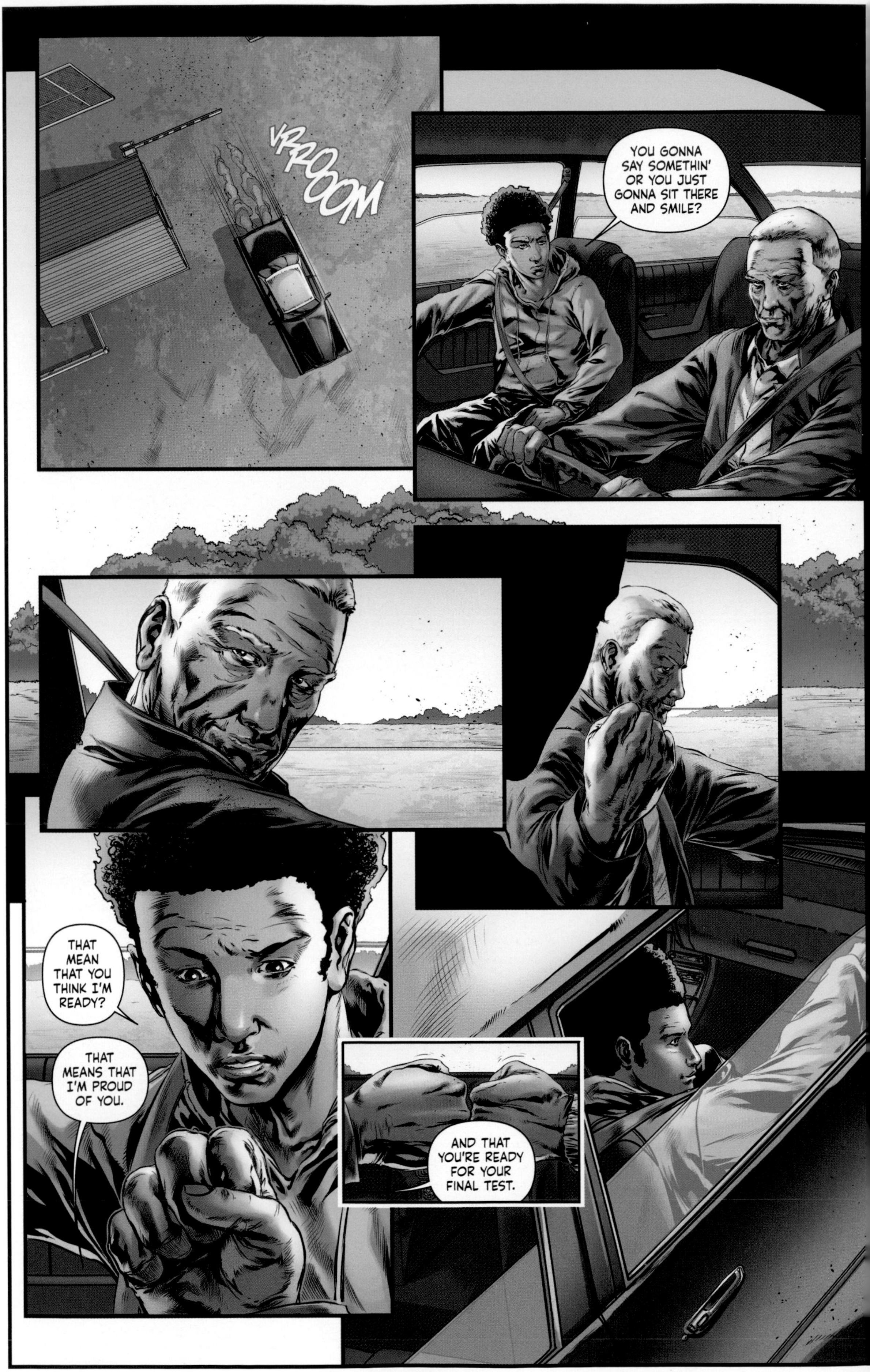
VRROOOM
YOU GONNA SAY SOMETHIN' OR YOU JUST GONNA SIT THERE AND SMILE?
THAT MEAN THAT YOU THINK I'M READY?
THAT MEANS THAT I'M PROUD OF YOU.
AND THAT YOU'RE READY FOR YOUR FINAL TEST.

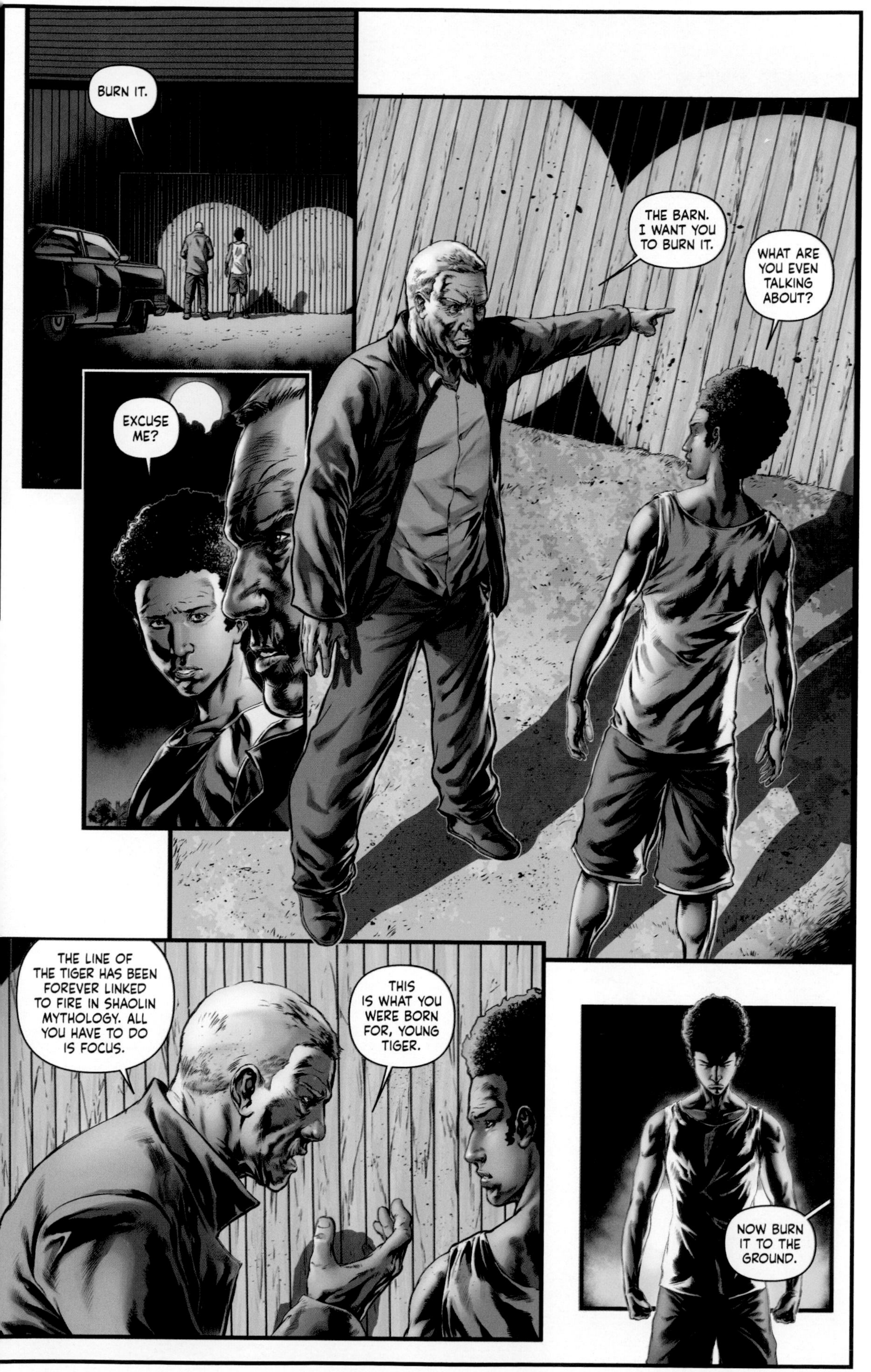
BURN IT.
EXCUSE ME?
THE BARN. I WANT YOU TO BURN IT.
WHAT ARE YOU EVEN TALKING ABOUT?
THE LINE OF THE TIGER HAS BEEN FOREVER LINKED TO FIRE IN SHAOLIN MYTHOLOGY. ALL YOU HAVE TO DO IS FOCUS.
THIS IS WHAT YOU WERE BORN FOR, YOUNG TIGER.
NOW BURN IT TO THE GROUND.

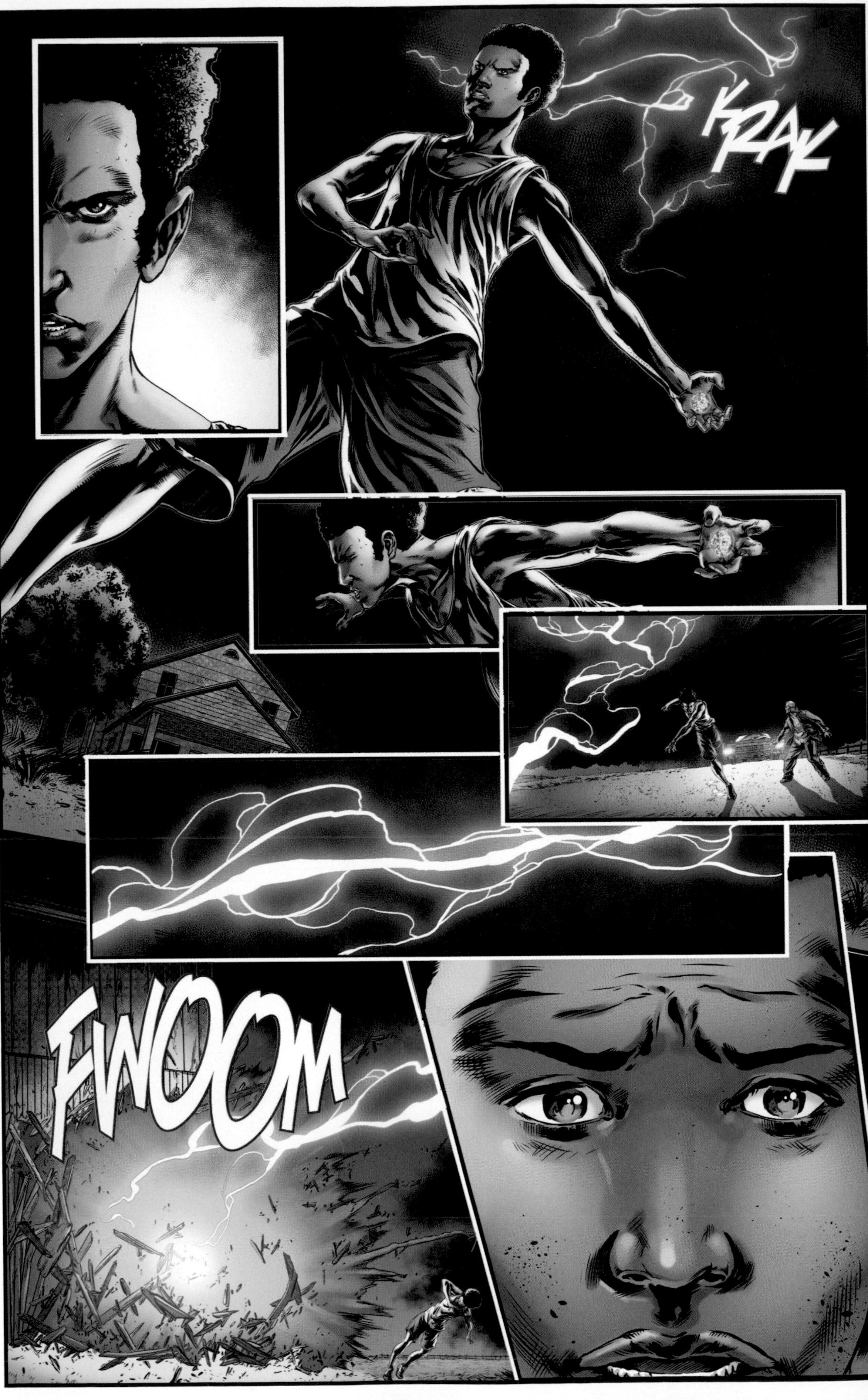
KRAK
FWOOM

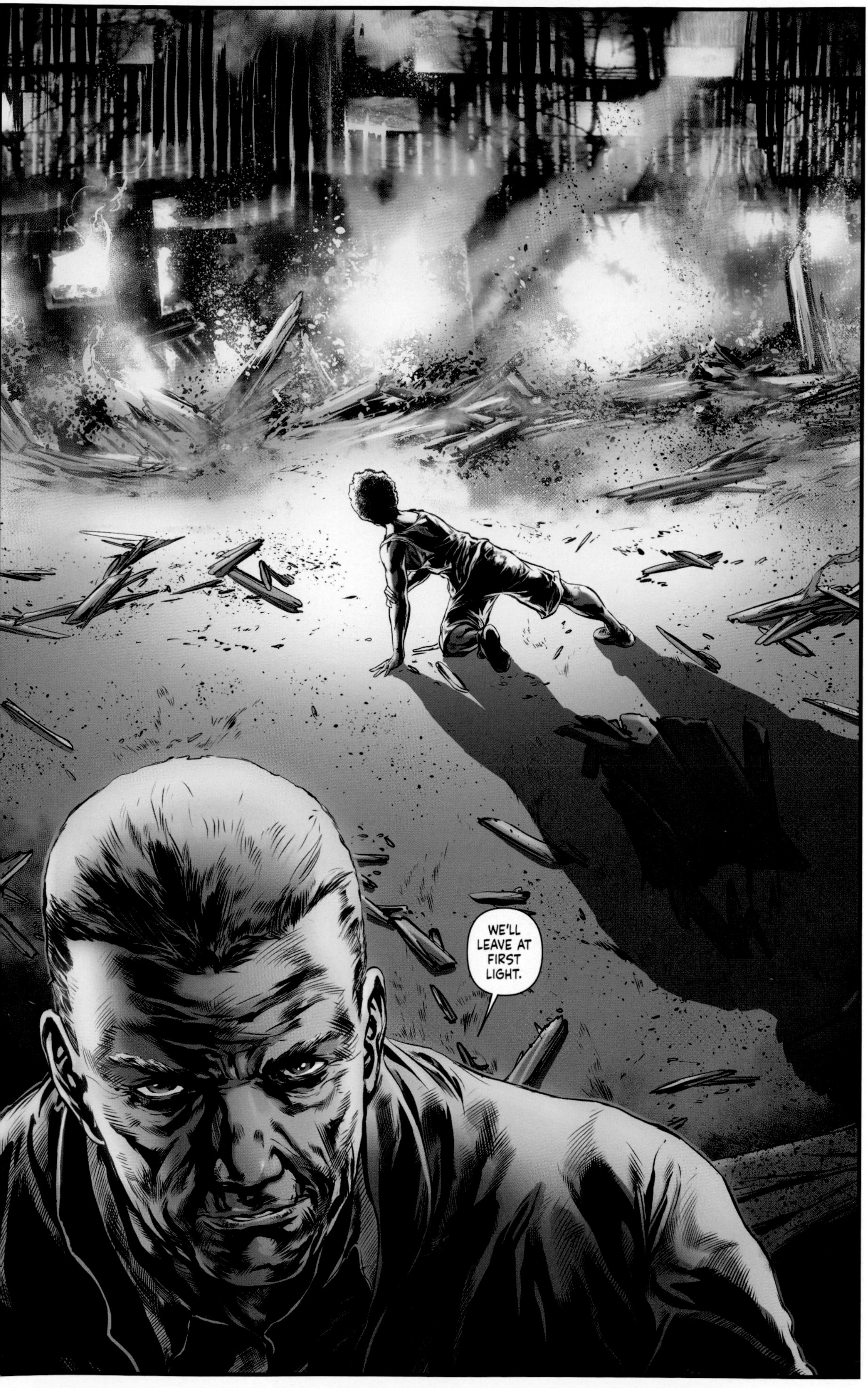
WE'LL LEAVE AT FIRST LIGHT.

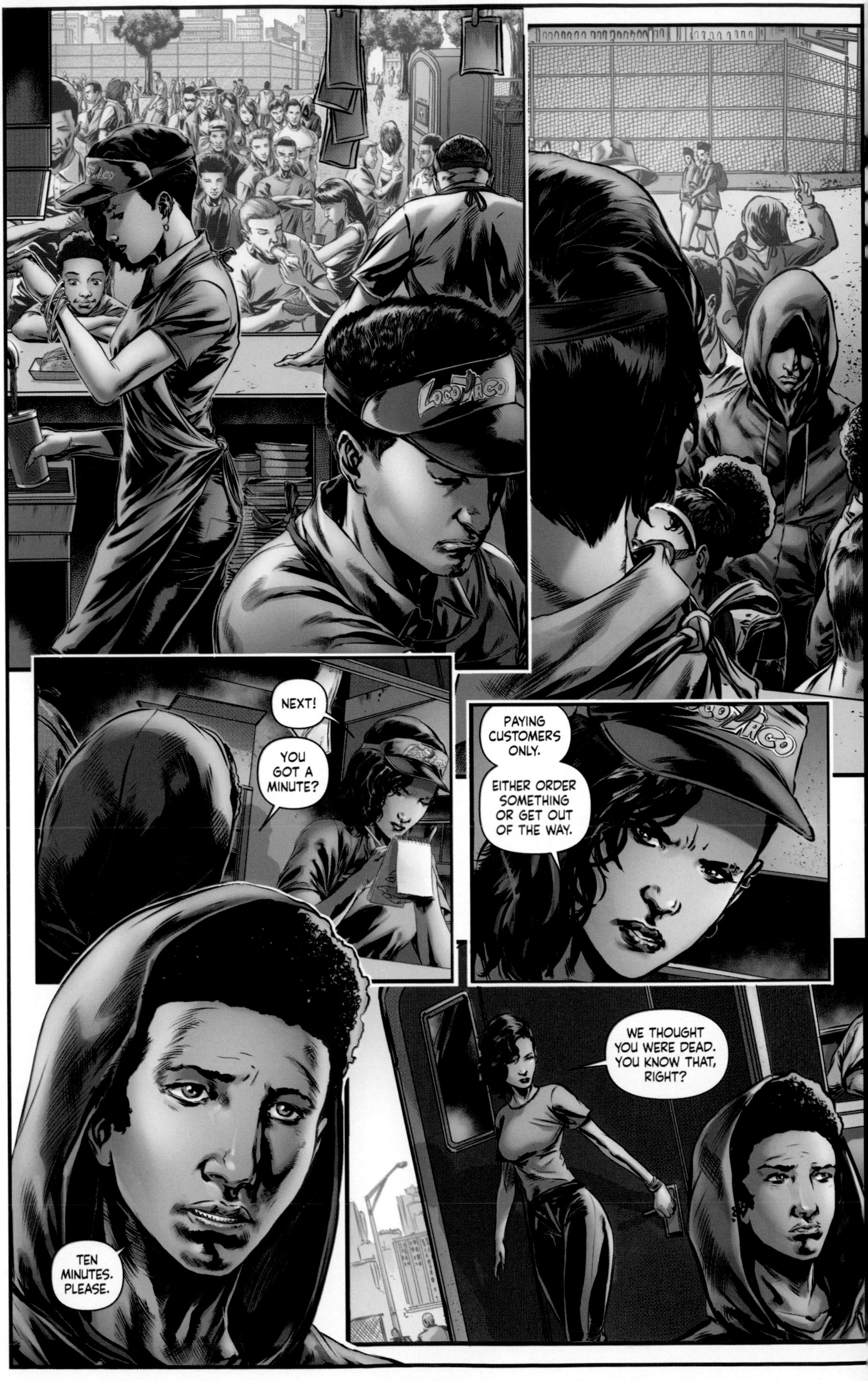
NEXT!
YOU GOT A MINUTE?
PAYING CUSTOMERS ONLY.
EITHER ORDER SOMETHING OR GET OUT OF THE WAY.
TEN MINUTES. PLEASE.
WE THOUGHT YOU WERE DEAD. YOU KNOW THAT, RIGHT?

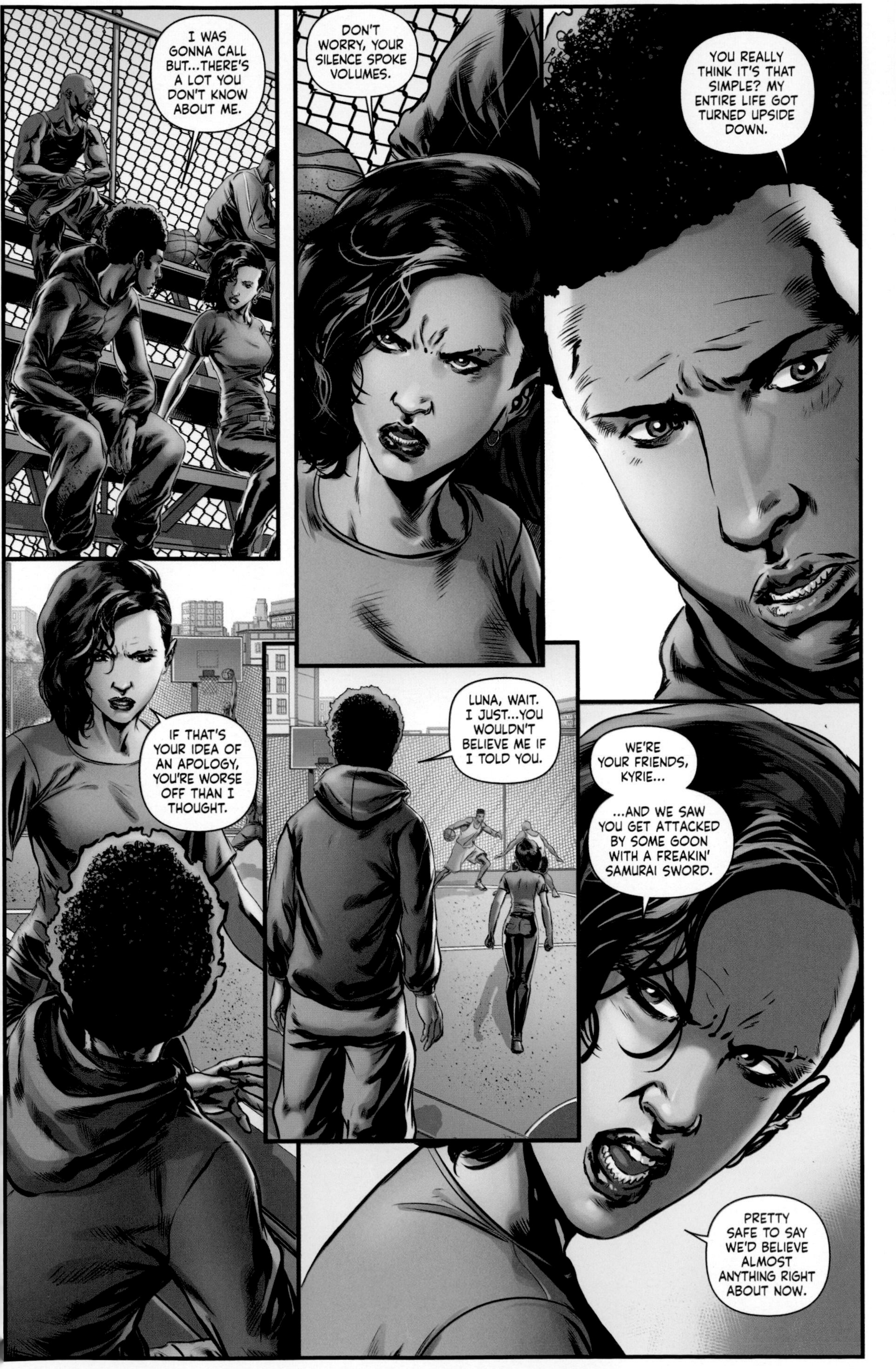
I WAS GONNA CALL BUT...THERE'S A LOT YOU DON'T KNOW ABOUT ME.
DON'T WORRY, YOUR SILENCE SPOKE VOLUMES.
YOU REALLY THINK IT'S THAT SIMPLE? MY ENTIRE LIFE GOT TURNED UPSIDE DOWN.
IF THAT'S YOUR IDEA OF AN APOLOGY, YOU'RE WORSE OFF THAN I THOUGHT.
LUNA, WAIT. I JUST...YOU WOULDN'T BELIEVE ME IF I TOLD YOU.
WE'RE YOUR FRIENDS, KYRIE...
...AND WE SAW YOU GET ATTACKED BY SOME GOON WITH A FREAKIN' SAMURAI SWORD.
PRETTY SAFE TO SAY WE'D BELIEVE ALMOST ANYTHING RIGHT ABOUT NOW.

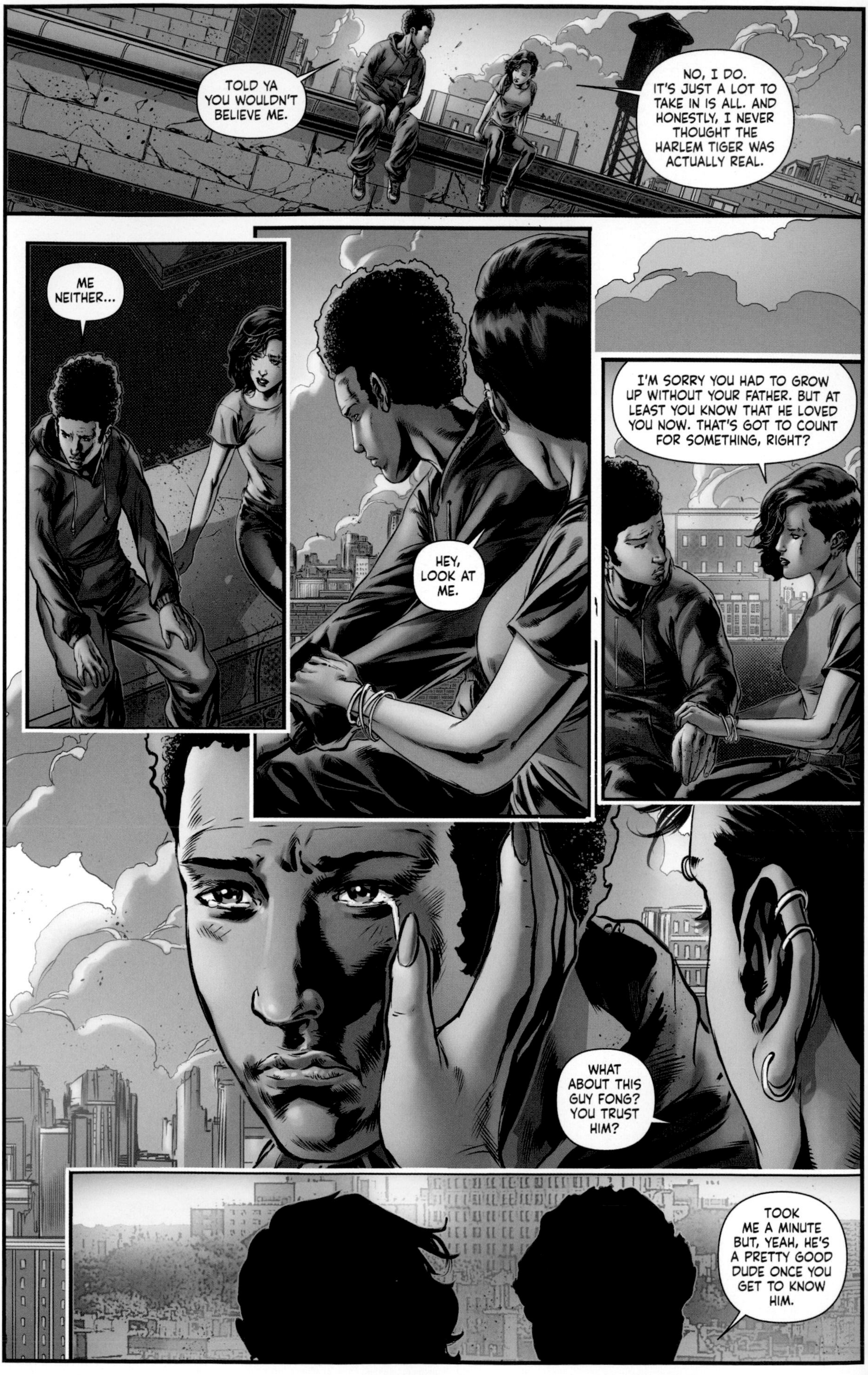
TOLD YA YOU WOULDN'T BELIEVE ME.
NO, I DO. IT'S JUST A LOT TO TAKE IN IS ALL. AND HONESTLY, I NEVER THOUGHT THE HARLEM TIGER WAS ACTUALLY REAL.
ME NEITHER...
HEY, LOOK AT ME.
I'M SORRY YOU HAD TO GROW UP WITHOUT YOUR FATHER. BUT AT LEAST YOU KNOW THAT HE LOVED YOU NOW. THAT'S GOT TO COUNT FOR SOMETHING, RIGHT?
WHAT ABOUT THIS GUY FONG? YOU TRUST HIM?
TOOK ME A MINUTE BUT, YEAH, HE'S A PRETTY GOOD DUDE ONCE YOU GET TO KNOW HIM.

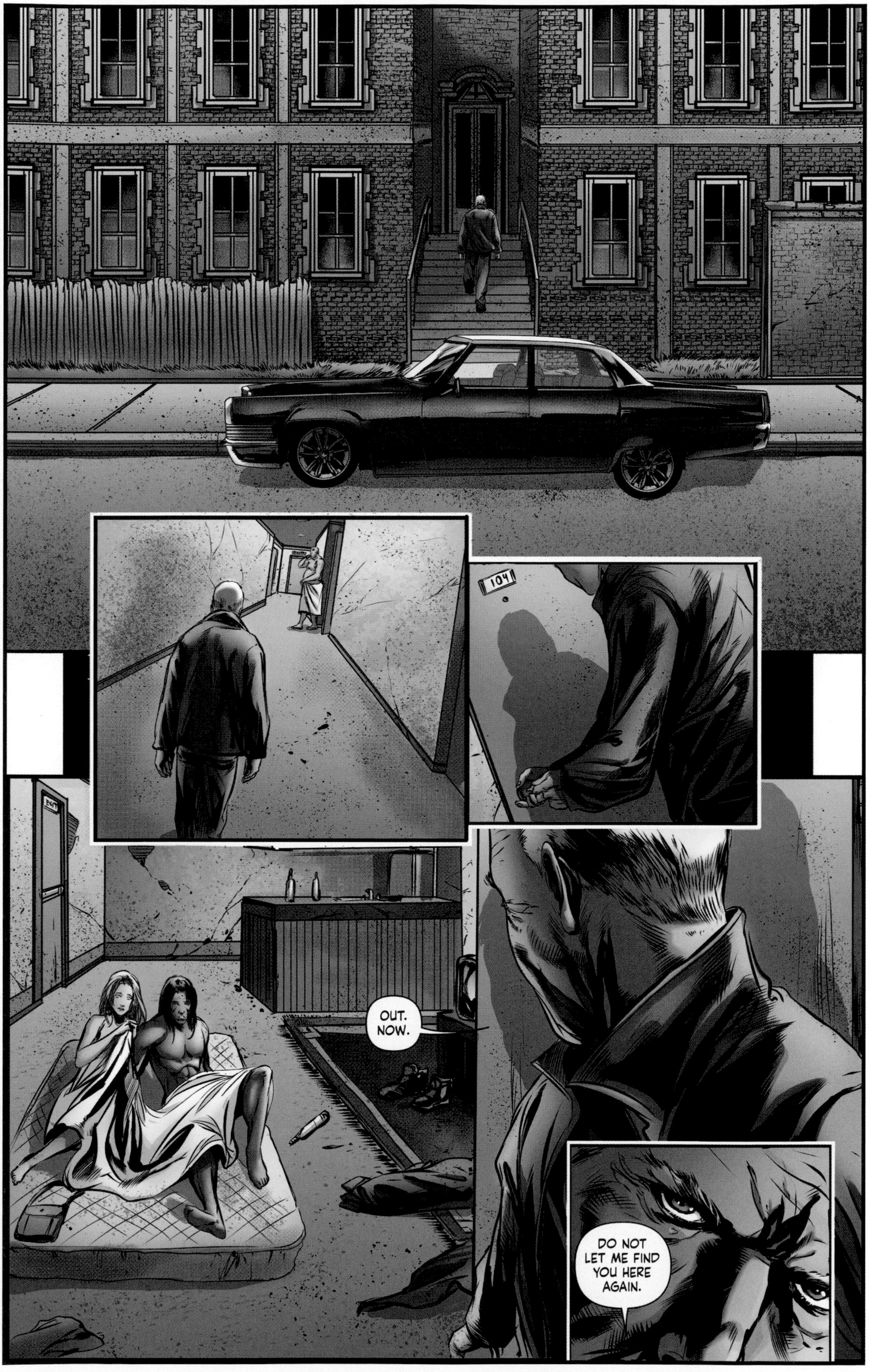
104
OUT. NOW.
DO NOT LET ME FIND YOU HERE AGAIN.

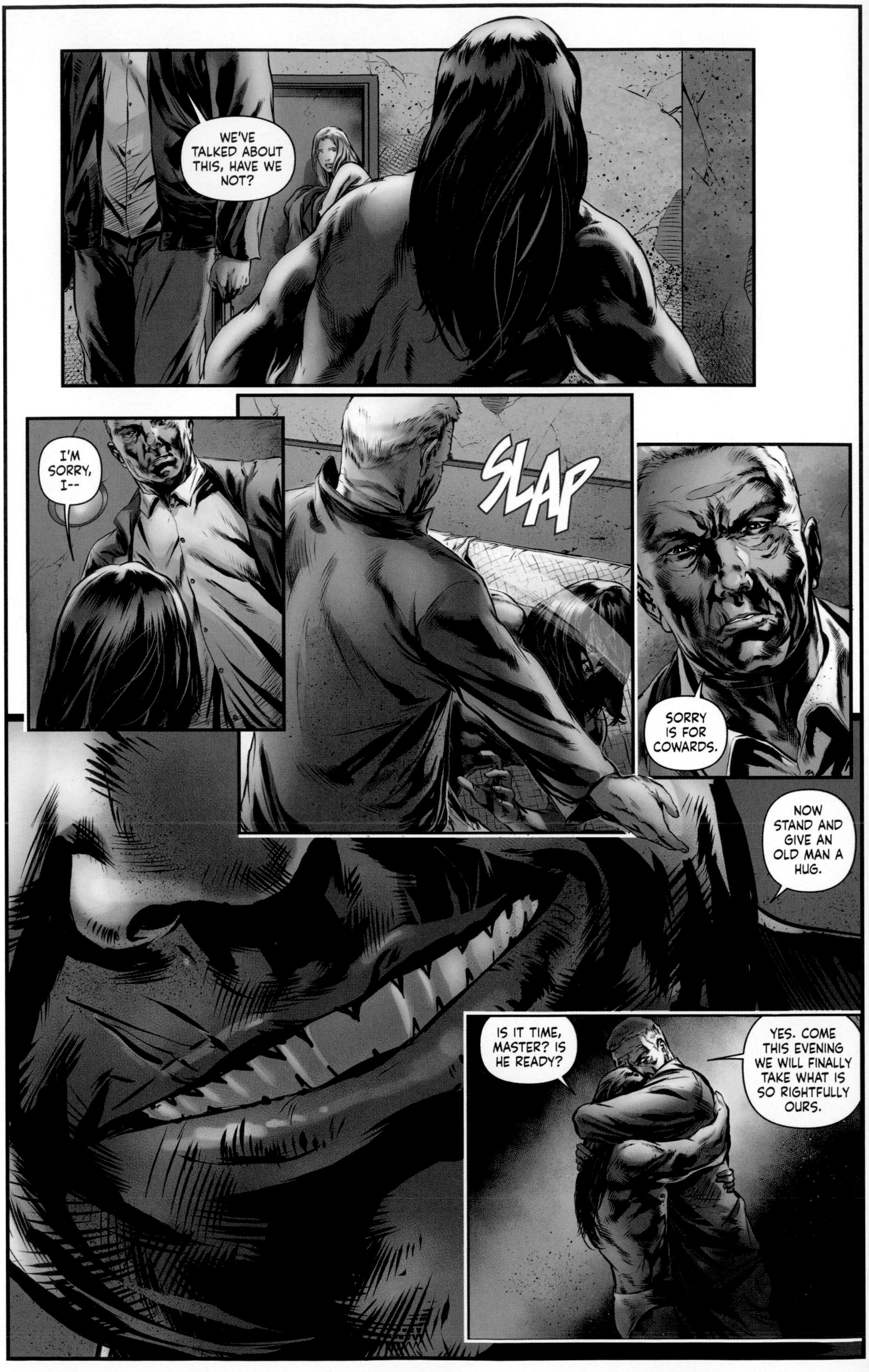
WE'VE TALKED ABOUT THIS, HAVE WE NOT?
I'M SORRY, I--
SLAP
SORRY IS FOR COWARDS.
NOW STAND AND GIVE AN OLD MAN A HUG.
IS IT TIME, MASTER? IS HE READY?
YES. COME THIS EVENING WE WILL FINALLY TAKE WHAT IS SO RIGHTFULLY OURS.

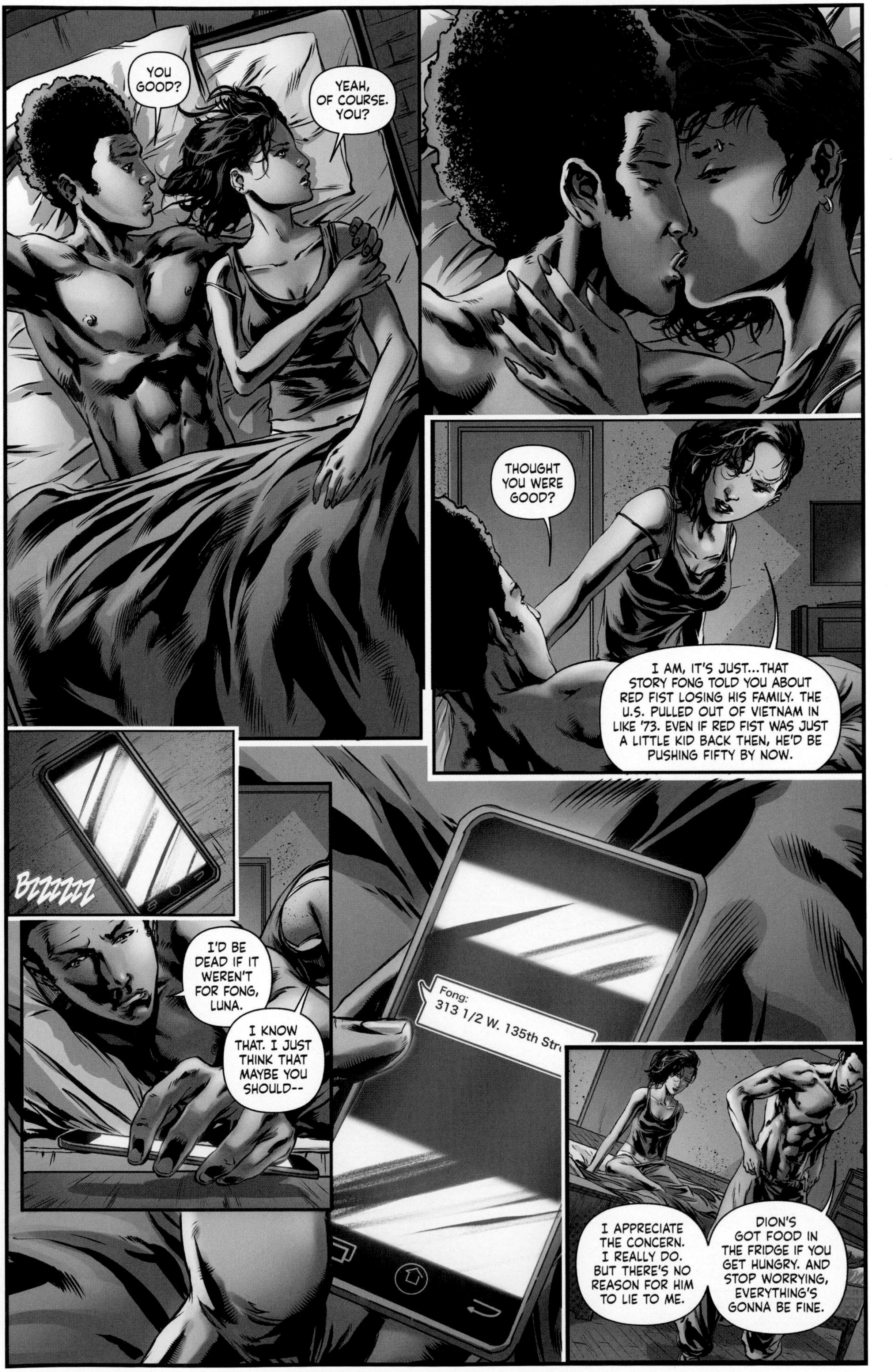
YOU GOOD?
YEAH, OF COURSE. YOU?
THOUGHT YOU WERE GOOD?
I AM, IT'S JUST...THAT STORY FONG TOLD YOU ABOUT RED FIST LOSING HIS FAMILY. THE U.S. PULLED OUT OF VIETNAM IN LIKE '73. EVEN IF RED FIST WAS JUST A LITTLE KID BACK THEN, HE'D BE PUSHING FIFTY BY NOW.
Bzzzzzz
I'D BE DEAD IF IT WEREN'T FOR FONG, LUNA.
I KNOW THAT. I JUST THINK THAT MAYBE YOU SHOULD--
Fong:
313 1/2 W. 135th Stre
I APPRECIATE THE CONCERN. I REALLY DO. BUT THERE'S NO REASON FOR HIM TO LIE TO ME.
DION'S GOT FOOD IN THE FRIDGE IF YOU GET HUNGRY. AND STOP WORRYING, EVERYTHING'S GONNA BE FINE.

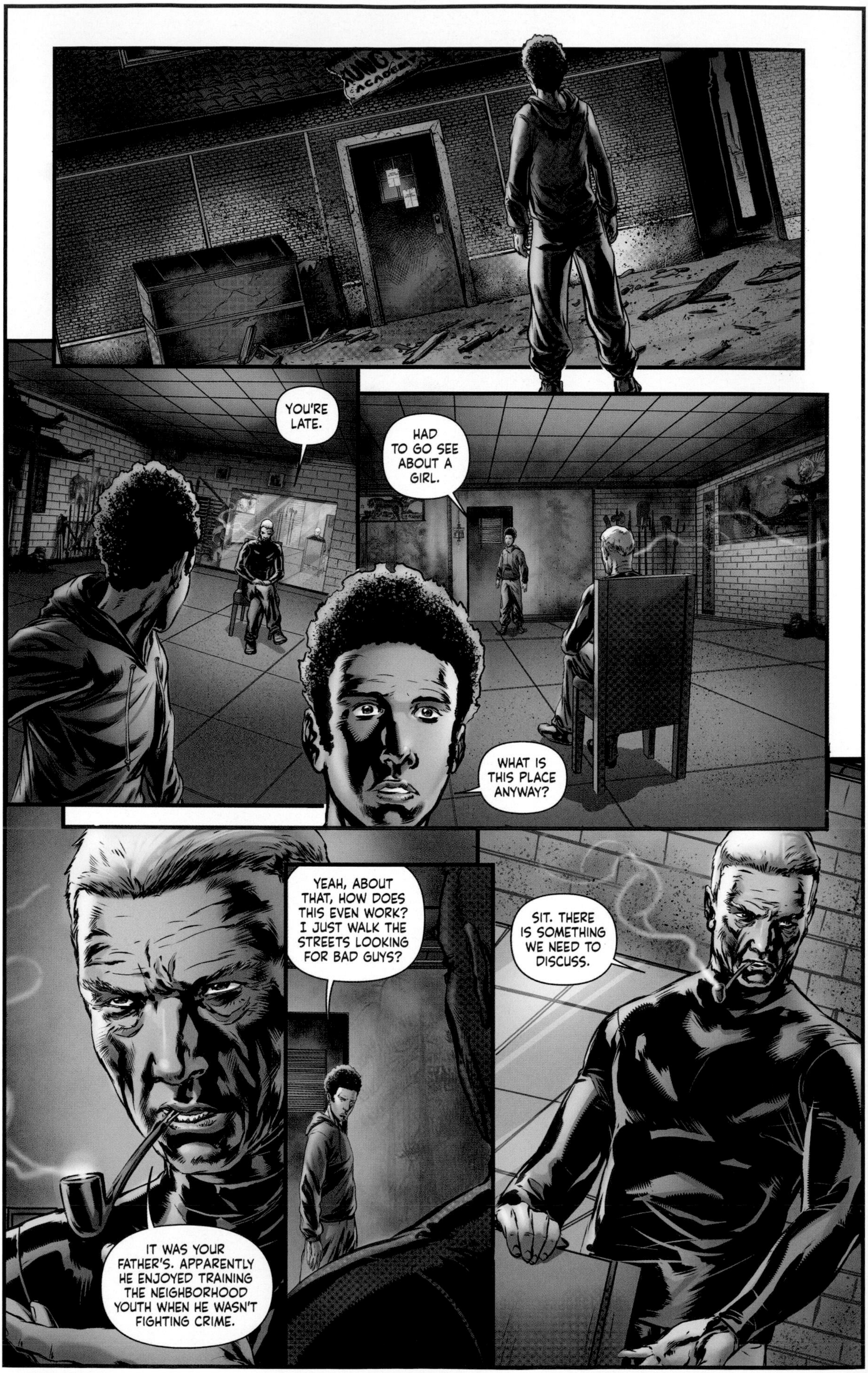
YOU'RE LATE.
HAD TO GO SEE ABOUT A GIRL.
WHAT IS THIS PLACE ANYWAY?
IT WAS YOUR FATHER'S. APPARENTLY HE ENJOYED TRAINING THE NEIGHBORHOOD YOUTH WHEN HE WASN'T FIGHTING CRIME.
YEAH, ABOUT THAT, HOW DOES THIS EVEN WORK? I JUST WALK THE STREETS LOOKING FOR BAD GUYS?
SIT. THERE IS SOMETHING WE NEED TO DISCUSS.

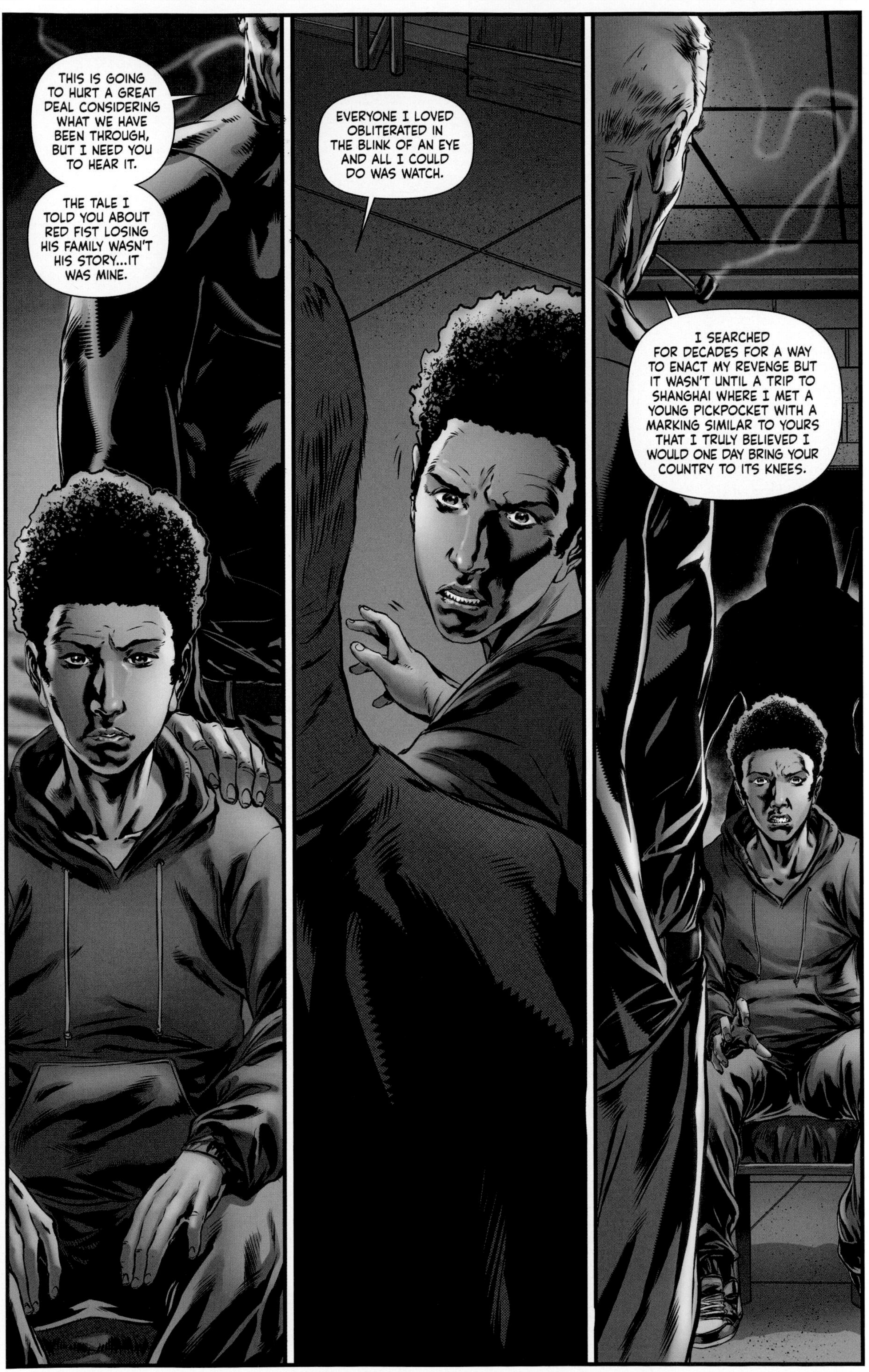
THIS IS GOING TO HURT A GREAT DEAL CONSIDERING WHAT WE HAVE BEEN THROUGH, BUT I NEED YOU TO HEAR IT.
THE TALE I TOLD YOU ABOUT RED FIST LOSING HIS FAMILY WASN'T HIS STORY...IT WAS MINE.
EVERYONE I LOVED OBLITERATED IN THE BLINK OF AN EYE AND ALL I COULD DO WAS WATCH.
I SEARCHED FOR DECADES FOR A WAY TO ENACT MY REVENGE BUT IT WASN'T UNTIL A TRIP TO SHANGHAI WHERE I MET A YOUNG PICKPOCKET WITH A MARKING SIMILAR TO YOURS THAT I TRULY BELIEVED I WOULD ONE DAY BRING YOUR COUNTRY TO ITS KNEES.

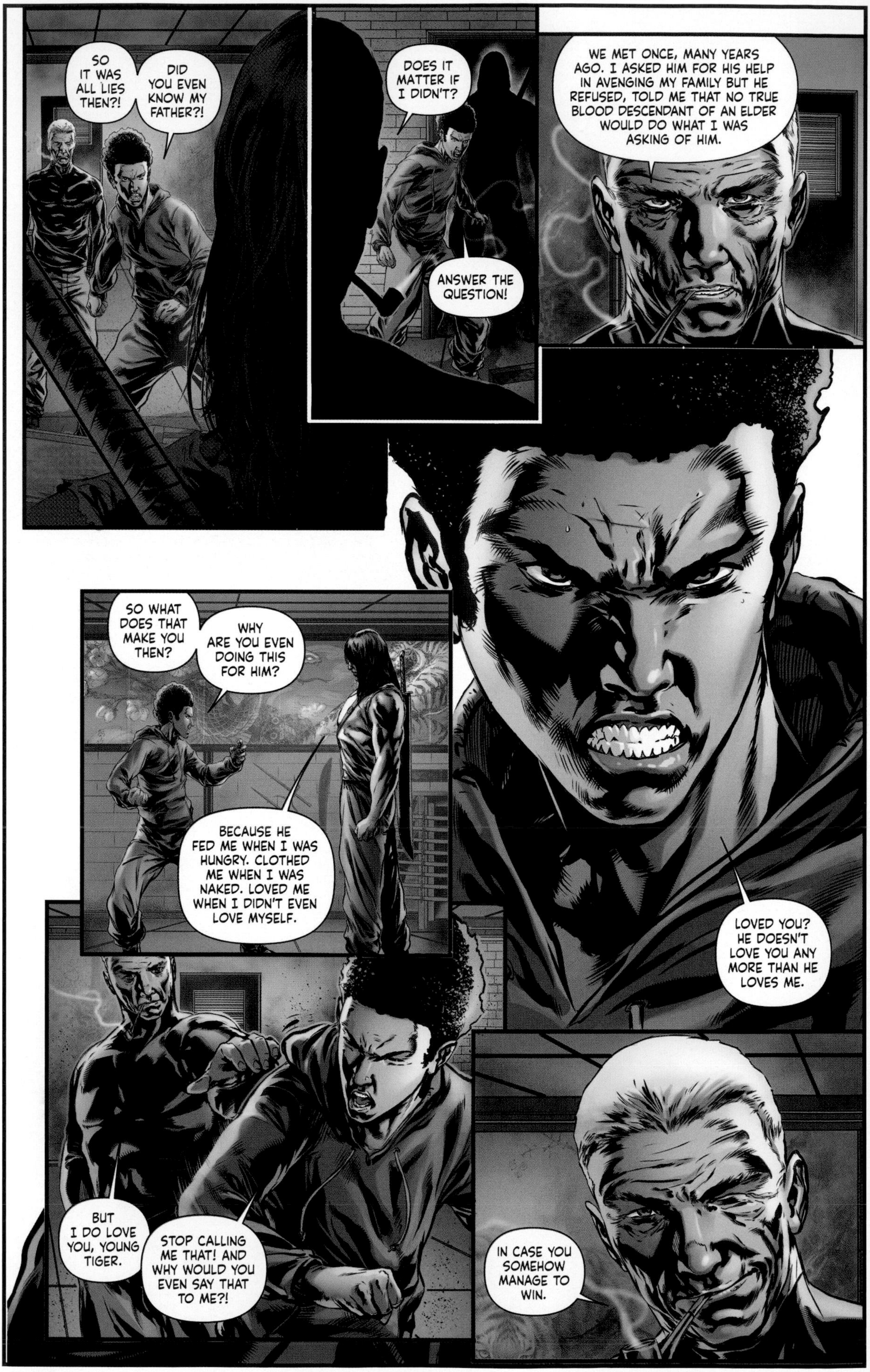
SO IT WAS ALL LIES THEN?!
DID YOU EVEN KNOW MY FATHER?!
DOES IT MATTER IF I DIDN'T?
ANSWER THE QUESTION!
WE MET ONCE, MANY YEARS AGO. I ASKED HIM FOR HIS HELP IN AVENGING MY FAMILY BUT HE REFUSED, TOLD ME THAT NO TRUE BLOOD DESCENDANT OF AN ELDER WOULD DO WHAT I WAS ASKING OF HIM.
SO WHAT DOES THAT MAKE YOU THEN?
WHY ARE YOU EVEN DOING THIS FOR HIM?
BECAUSE HE FED ME WHEN I WAS HUNGRY. CLOTHED ME WHEN I WAS NAKED. LOVED ME WHEN I DIDN'T EVEN LOVE MYSELF.
LOVED YOU? HE DOESN'T LOVE YOU ANY MORE THAN HE LOVES ME.
BUT I DO LOVE YOU, YOUNG TIGER.
STOP CALLING ME THAT! AND WHY WOULD YOU EVEN SAY THAT TO ME?!
IN CASE YOU SOMEHOW MANAGE TO WIN.

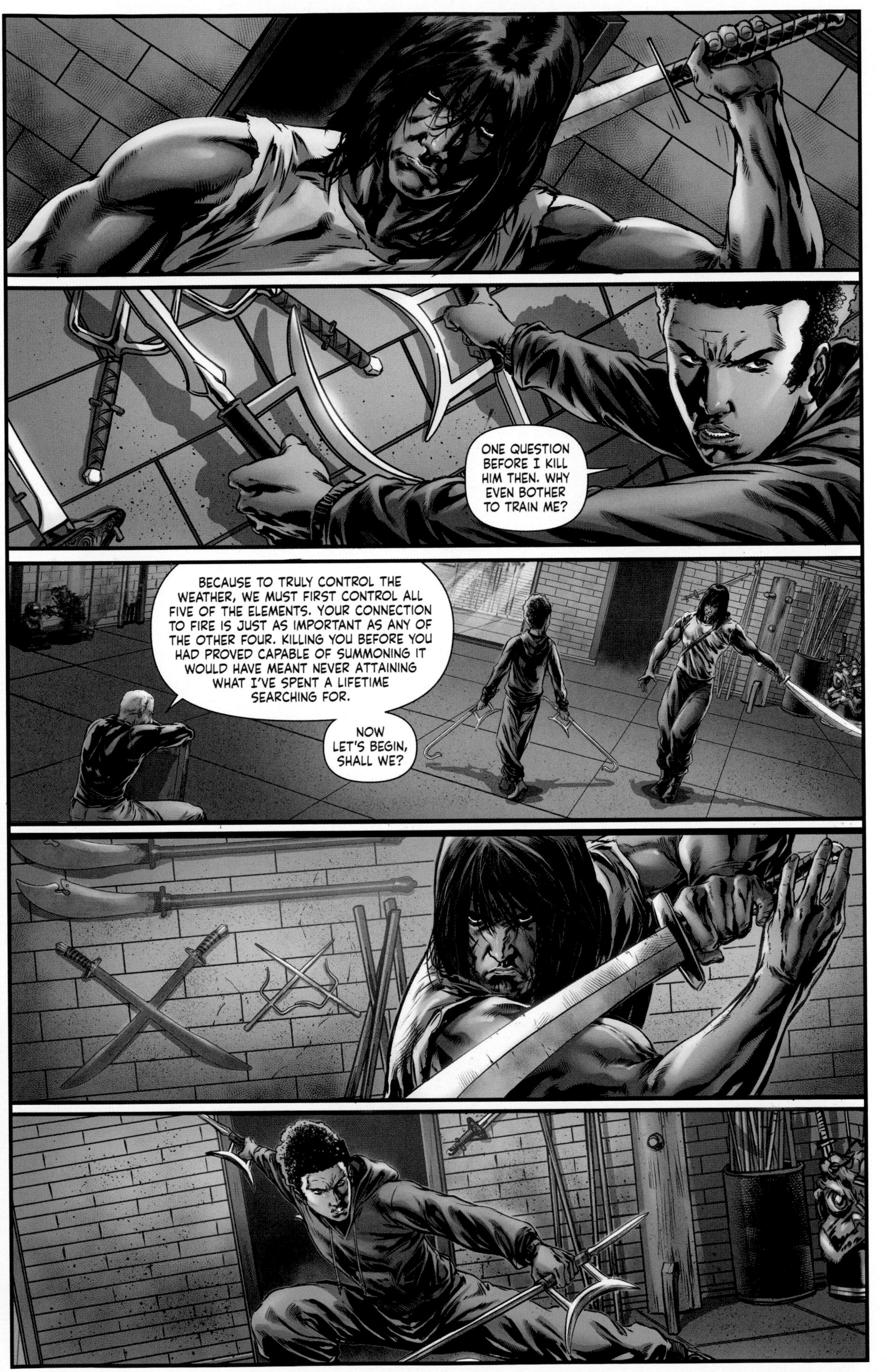
ONE QUESTION BEFORE I KILL HIM THEN. WHY EVEN BOTHER TO TRAIN ME?
BECAUSE TO TRULY CONTROL THE WEATHER, WE MUST FIRST CONTROL ALL FIVE OF THE ELEMENTS. YOUR CONNECTION TO FIRE IS JUST AS IMPORTANT AS ANY OF THE OTHER FOUR. KILLING YOU BEFORE YOU HAD PROVED CAPABLE OF SUMMONING IT WOULD HAVE MEANT NEVER ATTAINING WHAT I'VE SPENT A LIFETIME SEARCHING FOR.
NOW LET'S BEGIN, SHALL WE?

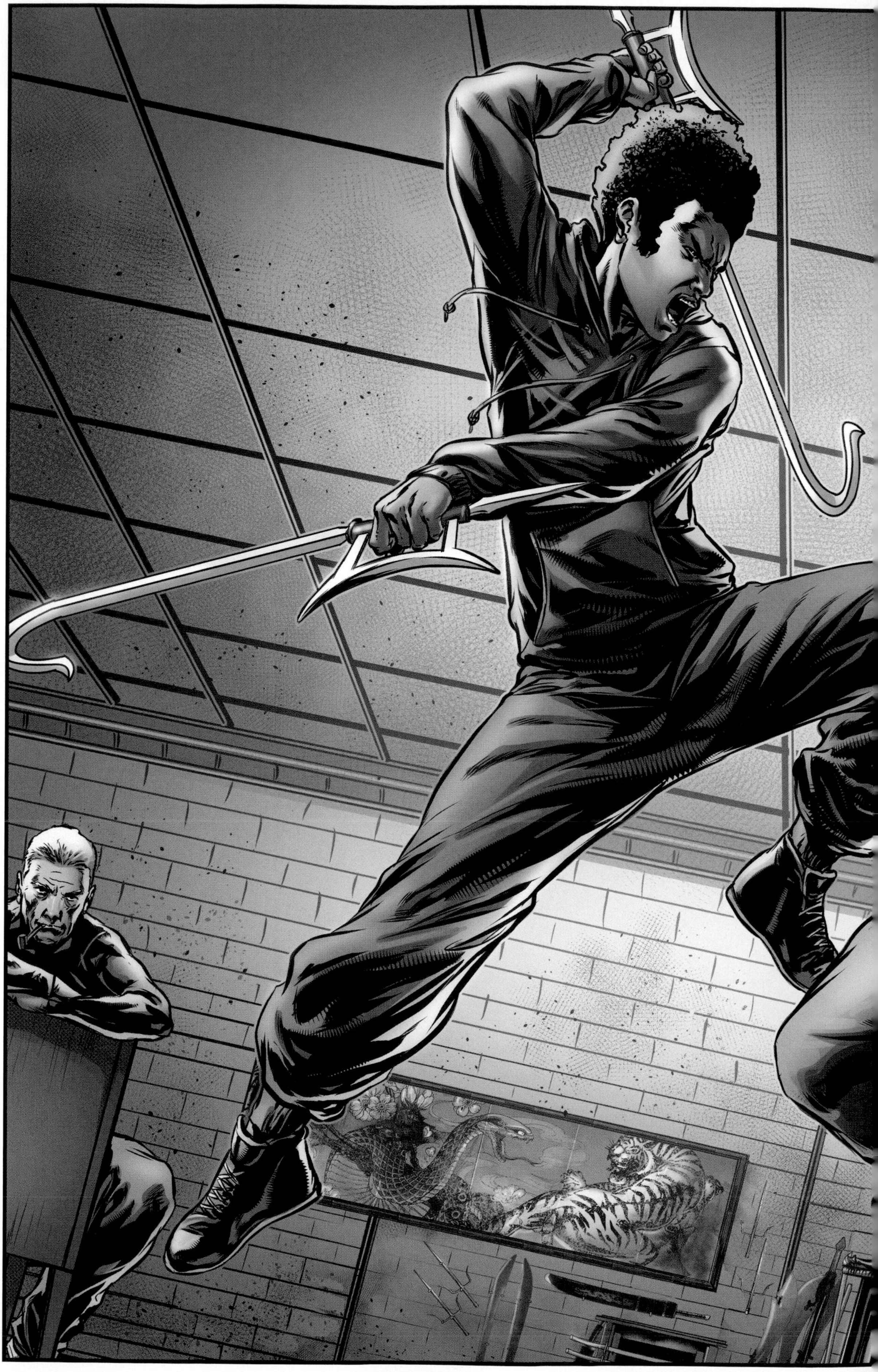

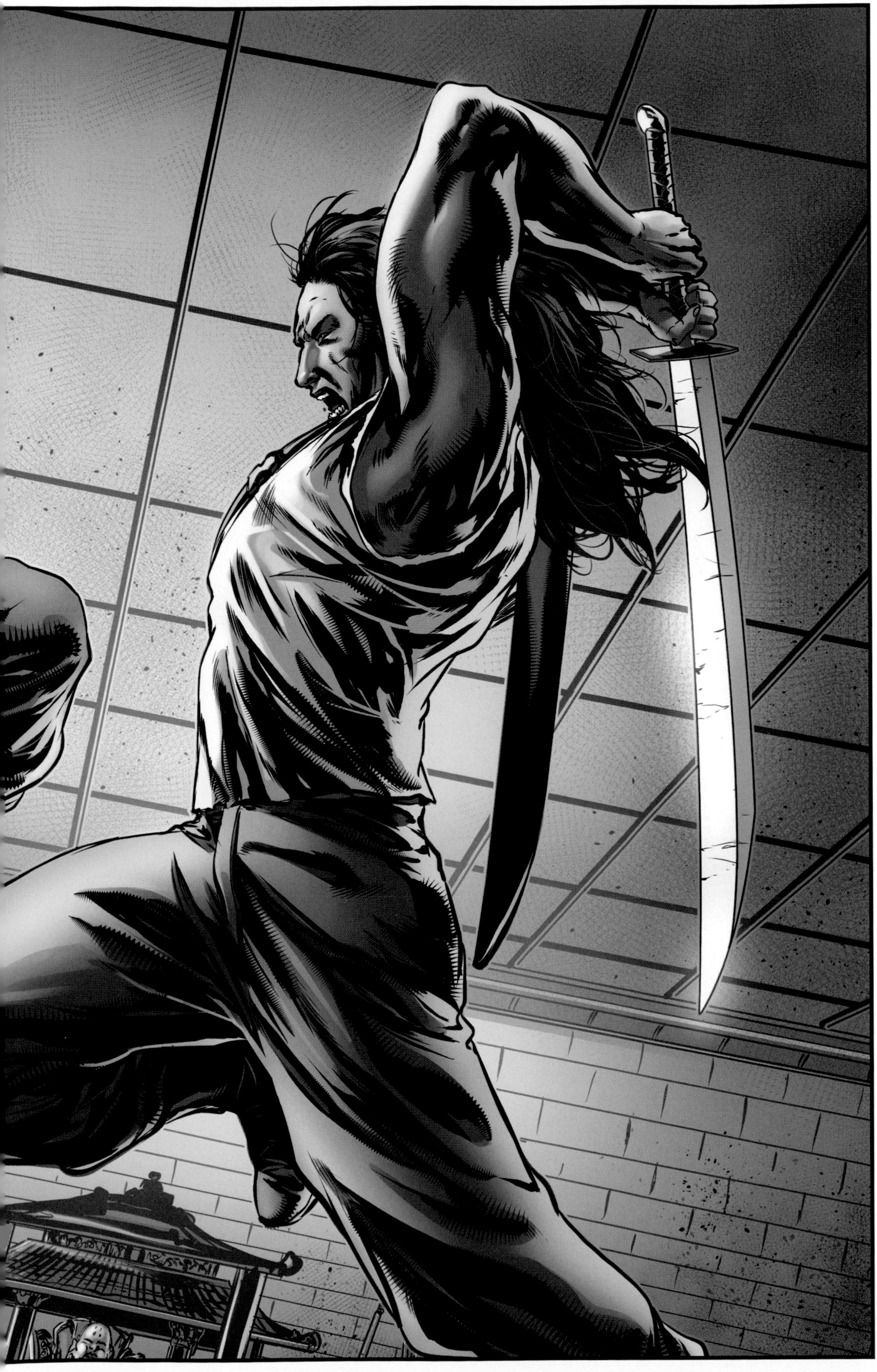

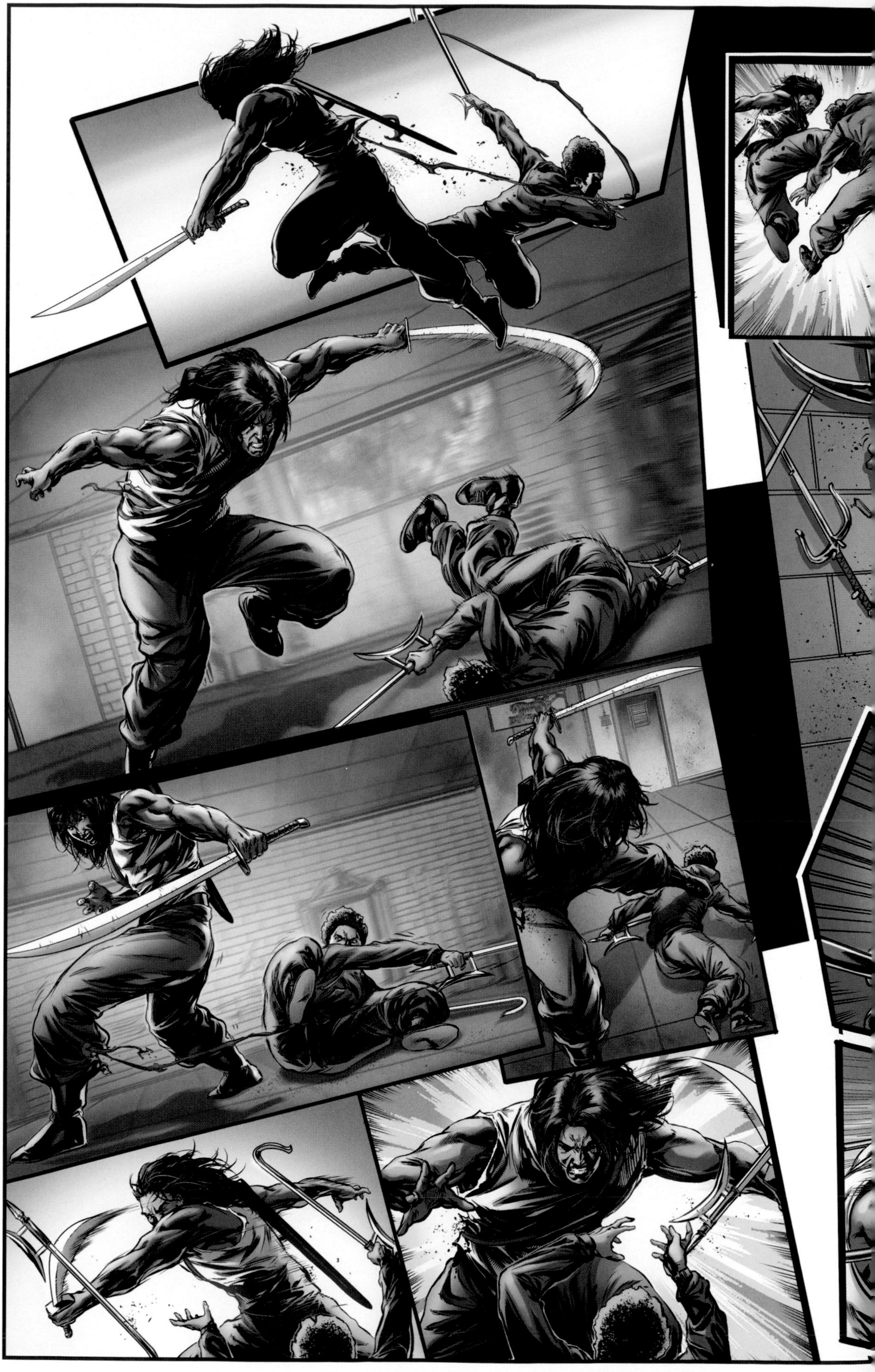

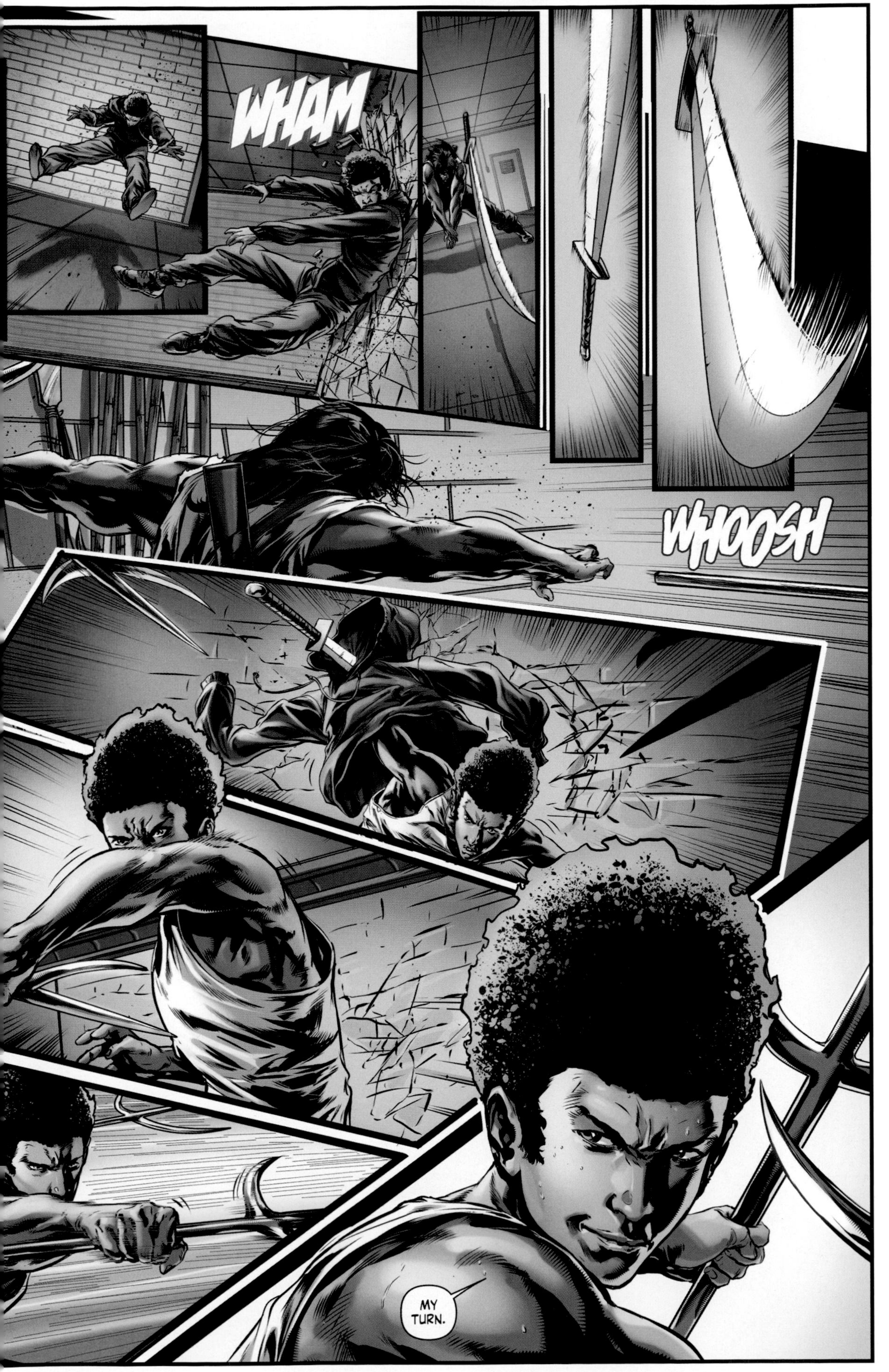
WHAM
WHOOSH
MY TURN.

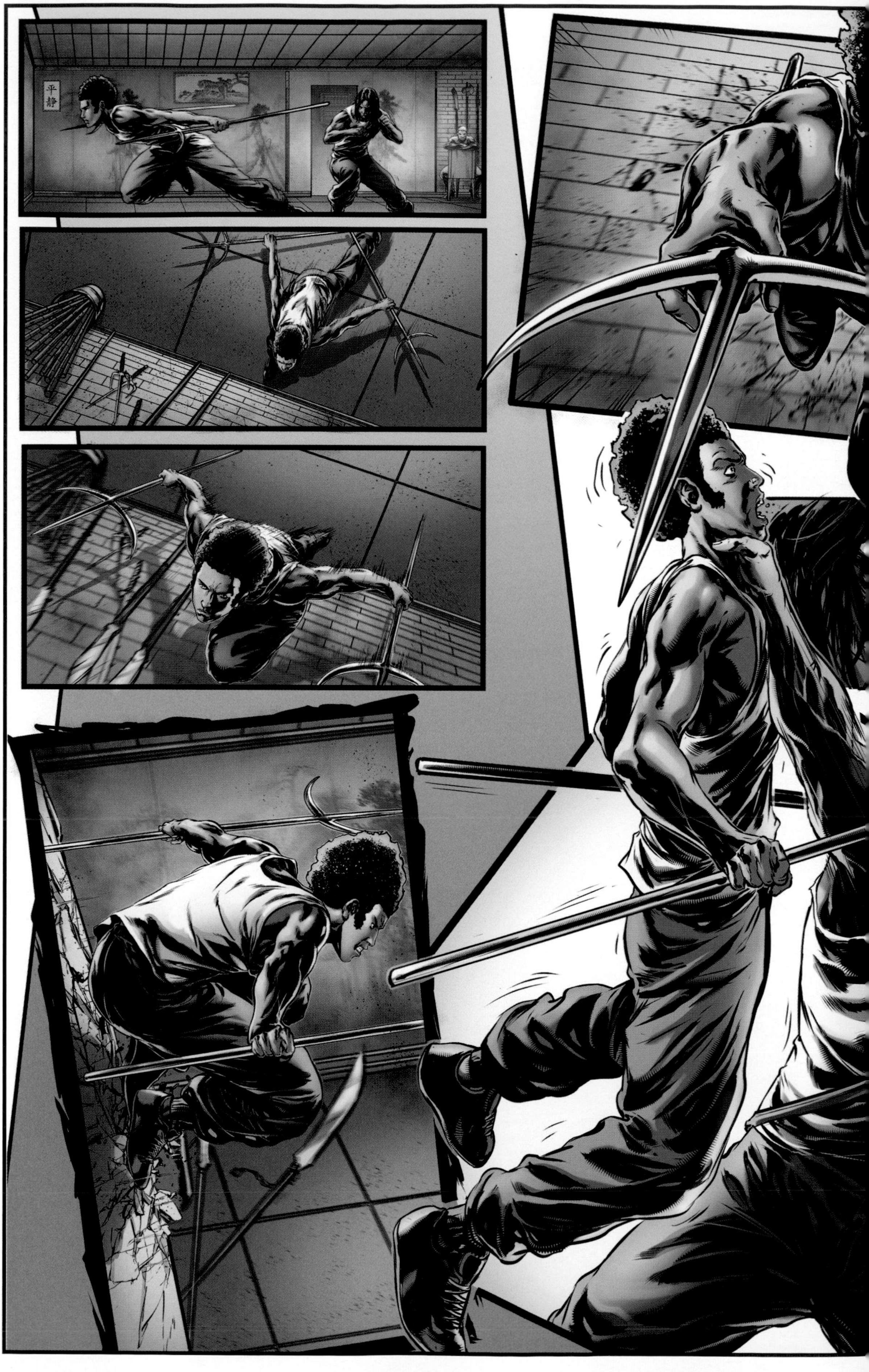
平静

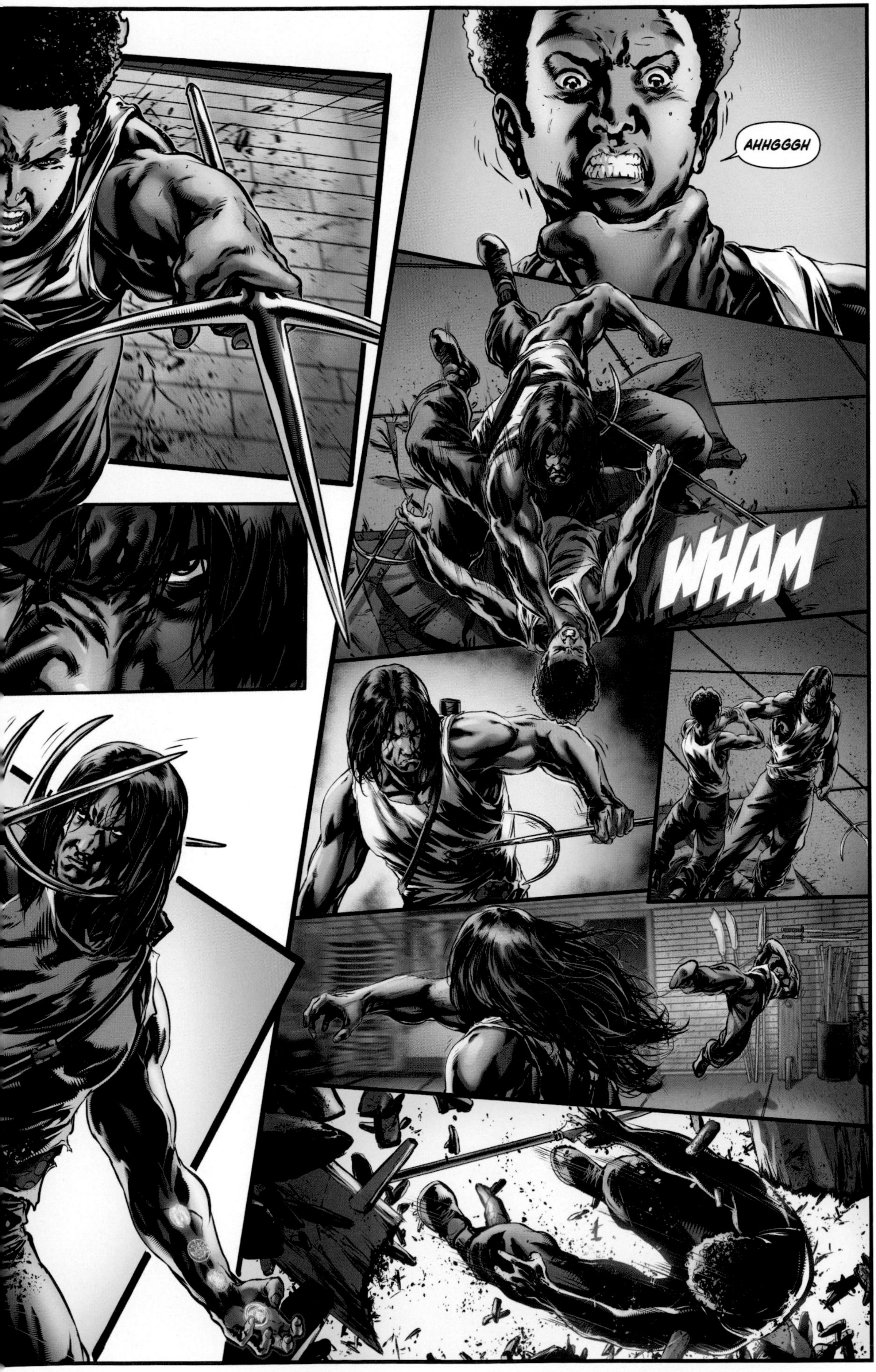
AHHGGGH
WHAM

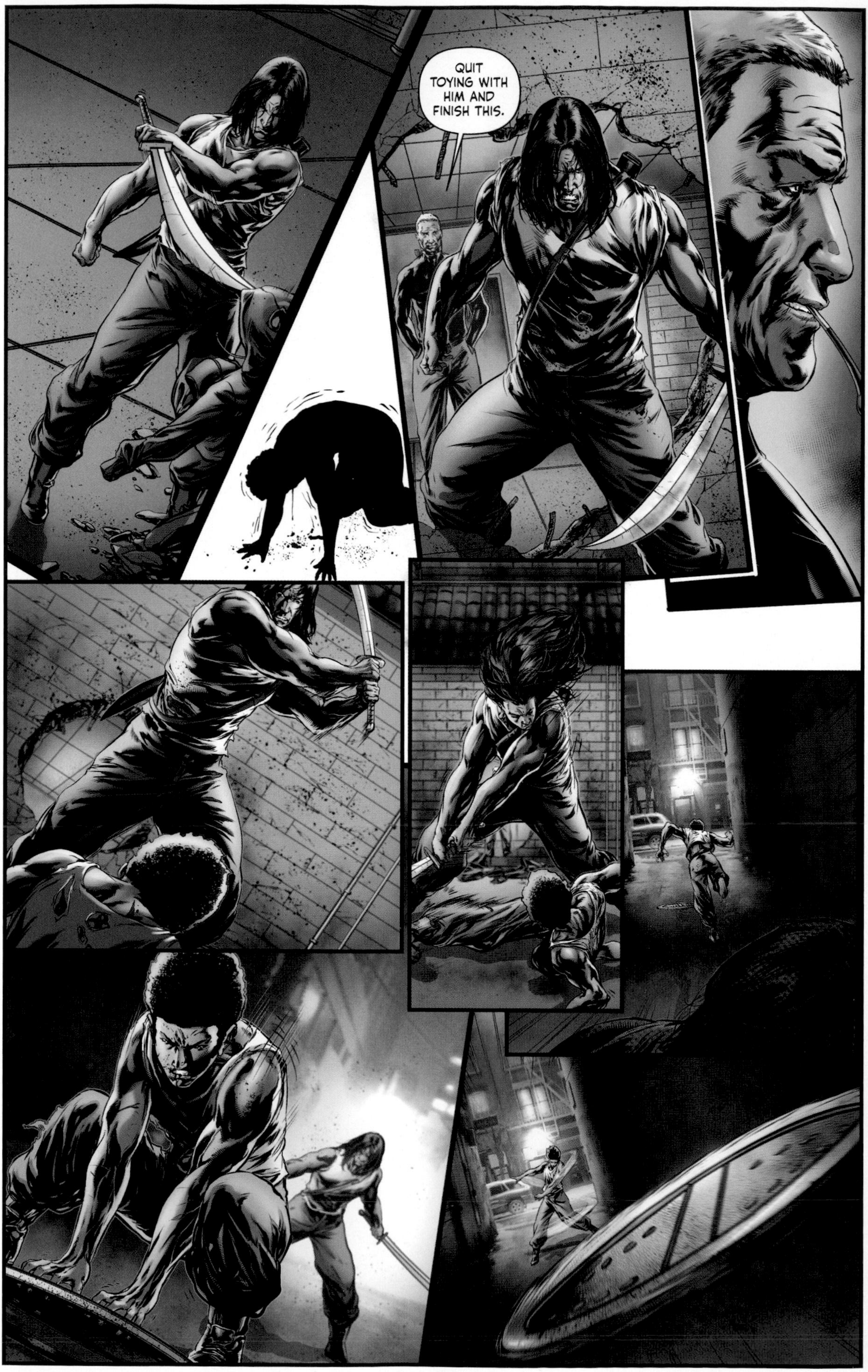
QUIT TOYING WITH HIM AND FINISH THIS.

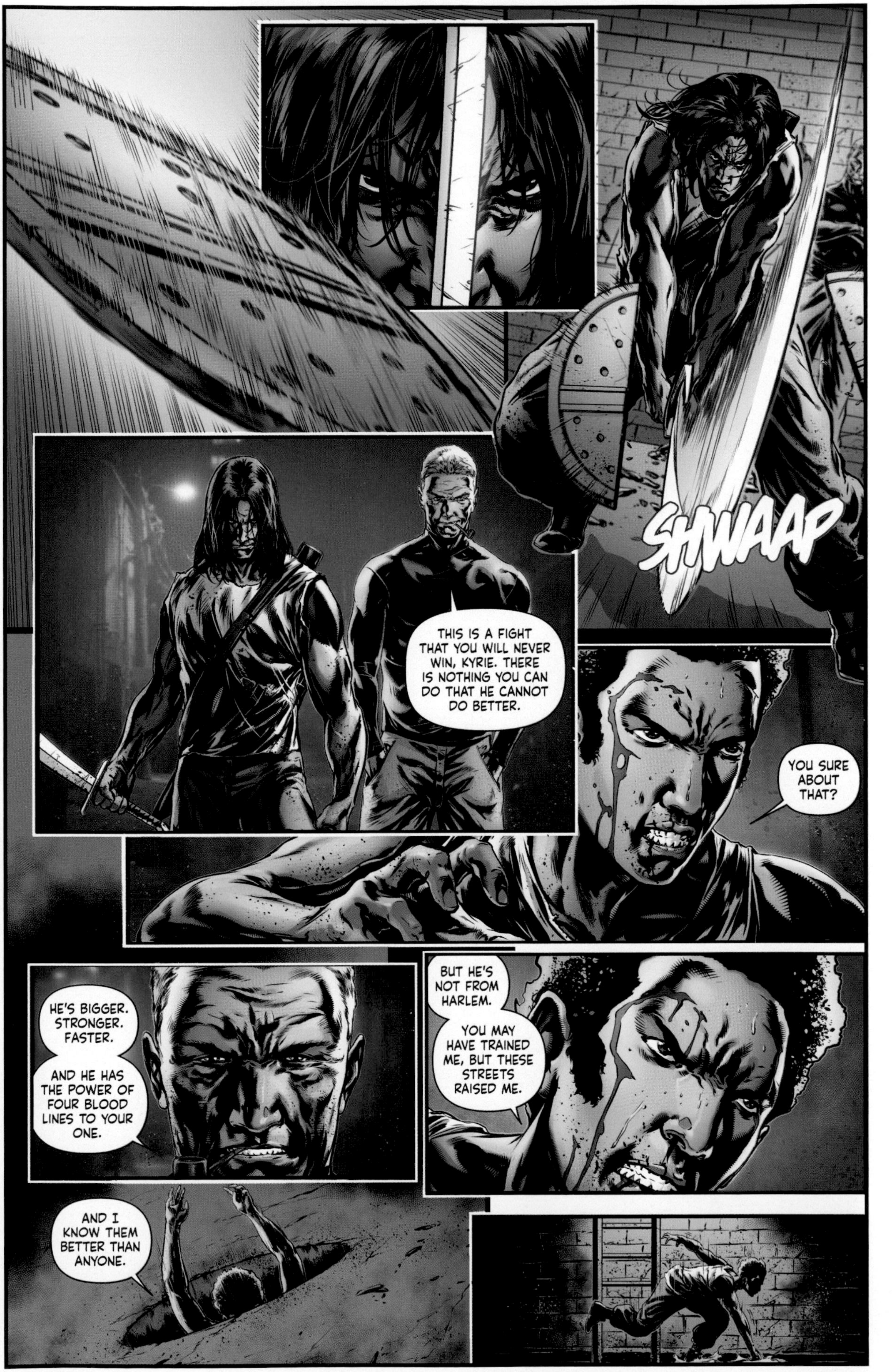
SHWAAP
THIS IS A FIGHT THAT YOU WILL NEVER WIN, KYRIE. THERE IS NOTHING YOU CAN DO THAT HE CANNOT DO BETTER.
YOU SURE ABOUT THAT?
HE'S BIGGER. STRONGER. FASTER.
AND HE HAS THE POWER OF FOUR BLOOD LINES TO YOUR ONE.
BUT HE'S NOT FROM HARLEM.
YOU MAY HAVE TRAINED ME, BUT THESE STREETS RAISED ME.
AND I KNOW THEM BETTER THAN ANYONE.

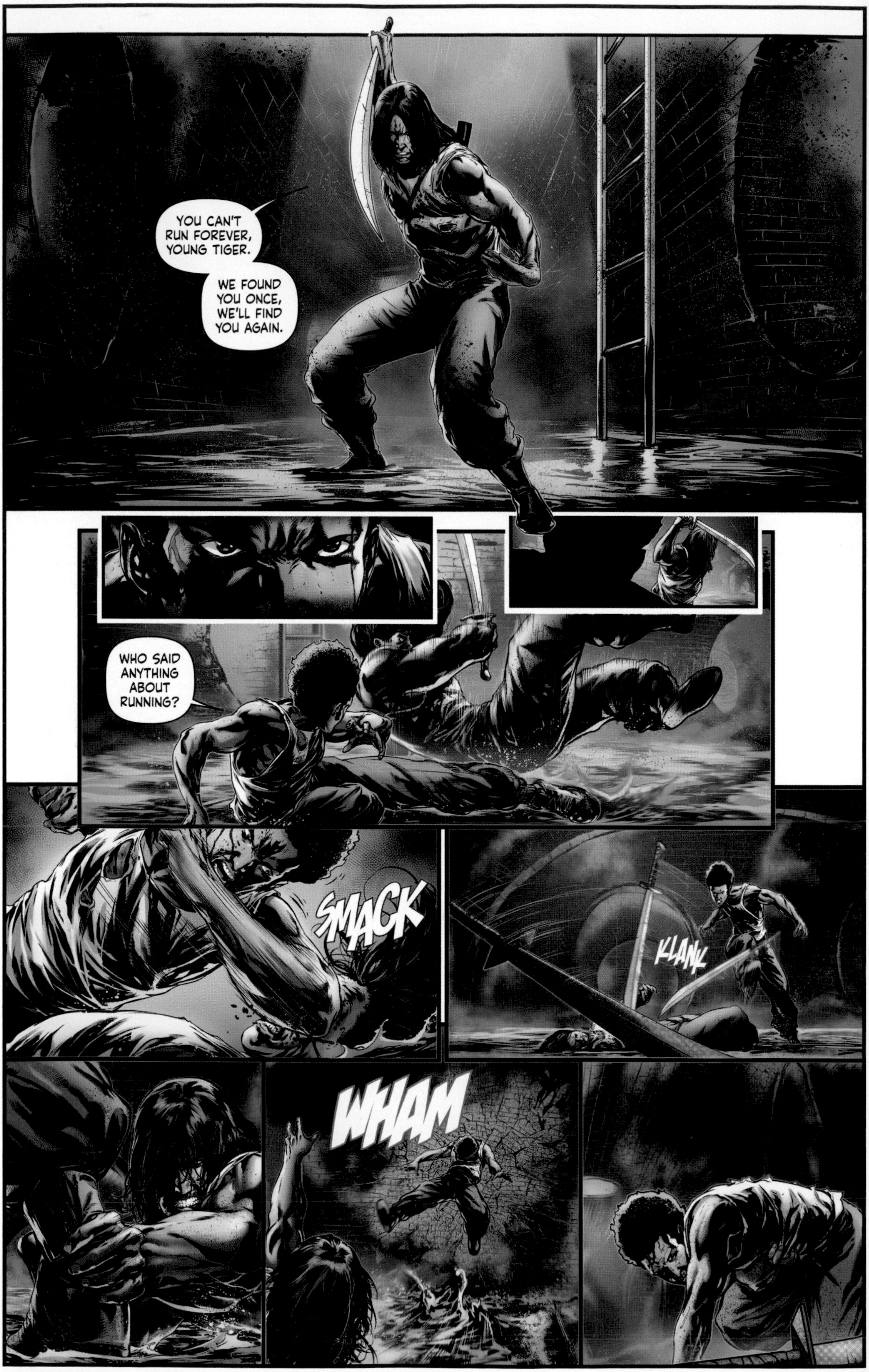
YOU CAN'T RUN FOREVER, YOUNG TIGER.
WE FOUND YOU ONCE, WE'LL FIND YOU AGAIN.
WHO SAID ANYTHING ABOUT RUNNING?
SMACK
KLANK
WHAM

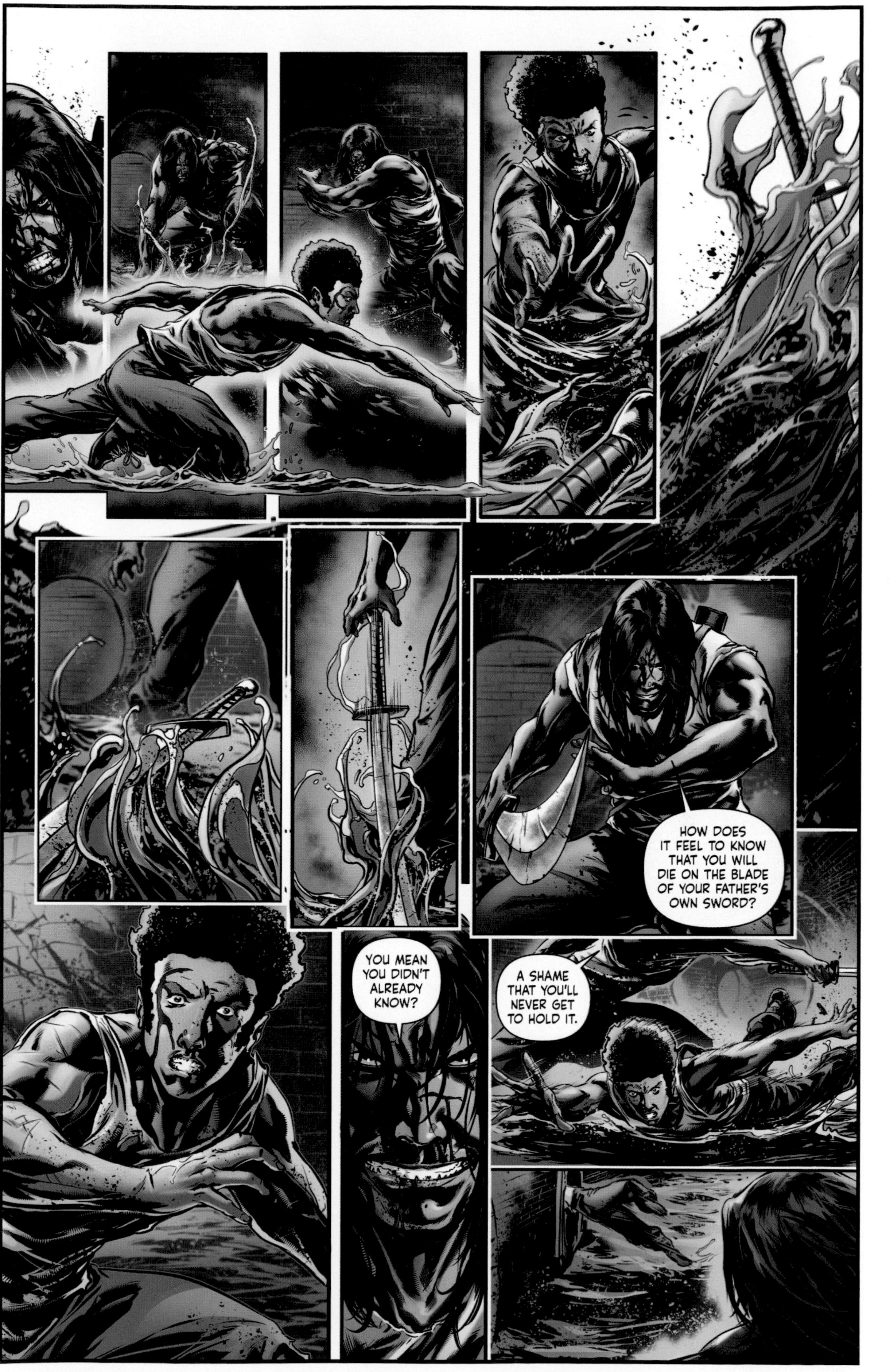
HOW DOES IT FEEL TO KNOW THAT YOU WILL DIE ON THE BLADE OF YOUR FATHER'S OWN SWORD?
YOU MEAN YOU DIDN'T ALREADY KNOW?
A SHAME THAT YOU'LL NEVER GET TO HOLD IT.

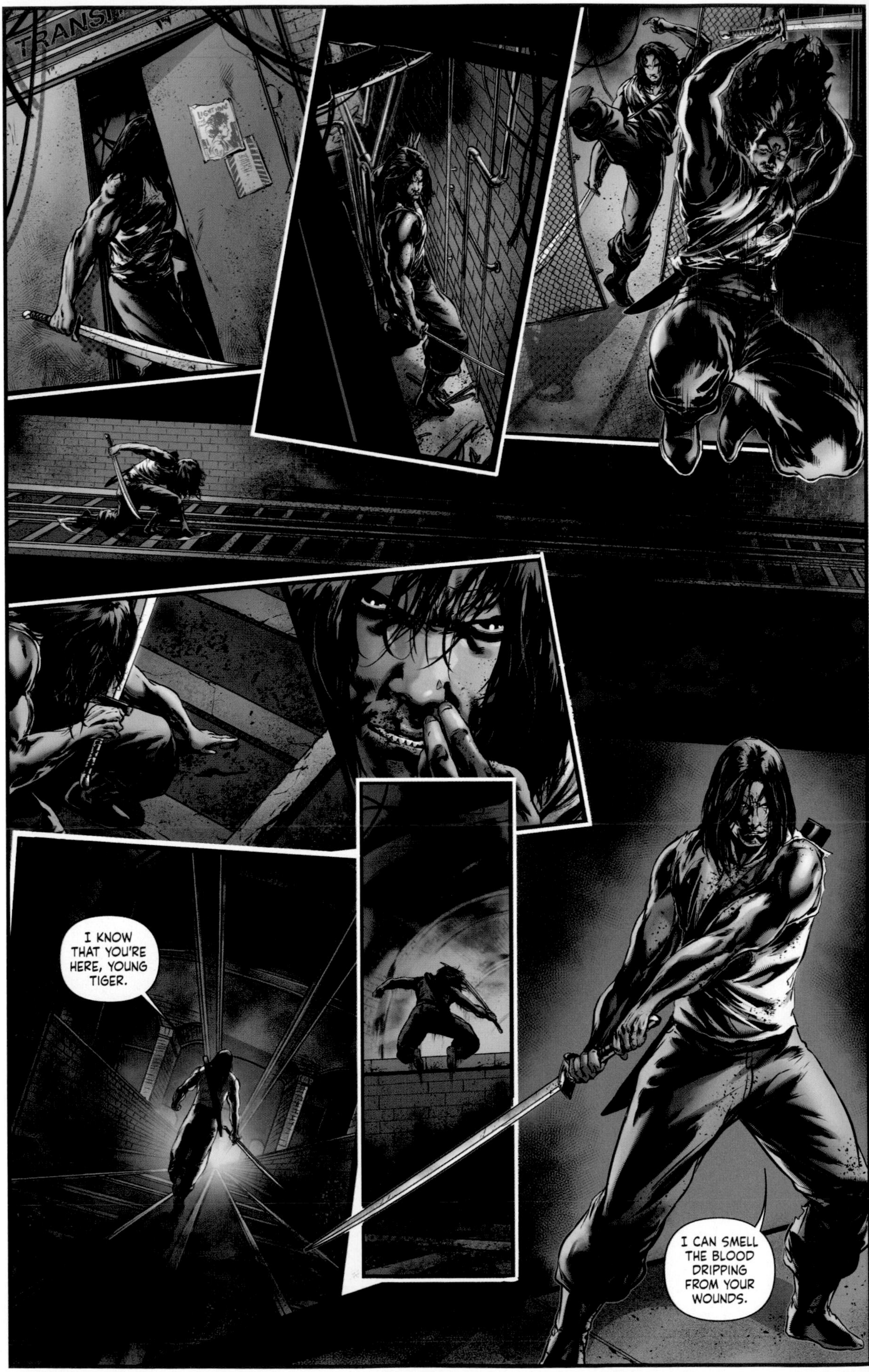
I KNOW THAT YOU'RE HERE, YOUNG TIGER.
I CAN SMELL THE BLOOD DRIPPING FROM YOUR WOUNDS.

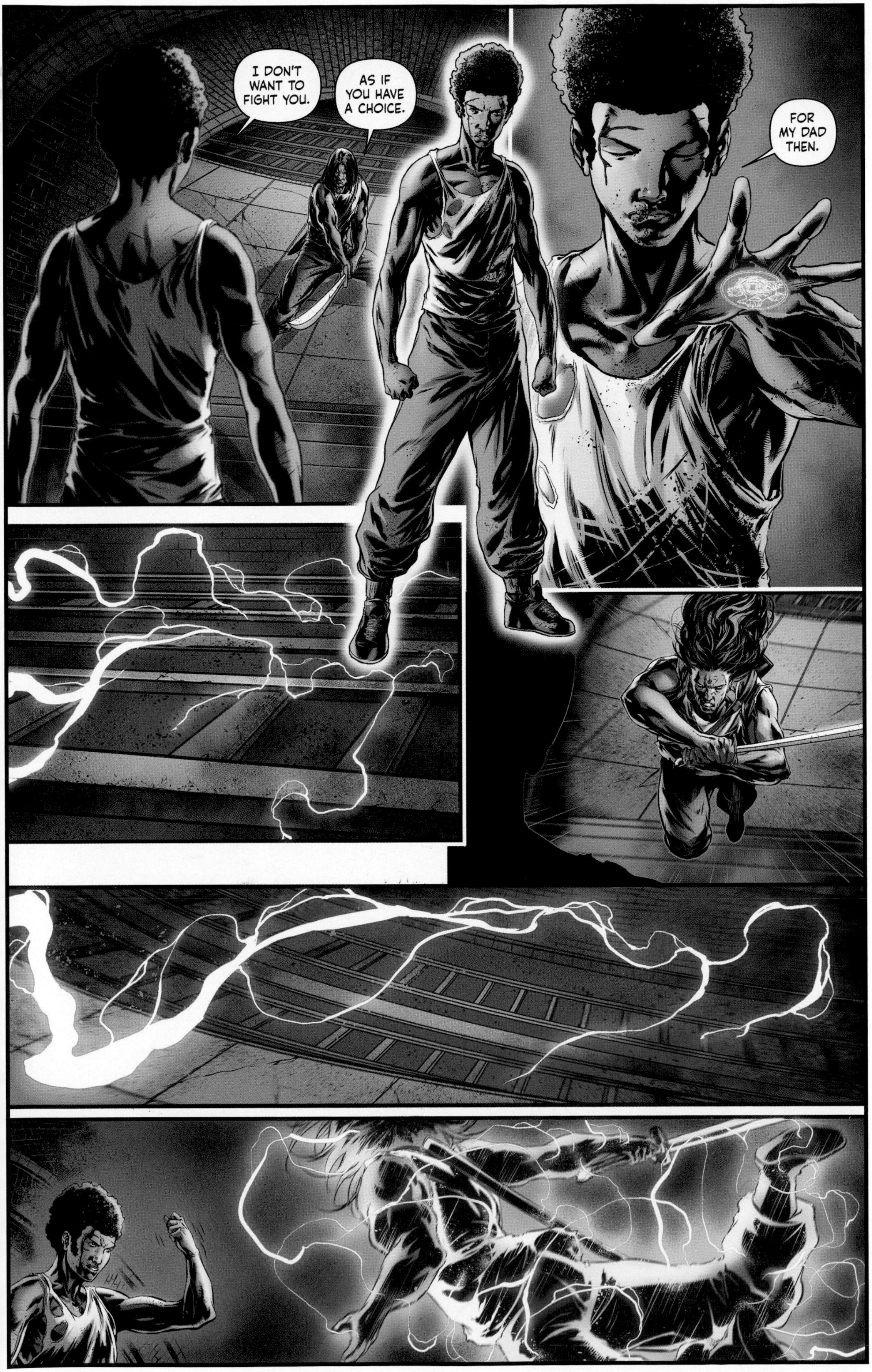
I DON'T WANT TO FIGHT YOU.
AS IF YOU HAVE A CHOICE.
FOR MY DAD THEN.

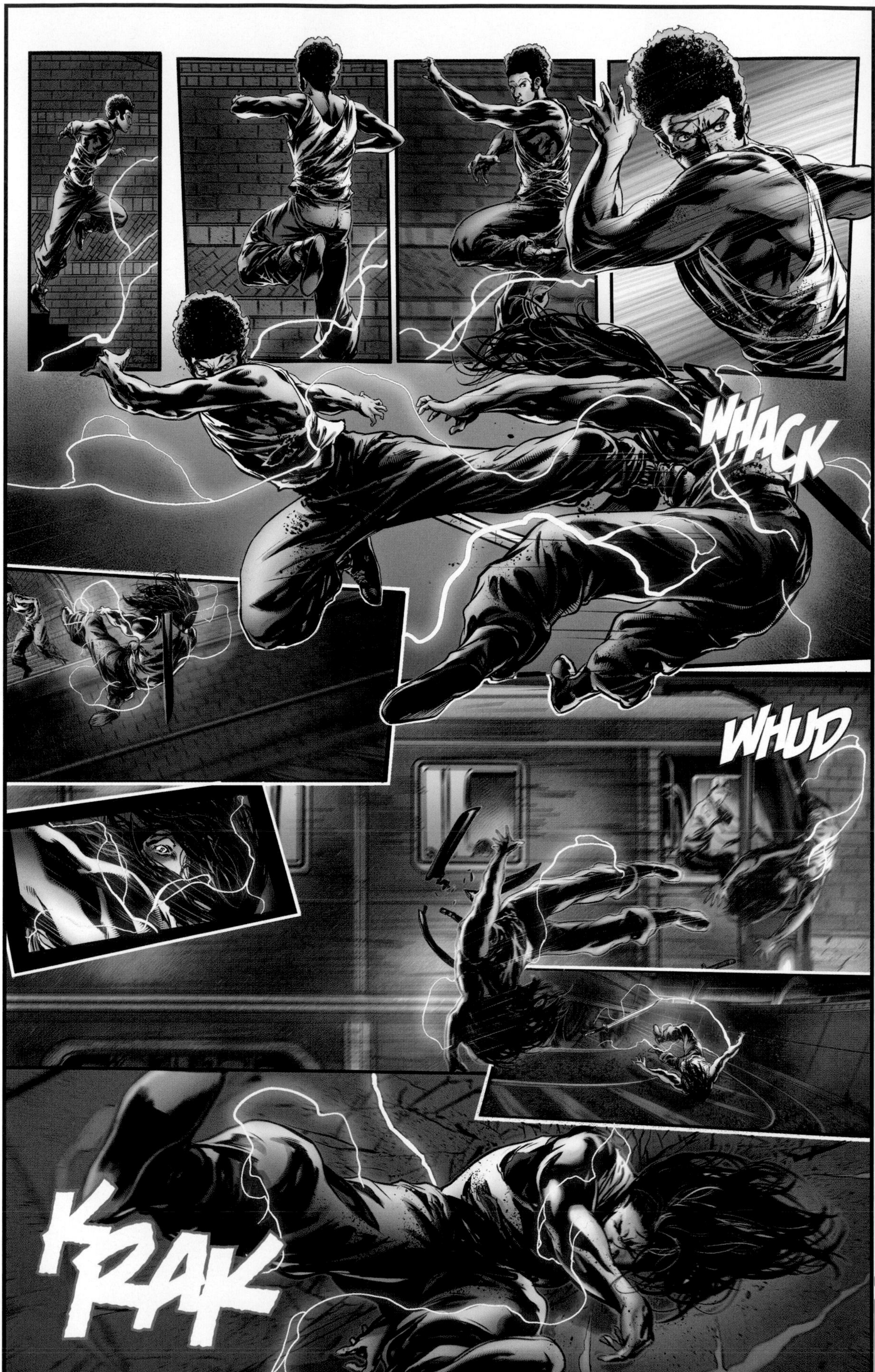
WHACK
WHUD
KRAK

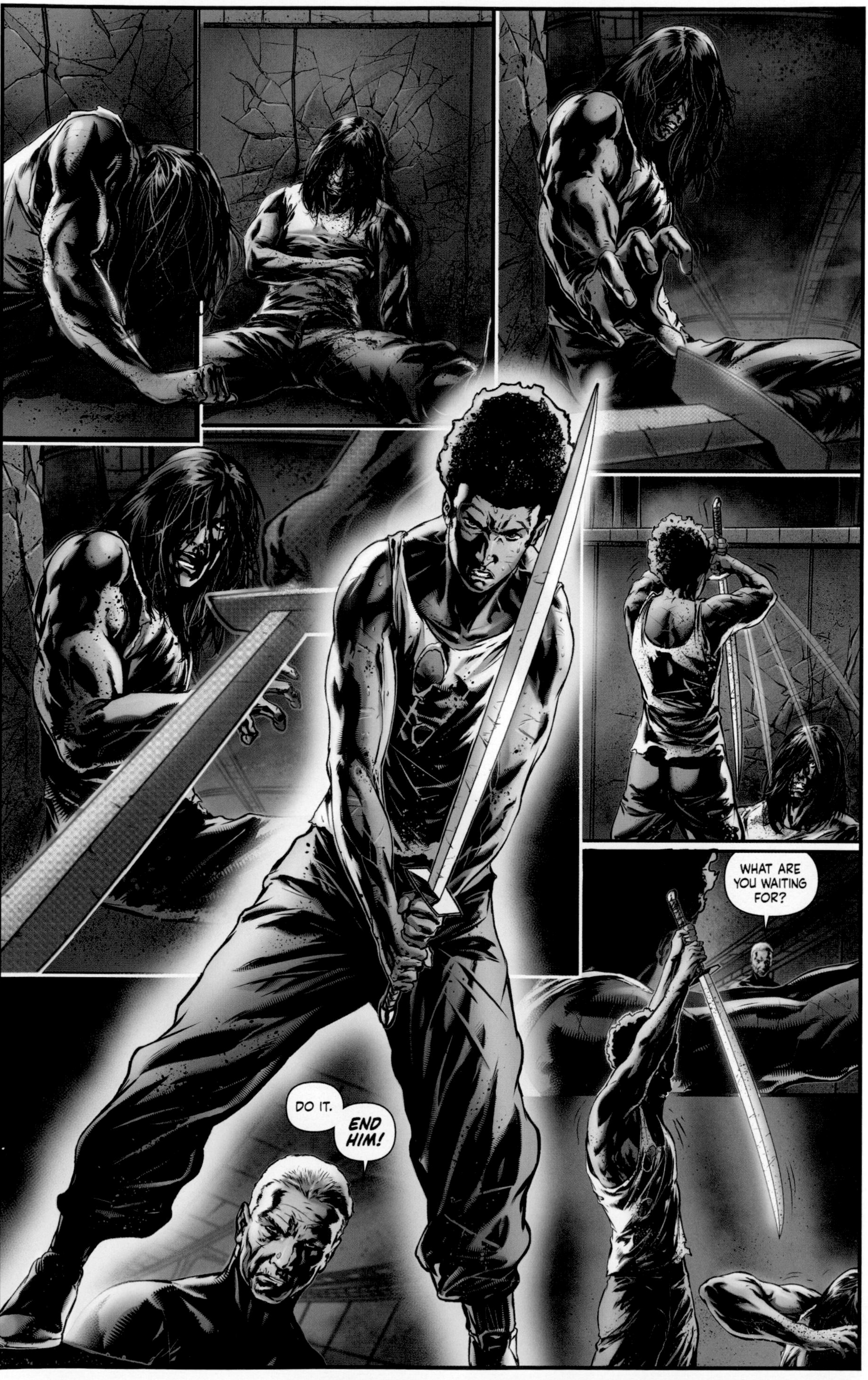
WHAT ARE YOU WAITING FOR?
DO IT.
END HIM!

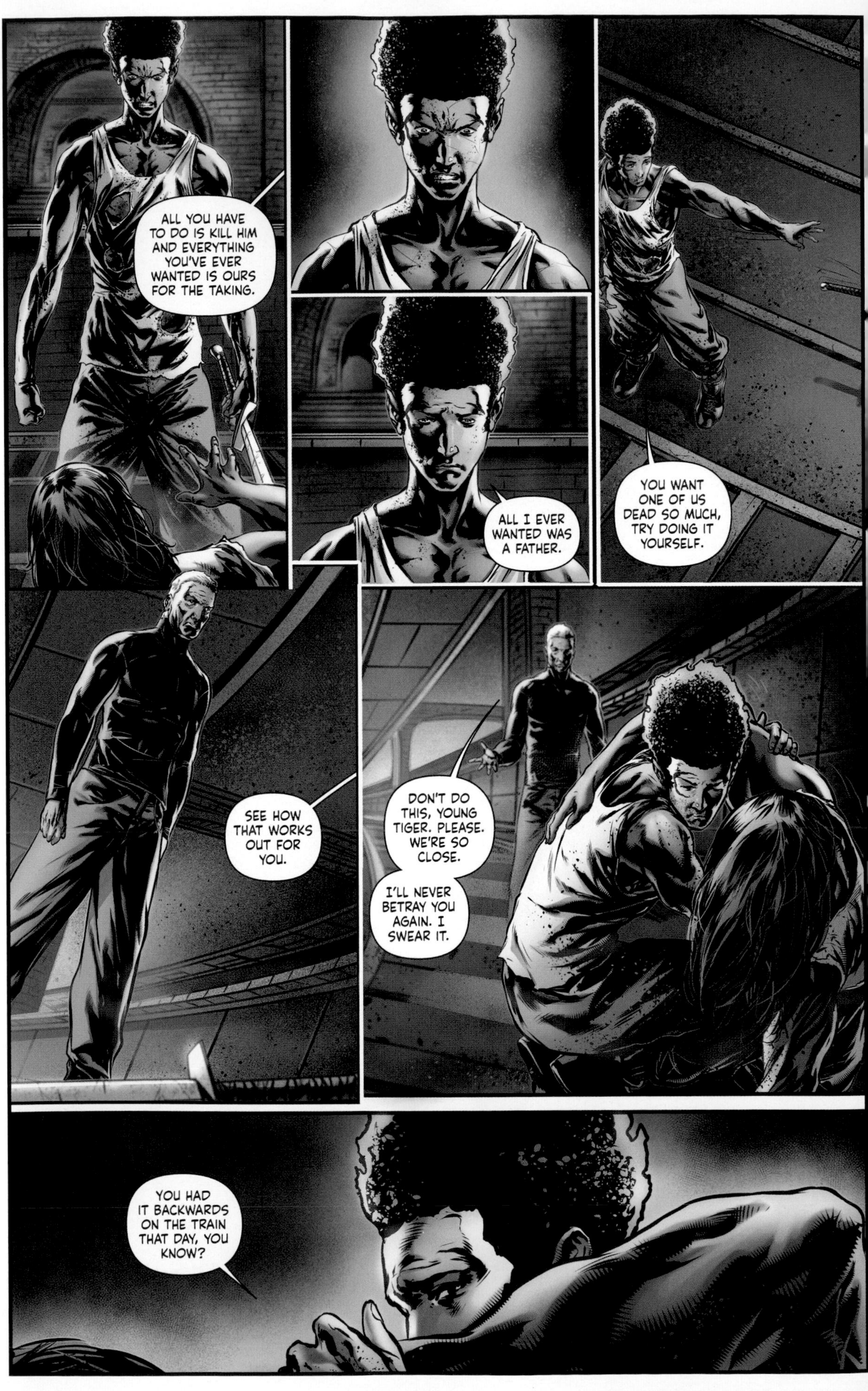
ALL YOU HAVE TO DO IS KILL HIM AND EVERYTHING YOU'VE EVER WANTED IS OURS FOR THE TAKING.
ALL I EVER WANTED WAS A FATHER.
YOU WANT ONE OF US DEAD SO MUCH, TRY DOING IT YOURSELF.
SEE HOW THAT WORKS OUT FOR YOU.
DON'T DO THIS, YOUNG TIGER. PLEASE. WE'RE SO CLOSE.
I'LL NEVER BETRAY YOU AGAIN. I SWEAR IT.
YOU HAD IT BACKWARDS ON THE TRAIN THAT DAY, YOU KNOW?

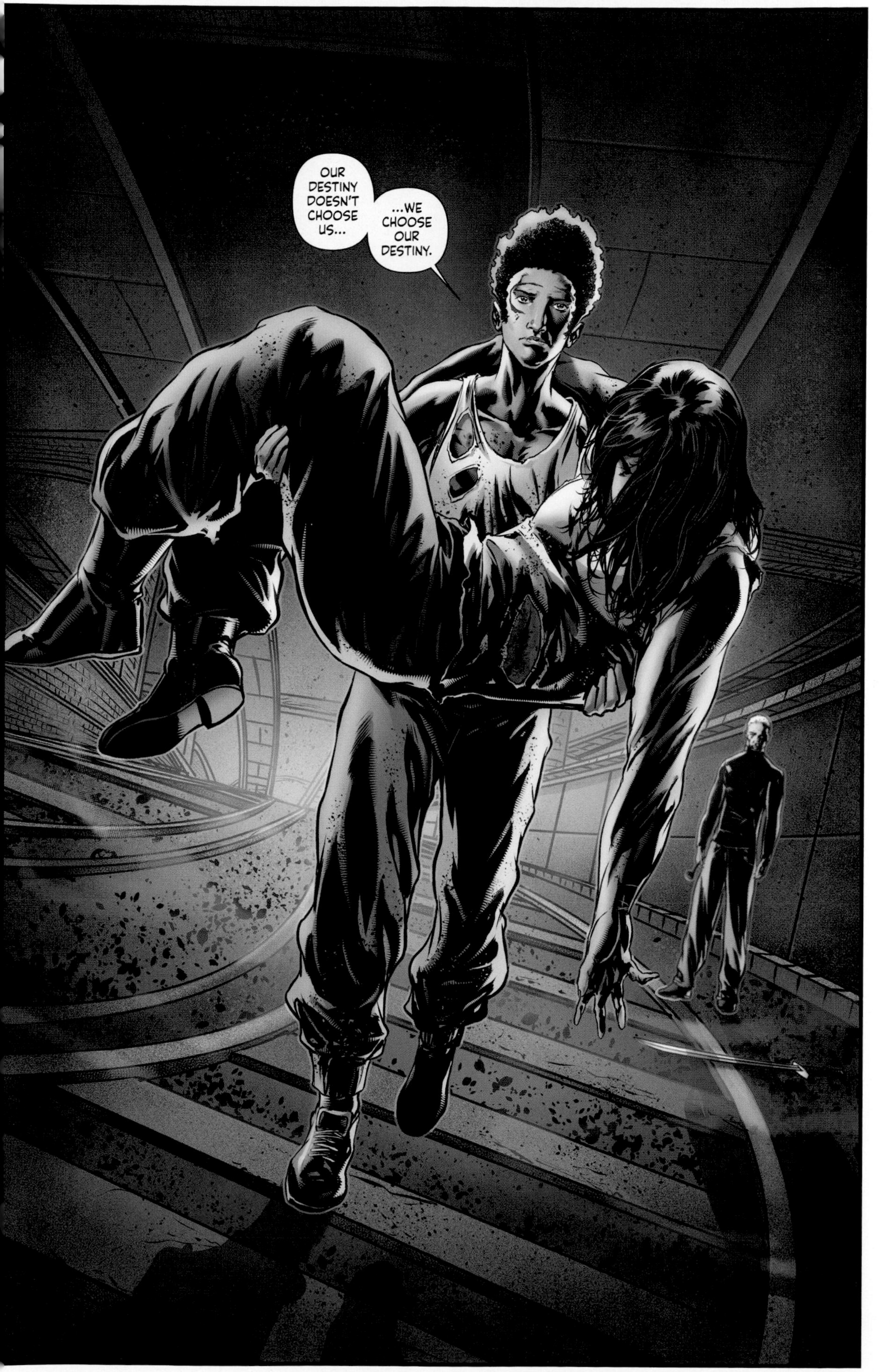
OUR DESTINY DOESN'T CHOOSE US...
...WE CHOOSE OUR DESTINY.

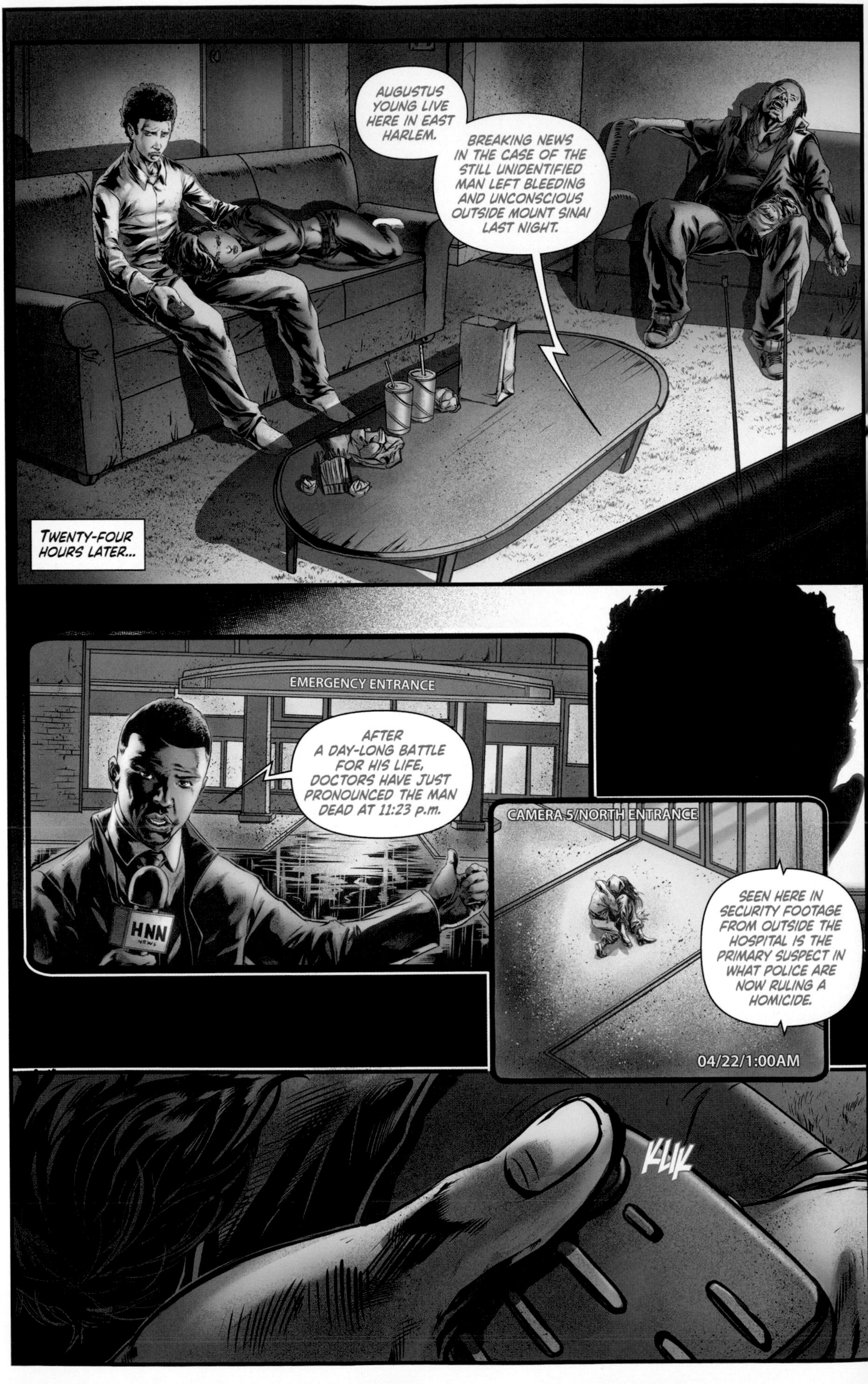
AUGUSTUS YOUNG LIVE HERE IN EAST HARLEM.
BREAKING NEWS IN THE CASE OF THE STILL UNIDENTIFIED MAN LEFT BLEEDING AND UNCONSCIOUS OUTSIDE MOUNT SINAI LAST NIGHT.
TWENTY-FOUR HOURS LATER...
EMERGENCY ENTRANCE
AFTER A DAY-LONG BATTLE FOR HIS LIFE, DOCTORS HAVE JUST PRONOUNCED THE MAN DEAD AT 11:23 p.m.
HNN
CAMERA 5/NORTH ENTRANCE
SEEN HERE IN SECURITY FOOTAGE FROM OUTSIDE THE HOSPITAL IS THE PRIMARY SUSPECT IN WHAT POLICE ARE NOW RULING A HOMICIDE.
04/22/1:00AM
KLIK

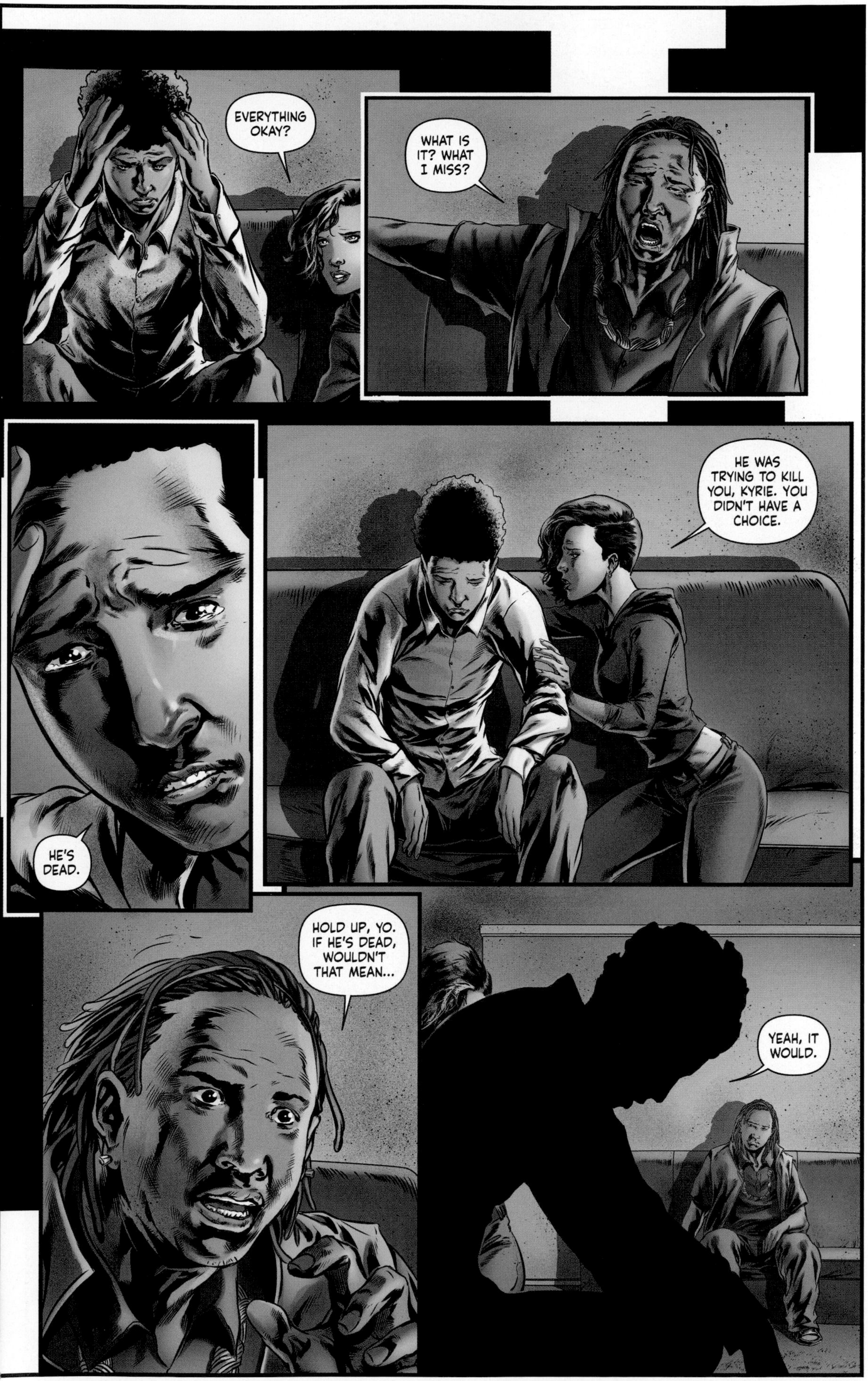
EVERYTHING OKAY?
WHAT IS IT? WHAT I MISS?
HE'S DEAD.
HE WAS TRYING TO KILL YOU, KYRIE. YOU DIDN'T HAVE A CHOICE.
HOLD UP, YO. IF HE'S DEAD, WOULDN'T THAT MEAN...
YEAH, IT WOULD.

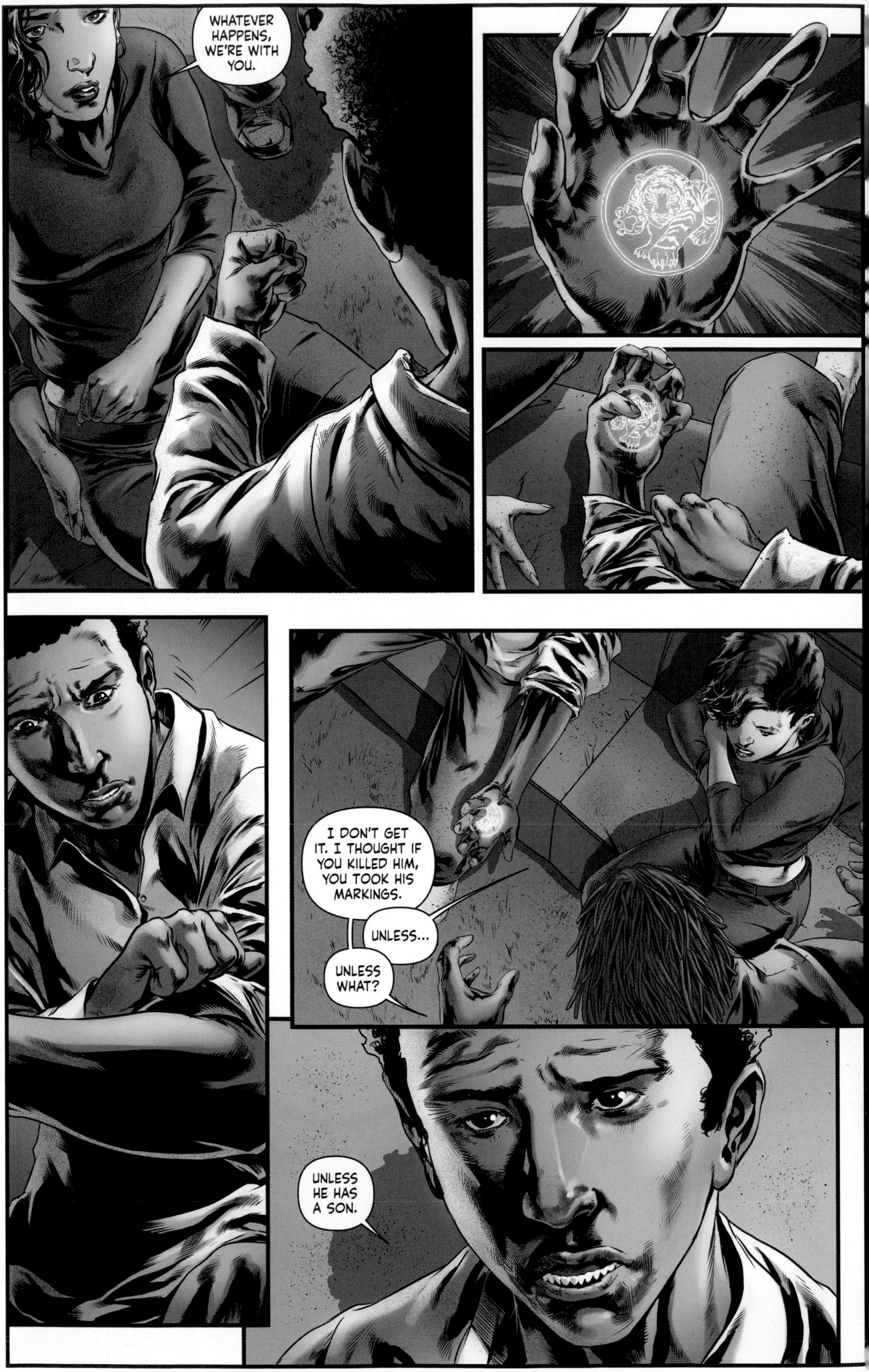
WHATEVER HAPPENS, WE'RE WITH YOU.
I DON'T GET IT. I THOUGHT IF YOU KILLED HIM, YOU TOOK HIS MARKINGS.
UNLESS...
UNLESS WHAT?
UNLESS HE HAS A SON.

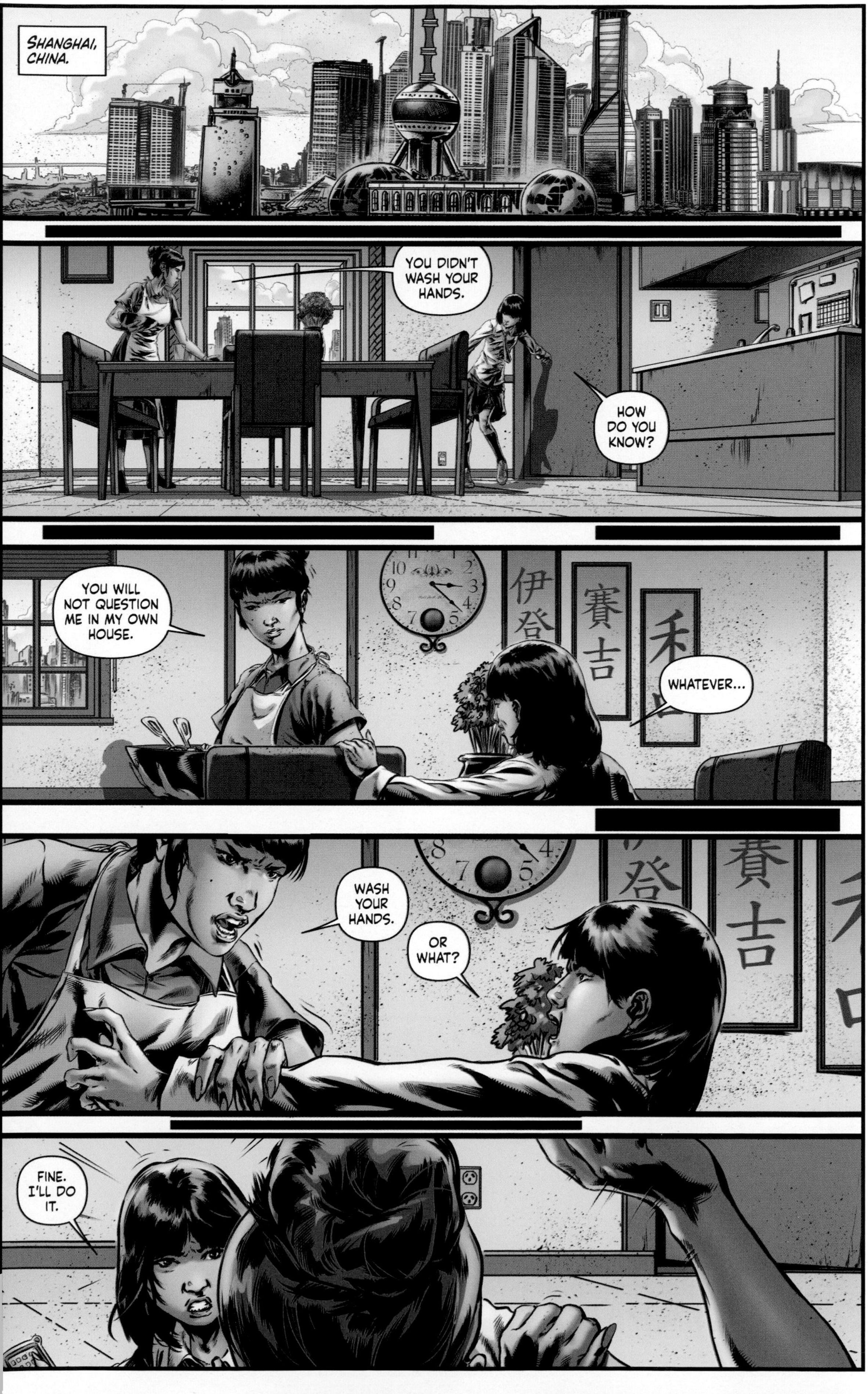
SHANGHAI, CHINA.
[redacted]
YOU DIDN'T WASH YOUR HANDS.
HOW DO YOU KNOW?
[redacted]
[redacted]
YOU WILL NOT QUESTION ME IN MY OWN HOUSE.
WHATEVER...
[redacted]
WASH YOUR HANDS.
OR WHAT?
[redacted]
FINE. I'LL DO IT.

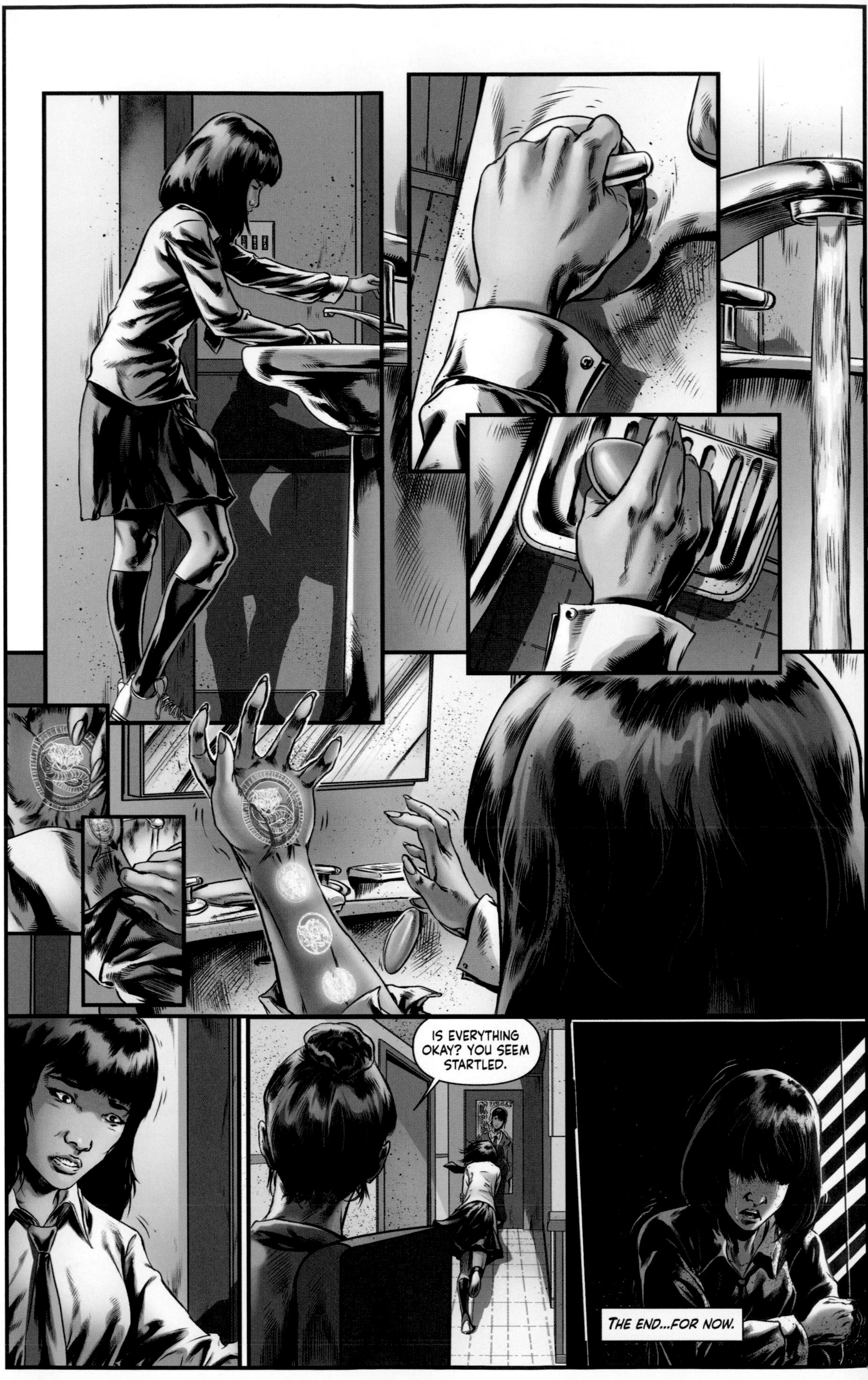
IS EVERYTHING OKAY? YOU SEEM STARTLED.
THE END...FOR NOW.

Biographies

Born and raised in Atlanta, **Jay Longino** first moved to Los Angeles to play in the NBA Summer League in Long Beach before playing basketball professionally in Mexico and the now-defunct USBL.

Following his passion for writing, Longino was subsequently able to make his mark in Hollywood writing and developing numerous feature film and television projects for Vin Diesel, Clifford "T.I." Harris, Sylvester Stallone, Liam Hemsworth, and director John Singleton, among others.

Longino's breakthrough came in 2016 with the release of *Skiptrace*, an action comedy starring the legendary Jackie Chan and Johnny Knoxville. Based on Longino's original story and co-scripted by him, the film became a runaway success in China.

Longino's latest project brings him full circle, returning to the world of basketball to write the script for the *Uncle Drew* movie, starring NBA All-Star Kyrie Irving.

Longino also recently formed Size 13 Comics, an offshoot of his Size 13 Productions, with partner Bernie Cahill in order to bring more of his stories to life in comics form.

Caanan White's career as an artist took off in 2006 when his art was published by both Dabel Brothers Productions and Marvel Comics.

Encouraged by the positive response, in 2008 White began submitting his work to various small press publishers, including Avatar Press.

Impressed with what he saw, Avatar founder William Christensen hired White to provide the art for two war-centered titles. The first, *Über*, was written by comics superstar Kieron Gillen and is an alternate history account of the events of World War II. The second, *The Harlem Hellfighters*, was written by Max Brooks and tells the World War I story of the entirely African-American 369th Infantry Regiment, whose acts of bravery helped turn the tide of the war and reshape the opinions of many Americans concerning African-Americans.

SON OF SHAOLIN is the first of four projects that White and Longino have partnered on. The other three are currently in production under the Size 13 Comics banner.

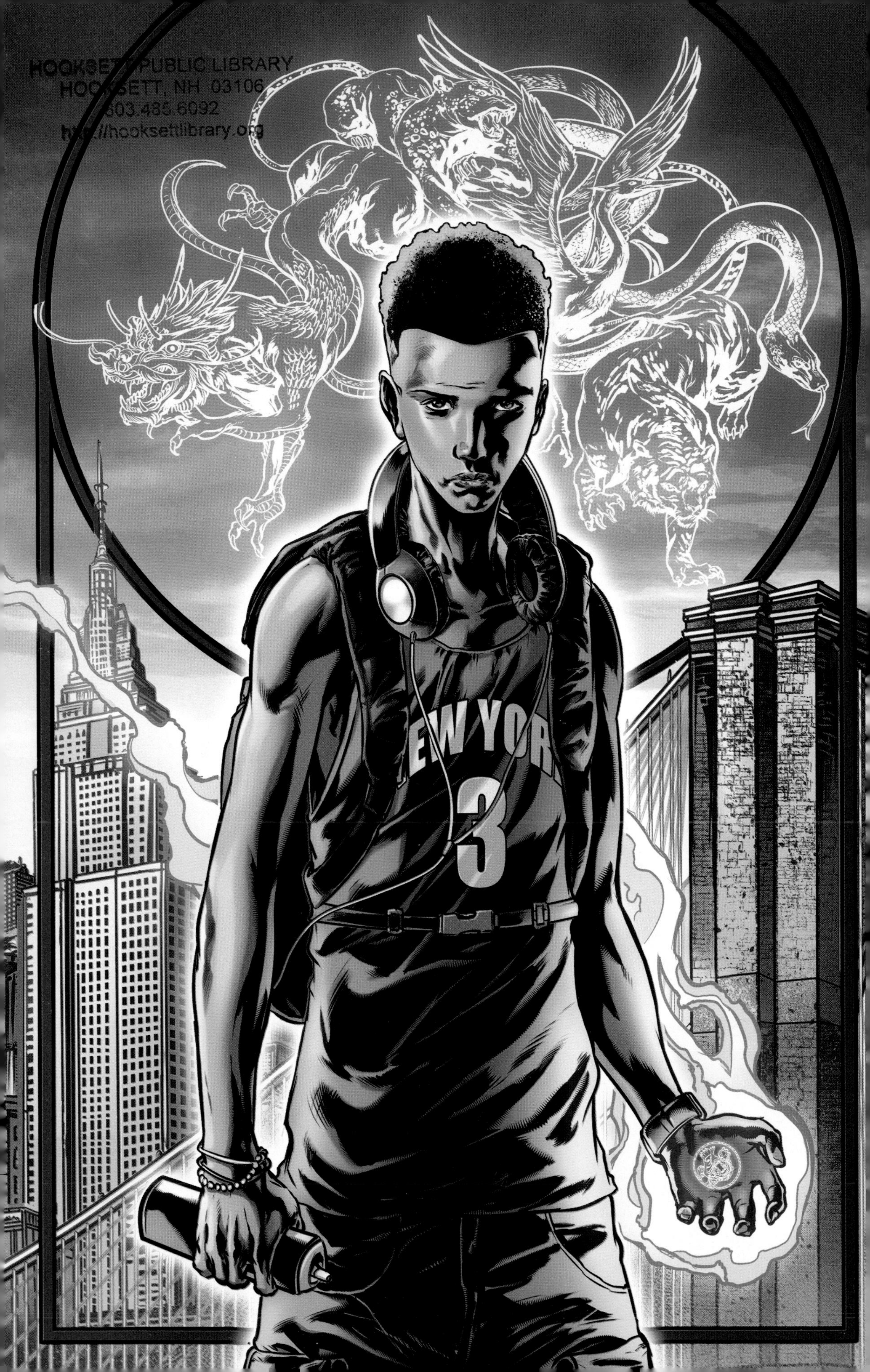
EW YOR
3